Where River Turns To Sky

WHERE RIVER TURNS TO SKY

Gregg Kleiner

AVON BOOKS ◆ NEW YORK

WHERE RIVER TURNS TO SKY is an original publication of Avon Books. This work has never before appeared in book form. This work is a novel. Any similarity to actual persons, places, or events is purely coincidental.

AVON BOOKS
A division of
The Hearst Corporation
1350 Avenue of the Americas
New York, New York 10019

Library of Congress Cataloging in Publication Data:

Kleiner, Gregg.
    Where river turns to sky : a novel / by Gregg Kleiner.
        p.   cm.
I. Title.
PS3561.L3769W48   1996   96-22024
813'.54—dc20   CIP

First Avon Books Hardcover Printing: November 1996

For Lori—
companion on the river, soul mate in the sky

To the memory of my mother,
Mary Elizabeth "Betty" Kleiner (1929-1995),
source of wisdom, source of light,
who lived the wonder.

☺

And to the memory of my maternal grandparents,
Grace and Joseph Sheehan,
who raised black-faced sheep, drove yellow school buses,
and made holly wreaths at Christmastime
to get by in this hard world;
and who passed their wisdom down.

ACKNOWLEDGMENTS

I want to offer my sincerest gratitude to the people who played a role in the creation of this novel by influencing my life at various times and in so many ways. First, to Betty and Bert Kleiner, for giving me a childhood filled with creeks and trees and sky, and always, *always*, a gentle, steady love.

To my siblings, Jeff Kleiner, Lori Kleiner-Schmidt, Julie Kleiner-Johnson, and Brad Kleiner, who shared that childhood with me, skipping stones on the pools of Lookingglass Creek, and swimming in the cool green waters of the Abiqua.

To the fine writers of my writers group, Rick Borsten, Charles Goodrich, and Anita Sullivan, who listened and had faith, who share writing, life, and so much more.

To Tom Spanbauer, who said "things align," and then without knowing so, nudged me and my '67 Volkswagen bus off a cliff on Highway 101 between Cannon Beach and Corvallis. And to all the Dangerous Writers up in Portland: Judy Allen, Stevan Allred, Helen Beum, Ann Buckingham, Kathleen Concannon, Helen Gundlach, Rachel Hoffman, Bill Hogsett, Rodger Larson, Ellen Michaelson, Candace Mulligan, Chuck Palahnink, Vera Peterson, J. Francis Rose, Cathy Thaler, Rick Thompson, Suzy Vitello, Cori-Ann Woodard, and all the others. A special thanks to Carolyn Altman and Nancy Palmer for reading the manuscript. And to Mike Taylor, for putting up with the woo-woo week after week.

Acknowledgments

To John DePasquale and Rick Martinez, who told me that late night in John's Chevy van to jump.

To Yung-hui "Chino" Cheng, Larry Clarkberg, Bryan Dawley, Martha Hankins, Marc Johnson, Julian Kilker, Evelyn Lee, Mike McPherson, David Ovellette, Marilyn Schwader, Martha Smouse, Jean Sullivan, Chris Walton, Carol Wenk, and the other dear souls at Terra Pacific Writing Corporation, for bearing with me all those years, and then cheering me on when I at last had to leap. Especially to Ted Wadman, for his long-term friendship, faith, and wizardry.

To Kris Dahl, my agent, who not only shared my same high school and hometown, but took me and this book on, and then kept gently saying, "all it takes is one."

To Jennifer Hershey, editor extraordinaire at Avon Books, for being that one, for her unflinching enthusiasm and faith.

To Elizabeth Udall, for her generosity (in the form of a Walden Residency through Lewis and Clark College), which afforded me the solitude and space to write on her hillside farm up Sardine Creek Road, and for her sparkle, spirit, and indefatigable dedication to the arts.

To Tracy Daugherty and Naomi Shihab Nye and Bill Stafford and Carolyn Forché, for their writing and guidance. To Duncan McDonald and Ken Metzler of the University of Oregon's School of Journalism. To Martha Gies, Teresa Jordan, Marilyn Krueger, Jon Sinclair, Marsha Weber, Tom Doulis, and Donna Henderson, who saw the very earliest drafts.

To Nikki Leary, Gary and Kirsten Oakley, and Kim Burke, for kind and gentle feedback on the manuscript. To Chris Johnson, Dawn Kleiner, Carrol Maurer, Penny Salus, and Jeff Schmidt, for being both family and friends. To Kari Margrethe Lende and Liz Coleman, for their friendship and passion for life. To Carol Ferris, for unlocking the secrets the stars hold. To Elmer and Roycille Paulson, for sharing their wisdom way back at the beginning in the hills outside of Lookingglass.

To Eli Asia and Sophia Hope—up at the headwaters, just starting out. To old people everywhere—downstream a ways where the water slows, flattens, and the sun and sky work their magic. And to all the others—may you know who you are—I thank you.

Finally, to Oregon—her trees, and salmon, and moving water. May they all survive until we learn to respect and hold sacred the natural world the way the Hopi and other native people have always held this earth.

And most of all to Lori, for standing beside me in the current all these years. For carving time out of the hollows of her being and handing that time to me. For helping stay the course when the water got too high to see the sky. And for being a wonderful mother, and true friend. This book is not mine; it is ours.

Youth, which is forgiven everything, forgives itself nothing;
age, which forgives itself everything, is forgiven nothing.

—George Bernard Shaw

PART ONE

North ○ Yellow

After I'm gone,
One eye with its film, one leg with its pain,
I'll still jog along inside the rain.
Already I'm older than my mother or father,
and I follow a river more strange than water.
A policeman asks if I'm lost this night—
why am I here in this dim first light?
I try to tell him why I have to run—
he's lost, he can't feel it, and I can't explain.
I jog on inside the rain.

    —"Near Dawn Some Time"
    by William Stafford

GEORGE CASTOR

THOSE TINY feet weren't Ralph's feet at the end of Ralph's bed. I knew that before I'd pushed Ralph's door all the way open and stepped inside his room, the smell of rainbow trout coming strong up off my hands. Ralph's feet were so big he had to feed them Purina Dog Chow. These feet were little feet, tiny as the Chinese women's feet in *National Geographic*, tiny as a kid's feet—the size of Jason's feet when Jason was still a boy. But I went on into Ralph's room, through that doorway I'd been through hundreds of times over the last couple of years, past the silver letter B and the silver number 24 nailed to the door at eye level. I kept going, knowing already it wasn't Ralph in the bed, but somehow hoping that maybe they'd just moved Ralph to another room, or another wing, or were helping him to the shitter or the shower.

The walls around Ralph's bed were stripped bare of the waterfalls and mountains and rivers I'd cut out of magazines and off of calendars and brought in. The snapshot of me and Ralph fishing was gone. Ralph and Eileen's black and white wedding picture was gone, too, and so was the framed picture of their farm taken from an airplane. The only things left on those blank walls were a couple of yellowed pieces of Scotch

3

tape and a handful of thumbtacks somebody'd missed. The only color in all that white was a short piece of purple yarn hanging down from one of the thumbtacks. Yarn I'd used to tie up a bunch of lavender I brought in for Ralph last summer and hung on his wall. The end of the little piece of yarn was all frayed out where somebody'd yanked Ralph's lavender off the wall.

I didn't know that those tiny feet in Ralph's bed were what was going to start the whole thing, turn my life upside down and dump it out, the way you'd empty an old wooden nail keg, all the crap inside tumbling out onto the floor around my feet, all the people I'd seen die during my life coming out, too, me standing there all alone—eighty years old and at the end of the line, standing on the riverbank.

I didn't know about the circle either. The circle came later, after Grace showed up soaking wet on my new front porch that Saturday morning just before Thanksgiving and started talking about spirits and sagebrush and telling strange stories.

Those tiny feet in Ralph's bed were what was going to make me do stuff I never thought I'd ever do. Loony stuff like buying a run-down mansion in the middle of town with money I'd never earned—death money's really what it was. Those tiny feet were why I got hauled in for kidnapping, too. Those feet and that promise—the second promise I made to Ralph because I broke the first promise all to hell, the one about not letting him die alone.

I looked again at the feet in Ralph's bed, then at the head on the pillow. Not Ralph's head. An old woman's head, maybe, but it was hard to say just looking at the face and gray hair, everything else covered except those feet. I wanted to grab the stainless-steel railing and shake the whole bed, yell at this person to tell me where the hell they'd taken Ralph off to. But I didn't, because right then Ralph's door swung open, the knob bumping hard into the plaster where the rubber stopper was missing. There she was. The Ad-ministrator. Breathing hard. That red dress with the big black buttons down the front filling Ralph's doorway. The Ad-ministrator swallowed so loud I could hear it. She glanced over at Ralph's bed, then back at me. I could tell she wanted me to step out into the hall so we could talk, but I wasn't budging out of Ralph's room. She must have sensed I wasn't, because she started in talking at me full throttle.

"I'm sorry, Mr. Castor," the Ad-ministrator said. "I planned to tell you the moment you came in, before you made it down the hall here. But today's Wednesday, so we weren't expecting you. You never come in on Wednesdays. And in the evening instead of midday? You never visit Mr. Pollux in the evening. Right after it happened, we tried calling. A couple times. But there was no answer."

She stopped to get breath. The buttons on her dress pushing out toward me, swelling bigger. Then she kept going, words flooding out of her again, the black buttons shrinking back down.

"Bingham & Bristol handled the arrangements. Everything went fine. We contacted some distant relatives who reside in Atlantic City. They said they didn't even know where Mr. Pollux was and were overjoyed to learn where he'd been living. Said they'd always wanted to see Oregon. Had heard the coast was just marvelous, but the timing for a trip out now was bad. So I personally tied up the loose ends over the phone. And Bingham & Bristol took care of the rest."

"Loose ends?" I said.

"Oh yes," the Ad-ministrator said. "You wouldn't believe how much there is to take care of when this happens. You know, even the little details add up. Paperwork and possessions. Of course, it's much more involved if there's no family around to help out. Which in this case—"

"Horseshit!" I said, and then my boots were taking me out of Ralph's room, the silver B24 on the door and those black buttons blurring past, me stomping down the hallway and out through those sliding glass doors that didn't open fast enough. I hit the right door so hard with my hand a spiderweb bloomed deep in the tinted glass. The four stacked words painted in silver on the glass cracked, too. Then the toe of my boot caught on the other door, popping it out of the track and setting off the loudest goddamned security alarm I'd ever heard. I stumbled outside, the clouds tearing open overhead, the smell and taste of rain coming in through my nose and mouth.

The gravel parking lot was a river boiling silver in the evening light, a river flowing past. Max was floating at the far side of the river, all the falling water and night coming on making Max's faded red paint dance and shimmer, making that old Ford truck of mine look new and shiny.

I had to get the hell away from the Gardens and back up to my farm in the foothills. Get away from that Ad-ministrator beating her gums at me about how she'd tied up Ralph's loose ends long-distance, how Ralph was already buried—not only dead, but already in the goddamned ground.

But what I really had to get away from was the promise I'd just broken all to hell. The promise I'd made to Ralph that day two years back when I found him in his muddy bathtub, just his mouth moving.

And what was I doing while I was breaking the promise? While Ralph was dying all alone here at the Gardens? I was fucking fishing for rainbow trout up at Odell Lake. *Fishing*!

Then those tiny feet kicked the hell out of me—as I was stomping across that parking lot flooded full of mud puddles, the sun already gone to coals behind the clouds somewhere out over the Pacific, rain coming down all around me in fifty-gallon drums busting open as they hit, soaking my boots and bad back, soaking my socks slid down inside my boots, soaking me clear through to the marrow. Those feet kicked me so hard I stopped stomping. Stopped splashing. Stopped breathing. I stood still in the darkness and water falling. Stared at the end of the line, at the river going by all around me, rain hammering the surface silver. The silver water already up to my ankles. Only a step or two away from floating on down myself. The river ready to take me away. *Me next.* Not another soul around anywhere. No Jason. No Dora. No Mama and Pa or baby brother. Nobody else on the bank. No Uncle Bill back in Omaha. No Bud. All of them gone on down the river. And now Ralph gone on down, too.

So I turned around. Just turned around in the middle of all that water boiling, night coming on fast, rain beating on the brim of my hat, my heart a herd of thunder-spooked Herefords in my head, that security alarm screaming louder still. I just stood there looking at the lobby, at those jammed-open doors with their words stacked one on top the other, the words I'd cracked: SILVER and GARDENS and NURSING and HOME. This place was no goddamned home. It wasn't a gardens either. And I wouldn't call it nursing what they do in there. The only thing I saw right about those four words was the first cracked word: SILVER. Silver for all the stainless steel. Silver for the chain-link fence they put up along the creek after that woman sleepwalked in and drowned. Silver for the color of most people's hair in there. Silver for how much it costs every day you spend inside.

I wanted to turn and run to Max and drive away. Or go straight up, into the rain coming down out of the dark, through the big ring in the sky the fir trees made around the edges of the parking lot, straight up to heaven the way Jesus was going up in the color picture in my aunt Bertha's black Bible back in Omaha. Aunt Bertha always showed me that picture whenever she talked about going up to heaven, where all of us were going up to someday if we were good, where my mama and pa had gone during that snowstorm. In the picture, Jesus was going straight up through a golden hole in the clouds, light all over the place, little chunky angels helping him go up, tongues of fire burning all around.

Standing in the gravel parking lot, half a continent and the better part of a century away from my dead aunt Bertha and her black Bible, there wasn't hardly any light anywhere, and no tongues of fire burning in the rain, no little angels to help lift me up, and no hole of blue sky where I could squeeze through. So I just stood there, my head back, my arms straight up in the air, my fists stinging full of fishhooks falling from heaven, my face and nose and ears stinging, too.

Then the security alarm stopped ringing, and all I could hear was rain coming down hard and the cattle in my brain.

My head came back up. Somebody'd turned on the lights in the lobby. I could see people watching me through the jammed doors, through those four cracked words. Then I saw the Ad-ministrator in her red dress trying to get people out of the lobby, shooing them back to their rooms with the silver numbers on the doors.

Ralph! I yelled, holding the name in my throat so long my throat went raw. I yelled Ralph's name over and over at those glass doors, those silver words. Two aides ran over and tried to get the jammed doors to shut. But the doors wouldn't.

More light blinked on down the windows of the B wing, one window at a time. Ralph's window blinked on. A rectangle of fluorescent white. *Ralph!* I took a couple of steps back toward those sliding glass doors, then remembered the tiny feet, and stopped. The light in Ralph's window washed to plain and dim and far away.

I turned and splashed on across the parking lot to Max, climbed into the cab, and sat looking in the butter dish of rearview mirror at the movement in the lobby, at people trying to gawk, the silver people trying to see who'd caused all the commotion, set off the alarm, and brought the Ad-ministrator charging out of her office.

It didn't take long for the windows and mirror to fog over. I wiped off the inside of the windshield with an old rag and fired the engine. Shag William looked over at me and whined, that basset hound face of his all baggy and sad. For the first time I saw flakes of gray in Shag William's muzzle, a growing blizzard blowing around his wet black nose. My dog was getting old. He stood up on the seat and thumped his tail against the passenger door. Then his tail stopped thumping and the rain screamed loud on the roof.

I pulled out of the parking lot, the tires squealing and Shag William falling against the door. My hand stayed shoved down hard on the horn for at least five blocks going out of town, the horn screaming Ralph's name, leaving a streak of honking horn hanging in the rainy night air behind me. I drove fast. Couldn't feel the pedals through my boots or the wheel against my hands. I knew the road so well I didn't have to steer. Max knew how to get home. The thirteen miles from tiny downtown Lookingglass up to my farm turned into two hundred. My brain tumbled and clunked and wouldn't work right, a drum plugging the little throat of each ear.

On the S-curves, Max's rear wheel dropped off the pavement into a pothole and all the shit I'd been shoving up above both sun visors for years came falling down all over me and Shag William. A shower of old parking tickets, beer bottle caps, hardware receipts, gaskets for who the hell knows what all. An empty can of WD-40 almost knocked my hat and glasses off. A plastic case of half-gone .22 shells dropped onto my knuckles and cracked open, spilling shells all over my lap and the floorboards, brass flashing everywhere. I didn't care right then if all those shells went off, tore through the gas sloshing in the tank behind the worn-out seat, turned the cab and me into one big fireball. Going out like that seemed pretty fitting. Fucking fishing.

I didn't know how many miles I'd gone when I saw Ralph standing on the shoulder in the rain and headlights, waving, trying to flag me down as I went by, that grin of his wide as the Columbia River. I hit the brakes. That son-of-a-bitch. This whole thing was nothing more than one of Ralph's jokes. Damn him. I pulled over and got out, hurried back behind the truck.

Nothing. Just the red glow of taillight, exhaust rising smoky through the glow, everything wet, dripping, and cold.

Ralph!

Nothing but the rain on the trees and blacktop. Rain on the metal of Max.

Ralph!

Nothing but my own breathing. The drum in my ears.

Ralph wasn't out here in all this rain. Ralph was gone on downstream and never coming back, just like all the others.

And I was a damned fool in such sorry shape I was seeing things.

I walked up to the front of Max and pissed into the shoulder. But in the light of the headlights, I saw darkness coming out of me. *Blood! Holy Jesus!*

And then I was back in Omaha, eight or nine years old, the baseball coming at me slow-motion through the July sunlight, the maroon stitching spinning, the white ball a line drive I couldn't lower my glove fast enough to stop, the ball popping me in the nuts so hard I thought I'd busted something for sure. I missed the rest of the game, and pissed blood into Aunt Bertha and Uncle Bill's toilet for the next two days.

But I was eighty now. Blood in your piss at eighty isn't the same.

Then, standing there watching myself pissing red wine into the night, the blood went away. The piss turned clear and yellow, steam rising up through the headlight beams. The headlights steaming, too. And then there was no more.

Maybe it was just the bad light, or me seeing things in the rainy night. I shoved myself back in and buttoned my overalls, climbed into Max, and pulled out onto the road.

I drove on for so long I should have crossed the border into Idaho. Except I wasn't going anywhere. I was sitting in the cab of Max in the middle of the road somewhere along those thirteen miles of Highway 214, lights on, engine off, nothing but the sound of steady rain on the metal roof above my head. I had no idea how far I'd come, or where I was exactly. I didn't know why I'd stopped, or how long I'd been sitting there in the middle of the road. But a string of words was piled up in my mouth, and those words came spilling out whispered into the dark cab: *I'll make this up to you, Ralph. I promise. Somehow, I will. I swear to you and God both I won't let anybody else die alone. And if I fail this time, friend, I'll shove the barrel of my twelve gauge into my mouth and pull the trigger.*

Sitting there in the middle of the road, knowing Ralph was gone down the river and never coming back, pulling the trigger and floating off downstream didn't seem a half-bad idea. Except I'd already made the second promise, trying to make up for the first promise I'd just broken. I had no idea how I was ever going to keep the new promise, but I'd figure out something.

CLARA PAULSON

THERE AREN'T many trees in Nevada, so I never saw music notes flying out of treetops down there. Nevada's where I lived most of my life, singing and playing piano in Vegas and Reno and all the little Podunk clubs in between, drinking White Russians, wearing feather boas, and being a fool-idiot with too many men. Men. Here in the Gardens, I can't sing or play. I can't even walk or talk. But I hear and see everything, believe me. Everything.

Right now I can see the dark green of the treetops up there through my window. Dark green against blue, sun already hitting the treetops. Going to be a nice day looks like. Nice. Sleep came heavy but baroque last night. Strange dreams. Cats and pianos and pearls bouncing on ice. At least I didn't have to pee. That's always a nice surprise. To wake up and realize you made it through the night without calling for help to the ladies' room. Help.

At least I have my treetops. My window's too high up in the wall to see much else from my bed or from this darned chair. Sometimes birds land way up there, resting I suppose, since flying must take so much energy. I like it when all the leaves are gone and blackbirds land in the bare branches of my treetops, then fly away again, music notes blowing off a page of sheet music. A blue sheet, or a gray sheet, depending on the weather. Sometimes I hear the notes when the birds fly away. Piano music in the sky. Sky.

Mornings like this one are okay. Seven-thirty and feeling pretty good for an old woman. I can't ever remember how old, exactly. Eighty-two, or perhaps eighty-five. Old, though, and only half of me working. It's Friday, so the aides are in good moods. The way they are when the Rhino's away on vacation. Good moods. Blue sky. Whistling while they mop. Jokes coming down the hall and into my ears.

If I want a better view of the outside, I ring my little bell on my chair for an aide to roll me out to the lobby where the windows are bigger and lower and the front doors are all glass. Glass. From the lobby, I can see whole trees outside, not just the tops. And bushes and grass growing around the gravel parking lot, and some days, if I'm lucky, I see blue sky.

I ring my little bell, write the letters LOBBY on my notepad, and wait. After a long time Johnny Q comes in.

"Mornin', Miz Paulson," Johnny Q says, exaggerating with his lips as if this will help me understand what he's saying. Johnny Q and the Rhino and all the others think I'm deaf. Deaf. But I'm not. I just can't talk. Which is why I'm allowed to sit out in the lobby. By the tone of Johnny Q's voice I can tell it's Friday, or payday, or else Johnny Q's in love again. Johnny Q's been here the longest of all the aides. He's okay. I ring my bell again, hold up my letters. Johnny Q's got his back to me, making my bed quick and sloppy, tugging and tucking. "Little bell's gonna fucking drive me insane yet," Johnny Q mumbles. "Ought to cut it off and throw it in the creek. I'm nobody's fucking butler." Johnny Q turns to me, reads my letters. "Okay, Miz Paulson," a fake smile on his face for a split second. "To the Lobby we go!" Then, as he's pushing me down the hall, I hear his breath muttering above me, "Ought to pry the fucking dinger out of it. She'd never know the difference." Johnny Q puts me over here near the drinking fountain, against the wall out of the way, then walks off, his shoes squeaking on the linoleum, a bounce to his step. Must be in love again.

The morning goes by. By. Lots of blue sky outside. Blue all over. Pieces of blue sky on the ground, too, floating on the mud puddles, little round mirrors with gravel frames. But no piano music, no music notes blowing out of the trees and flying off into all that blue.

$$\circlearrowleft$$

Oh, look. Here he comes across the parking lot. B24's friend. It's Friday. He always comes around noon. It's ten till. He's right on time. Smell of fish sticks already in the air. Always fish on Fridays for the Catholics. Fisheaters, Johnny Q calls them. I push myself back a little with my good leg until my wheels bump against the wall. I love watching people come in from the outside. Bringing nice smells in with them. Fresh air. Fresh-mowed grass. The smell of sprinklers in summer. Sometimes people track in leaves, yellow stars that stick to the big burgundy welcome mats inside the glass doors. The stars dry out and curl up on the mats. Sometimes when the doors slide open and the wind blows just right, the stars blow over around my feet and wheels, get caught in my spokes.

The automatic doors open with a little squeak—the same sound the doors on "Star Trek" make on the television in the dayroom—and B24's friend walks right by me the way he does all the time. Three days a week. Friday. Sunday. Tuesday. Today's Friday. B24's friend nods to the receptionist the way he always does and goes right down the hall to B24, and disappears through the door.

The fellow who lives in B24, he can't talk either, just like me. Shoot, what's his name? I hate it when this happens. Sometimes names just disappear and I can't find them. Zip and they're gone. Zip. Anyway, B24's worse off than me. B24's stroke took his other side out, bad. He just lies in bed, staring. Kind of like the mummies over on the A wing. I just call him B24 when I lose his name, like now. It works.

I jingle my little bell when I want to move someplace. How fast an aide comes depends on how busy they are. And their moods. I jingle a little right now, but not loud enough for anybody to come. I just want to hear the high tinkling. A star, or an icicle.

B24's friend usually stays in with B24 about an hour. Then he's gone again. Back down the hall and out through these sliding doors. Squeak. It's harder to watch people go back out. Most of us are here to stay. Unless you're over on the C wing. On the C wing, they've still got their bodies *and* their minds. That's the difference between B and C. Minds. The A wing, of course, is for the mummies. The mummies don't have minds or bodies. I've still got my mind, though. I just can't trust it a hundred percent. Ninety-five, ninety-six, perhaps ninety-four percent, but that's good enough. Probably as good as most folks living on the outside.

My stroke years ago changed everything. My stroke took my voice and half my body, too. And then there are the blank spots. The loose wires. That's what some doctor called it once, loose wires that never reconnected quite right. But I've learned where most of the blank spots are—that five or six percent—and try to play my way around them. My mind's fine. Right up here, working and watching, smelling and hearing everything.

I've watched B24's friend coming and going now for a year or maybe more. Sometimes I hear him talking to B24, but I can't tell what he's saying. B24's friend's voice is too low. He rumbles. Nobody else from the outside visits B24. Not many people visit the B wing or the A wing. If you wind up anywhere besides the C wing, you're supposed to be so far gone you won't notice that nobody comes. But this stocky little fellow with orange whiskers shows up three times a week to spend an hour or so in with B24. He's got a decent head of hair, B24's friend. His hair's always a little wild, like he just woke up. The color of chalk, except for his whiskers. His whiskers and his eyebrows are the color of rust, or a cheap violin. My room's right across the hall from B24. I live in B31.

My gone-for-good voice and dead half-body just make my eyes and ears and whiffer all the sharper. I see the little changes, like when they wash the windows, or turn the page on the VFW calendar behind the front counter. I hear whispers not meant for my ears, the aides talking about their lives, the Rhino talking about us, visitors talking about the outside. I smell everything, too: the bubble gum the day receptionist pops all the time, the smell of deodorizer that comes out of the men's room whenever an aide or a visitor goes in or comes out, the Rhino's cotton-candy perfume when she walks by, her hose rubbing hush, hush, hush between her legs. I don't wear hose anymore.

I remember the day B24 came in, wheeled down the hallway in a hospital wheelchair, eyes empty as two shriveled prunes. His room was ready and waiting. I'd been waiting, too. For almost a week. That's how long it had been since Beatrice disappeared out of B24. I say she disappeared because one evening Beatrice was there, and the next morning she wasn't. Gone. Nobody told us what happened.

Beds around here don't stay empty very long, so I was watching, waiting when they brought B24 in that day. That was the first time I saw this fellow with the orange whiskers and chalky hair. He was pushing B24 down the hall, escorted by two people from the hospital dressed all in white, and the Rhino in one of her red dresses, leading the way, marching along erect and happy as a drum major. They all went into B24 and put B24 in Beatrice's bed. The hospital people left with their empty chair, and the Rhino went back to her office—her cage I call it. But this other fellow stayed in there with B24 for most of the day, rumbling.

He didn't leave until after the lights in the rooms came on. But I could tell he'd be back. There was something between those two. I knew he wouldn't do the usual: drop in every few weekends at first, and then never. I don't know how I knew this back then. Perhaps it was because he was about our age. Usually the younger ones bring them in. Daughters or granddaughters. Seldom men. Men. I thought maybe these two were brothers. I knew he'd be back, though. And I was right. Three days a week for more than a year now. Friday. Sunday. Tuesday. I know it's been more than a year because of the stars. Two seasons of yellow stars on the burgundy mats since B24's friend started coming.

Depending on what you're doing, a year's a long time. Time goes pretty slow around here. Slow. Days are flat, the same things over and over. Breakfast. Lunch. Supper. Bath twice a week. Bingo once a month. Fish on Fridays. Time's gone so slow I'm not even sure how long I've been here. Long though. Ten years, perhaps twenty. That relative brought me. A few weeks after my stroke during that show in Vegas. I don't think I'll ever forget that show. One minute I'm singing, the lights are bright, the cigarette smoke thick and blue, the crowd real good. Then I hear myself playing wrong notes on the baby grand. Next I stop playing altogether. Stop. No more notes. My fingers aren't moving. Rings aren't sparkling. My voice stops coming out, too. Not a sound in that whole club, just smoke rising up through the spotlights. Then black blots swirl in behind my eyes and everything sags. Flashing lights and sirens, then the hospital, and then here at the Gardens ever since. No more singing or piano. No more cigarettes or White Russians. No more men.

But I deserve all of this. God knows I earned it. What I did to my Amy.

I didn't even know the relative who brought me here. In fact, I'm not sure how the hospital people got ahold of him. His wife used to send a card every Christmas with their signatures inside, but nothing else. They lived in Salem, Oregon, I remember that. The state capital. The hospital in Vegas must have telephoned them, and the relative arranged for me to come up here. To all this rain and wet and gray. I don't think I've seen the relative since. Don't even remember his name. Something about them moving to Hawaii for work. Oh, I don't know for sure. That's what's so darned hard. Always that little sixteenth note of doubt, that four or five percent, just big enough that I can never be a hundred percent sure. One of my wires.

Oh, there he goes out again. Out. B24's friend going across the burgundy mats and out through the doors. Squeak. White hair in the wind. Blue sky on the mud puddles. An hour gone by already. Lunch noises coming from the cafeteria, people in there eating fish sticks. Mealtimes are big deals here. But not for me. I think I'll skip lunch today. Just sit here instead and wait for somebody else to bring in more outside smells.

There he goes past the front doors, driving off in his beat-up red pickup truck, the same way he always does three times a week, that same dented garbage can rolling around in the back. It's harder to watch people go. Go. But the floor's nice and shiny today. The sky's blue. It's Friday. I wish I could play the piano again. Or have my Amy back. Or get drunk.

Moon on Wet Concrete

A small old woman walking through drizzle before daylight stops on the sidewalk in front of a house that breathes huge three stories above her. The house has been painted bright red, but in the charcoaled dawn of late November appears brown, the color of rust or dry blood. Beside the woman, at the end of a leash, a skunk noses the ground. The woman squints at something in her cupped hand, tips back a black umbrella, and looks up through the falling rain at the house. She looks back down at her palm, then begins digging in her bag, small pieces of turquoise attached to the leather fringe along the bottom of the bag clicking.

Gathering her skirt, the old woman squats down. The beads touch the sidewalk and go still. She lets go of the leash, but the skunk stays close. The woman hunches forward, as if to protect something fragile from the rain and air. Her two braids of gray hair hang down, brushing the wet concrete. Her body jerks twice, then a flame bursts orange between her legs, just above her ankles. The flame dims, almost goes out, then blooms into a yellow glow that pulses in the breeze. A wisp of smoke leaks up into the air above the chrome shaft of the umbrella. The skunk lifts its head high, sniffing the air.

The woman collapses the umbrella, lays it on the ground, and stands facing the house. On the sidewalk between her feet, a candle in a clear glass jelly jar now burns. Her dark skirt has dozens of round mirrors the size of dimes stitched to the fabric all along the hem. The tiny mirrors flash in the weak light. At her right wrist, the old woman wears a silver bracelet to which an oval lump of turquoise has been mounted. On her feet, rubber overshoes cover the lower half of a pair of high-top tennis shoes. White dots on the canvas at each ankle bone glow in the candlelight above the black rubber. For a long time the woman does not move. There is no sound other than the wind and a distant splattering of water through a gutter grate. A large bird glides past a nearby streetlight. A shadow streaks. The flame in the glass jar dances.

Now the woman extends both arms in front of her, her hands cupped and held together, and begins to turn slowly around, a yellow powder sifting down from between her hands. When she has turned a full circle, she stops, throws her hands into the air, and brushes the palms together, releasing a fine dust that floats away on the breeze.

She picks up the umbrella, opens it, and holding it out to one side, begins to spin around, her head tipped back, her face looking up into the drizzle. She is smiling. Drops of water fall from her braids and the blue beads on her bag as she goes around. The hem of her skirt floats out, the tiny mirrors blurring into a continuous hoop of silver that wavers at her knees.

Bringing her head back up, the woman stops spinning, stands still for a moment, then steps past the candle and limps up the brick walkway toward the red house. At the bottom of wide steps that lead to a cavernous front porch, she pauses, bends down, and whispers something to the skunk that has followed her. Then, using one small hand on the railing, she climbs the steps one at a time. At the top, just inside the shadow of the porch roof, she turns and looks back at the candle burning a shiny full moon on the wet sidewalk. Something sparks gold in her mouth, then she turns and disappears into the deeper darkness of the porch, the mirrors on her skirt winking away.

The sound of heavy door knocker echoes out. The knocking continues, steady, then stops. After a short silence a flapping noise emanates from the porch, the sound of geese taking flight off a body of water. Then the porchlight explodes white, and the moon on the sidewalk is blown out. The skunk has vanished.

GEORGE CASTOR

SITTING IN the dark cab pulled up to my mailbox I started thinking how I should have never gone away up to Odell Lake in the first place. Maybe then, Ralph wouldn't of died. Or if I'd only gone for two days instead of five ... If I'd stayed here going into Lookingglass to see Ralph the same as ever, maybe I could have done something to save him. Pushed his call button, got him rushed to the hospital, given him mouth-to-mouth right there on his bed. *Something*. But I was five hours east, floating my fly line out over the water. Tipping the good Doctor Jack that wasn't nearly as smooth without Ralph there tipping the bottle with me swig for swig.

I didn't know why I decided to go up to Odell Lake. Hadn't been fishing hardly at all since Ralph's stroke, and never away overnight. My whole life the past couple of years had pretty much been scheduled around those visits three days a week in to see Ralph at the Gardens, the thirteen miles down out of the hills, then back up again. Maybe I was tired of the trips, tired of the road. Or maybe it was the smell of the Gardens I was tired of, going in through those glass doors and smelling that same smell every single time. Not a breath of fresh air in that place. Or maybe I had just needed a break, needed to get away to some water and hear the line peeling off my reel, a big rainbow trout taking my fly deep.

But the Odell lodge was louder, the room Ralph and I always stayed in smaller and colder, the rental rates gone straight through the cedar shakes, and the fishing lousy.

Ralph and I used to go up to Odell Lake every spring for a long weekend. We took along a couple bottles of the good Doctor and fished our brains out. The Odell trip was our spring ritual, spring cleaning. Something about that high mountain air that put back in whatever it was the rains of this valley leached out during the wet winter. Ralph and I were on the lake before light, whipping flies until midmorning, smoking cigars and talking, water lapping against the underside of the boat. Then we'd come in and have a big breakfast at the lodge, coffee and eggs, home fries and bacon, more coffee. Coffee until they kicked us out to set up for lunch.

We'd go back out on the lake in the evening, fish until we couldn't see our lines, then sit in the boat talking and drifting and sipping Doctor Jack. Ralph and I, we used to talk about lots of things, about everything.

Until the stroke.

I don't know exactly why I'd driven down to see Ralph that damp spring day. Borrow some tool, or shoot the shit about the price of pork. But I knew something wasn't right as soon as I shut off Max and heard Ralph's John Deere moaning in the distance, the sound of diesel engine throttled too high and too steady. I ran past Ralph's house and down to the barn, following the sound of that wide-open throttle.

Ralph's tractor was rammed up against the lower barn doors, the doors splintered all to hell, the tractor seat empty, diesel exhaust blowing straight up, blazing a streak of soot on the silver wood. Ralph wasn't around anywhere. I throttled the tractor down. The engine coughed to a stop. Quiet rushed in all around. Nothing moved. No wind. No birds. Not a sound anywhere. Just the silver-gray layer of clouds overhead.

It took a minute before I saw the marks in the mud leading

back up toward the house, the marks that weren't a man walking, but a creature of some sort crawling, dragging itself along. I hurried, following those marks in the mud, mud up the back steps and across the floorboards of the porch, mud down low on the doorjamb and open door, mud across the kitchen linoleum, and on a couple of yellow kitchen chairs turned over, mud smeared along the bottom of the white Frigidaire I'd helped Ralph and Eileen move in years ago. The mud went under the closed bathroom door. I pushed the door open and that's where I found Ralph, curled in the claw-foot tub, a dying animal, Ralph's hair and face and clothes and big leather boots smeared with mud and cow shit, his mouth moving open and shut, dentures fallen out into the tub, mud on the gums and teeth, no sounds coming out of Ralph's puckered mouth, those ice-blue eyes of his staring out of the mud right on through me, watching something I couldn't see.

Ralph never said another word after that. I wasn't even sure Ralph heard my words at the Gardens. But I kept on talking to Ralph the same as ever.

Sometimes I thought I could see a high-desert horizon reflecting off Ralph's eyes. Other times, there was nothing but the yellowed whites and that deep-ice blue. A time or two, I swear I saw a wolf running across that desert on Ralph's eyes. Maybe that's what Ralph was staring at all the time, a wolf. Or maybe Ralph was watching Eileen setting an apple pie out on the porch railing to cool. Hard to say. Maybe Ralph didn't see or hear jack shit.

I stopped in to see Ralph on my way out of town up to Odell last Friday, to let him know I wouldn't be coming in for a few days. Ralph didn't say he was going to die on me as soon as I left town. Didn't even give a hint. Just stared straight ahead the same as ever while I sat there going on about the flies I'd tied up the night before. Dying was probably Ralph's way of getting back at me for going away fishing when he couldn't come along. One of Ralph's jokes again. Had to have the last laugh.

Steam was coming up off the wet hood, Max's headlights pointing out into the dark, my back aching worse than normal. Purple yarn and fly line and little angels tumbled around inside my head. Tongues of fire and tiny feet. Twenty-two shells and wolves. The black buttons on that devil-red dress.

I made myself move, lean across Shag William, roll down Dora's window, and reach out into my mailbox, rain on my wrist. I pulled a week's worth of damp newspapers and envelopes into the warm cab, flipped through the bills and junk mail.

An envelope at the bottom of the pile made me look close. The envelope had my name and address printed right on the paper—no mailing label stuck on crooked with my name misspelled, or with Mrs. Eudora Castor printed out as if Dora were still living up here on the farm with me the same as ever, baking her butter rolls and taking care of her chickens. This envelope also had a real stamp stuck to the paper up in the corner, an American flag waving above the White House. The string of names above the return address sounded like a circus show. But there was something about the names I recognized.

I worked open the envelope with my thumb and pulled out a letter printed on paper so thick it had sponged moisture out of the air. Nice paper. I unfolded the letter, leaned close to the dash light, and stared at the words. I tried to read the words in the bad light, but my eyes skipped down to a big number with a dollar sign out in front.

Farther down I read my son Jason's name on the paper, along with my own name, both our names all in capital letters. Then I saw the big words BENEFICIARY and DECEASED.

It had happened a year ago. December. Middle of the night. The floor was ice-cold and I was barefoot. Whoever was out there knocking on my door kept pounding as I felt my way through the dark, Dora's grandfather clock chiming out four long beats. Four in the morning. Not the right time for visitors. The bones in my right foot popping the way they always did, always louder first thing out of bed. I caught my toe on the molding coming around the corner at the bottom of the steps, bumped into the table under the mirror, and almost fell. I slowed down. It was probably just some drunk who'd run his car into the ditch up on the highway.

The porch light was burnt out, so all I saw when I opened the door were two patches of silver flashing in the cold night, one silver patch floating right out in front of my chest, and one higher up, both patches blurry because I'd forgotten my glasses.

A male voice came out of the dark. "Mr. Castor?"

I nodded, rubbing one eye. I didn't like being called mister.

"I'm Officer Franklin with the Oregon State Police."

The voice didn't have to say another word. Those few words explained everything. I knew why the trooper was here at this hour. They always come when it's family. Bring the bad news to the next of kin in person.

"I'm sorry, sir," the trooper said, his breathing white, lit up a little by a silver crescent moon hanging low behind him, just above the barn. The trooper's breath drifted up into the stars. He could have turned and left right then. I knew who'd been killed. It was easy math. One. The only family I had left. Jason. My boy. Jason gone.

"Jason?" I said, my voice so weak I could barely hear the name.

The silver patches moved, nodded. "A single-vehicle accident up on I-84. About seven o'clock last night. Looks like he hit black ice. Jumped the guard rail into the Columbia. He was dead when the divers got down to him. I'm real sorry, sir."

The trooper went on, husky words coming from between the blinking badges, bouncing off of me and falling to the porch the way flying ants do in springtime. But it was winter. Behind the trooper, the stars were bright silver blurs, the ones around the moon washed out a little. Clear and cold the weatherman had said last night, not much chance of a white Christmas this year. I wanted to tell the trooper he had the wrong place, the wrong George Castor. But it was too late.

"Divers had just finished pulling the driver out of a tractor-trailer rig about a mile upstream. So they were there right away. Went right down. Found your son's Jaguar in about fifty feet of water. Stereo still going loud. Seems impossible, but they said it was still playing. That's how they located the vehicle so fast in the dark. It's tough in that current. He was still strapped in." The trooper stopped talking for a second. The leather of his belt squeaked. "They're afraid the deceased might have been drinking," he said. "We'll know after the autopsy." The words kept bouncing off me and dropping in the doorway.

Jason was forty-some. Not a child anymore. Never married. No wife. No kids. Dead before his father.

I didn't know what to say to the trooper standing in front of the moon, his breath still floating off into the night. So I reached out a hand and touched the blurry metal of the badge above his heart, then stepped back inside and shut the door. I leaned against the door, listening to the car drive off up my long gravel driveway, and far away the murmur of a river.

Looking down at that letter under the dash light, I saw lots of other big words. Big words were why I'd dropped out of college after just a year and a half. I couldn't stand sitting around indoors all day learning how to use words to impress people. Big words were part of the reason Jason and I didn't get on too well. Jason learned lots of big words in law school back east and pretty soon Jason thought he was hot shit. He even said that once, "Dad, I'm a hot-shit attorney now."

Jason and I, we just didn't see living life the same way. That's all. He was a big talker, a playboy, liked living life in the fast lane and drinking spendy booze. Nothing I could say to change his mind, so I let him go. Dora couldn't, though. She blamed herself. But we'd done the best we could. We loved that boy. He just got off track somewhere along the line the way some kids do. Found fast living and big words. Making big money and buying nice toys, like that fancy green car of his that wound up in the Columbia. Jason living fast with too much tequila churning in his blood. They even found the goddamned worm out of the bottle in his belly when they opened him up.

The number with the dollar sign was big. I knew lawyers made good money, but Jason hadn't been working as a bigwig lawyer up in Portland for that many years. And before that, the crazy kid had gone to school forever, taking out loan after loan, buying clothes and cars. Nobody made this much money in that little time. Just shy of three-quarters of a million dollars. Jason three-quarters of the way to being a millionaire.

I counted the numbers before and after the comma again, including the thirty-seven cents. I reread the names of the circus show embossed into the nice paper. Lawyers taking care of legal stuff for other lawyers seemed a little odd to me. But undertakers probably had to bury other undertakers.

I'd never be able to spend this much money if I tried my damndest. I put the letter on the pile of junk mail and newspapers and pulled across the road into my long driveway. Halfway down, I shut off the engine the way I always did and let Max coast to a squeaky stop inside the carport. The rain was letting up a little. Glad to be home.

These hills were home. The same hills that flattened out down where little Lookingglass huddled along the same creek that flowed past the back of my farm. I'd lived in these hills for forty-some years. Been farming ever since I dropped out of college. Farming forever, it seemed. Blackcaps, barley, Southdown sheep, Nubian goats. Fifty head of holstein dairy cows at one point. I'd tried strawberries, rabbits, weaner pigs, and filberts. Goddamn filberts. I wished I were growing filberts now. Filberts were worth something now. Except they didn't call them filberts anymore. They called them hazelnuts. Supposed to be classier, makes them sell better.

One summer I even tried growing muskmelon. Heard farmers up in Hermiston planned to make a killing growing muskmelon that year because a freeze had knocked out most of the California growers. So I tried to get a piece of the action. It went well for the first month or so, vines and blossoms all over the place. I was finally going to make a few bucks farming. But the melons only got to be the size of doorknobs and then stopped growing. Just lay there in the dirt, hard as river rocks, and never got ripe. I finally plowed the damned things under, but they were so hard and green it took a couple of winters for those doorknobs to rot.

Used to be that a hundred or so acres was a respectable-sized farm. But these days, a hundred acres wasn't diddly-squat, what with the big boys farming thousand-acre tracts all around. Which was why most my longtime farmer neighbors—the real neighbors—had sold out to the big boys, or else to Californians, and moved away. Or died. Ralph had been the last of my real neighbors.

I gathered up the newspapers, junk mail, and that letter, and climbed out. Shag William followed me up the walk through the rain. I scraped the bottoms of my boots on the hoe head bolted upside down to the steps of the sagging porch and followed Shag William inside. I never locked up. Didn't even own a key to the place. Nothing to steal. Besides, the driveway was too long and the blackberries too thick. Blackberries grew up everywhere in these parts if you didn't keep them beat back or sprayed. I didn't need keys making a racket and taking up space in my pockets. You get to carrying too many keys around and you're in trouble. Jason's long fingers were always moving in his slacks pockets, jangling keys, jingling coins.

I turned on the light hanging down above the kitchen table and read the letter again. I was getting all the money Jason had made from using big words being a hot-shit attorney up in Portland. Death money. Jason gone on down the river, and me three-quarters of the way to being a millionaire.

So I yelled. Just yelled out into that dark old farmhouse. Yelled out that big number. The circus names. My own name. I yelled out BENEFICIARY, and Ralph's name. Yelled for no reason. Shag William came clicking across the floor toward me with his tail going, probably wondering if I was going loony on him, standing there yelling like that.

So I bent down and grabbed Shag William's front paws,

stood him up on his stubby hind legs, and started dancing that old hound all around the kitchen, Shag William licking at my fingers, whining and barking, tail going wild, back paws clicking on the linoleum, my boots trying not to step on him. I started singing while we danced, singing some song about Jesus dueling with the devil, and Judas and his dog cheering the devil on. I didn't know where that song came from. I didn't care. I just kept singing and dancing Shag William around the kitchen floor like a goddamned fool because singing and dancing seemed the thing to do right then.

Then I saw that dark color in the headlights and stopped dancing. But the room kept on spinning out in front of me. I let go of Shag William, thinking I was going to throw up or fall down. I swallowed and gulped air, reached out for a chair and sat down hard. I sat there sweating, waiting for the room to slow, for the darkness to go clear.

CLARA PAULSON

I'D LIKE to sing today. Sing. Somebody else could play the piano, if I could only just sing, hear my own voice coming out of me again. Words to music. I'd settle for a single song just one time through. *Singing in the Rain.*

I miss my voice. Days like this are worse. Cloudy and pouring outside. I haven't even opened my eyes yet this morning, but lying here I already know the weather's bad. I can tell by the light coming through my eyelids, and the rainwater gurgling in the downspouts outside. Mornings like this, I don't want to open my eyes at all, see the gray in my little window, rain falling past my treetops. Raining too hard for blackbirds. I just want to stay right here in bed all day long with my eyes closed, thinking about singing. But I can't. Sing or stay. The aides will be here soon, hustle me to the toilet, then down the hall for Cream of Wheat. I hate Cream of Wheat. On Sundays they let me have pancakes. Pancakes are okay. Today's not Sunday, though. I'd give up eating altogether for a single song.

I keep my eyes closed so no tears leak out, hold my dead piano hand in my good hand under the covers. Perhaps B24's friend will come in today to visit B24. But what day is it? Not

Sunday. No pancakes. I try to hum a little, but all I hear is the rain outside, the aides in bad moods banging buckets out in the hallway, bitching about work, about us.

૭

Sunny and yellow outside. Leaves on the parking lot. In the blue-mirror mud puddles. Stars back on the burgundy mats. Mats. Stale smell of fish sticks in my nose. I'm sick of eating. The food here at the Gardens is so flat you don't really taste it going down. Mashed potatoes. Creamed corn. Vanilla custard. And my tongue only tasting half of everything anyway. Half. It's hardly worth eating at all. Fish sticks are the worst. Thank God they only serve fish sticks on Fridays. For the Fisheaters.

I used to be one. A Fisheater. Went to Mass every Sunday when I was little, until I quit. So I know who the Catholics are around here. I've seen the crucifixes above their doors and around their necks. Henrietta's always pinching black rosary beads through her fingers, her lips barely moving, whispering hundreds of Hail Marys. When she sleeps, Henrietta wears a rosary around each wrist, plus the one she always wears around her neck. Only time Henrietta takes that rosary off is when she eats. She stretches the circle of black beads out all around her white plate, the silver cross upside down, pointing at whoever's sitting across the table from her. Some people say Henrietta was a nun. The aides call her Sister Henry behind her back. I never sit across from Henrietta.

I once did a show in the chapel of a Catholic convent outside of Reno or somewhere. Big beautiful pipe organ up in the choir loft and a big sad-eyed Jesus hanging on a cross behind the marble altar. I played a beautiful Baldwin upright pulled out in front of the altar, feeling that Jesus looking down at me from behind, blood running down his arms and ankles. I didn't sing too well that night. Never did another show in a Fisheater church, either. Too many stains on my soul, perhaps. Sin stains. Like that priest said years and years ago—

32

the priest the doctor called to his office to talk to me after I told the doctor I had grown up Catholic. As soon as the doctor stepped out of the room, the priest told me that not being married and in my condition was already a sin. Out-of-wedlock sin. Then he warned me that stopping it now would be the biggest sin of all. The type of sin that stained your soul bad. Black to the core. Mortal. The kind of sin it only takes one of to land you in Hell forever.

At that time in my life, though, I wasn't a practicing Fisheater anymore, so my sins weren't any of that priest's business. But perhaps, because of that priest, what I wound up doing was a dark-shade-of-gray sin, instead of black. Or perhaps it's black just the same. Or perhaps there's no difference between black and gray.

I wonder if my Amy grew up in a Catholic family, eating fish on Fridays. Perhaps she wound up in a convent. Sister Amy. Guess I'll never know. I don't want to think about Amy right now. I just want to sit here and look at the yellow stars on the burgundy mats, try to smell outside smells, instead of fish sticks and confessionals.

GEORGE CASTOR

I STOOD up to put the kettle on, my clothes damp on the inside from dancing with the damned dog and damp on the outside from standing too long in the rain in that parking lot. But I didn't want any tea or coffee or anything hot. I wanted something cold, beer or some Doctor Jack on the rocks, something strong. The kitchen counter was a mess: quart jars full of pennies and odd bolts, wooden matches tangled up in a wad of baling twine, empty beer bottles and dirty dishes piled up all over the place, a moldy heel of bread. The table was a mess, too, and the floor and cupboards dirty. Dora had always kept the place spotless, sweeping and wiping and dusting, always humming to herself. She loved this farm from the day we moved in up here from Cloverdale over at the coast when Jason was only two or three. I'd let everything go to hell since Dora died five years back. Old newspapers and *National Geographic*s piled up on the kitchen chairs, some papers slid off onto the floor. The cardboard kindling box next to the woodstove split open, wood chips and sawdust spilled out onto the floor, tracked everywhere. Dust and woodstove ashes all over everything. The whole place gone to seed, thistle and tansy down lying around in the corners, cobwebs everywhere.

The only bright spots in that whole filthy kitchen were the two daffodils I'd stuck in a ketchup bottle full of water and put on the table before I left for Odell Lake, those two flowers blowing yellow into the room.

I dug in a drawer for a candle and scraped a match. But I didn't touch the match to the wick right away. I just watched that flame working its way down the matchstick turning the white wood into twisted black charcoal, the ticks from Dora's grandfather clock coming loud down the hall. The flame got so close to my fingers I could feel the heat on my hand, my hand shaking a little. But I still didn't blow the match out. I let it burn until the burning came in through my skin and the flame went out on its own, the smell of burnt hide at the back of my throat.

Staring at that burnt matchstick, I saw the spine of the charred mouse Jason had found the day after our barn burned down.

Dora and I had seen the orange glow from down the road a mile or so. I figured it was somebody burning brush at night. But when we rounded the last bend before our driveway and I saw the flames, I knew. The house. The house we'd just plowed our whole meager life savings into. But halfway down the driveway, the Ford flying over potholes and loose gravel, I saw through a break in the trees that it was the barn burning. Not the house. The barn. The barn packed full to the rafters with that summer's hay, all the grain bins brimming full of barley and oats, harnesses and hardware hanging in the tack room, pumpkins and squash piled in the end stall, Dora's dried flowers and herbs and braids of garlic hanging from the loft joists.

Dora, Jason, and I came flying into the yard, and I saw a man stumbling out our barn burning bright behind him. The flames behind the man turned him black, his face in our headlights streaked black, too, soot-black as the night sky all around, everything black except those orange flames charging blow-furnace bright out through the barn doors, and up higher, more flames shooting out the hay mow.

Holy Jesus, I breathed out into my own reflection staring back at me from the windshield.

"I got the cows out, but the horses are still in there," the man shouted as I jumped out of the Ford. Then I recognized him. Ralph. Ralph Pollux, who'd come by with his wife Eileen after we'd moved in, brought us a warm peach pie.

"I'm sorry," Ralph was saying. "I couldn't get to the horses. I'm real sorry."

I couldn't say a thing back, watching those flames eating through the shingles high above Ralph's head, Jason standing beside me with his arm tight around my knee, Dora still sitting in the Ford holding her face in her hands, flames on the windshield, making it look like Dora was burning, too.

I just stood there next to Ralph, the heat against my face, no words in my mouth, burning shingles blowing away into the night, timbers glowing orange and caving in, sparks shooting up into the black sky.

That whole goddamned barn was going up in a fireball roaring and hissing so loud I didn't recognize the sound of horses screaming until one of them, the black brood mare we called Lady Luck, broke through the burning south wall and came charging out covered in a blanket of flames, shaking her head and bucking, hunks of burning mane and tail falling through the night air.

Lady was coming right at us, charging, her hooves beating the frozen earth, Jason's little arms squeezing tighter around my leg. I took a couple of steps back. Almost tripped over Jason. Backed into the car door. The door fell shut. Dora screamed from inside. I wanted to pull the car door open and push Jason in, too. But I couldn't take my eyes off that horse on fire bearing down right at us, throwing her head and bellowing like a banshee, flames burning up her legs and across her withers, over her flanks and back, flames all around the white blaze in the middle of Lady's face.

But right when that horse should have plowed into us, she turned and ran head-down away until she hit the woven-wire fence by the pump house and flipped. She fell thrashing, tangled in the wire, a burning heap, kicking and screaming like no animal I'd ever heard, sparks and glowing hair flying all over, wire squealing against staples.

Then, before I could even think to run for my rifle, Lady went still. Nothing moved. Just the flames burning brighter, the wire rectangles of the fence starting to glow red. Dora was out of the car, Jason sobbing in her arms, all of us watching that horse and barn burning up, heat coming through our clothes, nothing at all any of us could do except watch, Ralph rubbing Jason's head with his big hand, Jason's face pushed into Dora's neck, Dora's cheeks wet.

Then Ralph's hand was on my shoulder, his other arm around Dora and Jason, those big arms streaked black holding our family together.

The next morning early, Ralph was back with three other neighbors, all of them standing on our front porch with shovels, come to help bury the charred draft horses, help us clean up and start over. Ralph's wife Eileen was there, too, with a big pot of oatmeal, fresh-sliced pears, walnuts and raisins and brown sugar, cream and fresh butter, cinnamon rolls, and thermos bottles full of black coffee.

Back then, we were all young, working hard to make a go of it, the last thing on our minds getting old. But that was forty years ago. I was eighty now, living up here in the blackberries by myself, me and Shag William and the Gravenstein apple tree Dora and Jason planted on Lady's grave that next spring.

That apple tree was as tall as the house now. And I had more money than any human being has a right to, but not a soul to share it with.

I flicked the matchstick into the sink, where it landed in a tuna fish can full of greasy water. I lit another match, touched this one to the candle wick, and went out into the dripping dark.

It was cold for March, winter hanging on late. But walking the path that led down to the pond, I could smell spring trying to shove winter out of its way. Sap starting to move back up through the great trunks of cedar and Doug fir all around. The candle flame burned straight up bright. No wind. No rain.

But what the hell was I doing wandering through the woods in the middle of the night with a goddamned candle? I had a whole pile of flashlights back up at the house, and lanterns, too. Was I on my way to loony? It happened. I'd seen it. At the Gardens. People sitting around swatting at the air, talking words to nobody, wandering the halls wearing out the linoleum, grinning for no reason. Loony had to be worse than dying straightaway.

I almost threw that candle into the brush to prove I wasn't. But I saw something white on the ground, a piece of paper or a gum wrapper. I knelt down, held the candle out. A trillium! Glowing white. And close by was a violet, the edges of its petals already starting to fade. And all around my boots were handfuls of bracken fern fiddleheads, pale green violins nosing up out of the needles and moss. I breathed in the smell of rotting leaves and wet dirt, and then I heard music coming up out of the ground. Music, and one of Ralph's words, *wonder*.

The whole thing *was* a wonder. Seasons and sap coming and going year after year. That old ball of fire the sun coming up over the Cascades every single morning, never missing a beat. Why didn't this old earth just give up and stop spinning? Toss in the towel? Ball bearings all wore out, nobody greasing the old girl regular?

Right then, I wanted more than anything to be in a boat with Ralph out in the middle of Odell Lake, the sun gone down, the first stars poking through above The Sisters, the two of us talking about everything, talking about the wonder.

I walked on down the path and out into the clearing that held the pond. A single frog was croaking. The pond was deep, but not very big. A small spring on the far side let in enough fresh water to keep the algae down and the frogs alive, but that was about it. Years back I'd let three small koi loose here. Coppery orange and silver, darting from the plastic bag in my hands. Never did see those koi again. Herons must have got them.

The frog stopped croaking as I moved along the bank and went out on the dock I'd built years ago out of an old door bolted to cedar fence posts. I wedged the candle into a crack on top of one of the posts. A moth shit-faced with night air and spring coming showed up and started zigzagging around the yellow flame. The frog started in croaking again.

"Sing it out, slippery friend!" I said. "I'm listening. Go ahead and sing." My words echoed off down the valley through the dark. "I'm here." The frog stopped. No moon. No sounds.

I knelt down. The candle flame reflected on the black water below the dock, wavering and winking at me, laughing at me, a grown man on the verge of tears. *Pull yourself together, for crying out loud. You had it easy. Fishing for rainbow trout. Ralph's the one who died all alone, just the way you promised him he wouldn't.*

The moth moved down and was now going after the flame's reflection on the water. The moth fluttered just above the surface, waltzing with the flame, courting the flame, just daring that flame to burn its ass. What was it about light that pulled white moths out of pitch black, made moths go loony after light? Then, in a blink, the moth dipped too close, brushed the surface with its wings, and stuck fast to the black water. The moth struggled on the water, wriggling and twitching, powder coming off the moth's wings and spreading out on the surface.

The frog started in croaking again.

Then I was backed halfway up the grassy bank, sucking in as much of that winter-turning-to-spring air as my lungs would hold. And next I was going the other way, running full throttle back down the bank and all the way out to the end of that rickety door, sailing out over the black water, letting out a long holler, clouds spinning overhead as I hit the surface. I came up gasping, the candle sizzling and sputtering up on the dock, the dock dripping, the moth gone.

I treaded water, sucking in more night, coughing out water, ice-cold pond water pouring in everywhere, filling my clothes and boots and pockets. Water so cold it felt warm and thick as fresh cream. That black water held me. All around everywhere warm and smooth, the only cold spots those two places on my thumb and finger where that match had burned.

My breathing slowed and fell into rhythm with my arms and legs moving back and forth below the surface. The splashing went still. Time stopped. The candle up on the dock stopped sizzling, and the flame burned bright and yellow and straight up again.

I looked way up and saw a hole torn in the cloud cover. Stars were shining through, a handful of glitter somebody'd flung out across the night sky. So beautiful I knew this was it. My time had come at long last. Just like Jesus in the picture in Aunt Bertha's Bible.

While I floated there waiting to go up, waiting for that pond to change into a river and little chunky angels to come down, the stars turned into silver coins that floated on the water, blinking and bobbing all around my head, making me dizzy.

Wait up, Ralph!

But then the hole in the clouds blew shut. The silver coins melted and sank. The angels never showed up. No tongues of fire. Just the smell of pond water and mud, the tiny flame of the candle burning up on the dock, my own breath going in and out of me.

The frog started croaking again, and that goddamned moth came floating by, still struggling on the water, sending out little circles getting bigger and bigger, still trying to fly back up to the light.

CLARA PAULSON

B13'S BELLIED up to the front counter telling the receptionist the difference between a possum and a beaver. B13's name is Bert. Bert looks more like a bassoon than a beaver, tall and skinny, black-rimmed glasses and mussed-up white hair. B13's always full of nervous energy, moving and talking. The receptionist isn't listening because I hear papers shuffling back there behind her too high counter, her chair squeaking, drawers opening and closing. I don't blame her. We're all tired of B13's dead-animal stories. B13 was a taxidermist and is always talking about stuffing animals, or about a car he's got in storage across town. Today B13's trying to get the receptionist to let him go look for a possum he saw down by the creek sniffing along the fence they put up when Lizzie drowned. Lizzie. B17. I hate that fence. Fence. The floodlights, too. The floodlights changed all the shadows around this place.

"A possum's got a round tail, like a rat," B13's saying. "Except bigger, lots bigger. Bigger around than that Magic Marker you're holding right there in your hand, and yay long." B13 holds his bony hands a foot or so apart so the receptionist can see. His sleeves are too short, his wrist bones lumpy. "But a beaver's got a flat tail. For whacking the water when danger's near. Doing up the tail's always the trickiest part. Tail and the nose. You know why? I'll tell you. Because there's no fur to hide things under. Of course, I never did up a possum." B13 swallows. The skin on his throat moves up, then back down.

B13 drives me nuts going on and on all the time about stuffed animals or that car of his. But at least his words make sense, not like some of the other yakkers here on the B wing. I think B13's on the wrong wing, too, just like me. But B13 gets to go outside now and then. Outside. Somehow he finagles them out of a release and Johnny Q takes him across town to see that car of his. B13 can't drive it because he doesn't have a license. But he claims he has to start his car every few months. He calls the car his baby. Perhaps that's how he gets the release. They think he's going out to visit family.

When B13 comes back, he's always all full of himself and that car, announcing how his baby "fired right up and purred like a kitten," telling everybody all about what he saw out there on the outside. When he tells me about the outside, I listen and nod. I could care less about his car, but I like hearing about the outside. And when B13 first gets back, he always smells like the outside. So I don't mind listening. I close my eyes, smell the smells, pretend I'm outside. But the outside smells wear off Bert pretty fast. And then it's just B13 talking. That's when I ring my little bell.

"Just a quick gander," B13 is saying now. "I'll just go down and come right back, I promise I will. I haven't seen a possum in years. Please."

The receptionist keeps on squeaking her chair and banging drawers, letting B13 go on and on about beavers and possums. After a while B13 turns around and looks for somebody else to talk to. He spots me back here by the drinking fountain, but I close my eyes real fast, fake it like I'm sleeping. I don't want to hear about his Magic Marker tails. I want to hear ice cubes clinking inside glasses, people laughing through the curtain. Smell makeup and brandy and backstage smells. I want to hear the curtain going up. Feel the lights warm on my face and hands, my rings sparkly. I want to hear the hush, then the first few notes, and then singing. My voice. Me singing again.

GEORGE CASTOR

I⊤ WAS the hayfield that first caught my eye. A whole field of it getting ripe right there in the middle of downtown Looking-glass, houses and streets and sidewalks all around, the late May sun hot. I was driving to the bank to sign my name as the BENEFICIARY for what must have been the hundredth time since getting that letter a couple months back.

The banker who ran the Federal Security Bank in town was so excited about the whole thing, he nearly wet himself every time I walked in to sign my name again. He came rushing out of his office, waving his soft hand, calling me Mr. Castor and sir. Then he ushered me back to his office, his hand on my elbow, talking all the way about the weather and how nice it was to see me again. Funny how having money makes people start perking up and acting strange around you. Makes you wonder why everybody wants to get rich.

Driving back through town after finishing up at the bank was when I noticed the house—standing in the middle of that hayfield, a for-sale sign near the sidewalk leaning bad. Then Max was one tire run up over the curb, the engine idling, my door wide open, a couple of .22 shells rolling shiny across the blacktop down by my boots, and me standing in the middle of the street, staring up. I don't know why I'd never noticed this house before. I'd been driving right by it for years, every time I came into or went back out of town. I knew the house was there, of course. Everybody knew the Hogan House. But I'd never *seen* the house, not until right then, rising up out of that hayfield in front of me like a goddamned castle. The only thing missing was a moat and drawbridge.

Hallelujah! I yelled, right there in the middle of the street. I yelled out that word a couple of times. The same word my aunt Bertha used to whisper every evening right after grace as she crossed herself and unfolded her napkin.

Halleholylujah!

I took my hat off and sent it sailing across the street, spinning through the sunlight and birdsong, sinking out of sight in the middle of all that hay getting ripe. Then I stepped out in front of an oncoming Oldsmobile with California plates. The driver swerved and shot past me blasting his horn and yelling out the window something about me being blind. Goddamn Californians.

I went on across the street to have a closer look at the castle.

Just from the outside, I could tell the house was a beauty, heavy and hog-solid, the way they used to build all houses. The valleys and ridges of the roof sharp as the creases starched into Jason's shirtsleeves. No sags. The dormers pushing out of the third story each had a set of arched windows— eyes staring down at me staring up. And below just about every window in that place was a painted flower box. Dora would have loved the flower boxes. Up above the shake roof, two chimneys shot straight up into the sky, the bricks bulging out a little at the top making those chimneys look just like fists.

And then there was the front porch. The biggest wraparound porch I'd ever seen. A porch so pretty it pulled the breath right out of me. It was that porch that did it, made me fall in love with the Hogan House like a kid falling into infatuation for the first time.

I didn't care that the house had been empty for years, nobody living there or looking after it since the late senator Harry Hogan died six or eight years back. I saw that house only one way right then—the way old Hogan had always kept it: Lawn looking like a golf course. Shutters and shiplap siding and picket fence painted fresh. Flower beds perfect. I even saw Hogan's white Christmas lights burning right there in broad daylight—thousands of tiny diamonds running every which way up and down and all over the angles and edges of that old house. Those lights running up and covering a wooden star Hogan mounted to a pole way up above the highest chimney. Dora always liked driving past the Hogan House after dark at Christmastime. Sometimes she'd make me turn around and drive past another time or two, just so she could look at all those lights, see Hogan's Christmas star way up there blazing brighter than the star above Bethlehem, probably confusing the hell out of any angels or shepherds trying to find the manger.

I didn't care right then that the peeling picket fence was all fallen over, flower beds overgrown with morning glory and chickweed, dandelions coming up everywhere between the bricks of the front walk. I didn't care that the only thing growing in the flower boxes was thistles and crabgrass, that the flower boxes themselves were peeling bad and coming apart at the dovetail joints, or that a lot of the window panes were either broken out or boarded up. And it didn't matter that Hogan's golf course had gone back to its natural state: a hayfield.

Hallelujah!

And then I saw it was still there, the wood frame of Hogan's star way up above the highest chimney, still wrapped around with lights, the broken bulbs and frayed cord a tangled crown of thorns against the sky. Old Hogan would have shit himself if he'd known how his place looked now.

I yanked out the for-sale sign as I hurried back to Max and tossed the sign into the bed with a clatter that brought Shag William to his feet on the seat barking a blue streak. I got in, backed up, pulled a U-turn, and drove through town looking for the real estate office that matched the sign. For a town this small, there were more real estate offices than I ever would have guessed. The one I was looking for was on Water Street, only a block or two down from the Gardens. Just for the hell of it, I drove on up to the Gardens and pulled into the parking lot.

I drove slow toward the front doors and saw the new glass the Ad-ministrator had sent me a bill for. Besides the four hundred and fifty for the glass, the bill also included a hundred and some odd bucks worth of hand-painted letters, the words "silver metallic" in parentheses. I'd tossed that bill into the fire along with the rest of my junk mail.

I pushed in the clutch and let Max stop in front of the glass doors, that spendy new silver lettering bigger than before, and brighter, too. Inside, that woman in the wheelchair was sitting back against the wall, same place she always was when I came in to see Ralph. I let out the clutch and pulled on through the parking lot and out into Water Street.

At the real estate office, I cashed out the Hogan House that afternoon. I could tell the realtor, Will Richards, was dying to know what would make a widowed old foothills farmer like me move into such a big place right in the middle of downtown, but the $15,000 commission he was making for that hour or two worth of paperwork must have kept him from asking.

When we were finished, Will Richards the realtor stood up, dropped the keys into my palm with a smile, and said the wrong thing.

"Oh, before you go, Mr. Castor," he said. "Just this morning there was a couple from L.A. in here looking for a place in the country—out a ways, you know, peace and quiet, escape from all the craziness and earthquakes down there. Well I just now had a thought that maybe they should have a look at your old farm up in the hills. They want to build. Dream house, you know. Your place might just be a perfect location." Will Richards paused, pulled at his nose. "And I can personally guarantee you it would be a quick, and very lucrative, sale."

"Sure," I said. "I'll sell my farm ... just as soon as hell freezes over and the devil himself comes skating out singing Ave Maria. But you can bet your boxer shorts it won't be to any Californians wanting to build a goddamned dream house on prime farmland." I turned and left, slamming the door hard, hoping I just might break the glass in that door, too.

CLARA PAULSON

SUNDAY MIDMORNING, and everything's as still as can be. I'm sitting out here in the lobby. This is my favorite time of the week. Even outside it's quiet. Quiet. Everybody on the outside's at church, or else in bed sleeping off Saturday night. The way I used to. I'd wake up next to some strange man snoring into the pillow, the taste of too many cigarettes on my tongue, too many White Russians pounding inside my head. But the quiet this morning's interrupted by the chirping of songbirds, and an odd clicking.

A woman's standing on the burgundy mats. I didn't even hear the doors squeak open. She just appeared. A small woman. Old. About my age. Perhaps she's here to check herself in. She stands inside the doors, looking around. In one hand, she's holding a small metal cage with several yellow birds inside. Canaries, I think. Or goldfinches. Yellow. In the other hand, the woman has a skunk on a red leash. A skunk! But there's no smell. I used to wear lipstick the color of that leash. Did my nails up, too. The skunk's eyes are the color of her birds. Then the woman's eyes land on me. Her eyes are blacker than quarter notes. She looks at me a little too long, so I look away, pretending I didn't see her. But when I glance back, she winks real quick and something gold blinks in her mouth. I want to ring my bell and get the heck out of here, but I don't. For some reason, I just sit here, rolled back against the wall. When I look up again, the woman's on her tiptoes, back to me, talking to the receptionist across the counter. The woman's shoulder blades stick out, little nubs beneath her sweater. I listen for pieces.

But the woman with the birds is whispering quiet. So even my sharp ears can't catch any of her words. There's something about this woman that's not quite right. Out-of-place. Odd. Perhaps that's what keeps me from ringing my little bell. Her odd out-of-placeness. It's in the air now, spreading through the lobby all around me, the smell of woodsmoke.

Two long, gray braids hang down the woman's back, tied off with pieces of white string, her tan neck showing a little where the hair's pulled to the sides. Perhaps she's Mexican. On her feet she's wearing a pair of purple high-top tennis shoes. Over one shoulder she carries a leather bag with fringe along the bottom and little blue stones tied to the end of each piece of fringe. That's where the clicking's coming from.

"Stories?" I hear the receptionist say.

This skunk woman must think we're all a bunch of kindergarten kids. Just like everybody else. I bite down soft on my tongue, feeling the dead half, an eraser in my mouth.

The receptionist leans toward the woman to say something. I lean forward a little, too. This time I catch every word: "I'm afraid the majority of our residents here are beyond that, if you know what I mean," the receptionist says.

The phone rings. The receptionist squeaks her chair and answers it, loud and brassy, "Silver Gardens." The skunk woman turns and looks right at me again. Black eyes. Black. But this time I don't look away. I snap the fingers of my good hand three times, and wave her over, quick. She looks back at the receptionist on the phone, then comes across toward me, her eyes two holes so deep you could fall in.

I write two words on my pad: "HOG" and "WASH!" Then add five more, "SOME OF US R FINE," and hold it up for her to read. I smell garlic and dry leaves in the wind she brings. Her face is covered with wrinkles and tanned dark. She looks at my pad, but doesn't say anything. I check my words. Sometimes my spelling doesn't work right, but everything looks okay this time.

Then the receptionist apologizes loud and calls the skunk woman back to the counter, as if I weren't even in the room. I hit the pad several times with my good finger. The woman winks at me, quick, that flash of gold in her mouth again, then turns and crosses back to the receptionist behind the counter.

They talk even softer now. But a word comes across the room to me, hissing like it's being broadcast through an old amplifier: *Grace.* Then another word. *Nice.* And then a name that slices through me the way it always does, cutting deep as it goes. *Amy.*

The yellow birds in the cage go nuts, beating and flapping their wings against the shiny bars. The skunk lunges toward me, snaps its lipstick leash straight. Bird shrieks and woodsmoke and flying yellow feathers fill the room, suffocating me. I jingle the heck out of my bell, keep jingling until an aide comes and wheels me off. Down the hall to B31. Behind me, the skunk woman's hushing her canaries. Whispering to her skunk. Her blue stones popping. I blink. Yellow eyes and white stripes flash in the piano-black of my head.

GEORGE CASTOR

AFTER LEAVING the real estate office, I picked up a six-pack of Oly at the Thriftway Store and drove back over to the Hogan House. Pulled right up and parked on the concrete slab between the back door and the detached garage. The slab was a parking lot, really. Could have held a dozen cars. My concrete slab now. My parking lot. Sounded kind of funny. My house. My front porch. Being only one person and having two places didn't make a whole lot of sense, but I'd never sell out to Californians who would bulldoze my house to put up their dream.

That's what happened to Ralph's place, after he wound up in the Gardens. The Realtors got to his farm and diced it up into five-acre chunks, a dream house and a security light on each chunk. There must be fifteen dream houses on the land Ralph and Eileen farmed for a lifetime. Fifteen security lights burning holes in the night.

I twisted open a bottle of Oly and took down the whole thing still sitting in the cab. I opened another bottle, shoved a third in my hip pocket, and walked around to the front of Hogan's house. My house. I stepped back and took in that perfect front porch wrapping all the way around the front of the house, pillars the size of straw bales holding up the porch roof. The porch would cut out a little light, but front porches weren't made for winter. A few long summer evenings spent sitting on a good front porch more than made up for any loss of light. I believed in front porches. But front porches were getting fewer and farther between. Instead of front porches, most new houses had two-hole garages out front.

The porch on the Hogan House was one hundred percent pure American nod-at-your-neighbors-as-they-go-by tradition, and I climbed right up the front steps onto it. A couple of treads were on their way to rotting through and the paint was peeling bad, but it was a real front porch.

The front door was a six-foot oval piece of beveled glass set in solid oak. To the right of the door was a knocker—a brass barn owl, its claws still shiny from all of Hogan's political guests knocking at his door over the years. We had a pair of barn owls nesting in the barn back in Nebraska when I was a kid, their big shadows gliding in and out of the hay mow as night came on. The night before the snowstorm that took away not only my pa, but my mama, too, with my only baby brother or sister still inside her, I saw both those owls, winging fast off into the moon coming up big.

I dropped the keys twice trying to get my new front door unlocked, that owl staring right at me, eyeballs shiny as its claws. Inside the house, I smelled years of nobody living there. Found a world I'd never seen before, a world you needed money to know: dark oak molding and doors, oak floors, arched doorways, a cherry staircase curving its way up to the second story from the slate floor of the entryway. Through an arched doorway to the right was the dining room, its chandelier hanging a little lopsided and covered with cobwebs. To the left, the living room was a quarter acre, or bigger, a massive stone fireplace taking up most of one wall. I couldn't move. I just stood there on that slate smelling the smells of a house kept closed up too long, but good smells mixed in, too. The smell of wood, the smell of no roof leaking and everything dry inside. The good smell of something old.

I walked down the long hallway that ran back past the staircase to three big bedrooms and a bathroom the size of a small barn. At the far end of the hallway, through a door that was more panes of glass than wood, I could see Max parked out by the garage, my door still open.

Up the cherry staircase on the second floor, I found five more bedrooms and another huge bathroom. Up a smaller staircase, the third-floor attic was divided into four smaller bedrooms, all of them with dormers and the arched windows I'd seen from down below. I swung one of the windows open and looked down onto my new neighborhood, rooftops clean and new, lawns tidy patches of dark green, sidewalks white and straight, all the cars sparkling in the May sunlight. I couldn't see a blackberry vine or weed anywhere, except for the dandelions gone to seed in the flower box less than a foot out in front of me. And the funny thing was, I didn't see a single person moving down there in my new in-town neighborhood.

I drained the beer bottle and looked down at Max far below me. I'd never seen Max from this angle, how Max must always look to the birds. The top of the red cab was faded almost to white. The bed was full of junk, including the for-sale sign I'd forgotten about, bright blue, Will Richards's name in black letters so big I could read his name from all the way up here on the third floor. I threw the empty bottle out the window. But the bottle hit Max's hood and shattered, left a new dent in the hood and brown glass blinking on the concrete all around. I pulled the full bottle out of my pocket and threw it out, too. This time the bottle hit the sign dead on and exploded, beer foaming white all over the letters of Will Richards's name.

The kitchen was off the dining room on the main floor, behind a swinging door with a big chrome push plate. The kitchen was bigger than most living rooms, a maple butcher block the size of a foreign car standing in the middle. A dusty collection of copper and stainless steel utensils Hogan's kin must have left behind was hanging from a black iron rack bolted to the ceiling above the butcher block. Going up the walls were white cupboards with baby-blue ceramic knobs, the same knobs Dora always wanted me to put in our kitchen, except Dora wanted lavender. A blue tiled counter ran all the way around the room, stopping for a wide set of French doors that led outside, then stopping again for a stainless-steel sink hanging in the counter just below a big paned window, so much light spilling in through the glass of that window and those French doors, I had to squint.

I opened the French doors and stepped outside onto a bricked terrace. The air was good. I sat on an old concrete bench and looked out at the huge side yard that was all gone to hayfield, too. Hay all the way across to where a few Doug firs were growing this side of a neighbor's hedge, the hedge trimmed all straight and square, a bright green boxwood wall.

I sat there for a long time, the sun going down and night coming on. I had no idea what to do next, so I just sat watching the colors fade. I wished Ralph would show up with a bottle of the good Doctor. We'd sit out here all night, drinking and talking, Ralph giving me hell for getting a place in town.

But Ralph never showed up. Streetlights blinked on and ruined the light. The night got cool, and for the first time, what I'd just done started sinking in. I started feeling kind of sick as I sat there realizing I'd spent a third of Jason's money in a single afternoon on a house nobody'd lived in for years.

Right then, a shooting star took off, burned a white slit into the night sky high above, and I thought for sure I heard Ralph laughing the way Ralph always used to laugh, low and heavy and coming from deep inside him, rolling out across the dark water of Odell Lake, both of us laughing like a couple of goddamned kids with the giggles.

Candle Flame Through Chain-Link

Up the creek a half mile from a big red house, a candle moves along the other side of a chain-link fence in the dark. It is past midnight. No moon. The winter sky sparkles with stars. Whoever is carrying the candle walks just beyond reach of the sulfur vapor lights mounted to the eaves of a single-story building. The pattern of the fence wire passing in front of the flame causes the flame to tremble with the steady quiver of an aspen leaf in a light breeze. The fence itself appears to be in motion, sliding past the steel posts. But there is no sound. Just the gentle gurgle of creek water flowing around frozen rocks in the distance, the faint call of an owl.

The candle stops moving, then starts back along the fence. The flame now illuminates the ochre interior of a cupped hand leading the flame.

Inside the low building, the residents are all sleeping. One of the night aides has fallen asleep with his head on the front counter, yellow headphones from a Walkman plugged into his ears. The other night aide has gone down to the Circle-K to buy cigarettes and meet his girlfriend.

In one of the rooms, a woman stirs, wakes, and sits up. She holds one wrist, then the other, and finally clutches at something hanging at her chest. The woman gets out of bed, and shuffles down the dim hallway toward the lobby wearing a white flannel nightgown, a black rosary around her neck. The aide in the Walkman is snoring. The woman passes through the lobby and enters the dayroom. She crosses to the large windows that look out onto a mowed lawn that slopes down to a creek. The chain-link fence divides the lawn in half, the near side flooded with the metallic yellow light, the far side dark. The woman lifts both hands, and as she presses her palms against the window on each side of her head, more black beads strung through her fingers and around her wrists click against the cold glass. Her breath and moist palms steam the glass. The candle flame beyond the fence stops moving, then vanishes. The woman at the window rubs the fogged glass in front of her eyes with the fingertips of her right hand, a silver crucifix at her wrist clinking back and forth against the glass face of her watch that does not work and the cold glass of the window.

CLARA PAULSON

THAT WOMAN'S coming back today. The one with the birds. Skunk woman. I heard somebody talking. Talking. One of the aides, perhaps. Or somebody else. I never forgot the skunk woman after that first time she showed up in the lobby a few months ago with her skunk and lipstick leash. How could I forget her pointy little eyes, those staccato notes jabbing into me. She must have talked them into letting her tell one of her stories, because B13 told me she's going to tell one. A story. B13 says everyone's invited, even the mummies. But I'm not going. The skunk woman gives me the willies. I'm not going to sit in the dayroom and hear her talk to us like a bunch of kindergarten kids. I get enough of that just living here. Living.

I'm sitting out here in the lobby by the water fountain listening to the little refrigerator inside the metal case clicking off and on, keeping the water only visitors can drink just above freezing. I'll keep an eye on things from here.

I must have dozed off, because when I look up, I see the skunk woman standing on the burgundy mats, holding that cage of yellow birds. She's back. And just like last time, she looks right at me. Those black eyes stab so hard I feel pins going into me all along my spine.

I look down fast, see my dead hand lying on my lap. The skunk woman probably wants me to come listen to her story. I say no in my head. But I don't ring my bell to go back to my room, either.

I sit out here in the lobby near the open door to the day-room and listen. B13's in there, probably just itching to get his hands on one of her yellow birds, pluck it and stuff it, wishing the skunk woman had brought her skunk along today, too. From where I'm sitting I can hear almost every one of the skunk woman's words as she starts in talking, telling her story. My ears are sharp. But I don't look or let on I'm listening to anything. I just sit out here, real quiet, my hand heavy on my lap, my eyes getting heavy, too. Sleepy. Words floating. It's always so hot here in the Gardens. Hot.

Hope's mother was Paiute, her father Swedish, although he was born in Madras, Oregon. This is why the first word Hope remembered hearing was "half-breed." But at that age Hope didn't know what the word meant, or why the town people always said the word low, a raspy whisper.

Hope grew up on the reservation, which was basically an institution, except it didn't have any walls or bars like the other institutions Hope had lived in since. Hope's grandmother once called the reservation "a dry patch of desert a few white men figured was worth so little they could give it back to us." Her grandmother was who first told Hope about the hoop. But her grandmother died sitting against a tree one night when Hope was five. Hope's father said the grandmother was crazy. Hope's mother didn't say a word.

One of Hope's earlier memories was of her father coming home one warm August night, pulling up to the house and turning off his truck. She didn't hear her father get out of the truck. She wondered what he was doing. Hope could hear little ticking sounds the

59

truck made, as if the stars were clicking off one at a time outside, making it darker and darker. After a while, Hope thought her father must have fallen asleep in his truck. Maybe she fell asleep too, but then she woke up to his boots crunching up the driveway and his sloppy stomping on the porch. Hope stayed in bed and listened to her father staggering around the kitchen knocking stuff off the table and talking like he had a potato in his mouth, talking to nobody. Then her father went into his and her mother's bedroom and Hope heard the squishing sound of fist against flesh, flesh holding cries in, sounds Hope was never able to forget. Her father's muffled voice was slobbery and squishy, too. Hope never heard her mother say a word.

It was quiet for a long time, and all Hope could hear was her heart trying to get out through her mouth. She thought maybe her father had fallen asleep. Then the doorknob rattled and her father came into her room. He closed the door and filled the air around her face with the smell of sweated alcohol, engine oil, and grunting. Hope felt the rough calluses on his huge fingers pressing her teeth through her lip, releasing the slippery taste of iron onto her tongue. A taste Hope would always remember.

This was the first time. But not the last.

Each time, when her father was done, he always told Hope not to tell anyone, or her mother might bleed to death. He said her mother had a strange disease that caused her to bleed when she got too upset. Hope believed her father. Hope wasn't quite ten years old.

At fourteen, Hope left the reservation and never saw her family again. She went up to The Dalles where she worked washing dishes for the winter. One day she happened to see her mother's death notice in the paper. A little dab of text she wouldn't have noticed, except her own name jumped off the page at her like a kangaroo rat. Hope hitched down to the funeral home late that night and sat with her mother for a long time. Her mother looked more peaceful lying there in that box than Hope had ever seen her look before in her whole life. Hope thought that after she had run away, her father had given her share to her mother, which was probably what killed her. Or else her mother killed herself. Her mother was only thirty-

nine. That's what it said in the paper. But Hope knew one thing: her mother didn't bleed to death because of her telling anybody.

Now a young woman, Hope carried this stained secret of her father's around with her, not telling anyone, trying to forget. After two marriages, both to men who turned out to be just like her father, Hope realized she couldn't keep the secret quiet anymore. So she went to a hospital to talk to someone and wound up spending a year in the state mental institution in Salem, believing the doctors and nurses when they told her she was sick and needed help.

Then one day Hope woke up and knew it wasn't her who was sick, but her father, and some of his sickness had rubbed off inside her and was eating her up from the inside out. When she told the nurse that, the nurse said she needed rest—rest would heal her. All night Hope rested, staring up at the ceiling, planning her escape.

The following week Hope boarded a Greyhound bus bound for Arizona. She had to get away from the Oregon rain and the people who'd either made her sick or thought she was sick. She'd heard it was sunny in Arizona, and Arizona was near the top of the list of destinations posted on the wall at the bus station. So Arizona was where Hope headed.

On the way to Arizona, an old woman got on the same bus and sat down in the seat next to Hope. She told Hope her name was Dawamana. Then Dawamana told Hope she was pretty. Hope didn't believe her, but the next thing Hope knew, she was getting off the bus with Dawamana somewhere outside of Winslow. There was no bus station or buildings, just a burning dry heat, a ditch full of withered weeds, and a rattler run over flat on the pavement. After the bus roared off, the woman bent over and cut off the rattle with a little knife she pulled out of nowhere, tucked the rattle in a small bag around her neck, and buried the snake in the sand under a Juniper tree away from the road. Then the two women walked away into the desert far from the highway.

Dawamana's house was a dusty pile of stones high on a mesa. Inside her house, dozens of candles burned yellow cat eyes. Hope stood in the low doorway blinking, wondering who had lit all the candles. She thought maybe she should run. But the woman told her not to be afraid, that this was the safest, most sacred place in the whole world.

Hope spent the next half a year living in that stone house with Dawamana, rising at dawn to greet the sun, learning to grind corn, learning how the desert could help her. Hope started all over again. She wasn't sure if it was the desert light in the evenings or the color of the earth in that part of the world, but it was as if she became a different person. Dawamana taught Hope how to find water in the middle of nowhere, how to listen to her insides and to the birds, how to deal with white men. The most important thing Dawamana taught Hope was that there were spirits in the Underworld and all around who had the power to do just about anything. Lots of spirits. As many as the stars in the night sky. They were good spirits, willing to help people out. The trouble, Dawamana said, was that most people didn't slow down long enough to notice the spirits all around, didn't take the time to talk to the spirits and light candles and greet the sunrise.

During those months living in the desert with Dawamana, Hope learned to talk to the spirits. She also learned more about the hoop her grandmother had talked about so long ago, and why Dawamana didn't keep track of birthdays. And Hope learned about the power of corn. . . .

☺

My own snoring wakes me. A snort. Dribble on the dead half of my chin. Cold and wet. I wipe the dribble off fast with my good sleeve before anybody sees. The dayroom's empty, the skunk woman gone. I smell sage and think I'm back in Nevada. But outside I can see trees along the edge of the empty parking lot. A handful of blackbirds fly low past the glass doors. The little refrigerator in the drinking fountain clicks on down by my hip and hums. Just the Gardens. Always the Gardens.

PART TWO

East White

Wildflower seed in the sand and wind
May the four winds blow you home again.

— Jerry Garcia & Robert Hunter
"Franklin's Tower"
by the Grateful Dead

GEORGE CASTOR

It was getting late for a garden. I knew that well enough. But I also knew that living through the summer without growing at least a few of my own vegetables just wouldn't do. Not growing a garden was a sin in my book. No excuses.

But it was obvious from what I'd seen around my new neighborhood that these town folks were more concerned with flat lawns and flowering fruit trees than with growing food. I couldn't believe anybody in their right mind would grow fruit trees that had been genetically tampered with so as *not* to bear fruit. It made no sense. Went against nature. The only sign of a vegetable garden I'd seen so far was a handful of tomato starts growing in a planter box on the porch of a little pale yellow house down the street a ways.

I'd throw a garden in, better late than not at all, and hope for a long, warm fall. Growing vegetables did things for the soul you couldn't explain.

I hated to see all the ripe hay growing up in my new yard go to waste, but I also didn't want to take the time to rake and bale the stuff before putting my garden in. So I brought down my tractor and sickle-bar mower from the farm and cut the hay. I then hitched up my rototiller, engaged the power takeoff, dropped the tines to the turf, and churned it all under. It didn't take long to convert a chunk of Hogan's golf-course-gone-to-hayfield into what was a pretty decent garden plot.

The flower beds along the sidewalk were so overgrown and the picket fence in such sorry shape I cleared it all away with my front-end scoop and piled everything back by the grove of Doug firs to burn later that fall. The old flower beds tilled up easy, which made my new garden space even bigger than what I needed. But maybe some of my new neighbors might want to put in a few rows of corn or pole beans on my place.

I was working so fast, trying not to let the growing season get another day on me, that I didn't notice right away when a few people showed up on the sidewalk out in front of my new place and started taking an interest in what I was doing. Looked like some of my new neighbors come by to welcome me to the area. So I shut off Poppin' Johnny and climbed down. Pulled off my gloves and slapped them against my leg as I walked the stiffness out of my back over to where two men, a woman, and a couple of kids were standing.

"Howdy," I said, taking off my hat and wiping my brow. The woman wore an apron that was pressed so well and washed so white it looked like she was wearing a paper airplane. One man had a tie on loose around his neck and a little girl on his arm. The other man looked like he was either headed for a golf course or an operating room: white stretch shirt, white stretch slacks, and a funny glove full of little holes on one hand. A boy about five or six stood on the ground holding on to the edge of the woman's paper airplane.

"New landscaping project?" the man in white with the holey glove said.

"Oh, I suppose you could call it that," I said. "Just putting in a garden. Damn near too late, you know."

"In the front yard?" the woman asked.

"Yeah," I said, turning around to have a look at my tilling job. "Gets plenty of sun. Pretty decent drainage. Soil needs a good shot of manure, but in general it looks like it's going to work out just fine."

"Mister Hogan used to win the Neighborhood Yard Competition every summer, you know," the woman said.

"Yard competition?" I asked, turning back around.

"Our Neighborhood Association sponsors it," she said. "We have a committee that selects the best-kept yard in our neighborhood. Then we all get together and have a picnic. On the winner's lawn." She smiled, smoothing her airplane. "But nobody could ever beat Mister Hogan."

"You know who's moving in here?" the man in the glove asked. "Who you putting the garden in for?"

"Who do you think I'm putting it in for? *Mister* Hogan?" I laughed a little at what I thought was a pretty good line. But none of them laughed. I put out my hand. "I live here now," I said. "Name's George. George Castor. But George is good enough."

The man in the golf getup shook my hand, saying his name was Blankenship. He introduced me to the other man and the woman.

"Well, it's sure kind of you to come out and say hello," I said. "It's always nice to be welcomed by new neighbors." I remembered when Dora and I'd moved in up at the farm years ago. A couple of warm pies, halfdozen steaks, fresh-baked bread. Lots of handshakes. People had trickled by for two or three days, stopping in to meet the newcomers, wishing us well, introducing themselves and their kids, saying that if we needed anything at all, just to give a holler.

"You might want to check with City Hall about this," the man named Blankenship said. "There are certain restrictions about planting."

The girl dropped a doll that must have had a tape recorder in it, because the doll started laughing. The woman snatched up the doll and turned off the laughter. The boy giggled.

"Look, we just want the neighborhood to stay looking nice," the man in the tie said. "That's all."

"Well don't worry. I won't ruin your pretty neighborhood," I said. "But I am going to finish putting in my garden. So if you don't mind, I need to get back to work. Sun's going down." I turned and went back to my tractor.

☾

Knowing full well it was late to put on fresh manure, I stopped off at Ed Mumford's hog farm on the way back to town the next morning and had Ed put a scoop of fresh hog shit on top of the dry cow shit I had already scraped from my own barn and loaded into my manure spreader. Half an hour later, the spreader blades were throwing that old dry cow shit and that new sloppy hog shit all over what had only yesterday been Hogan's award-winning front yard. I got a little close to the house a couple of times and splattered the shiplap siding. But the house was peeling so bad the whole thing would need to be scraped before a new coat of paint would stick anyway.

When I was done, I shut off the tractor, climbed down, and breathed in. I'd underestimated the aromatic power of fresh hog shit. A half a scoop, or even a few shovelfuls, would have been plenty. I tilled the manure into the soil as fast as I could. But when I was done the whole place was still stinking pretty good. There wasn't much else I could do, except hope the wind blew straight up.

By the time I had most of the seeds and starts in the ground, I still had time to make a run back up to the farm and bring down my supply of six-inch aluminum irrigation pipe. When I got back into town with the pipe I was too pooped to pop and knew full well I should have quit right then and there, called it a day. But of course, just like me, I didn't.

After laying out lines of pipe on my new garden, my back aching bad and both knees burning to beat hell, I accidentally backed the pipe trailer into a goddamned fire hydrant some-body'd put at the corner of Hogan's front yard. A geyser went shooting through the air all the way across the street, filling up and overflowing out of a baby-blue convertible Chrysler New Yorker that I would soon find out belonged to the man with the holey glove. He had parked in front of the couple's house who were hosting a hastily called meeting of the Neighborhood Association, at which my arrival to the neighborhood was being discussed.

Standing there watching water overflowing out of that blue convertible, I knew I'd just disqualified myself from the neighborhood yard competition for good.

CLARA PAULSON

SOME DAYS I can forget all about little Amy. My Amy. Other days I can't get her out of my head. Guess that's what I get for doing what I did to her.

Sometimes I ring my bell for an aide to roll me out to the bulletin board and park me so I can see if there's anything new coming up. Up. Usually there isn't. Just the menu and maybe a newspaper clipping cut out of *Senior News* and tacked too high for me to read.

A few new people did move into the C wing. A man who wears a bow tie and walks down the hall in our wing now and then. Some woman who's so big around it must be hard for her to walk at all. Somebody else. I first saw the man in the bow tie talking to the Rhino about moving in here. He asked for a nice room, with a view of the creek, as if this were some fancy hotel and he was checking in expecting his lover to meet him later.

Sometimes I sit out in the lobby and try to pretend I'm staying in a fancy hotel in Vegas, but it doesn't work. There aren't any keys hanging behind the desk. No slots for messages. No luggage coming in and going out. No bellboys or elevators. And no lounge with music and cigarette smoke and laughter coming out.

B24 died. Disappeared. A few days ago.

His name was Ralph. Ralph. I finally remembered. He didn't last long here. Not really, not compared to some who have been here for years, waiting. Ralph was in a year or two, I guess. I didn't even know he was gone until I heard his friend out in the hall the other night yelling at the Rhino. I wanted to roll out and cheer B24's friend on.

B24's door had been closed for a couple days, but that wasn't unusual. I just assumed B24 was a little sick and the Rhino wanted to keep the germs contained. Which is a joke. Germs are everywhere here in the Gardens. The next thing I knew B24's friend was swearing and stomping out in the hall, aides running every which way, the smell of fresh fish and pine trees strong in the air, and the fire alarm going off loud— the most out-of-tune sound in the world.

B24's friend hasn't been back here since. Too bad. I didn't know B24's friend, but I sure liked seeing him come in and go out. Out. I liked the barnyard smells he brought in with him. I wish B24's friend would come visit me, especially when it's raining out and the mud puddles are just brown. Doubt I'll ever see him again now. Unless he checks himself in here someday. But he'll never do that now. He'd have to be nuts. He was so mad when he left he cracked the glass in one of the doors out in the lobby. The crack is a little starburst. Shiny and silver and pointy all around. Just like the star above the little cardboard nativity scene they set up in the dayroom at Christmastime every year. But the star B24's friend left in the door is getting bigger each time the doors squeak open and bump shut. Slowly rising, that star. My star.

GEORGE CASTOR

THE HANDS of my clock glowed four-fifteen. Shit.

I'd been waking up too early ever since moving into town for good a few weeks ago. Couldn't get back to sleep. I'd been blaming it on the streetlights, shining in the window making it look like the sun was on the verge of coming up all night long. But this morning I remembered hearing somewhere that the older you get the less you can sleep. Some people survived on only an hour or two a night. I rolled over and tried to force myself back to sleep. But that thought about only sleeping an hour or two a night kept buzzing around my head, a thirsty mosquito.

I rolled onto my back and lay breathing into the darkness. Outside, a robin started in, then stopped.

I thought about my old farmhouse thirteen miles away neck-deep in blackberries, about my new house here in town. The furniture I'd brought down from the farm barely made a dent in all the open space of Hogan's house. I wanted the wallpaper to tell me everything it had soaked up over the years. Tell me stories about Hogan. About the people who'd lived here before Hogan. Everybody had stories. I used to love stories. I remembered my mama telling me stories when

I was a kid, and then, after the snowstorm, my uncle Bill telling stories. Nobody told stories anymore. I hadn't told Jason many stories. Maybe that's what went wrong.

The ceiling had turned a grayish-pink, the real light coming on. The streetlights that burned all night would shut off soon, thank God. Outside, the birds were having a party, filling the air with song. I was glad birds lived in town. I decided to get up and go out for a walk with Shag William.

☉

Standing outside the wrought-iron gate of the cemetery at the edge of town, I thought about what my uncle Bill used to call graveyards back in Omaha: Marble Orchards. I thought about how I had slipped away during Uncle Bill's funeral when I was fifteen, how my last sight of Aunt Bertha was from the hill above the cemetery where I had stopped and looked back once, seen her hair spilling shiny as new pennies in a pool of black coats and hats and net veils. Then I'd turned and kept running for years.

On the iron gate, spiderwebs sagged frosty white with dew. I pushed the gate open and Shag William waddled through, nose glued to the ground. The sun coming up glowed behind the hills to the east, turning the undersides of clouds the color of coals. Walking down the narrow road that split the cemetery in half, I saw a tall white angel standing on a marble cylinder, leaning a little, staring at me. The angel's left wing was broken off, her face wet with dew. The angel was the last tombstone before the new section started, where the stones were all flush with the ground. For easy mowing. That's what they'd told me when I'd ordered Dora's. Pillars and the like that stuck up above ground were no longer allowed. All tombstones had to be flush, for easy mowing.

I walked out through the flat stones, thinking maybe I'd go see Dora's. Most of the stones were the same size, red or gray marble. Uniform. No fancy carving. No angels. Nothing but polished marble and etched names for acres.

Then my eyes caught on a small gray stone, letters across the top spelling out a name that made me stop breathing, stop walking.

RALPH EDWARD POLLUX

Holy Jesus. Here he was.

It was the cheapest tombstone they sold. I knew that from buying Dora's. "Modest" is what the undertaker had called it. Concrete and not much bigger than a brick, the name and birth and death dates the only things stamped into it. Nothing else. No fancy letters. No final words left behind for the living. Strictly utility. "For the less fortunate," the undertaker had said, flipping ahead in the catalogue. They didn't recommend it.

I tore out the grass around the edges of that cheap tombstone, the sound of roots breaking loud in the air, sow bugs dropping onto Ralph's name and curling up—fishing sinkers. Sweeping the sow bugs away with my hand, I noticed the tombstone rocked a little. I pushed on one edge, and it came loose, no bigger than a short chunk of two-by-four. I tried to stomp it back into place. But it wouldn't fit. The sun had crested the hills. The one-winged angel across the graveyard glowed pink.

I lifted the tombstone and scraped mud and worms off the bottom, then stomped at the hole in the sod until the edges were no longer sharp, stomped until it was just a patch of earth, a little bruised.

Carrying the tombstone the way my uncle Bill used to carry my aunt Bertha's Bible for her when the three of us went to Mass, I walked back into town. The tombstone pulled down on my arm, making my shoulder hurt. My right knee burned pretty good from stomping the hell out of that patch of marble orchard. The chill from the tombstone worked into the bones of my hand. A few cars went by, headlights still burning, weak and yellow in the dawn.

I walked right past my new house and was going across the bridge downtown when I stopped. The water of Lookingglass Creek fifty feet below ran deep, kept narrow by the steep basalt banks on both sides. A few spindly vine maple grew out of the rock walls, the leaves straining to find light. I put the tombstone on the bridge railing and rubbed my cold hands together. The sun was just hitting the copper flashing on the second story of Hamde's Hardware. The water coming out from under the bridge was sparkling a little with the first silvery light of morning. Goldfinches were singing to each other.

Then I lifted that hunk of concrete up over my head and threw it as hard as I could, watched Ralph's name tumbling through air and light, that stone taking flight. A single loud splash, and Ralph was gone. Just the creek flowing again. Nothing but circles floating on the surface. The current pulling the circles past the vine maple and on downstream, headed for the Pacific, that cheap tombstone sunk straight to the bottom.

But not for long. The first muddy floodwaters of fall would roll it along the bottom, knock the edges off, grind the letters smooth, and turn that modest chunk of concrete back to sand and river rock the way it belonged.

CLARA PAULSON

AN ORANGE cat's coming across the parking lot outside. Walking toward the lowest rays of my star. The Rhino hasn't fixed my star yet. Which is nice. Nice. I like watching my star getting bigger from all the bumping closed and squeaking open. So big the rays now reach out all around and clear down to the floor. Silver rays, thin as hairs.

Sometimes when the light's just right, the rays give off little rainbow sparks. Someday the whole piece of glass might collapse, my star implode. Too many rays. Too many bumps. If my star does that right now, the orange cat will be buried under a pile of broken rays and rainbow bits.

Earlier today I heard Bert, B13, talking to the receptionist about a storyteller coming tomorrow. Must be that woman with the black eyes and yellow birds. Skunk woman. I hope not. Not after what she told before. At least I think she told it. Something about a bus and a snake and circles. I hate snakes. But maybe it was just one of my wires. That's what's so hard. I'm never sure.

B13's so worked up about the skunk woman coming, he's telling everyone, even the mummies. He knows she might bring her skunk and birds. But I don't think I'll go this time.

I wish that orange cat would turn into B24's friend, walk in through my star. Become my prince charming. But the cat won't. B24's friend's only reason for ever coming to the Gardens has disappeared. Some days I want to disappear, too, shrink away into the middle of my star, into the diamond shining bright where all the rays come together.

GEORGE CASTOR

"I'VE ALWAYS liked red, Kenny." I knew Kenny from seeing him around town, and the few times a year I needed something at Chuck's Paint Floor 'N More, where Kenny worked. Pinned to his white overalls just below where his name was stitched in green was a little silver fish with the word Jesus inside. "Red's a color that stands up and shouts. Gets the blood going," I said. "Red's good for you, Kenny."

"You want to paint 'er red then, huh?" Kenny said, scratching at the back of his neck with his pencil.

"Damned right," I said. "Fire-Engine-red. Brighter'n hell."

Kenny stopped scratching his neck and cleared his throat. "What about the trim?" he said.

I thumbed through the paint cards and picked a yellow the color of dandelion in full sun. "This one," I said, holding out the card. "This yellow and that red."

"You sure about that?" Kenny asked.

"Sure as I'm standing here," I said. "Sure as hell."

"All righty. If that's really what you want." Kenny scribbled on a pad, then looked at a calendar tacked to the wall behind him. "Let's see, then, we can prep next week, and, depending

on the weather, probably prime the following Monday.
What's your address up there, George?"

"Three Thirty-three Ferry Street," I said.

Kenny started to write, then stopped and looked across the
counter at me. "That's right downtown here. I thought you
lived up in the hills, around Drake's Crossing."

"Not anymore," I said.

"You moved to town?" Kenny asked.

"Kind of," I said. "Bought the old Hogan House."

Kenny didn't say anything. He just looked at me. So I
winked at him. "Couldn't bear to see that house just sitting
there going to seed," I said.

"But the Hogan House is huge," Kenny said at last. "You
could put an army of God's soldiers in there."

"It's plenty big, all right," I said.

"What're you going to do? Open a bed-and-breakfast or
something?" Kenny asked.

"Hell no," I said. "I can't stand tourists."

Kenny kept looking at me. So I winked again. He looked
down and finished writing up the order, then tore off the
pink copy and handed it to me. "There you go. I'm sure
Chuck'll want to do an estimate for you. The Hogan House'll
take a few gallons. And I'm afraid it won't be cheap." Kenny
hesitated, working at his neck again with the pencil. "You're
sure about that bright red?"

"Why not?" I said. "The devil's not the only one who can
like red, is he?"

☾

Setting up the scaffolding took almost a week. Then the
prep took the better part of three more weeks, Chuck and his
boys scraping and sanding and making a hell of a racket.
When they finally got to the paint, it only took a day and a
half. The red looked wet even after it had been dry for two
weeks, and the yellow around the windows and doors shone
like gold leaf. Looked good. When the sun was out full boar,

even the garden and trees and irrigation pipe looked a little pink. I liked it.

But my new paint job generated a letter to the editor in the local weekly paper, *The Lookingglass Appeal-Tribune*, from a Mrs. Bernice Beasley. The letter claimed she'd lived in the neighborhood for "half a century," and that my color scheme was "abominable" and not "in keeping" with the vintage of the house. Just reading that much made me grin. This Mrs. Beasley then went on to say that if she wanted to live near a fire station, she would have moved closer to one. She ended by suggesting that this "newcomer" was either "on dope, or had absolutely no sense of artistic color." She demanded the Mayor look into painting codes and get back to her within ten days. I couldn't help laughing out loud.

But then my eyes locked on three of the words staring at me out of Bernice Beasley's letter: *half a century*.

Maybe she was the answer. Or part of the beginning of an answer at least. She had to be at least fifty. My new house was ready to go, paint and all. I read the letter again. The tone wasn't exactly encouraging, but I knew I had to start somewhere, take the next step. Ralph was waiting on me.

So I grabbed the phone book and looked under *B*. There she was, a Beasley, B., at Four-O-Five Ferry Street, only a block or so away.

೨

Turned out to be the pale yellow house with the tomato plants on the porch, the vines now lush and green and loaded with bright red tomatoes. The woman who answered the door was blonde and young, big plastic earrings tugging heavy on her lobes. She looked no more than thirty or forty—so young I almost turned away. "Mrs. Beasley?" I said. Her plastic earrings reminded me of the red and white tags I used to keep my milk cows straight years ago.

"No," the young woman said. "But I'll get her." She bellowed over her shoulder, *"Mommmm!"* then turned back to me, her ear tags swinging wide. "She'll be right here," she said.

"Nice tomatoes," I said, turning to the planter boxes. When I looked back, an older version of the younger woman was standing in the doorway. She was about half her daughter's height and wore sparkly earrings and a pink and turquoise getup kind of like the women in India wear.

"Thank you," she said, looking at me out of blue eye shadow.

"Hi, I'm George Castor," I said, offering my hand. "I believe we're neighbors."

"We are?" The woman didn't even look at my hand.

"I live in the red house," I said, pulling a thumb back over my shoulder. But I could see it didn't register. "The one you mentioned . . . in the paper," I said.

That hit home. Mrs. Beasley flushed pink, perked up straight, and started shaking a crooked index finger at me, the bright red nail blurring in the air below my chin. "So you're the one!" she said. "Great Scott, we'll all be killed. Where on earth did you learn to pick out colors?"

"I like red," I said, ". . . and dandelions."

"Dandelions? What are you talking about?" she demanded.

"The yellow," I said.

"Well, it's audacious!" she said. "Disgusting! I've never in all my life seen a house that calls attention to itself like Mr. Hogan's house now does. You must be crazy! What on earth possessed you?"

"Well, partly, like I said, because I like red. And partly, because of all you neighbors. The off-whites and pale greens and light yellows around here are pretty dull, don't you think? Boring and bland as lima beans straight out of a can."

"Why, not at all!" she said, making herself taller still. "It's very proper. Stately." She snapped her mouth shut, pushed her chin out, and turned her head a little to the side.

"Well, I just dropped by to introduce myself," I said. "And to ask if you'd like to join me this evening for dinner . . . in the red house."

Mrs. Beasley sucked air in so fast I could hear it going down. Then she stepped back and slammed the door in my face.

I looked down at the tomato plants and noticed that I was not only still wearing my bedroom slippers, but my fly was gaping wide open, the black and red plaid of my flannel shirt-tail poking out like a goddamned tongue.

CLARA PAULSON

I GO. Don't ask me why, but here I am sitting rolled up against the wall in the back of the dayroom. The skunk woman's up front already started in with her story. Story. I'm the only one here, besides B13 and a few mummies they wheeled in from the A wing. The mummies are already asleep, their heads bent over at odd angles like those flexible sweetheart soda straws. I look over at Bert. Sure enough, he's eyeballing her birds, leaning forward a little, rubbing his fingertips with his thumbs.

I haven't really been listening to the skunk woman's words until the word "hospital" comes zinging through the air loud and clear. So I listen up. At first, I think she's lecturing us about staying out of the hospital by keeping active, and exercising, and eating right. I've heard this sermon before and wonder why they waste their energy. But I'm dead wrong. This is no lecture about health. It's a story, and the skunk woman's already coming to the end.

"And at last the doctor came into the waiting room where the man dozed. The long, black night of waiting had exhausted him. A shadow of dark beard smudged his jaw and made him appear dirty. His hair was a mess. His skin the color of yogurt. The man was

ugly. The male doctor stood for a moment, watching the sleeping man, slid so far down in the chair it looked like he might slip off onto the floor. Then the doctor buttoned his white coat and cleared his throat. The man jerked awake. 'We have a baby girl for you, Mr. Paulson,' the doctor said. 'Congratulations.' "

My own last name shoots into my head like a rim shot. I jump so hard my bell jingles and I roll back into the wall. The skunk woman's staring straight at me. Not saying another word. Just letting my own last name and the words of her baby story sink in, little glowing coals. Coals. Searing deep. Too close to my dark sin. I ring my bell loud, keep ringing it. I want to scream at the skunk woman, tell her to stop messing with my mind, tell her to never come back.

An aide finally shows up with a question on his face. I scrawl B31 NOW! on my pad. He wheels me to it and leaves.

Times like now I can't stand this place and wish more than anything I could live in some little house outside Vegas where it's sunny and warm and I could have a Steinway and a porch with flower boxes overflowing with marigolds.

I pull my pillow off the bed onto my lap and push my face deep. B24's gone. And B24's friend will never be back in again. He's on the outside for good, and I'm going to be here in the Gardens until I die. Die. I want to cry, and keep crying, but I don't. Because I hear something, and listen. Yes! But it *can't* be. Not in this place. I hear piano music in the pillow darkness! It's one of the tunes I used to play! I haven't heard the tune in years. There's a piano in the dayroom, but the keyboard cover's always locked with a big metal padlock that's scratched a little half circle in the wood. Perhaps they've unlocked that piano! And somebody's playing it! But when I listen close, I know this music isn't coming from the piano in the dayroom. It's a grand, in a big hall, or a church. I can tell from the sound. I keep the light pushed away from my eyes, let only the footlights come up, slow.

GEORGE CASTOR

ONE OF the few nice surprises about living in town I discovered when I at last got around to resubscribing to the daily paper out of Portland was that *The Oregonian* was delivered the old-fashioned way: by hand, early in the morning, by a paperboy on a bicycle, right up onto my own big, wide front porch.

I looked forward to finding the rolled-up, rubber-banded bundle waiting just outside my front door every morning. The paper was regular, put a steadiness back into my life that had been missing since I'd been living among streetlights and jumpy neighbors. And because *The Oregonian* was hand-delivered, the way milk was before plastic jugs and waxed cartons, it was a daily reminder that a few things were still done the right way in this old world.

So I started sitting longer than usual reading *The Oregonian* every morning, drinking my coffee, letting the ink and caffeine start working together. I liked my morning ritual, the sound of coffee and newsprint kicking things into gear, boxcars being coupled in the freight yard of my belly.

Years ago, Doc Petit had told me coffee wasn't a good habit, said I should cut back, or better yet, quit cold turkey. But I

believe that just about everything in life is fine—in moderation. So I never did quit coffee. I did cut back, though, from
a dozen or so cups a day to no more than a quart.

It was my firm belief in moderation that every now and
again made me go out of my way to *not* read *The Oregonian*.
On those days, I dropped the rolled-up paper into the fire
and watched the green rubber band go gummy and snap, the
paper springing open a trifle, news of the world going up the
chimney unread.

I soon learned that the paperboy's timing was pretty close
to perfect: every morning within minutes of a quarter to six
The Oregonian came sailing through the air and landed on the
porch boards with a thud.

I was so impressed by the paperboy's timing that one late
September morning I stepped out onto the porch at twenty
till and waited in the dark. Pretty soon I heard the squeaking
of a rusty bicycle chain coming my way. Then I saw the boy,
yoked by dirty canvas bags, riding down the sidewalk at a
slight wobble. He passed my place and launched a paper into
the air without even stopping. I stepped forward and caught
the paper against my chest without a sound. The boy stopped
his bike and looked back. I stood there holding the paper over
my head with both hands, the breeze blowing through my
white nightshirt and hair.

"Nice throw!" I yelled.

The boy waited for a second, then pedaled on down the
dark street lobbing papers at houses, now and then glancing
back at me on my big front porch. I must have looked like a
goddamned ghost standing there in my nightshirt and bare
legs, hair not combed, my eyes probably shining bloodshot
red from no coffee yet and all the streetlight bouncing off the
red shiplap siding of my house.

Hallelujah! I yelled as loud as I could. But all I heard back
was the squeaking of that rusty bicycle chain fading away,
almost the same sound Canada geese make flying over in the
night. The streetlight by the fire hydrant blinked off.

I started getting up every morning in time to catch the paper. Pretty soon the paperboy had turned it into a game. He would pedal past the house as if he'd forgotten all about my paper, then wheel around and let one arc end over end all the way from the corner: *The Oregonian* airborne for what seemed a full minute. What an arm! Or the boy would arrive early, park his bike, and crouch behind the camellia bush by the sidewalk. When I stepped out onto the porch, he would jump out without a sound and fire the paper into the air. Somehow I managed to catch the damned thing every morning. The paperboy never said a word.

Sundays were different. No matter how early I came out onto the porch, the *Sunday Oregonian* was always lying there already, a bundle four or five times bigger than the weekday editions. Part of me was relieved. Catching the massive Sunday paper would have been like trying to catch a chunk of cordwood.

One Sunday morning I woke up at three-thirty, a dream about fishing with Ralph still washing through my head. In the dream Ralph and I were underwater, both of us tangled together in miles of bright orange fly line and purple yarn. We were trying hard to get loose and swim back up to the light at the surface, but we were sinking to the bottom fast, running out of air, Ralph starting to laugh bubbles.

I couldn't get back to sleep, so I got up and decided to see how early the paperboy delivered the mysterious, monster Sunday paper. It was a chilly morning, mid-October. I pulled a chair out onto the porch and sat bundled in an army blanket in the far corner. My breath came out of me thick. I waited.

After what seemed like hours, I heard the squeaky chain coming. But this time, the squeaking stopped and footsteps sounded on the porch steps. I stood up quiet. The boy struggled to the top of the stairs under the weight of his bulging bags, pulled out a paper, and let it drop to the porch boards with a slam that rattled the pane of glass in the front door.

"You're early," I said, standing in the shadows wrapped in the blanket. The boy shrieked, turned, and ran down the stairs, the loaded bags knocking and pushing and pulling him so bad he lost his balance and fell face-first on the grass at the bottom of the steps. The weight of the bags pinned him to the ground. He struggled and grunted in a panic trying to get untangled. I let myself down the steps, my knees stiff from sitting in the cold so long.

When I got to the bottom, the world had moved on, left me behind. It took me a minute to figure out what I was seeing. It was logical enough, but I'd never heard of such a thing. The paperboy was a girl. Her hair, tucked up under a baseball cap all these mornings, now spilled down her shoulders. And in the glare of streetlight, I could see her hair was the same coppery orange of my aunt Bertha's.

"Well, I'll be damned," I said. "Never heard tell of a girl paperboy."

The girl struggled to her feet and stood panting, glancing down at the bags as if they might still be alive. I could see freckles sprayed over the bridge of her pug nose and out across both cheeks.

"You all right?" I asked. "Nothing broken?" The girl shook her head and rubbed at her knee but didn't say anything.

"What's your name?" I asked.

She was silent.

"I didn't mean to scare you," I said. "I just wanted to see why the Sunday paper comes so early."

"Because Sunday takes forever!" she yelled, her face dark. "And now I'm going to be even later." She knelt and started shoving papers back into the bags.

"I'm sorry if I scared you," I said.

"You didn't scare me!" she said.

When she was almost done gathering up the spilled papers I said, "So you're the person who throws me the paper every morning," I said.

" 'Cept Sundays," she said. "Nobody throws Sundays. Sundays are like lugging lead. I hate Sundays."

"Well, it's a pleasure to meet such a talented pitcher," I said.

The girl stopped and looked up at me. "I love baseball!" she said, a smile starting to break across her face.

"With an arm like yours, I figured you must," I said. "I used to play, you know. Years and years ago, of course. Shortstop."

"Really? You played short?" the girl said, getting to her feet. "That's what I want to play!"

Then I saw the excitement wash out of her face. She went back to reloading her bags.

"Why don't you?" I asked.

"Because I'm a girl!" she said. "So my dad won't let me."

She put her bags on. "I gotta get going," she said, and hurried toward the street.

"Hey," I yelled after her, "you want to play catch sometime?"

She looked around. "I don't have no mitt," she said, getting on her bicycle. Then she squeaked off down the street.

"I don't either," I yelled after her.

One afternoon as I was racking my brain trying to figure out what to do next, how to get on with things, I opened a beer and started reading *The Appeal*. I don't know why I read the lousy rag every week, but I did. I read every word, all the classified ads, the church notices, the marriage announcements, and the sports page. I even read the obituaries—a word that I had always thought sounded more like a type of fancy cookie than anything to do with dying.

The names and ages in the obituary column were printed in bold type. Numbers and names. Years alive. Ink on paper. Why the hell did we keep track of age, anyway? Birthday after birthday. Another goddamned candle on the cake every year.

The oldest person listed was a seventy-nine-year-old woman named Marietta Maria Jakoby. Somebody else named

Harold Wadsworth Wermer was only fifty-three. Heart attack, no doubt. William Floyd "Willie" McVicar III was seventy-eight. His obituary had a photograph of a man who couldn't have been a day over forty wearing a uniform and medals, smiling at the camera. I recognized none of the names.

I put the paper down and looked out the window. The glass was spotted with rain and yellow honey locust leaves. The wind gusting pretty good. The clouds dark. Winter coming on.

Then I felt something slip, deep down in the dark of my gut. A trout. Trapped in my belly. Wriggling inside my stomach. Trying to get out of the acid and heat. Trying to find fresh water. *You won't recognize any more names! You don't know anybody your age anymore!*

I stood up so fast the edges went white. The paper floated to the floor all around me. Huge gray leaves. The trout twitched in my guts.

The rain was coming down so hard I could hear it pounding on the roof. Out the window, everything trembled. Then, through the pouring rain, I saw a wolfhound appear at the corner, pulling Mrs. Beasley down the sidewalk at the end of a leash. Mrs. Beasley was leaning back on her heels, braking the big animal with what little body weight she had. Her red hair showed through a pleated plastic rain bonnet, and a yellow rain slicker dragged on the ground behind her.

The trout went mad.

I jerked the front door open, knocking the half-empty beer out of my hand. The bottle hit the slate floor and shattered. But I kept going, stumbling sock-footed out onto the porch, through brown glass and foam, a hornet or thorn burning into my heel. The trout running out of air. I almost fell down the front steps, shouting and waving through the rain for Beasley to wait up. She saw me coming but didn't even try to slow down. I cut across the garden, my socks sinking deep into mud, and followed Beasley down the sidewalk until I'd caught up and was walking along beside her, so out of breath I could barely talk.

"I have to ask you a quick question," I said, the roar of rain loud all around.

"No!" she barked back, picking up her pace. "The answer's no. Heel, Sherlock. Come on, boy, heel!"

"It's not a yes-or-no question," I yelled.

"The answer's still no," she yelled back over her shoulder.

I caught up with her again, grabbed her upper arm, and spun her around. "I have to know, goddamnit! How old are you?" My words stayed between us, spinning in a white cloud, the rain beating our breaths apart. Everything but the rain stopped. Rain running down my bare head. Into my eyes and mouth. Down my neck.

"What?" Mrs. Beasley said, her eyes gone wide. "How dare you!" She pulled her arm loose, threw her head back, and was off again. The dog lunged into a trot, yanking her along behind at a full run.

I ran past her, took hold of the dog's leash, and jerked hard until the animal yelped and sat back on the wet walk. I turned to Mrs. Beasley.

"Listen," I said. "I don't—. I don't know anybody my age anymore." Mrs. Beasley didn't say anything. "I'm eighty, if that helps," I said.

"It doesn't," she said.

"Just tell me if you're younger or older," I said.

"What's it matter?" she said.

"I just need to know," I said. "That's all."

Mrs. Beasley didn't take off again. She just looked at my face. "Okay. Fine," she said at last. "I have no idea how old I am. How's that for you? My parents died on the way to this country. I've never known the date or year of my birth. Okay? Does that make you feel better, Mr. Dandelion?"

The rain let up. The air turned warm. The trout swam away.

"Well . . . ? Does that answer your question?" Mrs. Beasley said.

I just stared at her.

"I'd guess we're in the same ballpark, if that helps," she said. "Give or take a dozen years."

I wanted to grab her and start dancing across the soggy lawns! Dance Mrs. Beasley, B. back to the red house she hated, across the front porch I loved, past the barn owl, and in through the front door. Tell her she could have her pick of any room in the place.

But she spoke, and broke the spell.

"If you're finished with your little charade," she said, "Sherlock and I need to be going. And you'd better get out of this rain. You'll catch your death of colds. You're sopping wet. And no shoes?" She made a clicking noise with her tongue and teeth.

I stood there for a long time after Mrs. Beasley'd gone, the dripping trees the only sound in the air now that the rain had stopped. At last, I turned down the wet sidewalk and followed my muddy tracks back toward the house. That was when I noticed the roses, a red rose blooming in the heel of every other one of my footprints. And then my heel caught fire, and I was back on that dark gravel shoulder, pissing into headlights.

CLARA PAULSON

THEY FINALLY fixed my star. But I miss it. My star. Now my view out front is as bad as out back. The new letters they painted on the new glass are a lot bigger and fatter than the old letters. But it's the same four words. SILVER GARDENS NURSING HOME across both doors.

I still sit out here in the lobby, though, watching what I can see of the outside world through and around and in between the new silver letters. Sometimes I wish I had a razor blade. So I could scratch off the last two words so it reads SILVER GARDENS, clean and simple. Simple. I'd pretend I live in a beautiful botanical garden with lots of plants and flowers and waterfalls, where the air is moist and smells alive.

I'd rather sit in the cafeteria and look out back the way I used to do all the time, but the fence they put up a couple years ago when Lizzie walked off ruined that view. I still sit in the cafeteria sometimes, when nobody else is in there, and look out. At the metal fence, the trees. All the green is nice. Green. If I squint, the little diamonds the silver wire makes go away. And I pretend I could get up and walk down to the creek, the same way Lizzie did. Knowing the creek is down there beyond the fence is reassuring. Knowing there's moving water so nearby helps.

Of course, they didn't tell us what happened to Lizzie— little Lizzie from B17. Not official. But it didn't take me long to hear. The whole place was buzzing about it. That was the only thing the aides were talking about for at least a week. They said Lizzie walked into the creek sound asleep in the middle of the night. Somebody saw her body float under the bridge downtown, or else we might have never known where Lizzie went off to. Johnny Q said he heard Lizzie's nightgown was spread on the black water like a silk sheet when she went under the bridge. Just before Lizzie drowned, the Rhino changed Lizzie's pills, started giving Lizzie special blue pills. Lizzie told me she didn't like what those special blue pills were doing to her. I don't think Lizzie was sleepwalking that night. I think Lizzie knew where she was going.

Less than a week after Lizzie drowned, the Rhino had that shiny new fence up out back. Chain-link, Johnny Q called it. Set in concrete. And the floodlights, too. But I've gotten used to the fence and the floodlights by now. It's been a couple of years since Lizzie floated away. A long time. Lizzie used to help me with my bra and buttons, brush my hair every morning.

I'll get used to looking through the fat, new letters. The same way I've gotten used to squinting through the fence.

GEORGE CASTOR

Spend Thanksgiving with me, a man of age in search of good company of the same generation. I'll supply the bird, you bring your good spirits. Together, we'll carve out a nice afternoon, with all the trimmings! Call George at 873-2626.

THE AD had been running in *The Appeal* for three weeks straight now. I'd hardly left the place, afraid of missing a phone call. I must have read the damned thing a hundred times, checking to make sure the phone number was right, all my words made sense. It was, and they did. But nobody'd called. Not even a single wrong number.

I'd even bought a bird for the Thanksgiving dinner I thought for sure I'd be hosting. The fridge was so jam-packed full of food and wine and beer I could hardly get the door shut. But here it was, six-thirty in the morning less than a week away from Thanksgiving. I had no idea what I was going to do with all that food. Pull the plug and let it rot. Pour myself some good Doctor and toast the end of the whole thing. Admit my red house was history. A bad dream I'd wasted a good chunk of Jason's money and half a year's time on. Throw a few things in Max and drive back up to the blackberries without looking back, leave this whole god-damned place to rot with the turkey. It didn't much matter now. I was through. I'd failed Ralph twice.

My coffee water started screaming at the same time a knocking started coming loud through the house. I pulled the kettle off. Somebody was at the door.

I flipped on the porch light and pulled the front door open. Turned away from me, pumping the hell out of a black umbrella, was a tiny person, two braids of gray hair hanging down a bony back, each braid tied off with a chunk of string so white the strings glowed. The umbrella kept flapping, spraying drops of water turned white by the porchlight all over everything, including my bedroom slippers. The person turned around, still working the umbrella, eyes pinched shut against the spray.

A small woman with a wrinkled face the color of paper grocery bag opened her eyes and stood looking up at me. "Oh. Good morning," she said.

"Morning," I said. "What can I do for you?"

"Well, I'm here about the bird," she said, wringing water from the end of each braid, the drops tiny lightbulbs falling to the porch boards. "And the spirits." Her face pulled back into a grin of yellow teeth, the front two edged in gold, the gold flashing a little in the porch light, the smile making her whole face kind of shimmer. I had no idea what she was talking about.

Nice dentures, I thought, then saw a black gap where one of her eyeteeth was missing.

"Decided to drop by in person," she said, looking me straight in the eyes. "I despise telephones."

I couldn't say a thing. No words would come. The only thought going through my head was some memory of shrivelled-apple-face dolls Dora and I had seen years ago at a county fair. But this one was full-sized, alive, teeth flashing as she talked, standing right there on my own front porch before daylight. I could see the life coming out of her everywhere.

"It *is* your ad, isn't it?" the woman asked, pulling out a crumpled piece of paper and holding it out to me in the palm of her hand. Her hand was tiny, the lines of her palm dark with dirt, a silver bracelet at her wrist.

"Oh, that," I said. "Yeah, right, that's mine. . . . But I didn't list the address, did I?"

"No. But it's a small town." She put the piece of paper in her bag and tossed the umbrella down with a clatter. "You don't mind, do you?" she said.

"Oh, no. Not at all," I said. "I live here. I mean, this is the house. It's red. Please, come in."

She turned and propped herself against the porch pillar and peeled off a black rubber overshoe. "I hate these rubbers, but I hate wet socks worse," she said over her shoulder, pulling off the other overshoe and tossing both of them onto the porch. She was wearing purple high-top tennis shoes, red wool knee socks, and a skirt that had glass beads or bits of foil or something shiny sewed all along the bottom. The skirt fanned out a little as she turned back around, the pieces of foil spinning and blinking above her shoes. She brushed her palms together a few times and stepped close to me.

"My name's Grace," she said, offering me her tiny hand. "From up east of Tenmile."

"I'm George. George Castor. From up in the hills," I said. "And right here."

"Pleased to meet you," Grace said, pumping my hand, her hand a kid's hand in mine, except very warm. Then she stopped, held my hand still, looked right at me again, and asked, "It's not too early for you, is it?"

"Hell no," I said. "Come on in."

I held the screen door open with one arm, pushed the front door back with the other, and this woman named Grace walked by as if she'd been through my front door a thousand times, her head going past at my chest. She walked with a slight limp, and the air that followed her smelled a little like fresh hay. Something made a clicking sound as she moved past me, as if her pockets were full of marbles or seashells.

And as I pushed the door shut, I noticed that my hand left a pale dusty smudge on the wood.

"Nice place," she said, looking into the living room. "You live here alone?"

"Shag William and I," I said.

"Shag William?" she said.

"My dog," I said.

"Oh, what kind?" she asked. I now saw what was making the clicking noise: a row of turquoise pieces hanging all along the bottom of her bag, her little fingers moving the beads.

"Part basset," I said. "But mostly mutt."

"Best kind," she said. "They breed all the brains out of the purebreds." She looked around. "That stairway's incredible. How many bedrooms in this place?"

"Four down, five up," I said. "Plus a studio apartment out over the garage and an attic that could sleep another half dozen in a pinch."

"Holy moly," she said. "You must've had quite a family at one time."

"No. Actually I just moved in," I said.

"I see," she said. Then Grace went into the living room, took off her high-top tennis shoes, sat down on the couch, pulled her feet up under her skirt, and started talking.

↺

An hour later, as suddenly as she'd started, Grace stopped talking. Except her words kept bumping around in the sudden silence. The skin of my ears and face were tingling strange.

"So, let's hear about you," Grace said. "Why'd you run that little ad?"

My tongue was stuck dry to the roof of my mouth.

"Let me get us some coffee," I said, escaping into the kitchen. This had to be a dream. Who was this woman who'd marched in, made herself at home, and started talking non-stop about stuff I wasn't even sure I'd heard right, her kid-hands fluttering in front of her like a pair of cabbage moths all the while? I took a drink from the faucet, swallowed, wiped my mouth on my shirtsleeve. Who the hell was she? And what was she telling me about, going on and on? All her words now scrambled in my head. Something about a girl walking through the desert? The sun? Some bus? A ring?

I could smell sagebrush and juniper right there in my kitchen. I could taste dust in my mouth and feel the sun's heat even though it was pouring rain outside. Who the hell was she? Where'd she come from?

I poured two cups of coffee and carried the cups into the living room.

But Grace was gone, purple high-tops and all.

I looked down at the steaming cups, one in each hand. Or had she ever been here? I crossed to the mirror above the fireplace and looked at myself. My hair was a mess and I had a couple days worth of white stubble on my face. My big nose was more bent to the left than I'd ever noticed before. Maybe this woman Grace had decided to make a run for it while she had the chance.

I put one of the cups on the mantel and rubbed my cheek, stretched my skin tight, making the wrinkles disappear. Then I let go and watched all the wrinkles come sliding back into place. I squinted and looked at the crow's-feet around my eyes.

"Nice bathroom." Her voice made me jump, slosh hot coffee onto my hand, but I didn't drop the cup. "You could live in there," she said from the entryway. Her high-top tennis shoes were tied together by the laces and hanging from her belt.

I carried the cups across the living room and put them on the dining room table, on opposite sides. I pulled out a chair for her, then sat down myself.

"So, why'd you run that little ad?" she asked, sitting down, her beads rattling against the chair.

I took a sip of coffee, didn't answer right away. I wasn't sure I wanted to. Part of me had a mind to tell her to get out, that I was moving back up to the farm and forgetting the whole damned thing. But instead, I felt myself leaning across the table toward her, drawing a chestful of air. "Because I made a goddamned promise to a dear friend who's now dead! That's why," I said. "Okay?"

She just looked at me, her eyes the shiny black of wet rubber. A little bubble had formed in the gap between her teeth. But the bubble popped when her tongue flashed pink and she spoke.

"We all get to die, you know," she said. "You can't stop that."

"But we don't have to do it alone," I said.

"In the end, though, that's all you have, isn't it?" she said, looking right at me, into me. "Just yourself?"

"No!" I said. "Not if we pull together. Not if we surround ourselves. Nobody has to die alone. Nobody!" She just looked at me, the gold on her teeth showing a little between her lips.

"We've got a lifetime chalked up," I went on. "Decades of experience. Wisdom you only get by living." My open hand dropped to the table, a book slammed down. "And nobody gives a good goddamn! To the young folks, we're no more than rusty tin cans. Toss us in a nursing home and forget us. Well, I say to hell with the young folks. We have each other. We can take care of ourselves. We can live it up! We don't need goddamned nursing homes!"

She just kept looking at me. That look. Those eyes.

"You had a friend die in a nursing home, didn't you?" she said. "Alone."

"Well, I sure as hell won't, you can bet on that," I said, holding the table with both hands. "No way in hell I'm dying alone. You understand that? Do you?" She just looked at me. "Answer me!"

She smiled a little, raised both arms, and turned her tiny palms toward the ceiling. "I guess that explains this nine-bedroom palace, doesn't it?" she said, a spark flashing once in the dark of her mouth.

"Why the hell not? College kids do this all the time. A

100

whole slew of them living in one house all together. Tribes in Africa do it."

"Tribes on this continent do it, too, you know," she said.

"Damn right!" I said. "So why can't a handful of old folks? Why can't we?"

She leaned back in her chair without saying anything and looked away. I could tell she was somewhere else. Maybe back in that damned desert she'd gone on and on about. Or more likely, thinking I was loony. Same as Mrs. Beasley thought.

"So what time's the banquet?" she asked, her eyes dead on me again, her beads clicking below the table.

I stared at her, but it didn't fit. Or I hadn't heard right. "Banquet?" I repeated. Gears ground. *Banquet?* What the hell was she talking about?

"How about two o'clock?" she said.

I must have nodded, because she was on her feet, pushing in her chair. "See you then," she said. "I'll bring the spirits." She dropped a wadded-up piece of paper on the table next to the coffee cups, and was gone.

I snatched up the crumpled piece of paper, flattened it on the table. The ad! She was taking me up on my turkey dinner! The goddamned ad had worked after all!

I hurried to the front door and looked out through the oval window, but she was nowhere. No sign. The porch was empty, the street and trees gray and washed out in the early light. Even the red paint of the porch looked dull. Nothing moved. Fog hung low everywhere. Maybe I was seeing things that weren't there. Seeing whole mornings. Talking to myself and having coffee with people who didn't even exist!

But then something caught my eye. Color, movement on the red porch boards. I looked down. Two yellow feathers floated on a puddle of water, moving a little in the breeze. The feathers were the brightest yellow I'd ever seen, two slivers off the sun. And near the feathers, half sunk in the same shallow puddle, was a tiny piece of turquoise—a chunk of bright blue sky. *Halleholylujah!*

PART THREE

South ● Red

And now I am ready to keep running
When the sun rises beyond the borderlands of death.
I already see mountain ridges in the heavenly forest
Where, beyond every essence, a new essence waits.

You, music of my late years, I am called
By a sound and a color which are more and more perfect.

Do not die out, fire. Enter my dreams, love.
Be young forever, seasons of the earth.

   —from "Winter" by Czeslaw Milosz

CLARA PAULSON

WHEN THE lights on a cop car behind us come on and start streaking everything red and blue, I recall a little club I used to work in Vegas. At the end of the show, the guys on the spots would go nuts and swirl the lights all over the stage and me and the audience, blinding everyone. But this is no show. It's a real cop car, and I'm afraid my only real chance of getting out of the Gardens once and for all has come and gone. Gone.

I was a fool idiot to trust him, B24's friend—what did he say his name was? But it sounded okay a week ago, a way out. I'd watched him coming and going for those two years, so it was kind of like I knew him, although I don't know him at all. He hadn't ever come back to the Gardens since B24 disappeared six or eight months ago. So when he just showed up in my room a week ago and asked me if I wanted to leave the Gardens, of course I told him yes. HECK YES! is what I wrote on my pad. B24's friend said he'd be back in the next few days to pick me up. So I waited, and he did, sure enough—tonight, just a few minutes ago.

For some reason I trusted him as he wheeled me fast out through those Star Trek doors and across that crunchy parking lot, gravel pinging off my rubber wheels. But when I saw the skunk woman getting out of his pickup truck as we got close—those eyes of hers poking into me—I should have known. I should have said no. Put my feet down in the gravel. Scribbled, ROLL ME BAK N! But I didn't. Something in me said what the heck, throw the dice, woman. Perhaps you'll wind up back in Vegas.

The skunk woman helped B24's friend roll me up two planks into the back of his pickup truck. I smelled garlic and woodsmoke in the air near her face. George, that's his name!—George tied my chair to the pickup truck with yellow rope, and we were off. Only moments ago, we were driving through town, the ice-cold evening air blowing through my hair, around my ankles, up under my robe. Lights going by on both sides, all the houses decorated up with little Christmas lights. And way high up above the Christmas lights, the sky was decorated, too! Stars all over. We were driving through a magical land! I was out for good and never going back to the Rhino and her Gardens.

But it looks like it's all over now. B24's friend has pulled us to the curb, and the cop from the cop car is walking right past me sitting back here on my chair in the bed of the pickup truck. He must think I'm a department store mannequin, or a dummy they use when they test-crash cars.

I watch through the rear window, listen to the cop and George talking. Every now and then the skunk woman leans across George and interjects something, but I can't make out her words. When I hear the cop say "kidnapping" loud and clear, I know this whole thing's out of control and worse than I thought.

I want to roll myself lickety-split back to the Gardens so when the cop looks, the pickup truck's empty, all this never happened, and I'm waking up in my bed, in B31 with the too high window. With the treetops showing. I don't want B24's friend getting into trouble on my account, although it was his idea to begin with. So perhaps he deserves what he gets. Or was it hers? The skunk woman's probably behind the whole scheme. I don't think I like this George character after all, and I've never trusted the skunk woman.

Now, all of a sudden, I'm convinced this has to be one of my moments where the wires don't quite connect. I'm sitting up here on full display, feeling like a fool-idiot with the cop lights splashing my robe and chair every which color of the flag. But all I can do is just sit here watching the commotion and listening to George and the skunk woman trying to talk their way out of whatever pickle it is we're in.

I wonder how these two ever chose me. Picked me out of that decrepit crowd at the Gardens.

Now George is out of the pickup truck, arguing with the cop. Another cop car's just pulled to the curb in front of us and its lights are going nuts, too, coming through the cab window. Cars driving by are slowing down, people craning their necks, more people collecting on the sidewalks.

Then, out of the blue, I have an urge for a cigarette. Pall Mall. But it's been years. And I don't have a cigarette on me.

Now George is yelling at the three cops. He's shouting that the Gardens never was my home and that I have the right to live wherever I see fit. I agree and start beating on the side of his pickup truck with my good arm to cheer him on! Perhaps George and the skunk woman are okay after all—a modern-day Bonnie and Clyde! I wait for George to pull out a violin case and start shooting things up, get us out of this mess.

But the next thing I hear is The Word. Scripture. Booming all around me, loud as God himself. It's the skunk woman. She's tuned the radio in to some K-GOD station out of Portland and turned the volume up full blast. It's so loud I can't hear anything else, not even George yelling at the cops. I can see his mouth moving, and his face getting darker and darker, but I can't hear what he's saying. All I hear is this preacher's voice ranting and raging so loud the bass is booming up through the metal tubes of my chair, the thunder of a dozen kettle drums coming straight into my bones.

Traffic has stopped dead still now and people are getting

out of their cars, leaving doors open. One of the cops is trying to get the cars and people moving again. Another one's trying to turn down the radio. But the skunk woman's guarding that little white knob with her life. All of a sudden I burst out in a laughing fit that I can't stop. I laugh and laugh. It's been years since I laughed this hard. Hard. It feels fantastic, coming out through my face from way down inside somewhere. Now George is lambasting the cop for being such a sinner, telling the cop to get down on his knees and ask sweet Jesus Christ for grace and forgiveness before God himself strikes him down for his blatant infidelity.

☉

Blinking through my laugh tears, I notice it's all quiet again. No lights. The show's over. I look around. They're loading George and the skunk woman into the first cop car. Somebody shut her preacher off. The traffic's going again. Somebody's moving around with a camera shooting off flashbulbs that put cotton balls in my vision. A skinny man with a notepad almost like mine is trying to talk to George and the skunk woman, jotting on his pad and nodding. The cops are trying to get George to stop talking and get into the cop car.

All of a sudden, another cop shoves his face about six inches from mine and starts talking at me as if I'm a child. Child. The cop smells of sweat and deep-fried onion rings, and his neck bulges over the dark collar of his uniform as he talks. I can see a little fleck of rust where he must have nicked his Adam's apple shaving. For the first time in my life I can't stand men. Which is odd, because I've always loved men, thought I couldn't live without them. But this big smelly bull of a man shouting in my face as if I'm deaf makes me want to be sick. I pull back my good arm and watch my open hand slap his moving jaw with a pop that stings my palm and jiggles his jowls. But the cop doesn't get it. He just pulls his head out of range and talks louder, telling me that everything is going to be okay and that he'll take me back home to Silver

Gardens where I can rest. He doesn't have the slightest idea that the Gardens is the last place on God's green earth I want to go right now.

The cops lift me and my chair out of George's pickup truck and start discussing how they'll fit me into the other squad car. It's obvious none of them has ever been around a person in a wheelchair. They finally slide me into the backseat, toss my chair into the trunk with a clunk, and head back up Water Street toward the Gardens. Show's over. No spotlights. I'm going back. Back. B24's friend and the skunk woman are gone. The little Christmas lights outside are all dim and going by too fast. Nothing's funny anymore. The thought of a cigarette makes me sick.

Sitting here in the backseat watching the outside go by through this metal grate, I know what it must feel like to be a prisoner. Without my chair to hold me up, I slowly fall over onto my dead side, melt lower and lower into the shiny black seat. The officers in front talk about how I can't talk or hear, call me a poor old gal, call B24's friend a crazy old geezer, call the skunk woman his wacky wife. Then one cop asks the other if he saw some show on television last night, and they talk about that. They probably think I'm retarded. It happens. I'm mad at B24's friend for cooking up this scheme. And at old black eyes for helping him. Here I am riding through town in a cop car at the age of eighty-some. It's just as well. If this was a taste of what I was getting myself into with those two, I don't want to be a part of it.

But on the other hand, why not? I laughed tonight. And I haven't laughed in years.

GEORGE CASTOR

I was so mad about the article *The Appeal* ran yesterday I had to get out of the house. The picture was lousy, my mouth wide open, Grace's eyes glowing worse than coon eyes in headlights, the cop car in the background. And none of the words true about us trying to kidnap a poor old woman out of the "security and serenity" of her Silver Gardens world. It took us half the night down at the station trying to explain that we weren't kidnapping anybody.

I should have never let Grace talk me into going after Clara in the first place. The whole thing was bound to blow up in my face, just the way it did. I don't know who called the cops. I didn't see anybody around when I wheeled Clara out. Just the receptionist, nodding and smiling as I went by saying I was taking Clara out for a quick breath of fresh evening air.

I was tempted to boot Grace out of the house altogether for talking me into it, talking like she was sure this Clara would just jump at the chance to get out of the Gardens, and how once we got her here to the house Clara'd never want to go back. Grace said she just *knew* Clara's soul was ready. I didn't know Clara from Eve, so I trusted Grace. Turns out Grace had only met Clara a time or two, something about volunteering at the Gardens.

But I couldn't give Grace her walking papers. Having Grace here was better than nobody at all. And that's where I was a month ago: nobody but a basset hound. At least Grace was a start. I could put up with her quirks and the candles she was forever lighting for a while longer. But I had to find a few more people pretty soon. Knowing Grace, I might wake up one morning and she'd be gone, just as quick as she'd shown up on my front porch. And then I'd be all the way back at square one.

☺

Coming across the bridge after walking all over town for what must have been hours, I was still hot under the collar, and didn't have a clue about what to try next. But more walking was only going to make my knees and feet hurt worse than they did already, so I headed for home.

When I got there, though, I found a skinny old man, wearing a long coat and a ratty baseball cap with the bill turned backwards sitting halfway up the red steps of the front porch. Next to him stood a dirty army-issue duffel bag, stuffed to the gills. The man's eyes were shut, but he was sitting straight up, his head tipped back a little, a cigarette pinched between his lips, an inch or more of ash hanging from the end of his cigarette, smoke going up into nothing. But the man didn't move. I wasn't even sure he was breathing. His face was the color of harness leather, and hanging down from the tip of his chin was a long, scraggly billy-goat's-gruff goatee, pure white and shimmering in the sun—a wispy waterfall flowing right out of that man's face and falling into his lap. But then the inch of ash fell into the waterfall, and the man's eyes blinked open. He was Asian.

"Ah, you must be Mr. Castor," he said, blinking at me.

I felt myself nod.

"You look a lot better in real life than in that picture of you in the *Seattle-Times*," the man said.

"What?" I said.

"The story about you and the kidnapping. Decided to come meet you for myself. In person. Jumped the next freight south. And here I am. My name is Clayton. Clayton Liu."

To think the wire services had picked up the lousy story out of *The Appeal* and run it all over the goddamned country made me want to throw this crackpot off my property. But something stopped me. Maybe it was the water falling again from around his smile as he got up and came down the stairs with his hand held out. Or maybe it was Grace who showed up out of nowhere at the top of the steps, wiping her hands on some old newspaper.

But instead of blowing up at this stranger, I invited Mr. Clayton Liu to dinner. I even used the word mister. Then a wad of newspaper came bouncing down the steps, jumped over the duffel bag, and landed between my boots. When I looked up, Grace was gone, and I was staring into water falling fast and white, and the stale smell of cigarettes.

♋

At dinner, Clayton Liu told us how he'd been riding freight trains around the country for the past year or so. "Set free at last from a lifelong job in a Bethlehem steel mill by retirement," he said, smiling. "I am having such a good time I should have retired ten years earlier. Waiting until sixty-five got me nothing but a gold-plated watch with the words *Thanks for All the Great Years* engraved on the back—a watch just like the other fifty or sixty boys who were retiring that year got." Clayton Liu took a mouthful of mashed potatoes, chewed once, swallowed, and kept going.

"On my way home after the retirement party, you know what I did? I put that watch faceup on the railroad tracks and waited for the northbound eleven-fifteen to blast through," Clayton Liu said. "When I went over to see what was left of my new gold watch, all I found was the back, stretched out like a piece of chewing gum in a crosswalk. The only words I could still read were *great* and *years*. So I skipped that piece of metal across the oily water in the ditch and decided to have a close look at this country that is not even really my country." Clayton Liu smiled. "And the answer to how I was going to see it was right there in those railroad tracks."

Clayton Liu said he'd come to the United States with his parents from Thailand when he was a boy. His parents had worked hard running a laundry in Pittsburgh, but never made it big.

"No American Dream," he said. "Just lots of wash." Clayton Liu said he had never married, and never bought a house, because Pennsylvania had never felt like home. "Everything I own is inside that bag," he said, pointing toward the front door where his duffel bag was lying. "That green bag is my home now. I carry it on my back."

I had just taken a big swig of beer when his words about packing his house around on his back like a turtle reached up and slapped me right alongside the head. I sucked in and stood up so fast I damned near took beer into both lungs, then started coughing, beer foam and shouted words spraying out all across the table.

"Hang on!" I hacked. "You're home at last! Right here in this red house! No need to ever jump another train, ever! Welcome to the family, sir. Hallelujah!" Clayton Liu was staring at me, his mouth hanging open.

"We're looking for people just like you," I said. "You have to move in here with us. For good, goddamnit. What do you say? You can have your pick of any room in the place, including mine!"

Grace stood up and tossed her napkin on the table. "Except mine," she said. Then she turned and started to go upstairs.

"What do you mean?" I said.

She stopped and turned back.

"You heard me," she said. "My room's not up for grabs."

113

She glared at me, her eyes harder and more black than I'd ever seen them before. And then she was gone.

☺

Clayton Liu did decide to stay, to think it over, he said. But he only lasted three days. Every morning he went out onto the side yard and did what he called his "exercises." Bundled up against the fog and cold, Clayton Liu balanced on one leg, his arms and other leg moving so slow in the air he looked more like a lawn statue than a man getting any sort of exercise.

"Without my exercises every morning, I would not make it through the day," Clayton Liu said, smiling and stroking his beard.

I wasn't sure his exercises had anything to do with it. Because the minute he finished his lawn-statue routine, Clayton Liu came hurrying inside and chain-drank several cups of coffee without sitting down. Then he stepped out onto the porch and smoked two or three Camel straights, pacing back and forth, blowing smoke out his nose. Looniest morning routine I ever saw. But if I could put up with Grace and her candles, I could put up with Clayton Liu and his exercises.

On the morning of the third day, though, Clayton Liu came in after his cigarettes and announced he had heard a train whistle last night. Grace and I both looked up at him from the breakfast table.

"And when I hear a train whistle," he said, "I know my time has come at last." I thought Clayton Liu was saying he was dying on us.

"Time to push off to other places," he said. "Time to see some more tracks. Time to live it up a little. Time to leave."

I started in to say I was sorry, but Grace spoke up for the first time since Clayton Liu had arrived. "Checking out of the red palace, are you?" she said.

"I'm afraid so, ma'am," Clayton Liu said. "That train whistle last night told me it is time to go see the golden state for myself. I've never been to California."

Grace nodded once and went back to her eggs.

Clayton Liu packed his duffel bag, thanked us for our hospitality, and left on foot just as it started in to rain. I stood out on the porch, watching this wiry little man move down the sidewalk toward town, the weight of his duffel bag bending him almost in half. At the bridge, he turned back toward me and stood still for a second. The only motion other than the rain was the wind moving Clayton Liu's white waterfall. Then he disappeared on across the bridge.

"Just as well," Grace said, her voice so close behind me I jumped. "He smokes too much." A smile was taking up most of her face. "Close," she said. "But his soul just isn't ready for this palace yet." She turned and went inside.

What the hell did Grace know about souls being ready? She'd been wrong about Clara's soul. Grace sounded like that undertaker, after loading Dora into his van. "Her soul must have been ready," he had said, lighting a cigarette. He didn't even know Dora, and there he was taking her away from me forever.

Before I'd even opened my eyes, I knew. Because of the silence in our bedroom. I looked over at Dora, the first shades of dawn brushing her face. Everything was okay. She was just sleeping. I reached out a hand and touched her shoulder, shook her a little, whispered her name. Her head rocked back and forth on the pillow, but she didn't stir. Her face was calm, almost a smile. She was kidding with me! Dora'd always been a joker. I wanted to grab her and tickle her the way I'd done when we were younger. I got up onto my knees, and that was when I saw the dark gap between her lips.

Dora.

I lowered my head to the gap to listen. My ear touched the coolness of her lips. They were my mama's lips. I was five years old again. The blizzard bayed outside across the Nebraska prairie. I smelled ice and dead ashes. Wondered why

Pa wasn't back with the doctor yet. Then felt the dark stickiness on the sheet between my mama's cold legs.

I climbed over and straddled Dora, shook her by both shoulders. Her head flopped back and forth. The black gap opened and closed. I saw her teeth, the teeth I had so often touched with my tongue. I heard her high, sweet laughter. Saw sunlight on her brown hair and bare shoulders as we walked on the beach in the wind. And then there was nothing but the ticking of our bedside clock.

I got dressed and went downstairs. The stove was out cold. I took my coat from the hook behind the door and went outside. It was time to leave. The sky behind the ragged horizon of Doug fir to the east was a translucent red-orange, the color of salmon eggs. The barn roof black against the sunrise.

I walked past my truck, and, instead of driving off somewhere forever, walked down the east property line toward the creek that flowed through the brush at the bottom of our land.

Years ago I had come this same way. For a drink, for shade, to take a break from plowing the lower twenty-eight in the hot August sun. I'd heard a thrashing in the shallows, and seen the large coho salmon a few feet from my boots. The fish was battered but breathing, gills moving above sand, swam all the way up from the ocean. I reached down and grabbed the fish, pulled it out of the water by its tail, the silver sides flashing in the filtered sunlight. Then I had killed the fish, slit its belly open with my knife. I'd surprise Dora with dinner. But when I lifted the eggs from the gleaming red cavity, I'd wished I could have sewn the fish back up, put her back in the water, watched her swim away. I laid the eggs on a bed of gravel at the bottom of a pool.

And now I was headed back to that same creek, walking through wet grass this time, instead of dry plowed earth. My wife dead in bed in my house behind me. I squeezed between strands of barbed wire near the creek, tore my jacket, pushed dripping vine maple and alder branches out of my way, and at last came to water moving over and around rocks. The water flowed at a good pace, but was clear. Late fall. I stood watching the water as daylight gathered strength, painted highlights on the riffles and eddies. Fallen chittim and maple and alder leaves floated past, spinning on the current, some leaves resting on the bottom, or wrapped around sunken sticks. The trees along the creek were all bare, the limbs black against the steel sky.

And I again heard the thrashing I'd heard that summer. In the water near my feet. I looked down, expecting to see the salmon's dark tail and dorsal fin cutting through the water between rocks, the flash of silver scales. But I saw only the smooth surface of the water running, and a few yellow leaves lying on the bottom.

Then my own reflection blossomed on the surface, a dark space between my own lips, and I ran, falling on the slippery rocks, blackberries and devil's club tearing at me, vine maple knocking against my forearms and shins. I crawled through the fence again, this time cutting the heel of my hand. The cuff of my overalls caught and I fell forward into the wet grass. I picked myself up and ran all the way back up to the house, my throat sanded raw, my legs numb, me stumbling in through the door to stand panting in the cold kitchen, calling her name.

Hours passed right then. Days. Maybe a whole year. I didn't move. Just stood fighting the urge to go. To leave the farm behind forever. Find something else to do. Find another life, the way I'd always done for years after running away from Aunt Bertha at the funeral.

I went to the phone and dialed the police.

A woman's voice asked me questions, asked if I was sure my wife was no longer breathing. I wanted to drop the phone and hurry back upstairs to our bedroom and check, wake Dora up. Or maybe Dora would jump out from behind the bedroom door, grab me, and we'd both fall onto the bed laughing, kissing, and holding each other tight.

But I said yes. I was sure. The woman said she would contact the funeral home. Someone would be up right away.

And they did, two men in suits and ties, with a chrome

stretcher on silver wheels. I let the men in, led them upstairs
to our bedroom one step at a time. Dora was still there, lying
in the middle of the tangled blankets, her gown open a little
at the neck, the whiteness of one breast showing. I wanted to
button the gown up, kiss her, hold her head, tell her good-
bye. But there was no time. The men put Dora in a white
plastic bag and zipped the bag closed. They strapped the bag
down to the stretcher, and carried Dora downstairs, head
downhill. They carried Dora out the front door, folded the
wheels up, and rolled her into the back of a black van.

One of the men said they would need a photograph of
Dora, if it wasn't any trouble. He could go get it, if I just told
him where it was. The other man lit a cigarette and said he
was sorry, that he knew how hard it was to lose a loved one.
But her soul must have been ready, he said.

Then the van doors slammed shut and the van was driving
away, Dora being taken away from our farm by two men I'd
never seen before in my life. They were taking Dora away
from me just like that. No different from how it was when
you sold a heifer. I started to run after the van, shouting for
them to bring Dora back, but the van was gone, the sound of
the engine accelerating up on the highway. And farther off,
a hushed murmur, the strange whisper of a river flowing.

No, Grace didn't know about souls. And now we'd just lost
Clayton Liu thanks to her scaring him off. Thinking she knew
his soul, too.

ᘒ

The following week another letter to the editor showed up
in *The Appeal*. Except this time the letter wasn't from Mrs.
Beasley. And didn't have anything to do with the color of my
house. This letter referred to the front-page story about Grace
and me. "Maybe they should check into Silver Gardens themselves," the letter read. "There comes a time when old people
can no longer take proper care of themselves and they become

a burden on the rest of us. That's why we have facilities like Silver Gardens in the first place."

I wadded up the whole goddamned paper and thew it in the fire, snapped off the brass reading lamp and stood there in the dark. Shag William shifted in his box in the kitchen, the jingle of his tags coming under the swinging door. Dora's grandfather clock ticked loud. Outside rain was falling hard through streetlight. But Grace was here. Grace and her candles and skunk and yellow birds. Grace and her soul.

CLARA PAULSON

SOMETIMES I think the other night was just one of my wires. Cops, Christmas lights, and everything. I haven't heard from B24's friend or the skunk woman since. Perhaps the cops locked them up. The aides have been watching me a little closer. I can tell. And the Rhino had a doctor come in and check me over a few days ago. Now I get two special pink pills every morning. But I don't swallow the pills. I hold them under my tongue until I'm on the toilet and the aide turns his back. Then I spit the pills quick into a wad of toilet tissue, squeeze to be sure I got them both, wipe myself, and drop the whole works between my legs.

I hope the cops didn't lock up B24's friend. Anybody nuts enough to try to kidnap me out of this place can't be too bad. They changed the water bottle on the fountain today, put a red bow on the faucet. They also fixed the light in the ceiling of the lobby that flickered all the time. The nativity scene is all set up in the dayroom, too, except for the aluminum foil star that normally shines above the cardboard animals and manger. Somebody forgot to put the star up this year. Tomorrow's Christmas.

Goldfinches and Red Scarf

The old woman is walking across a bridge carrying a dome-shaped birdcage draped with a red scarf. Her gray braids sit coiled high on her head, held in place with what looks to be a white chopstick or a thin bone that's luminous in the low evening sun. The woman stops halfway across the narrow bridge, shades her eyes, and looks up, as if she sees something on the roof of the old building that houses the hardware store. An advertisement for Silver Creek Stoneground Flour is painted high on the brick above the creek, but the letters are faded and peeling. The woman tips her head back more, arching her body to look higher in the sky, the way a child would watch an airplane going over, or a balloon floating away. She does not move, but a silver bracelet slides slowly down her forearm from her wrist toward her elbow. After a long time, the woman lifts her hand from her brow and raises it into the air, as if she's hailing someone in the sky.

She lowers her hand, and the silver bracelet drops

back down to her wrist. She sets the cloth-draped cage on the sidewalk, then squats beside the cage. Her hands work at the cloth, untying something. She stands again, then, using both hands, lifts the cage and places it on the railing of the bridge. She pauses, bows her head, then lifts the domed top of the cage away, trailing the red scarf. From the cage, a ball of shimmering gold rises into the air, hovers for an instant above the bridge, then shatters—goldfinches darting away into a sky carved out of turquoise.

After many minutes have passed, the woman raises the red scarf and waves it in the air. The birds reappear out of nowhere, fluttering back down into the open cage. The woman replaces the top and begins carrying the cage back in the direction from which she came. Below the bridge, the red scarf alights on the moving water and floats out of sight downstream.

GEORGE CASTOR

"Do I look like me?" I asked, coming down the cherry stair-case, slow, so Grace could get a good view of me from where she was sitting in the dining room. I was wearing a panama hat, a trench coat with the belt cinched tight, and a bright red handkerchief knotted around my neck and tucked inside the coat collar. I'd used mascara to turn my eyebrows and side-burns the color of mud, and I wore a pair of dark green aviator glasses I'd picked up at the Thrifty-Bee Thrift Shop, same place I got the panama hat and black wig. I thought I looked pretty sharp.

"Where's the violin case?" Grace asked, looking my getup up and down. "The wig's iffy, but nobody'll know it's you, that's for sure," she said.

"And that's all that matters, right?" I said.

She tugged on one side of the wig, tucked her fingers up under it next to my skull. "But you don't want any of your white stuff showing," she said. "That would give you away in a minute."

"See you in a few," I said. "If everything goes well." I went out the back door to Max.

January already. A new year. Me a year older. It had taken

Grace and me since Christmas to come up with another plan. The cops had warned both of us to stay clear of the Gardens, but Grace still believed that was the best place to start. And I agreed, mostly because we couldn't come up with another plan that held water, besides trying another ad. And I didn't want to give another dime to *The Appeal*. Grace still claimed Clara was ready. I wasn't so sure Clara would want anything to do with either of us ever again. But Grace said she could feel that this was the right thing to do. So I went along.

I parked Max on the street a couple blocks shy of the Gardens and walked the rest of the way. In the lobby I was relieved to not recognize the woman behind the counter who looked up. "May I help you?" she said. I wanted to take my panama hat off, to be polite, but I was afraid the wig would get hung up in the hatband and come off, too.

"I hope so," I said, touching my fingers to the brim of the hat. "I'm with Senior Support Services, and I was just wondering if I might put up a flyer or two about an evening of activity we're putting on here in town next week?" The woman looked at me. I thought something must be wrong with my getup. The wig had slipped, my white stuff was showing.

"It's for seniors," I added.

"Sounds fine to me," she said. "But don't expect too many people around here to be interested in much activity." She went back to a pile of pink slips on the desk.

I thanked her and moved down the main hallway, trying to walk so my wet boot soles didn't squeak so loud on the linoleum. At a bulletin board I stopped and glanced both ways. Borrowing a thumbtack from a poster about living wills, I pinned our flyer to a vacant patch of board below the words *Employee of the Month*. Both the month and the employee were missing, so I didn't think anybody'd mind.

I stepped back and read our flyer:

JOIN US FOR AN EVENING OF INFORMATION AND LIGHT.
GUEST SPEAKER: DR. WILLIAM SHAG,

A LEADING SENIOR CITIZEN REPRESENTATIVE FROM WASHINGTON, DC,
WILL SPEAK ABOUT GROWING YOUR OWN VEGETABLES
IN POTS AND WINDOWBOXES,
AND ABOUT HOW HOME-GROWN EATS ARE BETTER FOR YOU.

DR. SHAG'S BRIEF PRESENTATION WILL BE FOLLOWED BY CANDLELIGHT
REFRESHMENTS AND DISCUSSION.
TIME: 7:00 P.M. JANUARY 27TH.
TRANSPORTATION TO AND FROM THE EVENT PROVIDED.
MEET IN FRONT OF THE LOBBY AT 6:45 SHARP.
ALL ARE WELCOME.

Grace's touches about candles and light were a bit much, but I was pleased with how official our notice sounded. This should bring people out of the woodwork.

At the end of the hall I came to a red metal door marked *Emergency Exit Alarm Will Sound If Opened*. I considered pushing the bar down, unlatching the door, just to see what would happen, but I didn't. A fire in this place would be hell. I duct-taped another flyer to the door's narrow window.

At eye level, I taped a third flyer to the swinging doors of the cafeteria, then pushed one door open and took a look inside: the air smelled of vanilla pudding and piss. On the far side of several rows of long tables and a few scattered chairs, two white-haired men sat in wheelchairs against the wall. One of the men looked to be asleep, his head bent forward. The other man was humming "America the Beautiful" while he saluted the wall with a hand in a white glove. I pulled my head back out and retaped the flyer a little lower down on the door.

Halfway down the hall of the B wing, a silver B24 shining bright stopped my legs from working. *Ralph's door.*

I started to leave, but saw Clara in the room across the hall, sound asleep. Clara was why I'd come back here in the first place. I had to tell her about the seminar. But I didn't want to wake her up, scare her. She might yell, bring the aides running.

I stood there in the middle of the shiny hallway, the silver letters on Ralph's door behind me, the stainless steel railing around Clara's bed in front of me. Lights buzzing overhead. I looked both ways. The place was deserted. I'd leave a quick note.

I tiptoed into Clara's room and was digging for a paper and pencil on her nightstand when I knocked over a half-full glass of water. I grabbed the glass before it rolled off and hit the floor, but a whole stack of magazines and music went sliding off onto the floor one by one, slapping the linoleum loud.

Shit!

Clara woke up and looked right at me, blinking, her eyes only a foot away from mine.

"It's me, George. Remember?" I said as fast as I could, keeping the words to a whisper. "Red house. Red truck. Remember?"

Clara was feeling for her glasses on a chain around her neck, her eyes still blinking, nothing but bewilderment all over her face.

"Of George and Grace and the pickup truck," I said. "Remember? We took you for a ride a few weeks back." Clara had every right to tell me to go straight to hell, or else start screaming and get me kicked out. But she didn't. She pushed her glasses onto her face, looked at me, then wrote "U R NOT GEORGE!" on a pad of paper lying on her stomach and held it up.

"Oh, hell, sorry," I said, pulling my aviator glasses down and lifting one side of the wig to show some of my white stuff. "Figured this was the only way I could get in here without being spotted. You know, after the other night . . ." I shutup and handed Clara one of our flyers. "Grace and I are Dr. Shag," I said, winking. I could tell Clara knew I was me now. And she seemed okay with it. "Pass the word to anybody else who wants to come along. We'll pick you up at six forty-five, sharp. Okay? Be watching for us out front."

Clara scanned the flyer, then wrote, "U 2 R NUTS!" She underlined the word nuts twice.

"Maybe," I said. "But we think you're worth it."

Footsteps echoed out in the hall. I wondered if Clara'd pressed her call button. I looked around her room for a place to hide, then remembered my getup. I'd say I was an old friend of hers from Florida, just passing through. An aide went walking by outside pulling a mop bucket along behind him, the wheels of the bucket in sorry need of a good shot of WD-40. But the aide kept going. Everything was still again.

"I'd better get out of here before they catch on," I said. "See you next week, six forty-five. Okay?" I patted the foot of her bed, and went out.

I knew I should have kept going across the lobby and out through the glass doors, but I got a wild-hair idea and stopped. The woman behind the counter looked up at me, stopped in the middle of the lobby, and said, "Yes?"

"Coconut," I said. Of all the words in the English language, I had no idea why I picked that word to say right then. But that's what came out.

"Pardon me?" the receptionist said.

Then I was being pushed closer to the counter, the words of a lie spilling out of my mouth, nothing I could do to stop it.

"You know, I was just talking to Mrs. Paulson down the hall," I said. "And she was telling me how much she misses living in Florida. That's where her family's from, you know." I didn't have the foggiest clue as to where Clara's family lived, or if Clara even had any family. I didn't know where the word Florida came from, but there it was, in the air between me and the receptionist, along with coconut and all the other words.

"Is that right?" the woman said, paper-clipping a pile of forms together without looking up.

"Anyway," I said, "Mrs. Paulson went on and on about how much she *loves* Florida and the weather and how *good* the coconut is down there. She says the coconut we get up here just isn't the same after coming all that way in a refrigerated truck. She even said she misses the cockroaches. Can you believe that? *Cockroaches*! Anyway, she's such a sweet person, I thought it might be nice if I arranged for her family in Florida to ship her up a fresh one."

The woman looked across the counter at me, tipping her head forward a little so her eyes could see over the top of her half glasses.

"A coconut," I said again. "You know. Don't you think a fresh coconut would cheer her up?"

"That sounds just peachy," the woman said.

"You see, the problem is," I went on. "I'd kind of like to surprise her with the coconut. So I was wondering if I could get the phone number of her relatives down there. That way she wouldn't have any idea what I was up to. You know, everybody likes surprises."

The woman rolled her eyes behind her half glasses, sighed, and swiveled around in her chair. She pulled open a large filing cabinet drawer marked CURRENT RESIDENTS, then jotted down a phone number on a scrap of paper and handed the paper across the counter to me.

"It's Hawaii, not Florida," she said.

That almost threw me off. Wrong states. Opposite sides of the world. I thought for sure she was on to me now. I'd been caught, wig, aviators, and all. But more words kept coming up inside of me, so I kept moving my mouth, to let them out.

"Oh," I said. "Well, they grow coconuts in Hawaii, don't they?" The woman didn't answer me. She was busy with her paper clips again. Looked like I was safe. I thanked her. Then a few last words tumbled out. "I'll tell Mrs. Paulson you helped me keep the nut a secret," I said. I touched the brim of my hat and went out through the sliding glass doors.

C L A R A   P A U L S O N

I TALKED to Bert from B13 about this vegetable seminar. He saw the poster and asked if I was going. I shouldn't have told him what's behind the whole thing, about B24's friend and the big house. But I did. B13 got all excited and said, "I'm going now come hell or high water." He said, the word hell so loud I heard Henrietta the Fisheater down the hall exhale *Lord Have Mercy*. At supper Henrietta worked her black beads faster than normal.

B13 claims he knows a married couple in the C wing he can talk into escorting us out the night of the vegetable seminar so we don't have to take an aide. The C wingers can come and go as they please. I don't believe B13, though, because I've never heard of anybody living here at the Gardens with their husband or wife. Here most everybody is a widow or a widower, or else so much of a mummy they don't know if they're married or not.

I don't really care, though. I've decided I'm not going. From the lobby, I'll just watch B13 and his imaginary married couple from the C wing go out through the doors. Or perhaps I won't. Perhaps I'll slip a note under the Rhino's door. Tip her off and watch B13 get caught, along with B24's friend and the skunk woman.

Oh heck, I don't know what I'll do. I just wish somebody would unlock the piano in the dayroom so I could touch the smooth keys with the fingers of my good hand. Just touching the creamy whites and shiny blacks would be enough. I wouldn't even press down. Just touch. One touch would help me make it through another year or two here.

GEORGE CASTOR

I PULLED the twelve-passenger rental van to a stop in front of the glass doors. Except out a ways. Didn't want to be too close, just in case things didn't work out. I shut the lights off and shifted into park, but left the engine idle. The lobby glowed in the night, all that glass and fluorescent light. But the lobby was empty. No crowd waiting for us. Not a soul. Not even Clara.

Damn.

"Maybe they're just running a little late," I said to Grace who was riding shotgun. Grace didn't say anything back. She was digging in that bag of hers. "Maybe they did some research," I said. "Checked into Senior Support Services. Found out we're phony. Maybe they tore down all our flyers. Or maybe the receptionist the other day recognized me after all and now they won't let Clara come."

"Give it some time," Grace said. Then the windows all around us burst into flame, and I was blind. I blinked. But it was just Grace, lighting a goddamned candle right there in the van.

"What the hell are you doing?" I asked.

"Patience," she said without looking up. "And a flame for

faith." She cupped the candle in her tiny hands. This was all
we needed, somebody inside to see us waving an open flame
around out here in the parking lot. But I didn't say anything.
Grace was hunched over the candle, keeping the flame low,
her face orange below the side window.

I'd worn my getup again, on the off chance I'd have to go
in. I pulled down the aviator glasses and scanned the lobby.
Something moved inside. A bent-over woman in a nightgown
and frizzy gray hair hanging down all around was working
her way across the lobby, pushing a walker along in front of
her in low gear. The woman turned down a hallway and out
of sight. This one hadn't signed up for our seminar. I took a
deep breath, held it, then breathed out. The candle flame
flickered. The green numbers of the clock in the dash showed
six fifty-four. *Shit.*

But maybe everything was okay. Hell, maybe the whole
place had decided to come to our seminar! They were all in
the cafeteria right now dividing up into small groups. Maybe
there would be so many people, I'd have to make a few trips
back and forth to the house! A regular shuttle service. Or
maybe they'd all want to walk to the house, get some fresh
air and exercise on the way. I could just see the Ad-ministrator watching me leading all her residents out through those
front doors, a pied piper in a panama hat. Nothing in the
world she could do. We'd all parade back through town,
south across the bridge, and right up the front steps into the
big red house. There might be so many takers we'd have to
add on, or maybe buy another house or two down the street
and paint those houses red, too, tie it all together.

I kicked my mind out of gear. I'd be lucky if Clara showed.
I wouldn't blame her a bit if she said to hell with me and my
whole red house idea.

Movement inside the lobby made me look. Grace looked,
too. There she was! Clara! Rolling around the counter, dressed
in a yellow robe, earmuffs, and hot pink slippers. *Hallelujah!*
"What'd I tell you," Grace said. She blew out her candle,

kissed it, and put it back in her bag. "Just have to have a little faith in the spirits, and a pinch of patience."

The man pushing Clara was too old to be an aide—skinny as a rail, with black-rimmed glasses and a dollop of whipped-cream-white hair up on his head. Right on the heels of Clara and her skinny chauffeur, was another woman—a big woman, one of the heaviest human beings I'd ever seen, waddling along draped in white polka dots the size of pancakes.

The fat woman went up to the counter and handed some-thing to the receptionist. The receptionist nodded, and all three of them came out through the glass doors rolling apart to let them through.

Hallelujah! The parade was under way at last.

But nobody else showed up. Just the three of them standing there, this side of those doors slid back shut, looking out into the dark the way you'd wait for a bus.

Then I remembered that I was driving the bus they were waiting for. But I wanted to go the other way. Shift into gear and get the hell out of the parking lot. Get away from those three stooges standing there waiting for us. But I didn't. I got out of the van and waved the three of them over, earmuffs, pancakes, whipped cream, and all.

"Is this everybody?" I asked.

"Fred's coming yet, but he'll be late for his own funeral," the fat woman said in a brassy, out-of-breath, East Coast ac-cent. "I'm Emma," she said. "And this here's Bert. I believe you already know Clara." Emma's hand was bread dough in my grip, Bert's a handful of bird bones. I nodded down at Clara who didn't seem too sure about the whole thing, but at least she was here, bless her heart.

"I'll take any chance to get out of this hellhole," Bert said, his words high and screechy. He blinked and pulled at his ear. The thick lenses of his glasses gave him owl eyes. "So what's next?" he asked.

"Well," I said. "Let's load up and get out of here."

Grace helped me get Clara rolled up the planks and loaded in through the back doors of the van. Bert and Emma got in through the side door, the van rocking hard when Emma pulled herself in. Grace sat in back with the others, and I climbed in behind the wheel again. There we were, five of us, sitting in the van, the engine running, waiting for somebody called Fred.

And right then a tiny man dressed in a black dinner jacket came running around the counter, both hands fiddling with a red bow tie at his throat. He stopped and looked around the lobby. Then his hands went slow down to his sides, and his shoulders melted.

Emma stood up, reached past me and leaned on the horn, her fleshy arm against my cheek, her body odor and perfume coming in through my nose. The man in the lobby jumped a little, then bent at the waist, squinting and shading his eyes to see outside. He must have spotted us, because he waved as if hailing a cab, did a slight bow to the receptionist, and came hurrying out through the glass doors.

"Sorry I'm late," he said, climbing into the passenger seat next to me. "Couldn't quite get the tie." He was the size of a boy. I thought I smelled whiskey, but couldn't be sure on account of Emma's perfume, so strong my eyes were watering.

"This is Fred," the fat woman's voice said out of the dark from behind me. "My ever-tardy husband. Fred hasn't been on time for anything—including our first date fifty-two years ago."

"Oh, be fair, Emma, will you?" Fred said without looking back. "Neither of us are the most punctual of people. You know that."

"I'm *never* late," Emma snapped. "And I get sick and tired of you constantly denying the—"

"Let's go!" Bert shouted from farther back in the van, slapping on the vinyl seat. "Let's go, let's go, let's goooooo!" he yelled.

Bert had it right. I shifted into gear and punched it. The van lurched. Bert clapped his hands and cheered. Emma started talking about somebody at the Gardens named Blitz who'd walked in on her in the showers yesterday. Fred snuck a quick pull from a silver hip flask that glinted as a streetlight went over.

Headed down Water Street into town, I thought maybe I should just keep on driving, go right through Lookingglass and keep going the twenty miles on over to Salem and deliver my cargo to the State Hospital, Grace and her candles included. But this was the closest I'd come so far to keeping the promise. So I headed for the Hogan House.

Going slow past City Hall, I saw Clara's eyes watching me in the rearview mirror, the neon POLICE sign sliding by outside, those letters burning a bright red hole in the night.

☽

It wasn't until everybody was out of the van and standing in the driveway that I first thought about all the steps. Every door leading into the house was at the top of at least a dozen steps. And Clara was sitting there in a wheelchair. *Shit.*

I looked around for Grace, but she was gone. A shot of lightning flashed the sky white. I thought about using the planks to rig a ramp up onto the front porch, but knew the ramp would be too steep. We couldn't carry Clara up. Fred was tiny; Bert a fence picket. None of us spring chickens. That's all I needed now, somebody dropping of a heart attack on the front steps of my place. They'd lock me up for sure.

Thunder shook loud. More lightning arced white, making the night seem darker. Then it started in to pour. Bert stood looking up, grinning as if he had never before felt rain on his face. Clara sat in her chair with her hands in her lap, the chrome of her wheelchair glowing blue in the dark. The rain picking up steam turned everything shiny. Emma yelled something about her hair getting wet and climbed back into the van, shoving Fred in first. And then I figured it out— hardware, rope, hydraulics—and hurried off to get Poppin' Johnny.

Roaring back around the house full-throttle, the tractor throwing hunks of mud high into the night behind me. I stopped and lowered the front-end scoop to about a foot above Clara's head, got off the tractor, tied Clara's wheelchair to the tines of the scoop with a tangle of rope, then pushed the lever. The scoop went up. The ropes got tight. Clara and her wheelchair tipped back and a little to one side and came off the ground. The rain was coming down in milk buckets now. I raised Clara a little higher off the ground. Up, down, up. The ropes would hold. I revved Clara high up into the night, one arm and one leg of hers flailing from hell to breakfast, the chain on her glasses catching the lightning.

I backed the tractor around and was working Clara over toward the back porch when I noticed the candles: one burning in damned near every window of the house. Grace was at it again. She'd burn the place down yet. Bert was grinning like a kid now, his wet clothes making him look all bones. I thought I heard Emma's voice coming muffled from the van, but I didn't bother to look around.

I eased the tractor closer to the back porch, Clara dangling out in front of me, her arm and leg still going, one pink slipper streaking circles through the air. Then Grace showed up on the back porch wearing a yellow sailor's rainhat and carrying a lantern. She waved one of her tiny white hands, directing me. More lightning cracked, sparks fell from Grace's mouth, and the rain poured harder still.

I lowered Clara onto the porch and let some slack into the ropes. But before I could climb down to untie the ropes, something streaked silver. Grace had slashed the ropes with a single stroke of a kitchen knife. Then the porch was empty, just some pieces of rope hanging down from the scoop tines, dripping and blowing in the wind.

And as quick as it had started, the rain stopped.

I parked the tractor and ushered the others in the back door and down the hallway single file, all of us coming into the living room where Grace had Clara wrapped in a blanket and was toweling her hair dry in front of the fireplace. Candles burned along the mantel. Nobody said a word. The candles flickered, threw shadows on the walls, and on all of us standing there.

"Power's out," Grace said, without looking at me, those two words the only sound in the room other than six wet bodies breathing. Clara's eyes were on me, staring through steam rising up out of a cup of tea she was holding just below her nose. By her eyes I could tell Clara was anything but happy to be here, Emma was mad, close to boiling over, her face puffed up and frowning hard, her fingers trying to fluff up her wet hair, her polyester pancakes gone soggy. Fred was still messing with his bow tie, looking like maybe Emma'd chewed his ass pretty good out in the van. Bert was a wet puppy, still grinning earlobe to earlobe, candlelight on his glasses and teeth.

The odds of any of them wanting anything to do with me or my big red house now were no doubt pretty slim.

CLARA PAULSON

WHEN WE'RE all ready, we ask the receptionist if we can see the Rhino. The receptionist buzzes the Rhino's cage, then tells us she'll be out in a minute. We wait out here in the lobby. In silence. It's hard to hear the fountain clicking on and off, because my heart's beating as hard and loud as I've ever heard it. Forte.

The past two weeks have been all waiting. Every day seems to take a week to go by. By. Every minute slow since B24's friend dropped us back here after his and the skunk woman's so-called seminar, which had nothing at all to do with vegetables. The waiting had been so long, I thought for sure they'd both decided to forget us, decided we didn't qualify for their house. They had seen how my body only halfway works, and how I can't talk, and decided I would be too much of a burden. Burden.

But yesterday B24's friend showed up in that silly wig with a letter for me from the relative who put me in here. A letter and a coconut, of all things. He had a letter for B13, too. Our official papers is what B24's friend called the letters. But I'm not sure it's going to work.

After a long time, the Rhino follows a young well-dressed

couple out of her cage, and the three of them stand in the
lobby. The Rhino's wearing a red dress with three black buttons the size of cookies up the front. She must think she's
Nancy Reagan. Just say no. That's all she has to do. One word,
two little letters, N and O, and we're all stuck right back
where we started.

The couple and the Rhino laugh short splurts, the way people do when they're nervous around each other. They all
make polite departing comments as the man jangles his car
keys. In her client-relations voice, the Rhino assures the couple
that everything will be taken care of, that the transition will
be very smooth, that whoever they're committing to this Hell
will be in good hands. I can see the couple buys it. They all
shake hands and laugh some more. We sit here in the lobby,
all of us invisible, watching. My teeth are ice in my mouth.
I'm sure Bert and Emma and Fred wear dentures, too. Seems
everybody in this place does. I know, because I see teeth soaking in all the rooms. Henrietta soaks hers in a pint jar, along
with her rosaries, sunk to the bottom, black beads draped
over pale pink gums and white teeth.

The couple finally thanks the Rhino for her time and leaves.
The Rhino whispers something to the receptionist, who points
to us with her chin.

"What seems to be the problem?" the Rhino asks, her voice
back to normal, everyday. We're not clients.

"There's no problem," Bert says. I can see he's about to
burst at his seams.

Lucky for us, Fred jumps in. "We just wondered if it might
be possible to meet with you," Fred says, clearing his throat
several times, hard. "It won't take but a minute of your time.
I promise."

The Rhino looks at the big watch on her wrist. "I've got
another appointment," she says.

"This shouldn't take long," Fred says.

"Yeah," Bert shouts, getting to his feet. "And we can do it
right here in the lobby, if you'd like." As if what we're about

to do is going to be some dirty display the aides will have to mop up.

The Rhino glances around. Snorts. "Okay. Come in," she says. We all follow her into her office. The others sit on a long leather couch that smells new. The Rhino sits behind her big walnut desk. I stay in my chair where I always sit.

Bert can't hold back any longer. "We're leaving!" he yells out, standing up and pushing his wrinkled official paper across her desk. "Read this! We're leaving. We're out of here!"

I'm sure Bert just cooked our goose, but Fred nudges me. So I give Fred my official paper. Fred takes my paper, unfolds it, and puts it on the Rhino's desk next to Bert's official paper. Then Fred puts his and Emma's letter next to our papers. The Rhino scans the three white sheets lying there one next to the other. Her face doesn't show a thing. She looks up, eyeballs each of us, one at at time, down the line. "You realize it's against the law to operate a nursing home from a private residence, don't you?" she says.

None of us says a word. Not even Bert. It's perfect. We all just look at the Rhino.

"This isn't a wise step you're taking," she says, so calm I want to kick her. "If you leave here, we can't guarantee you a bed when you have to come back."

We all hold our tongues. Tight. It's incredible. I can't believe B13 or Emma haven't blown it.

"And it's only a matter of time before the authorities close it down," the Rhino adds. "And then you'll *have* to come back."

I see those words make a direct hit on Emma. She swallows and looks at Fred. "Maybe we should think this over some more," she says.

"No, dear, we're leaving," Fred says, mustering all the voice he can out of that little body of his. I want to cheer him.

"You might want to listen to Emma," the Rhino says, her voice all of a sudden calm and sweet, almost back to the way her voice was with the couple out in the lobby. "She has a point, you know," the Rhino says. "I'm not sure Mr. Castor himself has put much thought into this scheme of his."

The Rhino's more wicked than I ever thought. You can hear it coating each word. I want to poke her with my pencil.

"Well, I'm not doing any more thinking," Bert announces, standing up. "I've had ten years to think about this day, and I'm leaving. Let's go!" He turns and starts to push me toward the door.

"Mrs. Paulson, I'm surprised at you," the Rhino says, her voice and my own name, snakes wrapping around me. "After all we did to help you just before Christmas when this same Mr. Castor tried to kidnap you."

I ignore her. The bitch. Bert pushes me on out into the lobby, away from the Rhino behind her big desk. I hear the Rhino get up, the hush of her hose. She starts to say something, but doesn't. When I look back, she's standing there, her open mouth a black hole in her face the size of the cookies on her dress.

The sunlight streaming in through the letters on the glass doors and reflecting off the linoleum is the brightest I've ever seen. So bright we all have to squint. So bright my eyes water, and I think for a minute I'm onstage again, footlights coming up fast, the sound of curtains parting and the clinking of ice cubes all around.

GEORGE CASTOR

I WENT out onto the front porch and sat on the steps. The night air was cold, heavy overcast, everything wet and shiny under streetlight. Typical February weather. Breathing the damp night in deep felt good, smelled good, cool against the roof of my mouth.

My low back ached worse than normal, and my knees and feet throbbed. Too many boxes lifted and lugged. Too many trips upstairs and back down. And then most of last week building Clara's ramp up onto the back porch. But the aches and pains were worth it. The ball was rolling now at least. Four other people and Grace were living here with me in my red house. Ralph was no doubt laughing that laugh of his, taking a long swig of the good Doctor, fish rising through clouds up there in heaven. And down here we were six.

Hallelujah!

"You hear that, Ralph?" I said. "We're six, goddamnit! Six of us living here in this big old red house. *Living*, I said. Not dying. None of us wasting away over in the Gardens waiting to die all alone. You hear me, buddy? Nobody's dying alone here. I told you I'd make it up to you. You hear me, Ralph?"

I stood up, took another chestful of night air, and went

inside. It was late, time to rest. I closed the front door and stood at the bottom of the staircase, listening. There wasn't a sound in the place, other than Dora's clock ticking. Everybody sound asleep. Clara and Emma and Fred downstairs. Bert and Grace upstairs with me. Then I heard the breathing. The whole house breathing slow and steady.

Across the living room carpet, Clara's wheelchair tracks glowed in the streetlight coming in through the windows. I smelled my aunt Bertha, mixed in with the smells of the rice and lentil stew Grace had made for supper. Our first supper. All six of us sitting around the big oak table under the chandelier—six strangers dropped into dinner with each other out of the sky-blue nowhere. Who knows why. Nothing in common but our gray hair, and skin gone slack.

I climbed the staircase and headed to my room. But going past Grace's room, I noticed a crack of yellow light glowing under her door. I stopped. The crack of light flickered, wavered a little. *Shit*. Grace had fallen asleep and left one of her damned candles burning. Too tuckered out from all the action today. Or maybe she was still awake? I wasn't sure what time it was. I didn't want to bother her, but I also didn't want the place a pile of ashes in the morning, all six of us burnt up in our sleep without even a full day together under our belts.

I turned the knob and pushed Grace's door open a crack. Sure enough. On her dresser in front of the mirror, a candle flame bobbed—two flames, one a reflection in the mirror. The birdcage beside Grace's dresser was draped with a scarf. I pushed the door open and went over to blow the candle out. Then I saw Grace's empty bed and stopped walking. Froze. Where the hell was she at this hour of the night?

"I'll blow it out." Her voice hit me out of the dark. I let out a bark. The birds behind the scarf flapped, a tiny bell in the cage dinging a little. Grace was wrapped in a blanket, sitting in her big stuffed chair pulled over to the window, her skunk a shadow curled on her lap.

"What the hell are you doing?" I said. "Trying to burn the

place down?" She was smiling, most likely pleased with herself for scaring the shit out of me.

"Not at all," she said. "I'm just sitting here. Enjoying the candlelight. Listening."

Listening to what? I wondered, but didn't dare ask. I knew Grace heard things I couldn't. Sounds in the burning wicks of all her candles. Sounds in her head. I'd heard her talking to herself before, the way loony people do. I had no idea what Grace heard, and I sure as hell didn't want to encourage her by asking now.

"Looks like it's coming around," she said. Her words floating out of the dim light. "There's life in the palace!" Then she started laughing for no reason.

The last thing I needed was Grace going off the deep end on me just as we were getting going. I said good night and headed for the door.

But as I touched her doorknob, everything went black. On her dresser, the candle was out, just a tiny orange dot glowing, pale smoke coiling up through streetlight in the mirror. But Grace was still sitting in her chair, the eyes of that skunk on her lap glowing. I pulled her door shut so fast it slammed in the dark. Through the wood, I heard Grace laughing again, those birds of hers flapping under the scarf, and that tiny bell jingling. The bell making a sound I hadn't heard for seventy-five years. The same sound the bridle of my pa's horse had made when I opened the front door and saw it standing chest deep in snow, shaking its head in the freezing Nebraska air the morning after the storm. The horse's muzzle frosted white, the saddle empty and wet and dark. That was when I knew Pa was gone, too. He'd never made it through the blizzard to the doctor's the night before. Mama was inside the house, dead in bed, my baby sister or brother dead, too, still inside her. I was all alone in the world, standing in the doorway looking at my father's empty horse, just the jingling of the bridle in the clear blue ice-cold air.

I had no memory of leaving. Only of arriving, jumping

down from the train into a swirling cloud of steam and people rushing past, more people in one place than I'd ever seen, mostly big people—grown-ups wearing strange and wonderful clothes and hats. I stood on the platform looking at the big people appearing and disappearing in and out of the steamy cloud. Pinned to my jacket was a rumpled piece of paper with the letters of my name written on it. I had no idea where I was, who had sent me, or why I was there.

A whistle blasted loud. The cloud churned warm and thick. All the people hurried away. Then, out of the whiteness, a big red-haired angel descended, crying my name, lifting me off the ground, pushing my face into the flowers on her bosom with so much force I had to struggle to get air. I arched back for light and breath, but this woman kept pulling me into her, pushing my face into the skin of her neck and the sweet flowers, crying my mama's name over and over.

I lived with my mama's only sister Bertha and her husband Bill above their hardware store in downtown Omaha for the next ten years. My uncle Bill became my second father, teaching me the secrets of every piece of hardware in that store with the dark oiled floors and worn silver nailheads. But my doting aunt Bertha never did replace my mama.

During the summer of my fifteenth year, I watched my uncle Bill wither and die of cancer in an upstairs bed. I stayed only long enough for the funeral, sweeping the floor as usual that morning, the silver nailheads blinking at me from under the broom.

As the priest droned his closing remarks at the cemetery on that sunny fall day, I slipped over the hill and never saw my mama's only sister again. For the next fifteen years, I wandered all over the West working various jobs: row crops in the San Joaquin Valley, logging near Forks, Washington, trapping in British Columbia. But I always moved on. After working a season in the orchards at the base of Oregon's Mount Hood, I settled for almost three years on an isolated ranch at the opposite corner of the state, in the high-desert country near the tiny town of Frenchglen. That was where I met a fellow hand on the ranch named Bud Tipton. Bud became the closest I ever got to having a brother. He was a big man, full of vinegar and stories. He had hair the color of ripe peaches, red cheeks and blue eyes, and seemed to be forever smiling. I worked alongside Bud almost every day for the better part of three years. And every other Saturday night, we'd head into Burns, where Bud taught me how to raise hell, how to dance with women, and how to hold my whiskey. But one hot day in the corral, a dark red Santa Gertrudis bull got Bud, gored him through the back.

I packed up and went as far west as I could go, stopped only by the Pacific Ocean washing in around my ankles. I wanted to keep going, swim out beyond the breakers and keep swimming to where there were no blizzards or corral dust or shiny nailheads.

But I wound up in the Willamette Valley, at the Oregon Agricultural College in Corvallis, which was where I met Dora, who was young and light and laughed a lot. I fell hard for her. After I dropped out, Dora and I moved over to the coast, near Cloverdale, where I got a job on a dairy and Dora waitressed at the local café down the road in Hebo. When Jason was going on three, we used what little money we'd saved up and bought the farm in the hills above Lookingglass.

CLARA PAULSON

I THINK I'm awake. It's morning. But now I look around and think again. I must still be in a dream. Dream. Pale purple rosebuds twist up the wallpaper from floor to ceiling through faded white lattice. Out the window next to the bed, I can see entire trees—not just the tops—and a light scarf of fog blowing across a lawn. A green lawn. No chain-link fence for Lizzie. A tractor parked under one of the trees, black tires coming up out of the fog. This window's big. The bedsheets have that line-dried roughness and smell of dew and sunlight. I have to pee.

But wait! I can't find the call button. And the stainless steel railing around the bed is gone, too! Just four oak spindles capped with carved lion heads rising into the air above me, the mouths frozen wide in midroar, the eyes little yellow marbles with tiny flames burning inside. No railing, no call button, no too high window! Just four lions staring down at me. This has to be a dream! I don't want to wake up and spoil it all. All. So I lie still, with my eyes closed.

I listen for aides out in the hallway. Coming in to take me to the toilet. But instead, I hear laughter, and dishes clinking somewhere in the distance. Real dishes. The cafeteria? But they don't use real dishes in the cafeteria. Only plastic. This is the sound of porcelain, or bone china. Not plastic. The sound of silverware. I smell coffee and know it can't be the cafeteria. They only serve coffee in the staff break room. Behind a metal door that locks automatically when it falls shut with a bang, an echo, that sign in big black letters staring you in the heart: *Staff Only.*

I run the fingers of my good hand up one of the bedposts, press pointy wooden teeth, breathe in the coffee smell, and wonder if this is heaven. Heaven. But there's a knock at the door and a man pokes his head in. Chalky hair all wild. Red whiskers. It's B24's friend. George. What's he doing here? Come to visit B24?

"Rise and shine!" he announces, all loud and happy. Now I remember the vegetables, the rain and thunder and tractor smell, our official papers on the Rhino's desk, and I know where I am.

"How'd you sleep?" George's voice is too cheerful. He comes into the room toward me. This big room with no railing. I pull the covers up around my throat. George stands there waiting for the answer like an off-duty department store Santa. I can tell he's forgotten I can't talk.

I nod, fine.

He still doesn't get it. Then he remembers. I see it cross his face, the shadow of an airplane going over. I see everything. I can see people thinking.

"Well, breakfast is about done," he says. "Come on out. Hup-hup." He disappears and the door bumps shut. He's forgotten I can't walk either.

I've joined the army or the marines, and Saint Nick is the drill sergeant making his way through the barracks rousting everybody out at the crack of dawn. I've signed up for the rest of my life! I hear George barking in the next room. Hup-hup. Hup-hup. Rise and shine.

I struggle up onto my good elbow and pound on the rose-buds and lattice above the headboard. I need my blasted chair, the fool-idiot! Then I regret pounding. Hope he didn't hear me. Hope I didn't hurt the roses. Everything's too fuzzy still. I better just lie here for a while. Real quiet. Wait for the fog to burn off. Off. I don't want them giving me more pink pills.

But George's head pops back in. Not the Rhino's. "What's up?" he says, pushing the door open and stepping back inside. His thick body comes across the room toward me. I scribble, hold up my pad, a shield with two words and an exclamation point: MY CHAIR!

George stands there, his big hands hanging at his sides. I'm living with George. A man I don't know. In his house. Alone. I jerk the blankets up over my face. Breathe darkness. Taste wool and the faint breath of mothballs. I wait for the lions to come to life, roar, and spring from the bedposts.

"Tell you what." His voice is muffled through the covers. "I'll get Grace. She'll be better at this. She used to work in a hospital." The floor squeaks as he turns to leave. Oh no! Not her! Not the skunk woman with the black eyes! I lower the covers, look out, slap the mattress, hard with my good hand. Twice. Pop. Pop. George stops, turns, flannel shirt and overalls. We both hang there for a minute, two dumb puppets, a few feet apart. I scribble on my pad that it doesn't matter who helps me. George leans closer, squints to read my words. I see tiny purple veins frayed in his nose and cheeks, tufts of red hair growing out his ears.

I scribble again. Hold up my pad: IT'S OK! I DON'T ZZZ NUDE!!! Three exclamation points.

Then a wire arcs in my head, my good arm throws back the covers so hard the blankets billow through the air and land in a heap on the floor near his feet. *See*! I want to scream, but nothing comes out. Just dust flying through sunlight and silence. Him standing there staring at me in my thin nightgown, me holding up my little pad. What's he thinking? Flipping through pages in his head for the right words? What do you say to a person who can't get out of bed by herself? Who can't talk? Who used to sing and play the piano and laugh and dance, but now can't even say her own name?

The air is cold up under my nightgown, around my legs. Then I know what he's thinking: I'll be a burden! My dead half body. Rubber tongue. B24's friend is standing there wishing he never got me my official papers, or at least never gave the papers to me. I can see the Rhino pushing me out to a van waiting at the curb. Nobody on the front porch of this house, waving. It's raining and I'm going back to the Gardens. To B31, the stainless steel railing, the too high treetops. The Rhino won.

"Hang on a sec," George says. The latch on the bedroom door clicks as he closes the door behind him. The click echoes in the tiny, wooden lion mouths carved around me. I think about what I wrote on my pad about sleeping nude. My face flushes hot. Too many men. I'm glad this George is gone. But perhaps he's calling the Rhino to come get me.

A few minutes later, the door opens again. But it's not George or the Rhino. It's her. The skunk woman. Grace. Coming toward me. A mouse whisks up my spine. But she's carrying two cups of coffee, sipping one. Those quarter-note eyes above a thin band of gold going around the rim of a white porcelain teacup, painted pink roses below the gold. I haven't had coffee in so many years I can't remember what it tastes like. Things clear up a little. I remember Emma and Fred, and B13, too. The sun's pouring in through the big window next to the bed. Everything's shifting back. The fog out in the yard's all gone. Whole trees. That tractor with its black tires and yellow scoop.

"Good morning, Clara," the skunk woman says, putting the white cups on the dresser and gathering the blankets from the floor in a single motion that seems effortless. Grace has a purple bandanna tied around her head that's pinching the skin on her forehead. The bandanna looks too tight, painful. I notice her eyes again. Clarinet black. Black. Her gold teeth make her eyes even blacker.

Grace helps me into my robe, out of bed, and into my chair.

She straightens my nightgown and robe, pats my dead leg. I think of the aides at the Gardens shoving and jerking to get me out of bed. Looking where they shouldn't. She's good at this. I give her my good thumb up. She winks, hands me my cup of coffee, gold handle first, and starts making the bed. I can feel the heat of the coffee in the cup's handle coming into my good hand. I don't take a sip right away. I just sit here, breathing the coffee smell, watching the pink light fixture up on the ceiling floating on the black pool inside the cup. Inside the thin gold ring.

At last I take my first sip, hold the hot liquid on my tongue, swallow. Just the way I've always liked my coffee. Black, with a hint of sugar. There's something about the skunk woman that gives me the willies, though. Like when she winked a minute ago. Or the sugar in my coffee. It's as if she knows more about me than she lets on. Like she's talked to somebody about me. But perhaps it's just my mind again.

Then, out of the blanket sounds, I hear the skunk woman asking me if I have any children. Her question stops my breath. A hospital door flashes when I blink. I feel hot coffee dripping onto my lap. She can't know about that! Or did I say something without knowing it? I want to get away from here, from her.

Out the window, the fog's blown back in all over the lawn again, thick as cream soup. No tractor, no tree trunks.

NO KIDS, I write and show her, my pad shaking a little, the corners doggy-eared. The lions all stare down at me holding up my lie. The yellow flames in their eyes flicker and spark. Grace stares at me, too. I look away, want to ring my little bell. My good hand finds my robe and gathers the collar closed at my throat. The pink light fixture trembles inside my teacup balanced on the arm of my chair.

"Me neither," the skunk woman says. "Let's go have breakfast. Everyone's waiting."

She wheels me down the dark wooden hallway. I smell bacon, now, and toast, feel the skunk woman's breath, light and warm and moist, on the back of my neck.

151

෧

Breakfast is over. George and Grace cooked. Real food.
Bacon and fried eggs, hash browns and toast. Orange juice,
too. And more coffee. I write D-LISH! on my pad, hold my
pad up, and smile my half smile. George and Grace start
clearing the table. Bert wheels me into the living room.

What I see makes me stop breathing. I know now this is
no dream. Heaven, perhaps, but not a dream. Sitting over
against the wall is a shiny black Steinway! A baby grand! Bert
rolls me over near the fireplace and goes out. Sitting here
staring, the morning sunlight pouring through the windows
in slanted golden shafts the size of telephone booths, I watch
this ebony piano come to life, shine, call out to me! No padlock on the keyboard, no scratches. I really am out of the
Gardens! The ivory keys are radiant below gold-leaf letters.
The black lacquer finish is so dark and deep I want to swim
in it, drink it up, pour it all over me. And the stool! At the
bottom of each leg, tarnished talons hold a moss-green ball
of glass. And inside the glass balls, tiny bubbles of air are
trapped, forever.

Of course, I could never trust myself to play the piano. Not
now. Not after so many years of no voice and only one good
hand. Not after a life of nothing *but* music, and then none.
But just knowing this piano is here makes me want to cry. A
piece I once played flares in my head. But the notes get all
tangled up with treble clefs and staffs and sharps, everything
twisted together and poking and going every which way—
scrap metal in some Nevada junkyard. Not music.

I wonder why I'm still alive. I always thought that without
my music there would be no reason to go on living. Living.
But a stroke changes everything. Changes perspectives. And
here I am still alive—or at least half-alive—after all these
years. I don't remember how long. That's the worst loss, after
my voice and fingers. The little scraps of memory I can't find
anymore. I deserve it, though. All of it.

But right now, there's a piano in this huge house! A beautiful black baby grand Steinway. At this single moment in time, I'm happier than I've been in years. I want to stop time, stay here in this moment forever, like the bubbles in the glass balls.

GEORGE CASTOR

WHEN BERT walked in one day carrying an antelope head mounted to a walnut plaque and hung the whole thing on the wall above his bed, I assumed Bert had done some hunting in his day, and this was his prized trophy—a mounted reminder of the great hunt that he couldn't bring himself to part with. But a few days later when Bert showed up with a stuffed Siamese cat and put the dead cat on the dresser beside his bed, I started to wonder about Bert. And wondering about Bert made me start to wonder about the other folks who had been sharing my big red house with me now for the better part of a month. Bert's dead cat made me start to wonder about myself.

"That there's Tye-Boo," Bert said when I went into his room to have a closer look. "Best cat the wife and I ever had. We decided to keep the ol' boy around. You know, forever." Bert was glowing, pride oozing right out of him.

I wasn't sure what to say back. I'd never heard of anybody stuffing their pet cat for a keepsake.

"Tye here sat on our television set for years," Bert said. "Watching us watch it. Except for when the wife put him outside a couple times a year to air out in the sun. The ol'

154

boy collected dust something awful. I've had him in storage since the wife passed away and I went into the Gardens. They wouldn't let me keep Tye in my room there. No pets allowed, they said. Except for Mrs. Lockhart over on the C wing. Somehow she talked them into letting her keep a bird in her room. A yellow bird in a wicker cage."

I couldn't believe I was now living with a man who had not only skinned and stuffed his pet cat, but had kept the damned thing around for God knows how many years. Bert adjusted the cat on his dresser, scratched the cat's chin, made a little purring sound with his mouth.

"I had a shop, you know," Bert said, turning around to face me again. "Taxidermy. Doing up Tye here didn't cost us a penny." Bert stopped talking for a second. "But these two are all I got left now. Nobody ever came back to get the pronghorn there. Too bad. He was one of the best jobs I ever did. Fella forgot all about him, I guess. So I hung on to him. And then Tye here. He's a fine cat."

"These eyes look real," I said, leaning closer to inspect the dusty blue cat eyes staring back at me.

"Glass," Bert said. "Marbles. Mail-order supply house. They got everything you can imagine."

"No kidding?" I said.

"You name it," Bert said. "Eyeballs, claws, teeth, plastic skulls and tongues, rubber noses. They even got individually wrapped whiskers. All I ever really needed was the hide."

I'd read about artificial hearts and hips for humans. It probably wouldn't be too long before they'd have mail-order parts houses for us. A toll-free telephone call would get you a new set of eyeballs or eardrums shipped out UPS in a brown paper package. You'd just pop the new ones in and toss the old ones out. Replace anything you wanted. Except your hide. Hell, it probably wouldn't be long before they'd have new suits of skin too, complete with zippers or Velcro, and not a wrinkle anywhere.

"How'd you get into it?" I asked, sitting down on Bert's bed.

"What, stuffing critters?" Bert said.

"Yeah," I said. "Taxidermy."

Bert shoved his glasses up against his forehead with his knuckles and blinked through the thick lenses. "Well, let's see," he said. "My dad was a trapper. He had five or six lines going all winter long. So he was always coming home with different critters. I learned how to tan hides real young. The heads weren't good for much. So I started mounting the heads on sticks or shingles and selling them to kids at school." He looked at me. "Wound up spending my whole life at it."

"Any regrets?" I asked.

"Regrets?" Bert pulled at his ear.

"Yeah," I said. "Ever wish you'd done something else? You know, been a rodeo clown or a reporter overseas?"

"Oh no. I didn't mind stuffing critters. It was good work," Bert said. "Why's that? You didn't like farming?"

"Oh, I love farming," I said. "It's harder than hell at times. But there's something about shoving your hands into dirt that does something for the soul. That's part of what we've lost, I think, the soul-dirt thing."

"So why'd you ever move into town and stop farming?" Bert asked. His words piled into me. "Why'd you quit doing something you loved?"

Bert stood there next to his dead cat blinking at me, waiting for an answer. His dead cat stared at me, too, those two blue marbles boring into me. But I didn't have an answer. I'd never looked at moving to town as quitting farming. But Bert was right. I wasn't a farmer anymore. I'd quit farming. Left the land for a goddamned city lot. And here I was, talking to a man with a stuffed cat sitting on his dresser and an antelope head hanging above his bed. A man I didn't know from Abraham Lincoln. Living in the bedroom next to mine. In my house! Me living with a whole houseful of loonies! A woman in a wheelchair who couldn't say a single word. A couple so mismatched in size and stature they could have signed on with a freak show. And a woman who was either a witch or a closet firebug, or both. Here I was *living* with these people.

In the middle of downtown Lookingglass, thirteen miles away from the land I'd farmed for forty years. What the hell was I doing?

The blue marbles turned into Ralph's eyes. I heard hooves pounding and Bud's cry. Smelled ashes and snow. Saw a muddy bathtub sitting on the floor of Uncle Bill's hardware store. The tub brimming full of blue marbles and salmon thrashing. And all over the floor, silver nailheads burning bright as stars.

Then the floor went to wet gravel, my own boots soaking wet, the smell of warm piss and exhaust making me gag.

I stood up so fast the edges went white. Almost fell trying to get out of Bert's bedroom and down the staircase—away from that dead cat staring at me. Ralph's eyes. Bud's eyes. Going through the downstairs hallway headed for the back door, I saw yellow eyes glowing. A streak of white fur. But I made it to the door, pulled the door open and fell out into sunlight and fresh air.

CLARA PAULSON

AFTER A few weeks here, I don't wake up wondering where I am anymore. This place is real. The Big Red House, George calls it. Seems too good to be true, though. True.

There's something about Grace I still can't figure out, though. It's like she's here, but she's somewhere else too. She's the one who helps me in and out of bed. Helps me get dressed. Go to the toilet. I never asked her to. Grace just started doing it. Which is nice. I guess she used to work in some hospital. Grace doesn't say much, which is fine with me. I haven't seen her yellow birds yet. But I think I've heard them. Her room's upstairs, so I can't get up there. I see her skunk now and then slinking through the house, black and white. But no smell. The other day I noticed her skunk's got a tiny silver pig hanging from its collar. Like a charm off a charm bracelet. The pig jingles a little when the skunk moves through the house. The pig must have a tiny bell inside its belly.

But this house! It's a castle! Such a change from the Gardens that I sometimes catch myself looking out through the big oval window in the front door half expecting to see the Rhino herself sneaking up the brick walk with a couple of aides behind her dragging straitjackets and rope. But it never happens. The daffodils along the walk just get bigger and brighter. Little yellow baritones tooting toward the sun, making music I can almost hear!

These first weeks have been the slowest of my whole life. It's not boring, though. Each day just takes a long time to go by. Which is nice. Nice. I don't want time to ever speed up again. But routine is starting to settle in, and routine always makes time go faster. Too bad. Living here in George's Big Red House, I see no reason to rush on to Hell.

So far, I've spent most afternoons out on the front porch sitting in a state of semidisbelief, watching the neighborhood go by, listening to the wind playing George's chimes. Although they're the ugliest-looking things I've ever seen, George's wind chimes do make a range of beautiful melodic sounds. George says he made the chimes out of an old milking machine. One thing I've learned already: George can fix or build just about anything he sets his pigheaded mind to. He'll disappear off in that beat-up pickup truck of his and come back with the bed full of metal parts or boards he's scavenged up somewhere. Next thing you know, George has rigged up some contraption to plant peas, or open the back door for me and my chair. And like his wind chimes, these things seem to work.

George is a pack rat. Addicted to collecting all sorts of stuff—junk, as far as I can tell—that he piles in the driveway and stacks out around the garage. Just since I've been here, he's added two porcelain toilets, a pallet of bent metal fence posts, and an old gas station pump to his collection. I can already tell the junk's getting on Fred's nerves. Fred's a neat-nick it turns out. Picks at his teeth all the time. I admit, the junk's kind of an eyesore, but I'll never say anything to George about it. Not after the other day.

He came up to me after breakfast and said, "Clara, I've been thinking. Seems to me you'd be better off navigating yourself around here under your own power, don't you think?"

On my pad I wrote, PEOPLE N HELL WANT H2O, 2. George laughed a little, but kept going.

"You've got one good arm and a good leg, right?" he said.

And a mind that's good ninety-eight percent, I thought. But before I could respond, George wheeled me out onto the driveway and left me sitting there in my robe and curlers, the sunlight warm on my face. A few minutes later, he came back with a bunch of metal pipes, pulleys, and rope in a beat-up wooden box that he dumped out at my feet and went to work. Work. That's kind of how George is, I'm learning. He gets an idea in that head of his and just barrels through with it, regardless of what anybody else thinks or says.

In less than an hour, George had rigged up what vaguely resembled a metal spinning wheel and bolted the whole thing to the left side of my chair. It looked ridiculous and I was convinced he'd bitten off more than he could chew this time. But he stood back and told me to spin the wheel. Spin. So I reached my good hand out and took hold of the glass doorknob he'd attached to a weathered black steering wheel on the contraption.

"Go ahead," he said. "Give 'er a crank."

I turned the wheel a little, and me and my chair moved forward. But instead of turning sharp to the right and going nowhere like my chair normally does when I push with my good arm, my chair rolled straight ahead, both wheels moving in unison beside my thighs. I spun the wheel a little more. Rolled straight ahead again. I couldn't believe it! I gave the wheel a good spin this time, and me and my chair rolled down the driveway picking up speed. The air moving past my face felt nice! I was sure George had to be pushing from behind. So I looked around. But he wasn't! Wasn't. George was just standing back there grinning. The thrill of rolling under my own power set an entire pit orchestra going somewhere inside me. I wanted to go on forever. Roll all the way back to Reno! Pull into the Starlighter, wheel right up to the bar, and order three or four White Russians. Line them up and keep them coming. I cranked a few more times, real hard, until the air rushing by was whistling a little up in my curlers.

I was getting close to the end of the driveway, so I reached down for the wheel lock. But the handle was gone! I looked back and saw George running after me, the grin gone, waving my handle in the air like some nutty conductor chasing after his runaway orchestra.

Out the corner of my eye, I could see a vehicle approaching up the street. I waved for it to stop, and tried to jam my good foot down under the chair to slow me, but I was going too fast. Just whipped my slipper off. I turned again to see if George was gaining on me, and when I did, the whirring black steering wheel tore a half-dozen curlers from my hair and launched the curlers into the air in front of me, pink plastic bullets.

Just before I hit, I saw a final handful of curlers ricochet off the yellow metal fender of what I thought was a school bus. I slammed into the bus. Tires screamed. Everything jarred. My chair spun sideways and lodged hard. When I opened my eyes, I saw long scratches all along the side of the school bus, the paint hanging down in fine little curlicues. I thought I was dead now, for sure. Finally headed for Hell.

But the driver's door opened, and a wave of perfume more potent than anything Emma wears washed over me. A short woman wearing a bright purple gown with a flow-ered sash struggled out of the driver's seat and stood glar-ing up at George, her fists pushing into the blossoms on her hips, George panting like a dog, his hair wilder than ever.

"If you think this is a good way of attracting my atten-tion, Mr. Castor," the woman said, "I don't think it's funny in the least. You could have killed this poor woman." She glanced down at me, still jammed against the fender. "And look what you've done to my car!" She swept a hand of rings sparkling and bracelets tinkling through the air in front of me.

This is how I met Mrs. Beasley and her school-bus-yellow Cadillac. She lives just down the street and seems to keep an eye on this house, The Big Red House. But I think she has an eye for George. When George offered to pay for the damage to her yellow Cadillac, she waved him away, jangling her bracelets and saying that her insurance, which she said she had plenty of, would more than cover it.

George unwedged me and my chair from the dented fender and limped us back across the street and up the driveway. Mrs. Beasley roared off in her Cadillac. I wanted to call it quits, but George was determined.

"Have to get back on the horse!" he said. I couldn't scream at him or tell him I thought he was nuts all the way through, because I'd lost my pad and pencil in all the commotion. So I got back on the horse, my chair that George had converted into a horse that galloped.

In hindsight, I'm glad we stuck with it. Because now I can go anywhere in the house, except upstairs. My wheelchair ornament's not the prettiest sight, but it works. I like the glass doorknob. Sometimes, if I'm sitting outside, or near a window, and the sun hits my doorknob just right, the glass sparkles and shines, a big diamond sitting there on my black steering wheel. Kind of reminds me of my star in the door back at the Gardens.

So, I'll never complain about George's piles of junk. Just the other day he said something about rigging up a trailer for me—a chariot is what he called it. Whatever he means by that. Who knows? Perhaps George's chariot will swing low and take me off somewhere. Up into the fluffy white clouds where there's harp music and pianos are made of solid gold. Or more likely, this chariot will swing low, scoop me up, but keep on going down, into the flames and glowing rock, the pitchforks and red tails whipping, down where I earned myself a front-row seat forever.

GEORGE CASTOR

ONE DAY Bert asked me if I'd be willing to help him out with a small favor, at the ABZ Mini-Storage across town.

"Time to get Gertie out," Bert said. "Time to bring the old girl home for good."

I figured Gertie was another stuffed animal Bert had been storing for years. Probably his dog this time, some black boxer sitting up on its hind legs begging for a bone. Grace would have a fit. She'd already made Bert promise to keep his bedroom door shut.

"Who's Gertie?" I asked.

"My girl," Bert said.

"Your girl?" I said. If Bert had a stuffed human being in storage, I was throwing his ass out.

"Never had the heart to get rid of her," Bert said. "The wife and I, we never had any kids. We tried a lot, but it never took. Just the way things were, I guess. So we got Tye-Boo. Of course, Tye was just a cat. And Gertie, well, she's just a car. A Hudson. But she's like a kid to me, George. She's my baby." The way Bert was saying the words, I could tell he'd been a good father to his cat and his car. "When I went into the Gardens ten years ago, they told me my eyes were too far gone for driving. Took away my license. So I haven't driven Gertie in ten years. But I think now it's time to bring her home, here, if that's okay with you, George. Will you drive my baby home for me?"

"Sure, Bert," I said. "But if it's been sitting for ten years, I doubt we'll even get the engine to fire."

"Oh no. She'll start right up," Bert said. "You see, every three or four months I got a one-hour release. The same aide always brought me down. I'd climb into the driver's seat and start Gertie up. Let 'er run and just sit inside listening to the radio, wiping off the dash, polishing Chris."

"Chris?" I asked as we went past Chuck's Paint Floor 'N More.

"Saint Chris," Bert said. "He was pinned to the headliner when the wife and I first bought Gertie. The couple who sold her to us said they'd never had a wreck. Put full credit for that safety record on the fact that Saint Chris had always been a passenger, had always been up there watching over them. So I never threw Chris out."

We pulled through the open gate at the mini storage and Bert directed me to stop in front of a metal door numbered one-forty-five.

"She's in there," Bert said. "Sealed up tight."

We got out and Bert rolled up the garage door. Sure enough. Nosing out of the darkness was a chrome bumper and grill gleaming from here to Texas. And above the grill was a wide, shiny, black hood soaking up most of the daylight going in through that open door.

"Gertie, this here's George," Bert said, holding his hand out my way, as if that damned car were living and breathing just like the two of us. "George, this is my baby girl, Gertrude."

After I'd pulled the car out into the sunshine, and Bert had closed the garage door and climbed into the passenger seat ready to ride shotgun, I shifted out of gear, set the brake, and got out. It was a crime Bert wasn't allowed to drive his own car. We were just going across town, and the day was one of those late-winter treasures: so damned warm, so early in the year, it made you wonder why all the trees didn't just go from bare limbs to full foliage overnight. The engine idled, the drone low and perfect. Drops of water fell from the chrome tailpipe in little splashes that flashed when they hit the concrete. I walked around the car and opened the passenger's door.

"You drive her on home the rest of the way," I said.

"I can't," Bert said. "They say my eyes are too shot for that."

"Can you see me?" I asked.

"Of course I can," Bert said.

"Can you see that sign down the street there?" I asked, pointing.

"That stop sign? Sure," Bert said.

"Then slide over and get behind that wheel," I said. "It's your only child, remember? Besides, we're just going across town, not more than a mile."

Bert sat there, blinking through a frown. "I better not," he said. "It's been a long time."

"It's your car, right?" I asked.

"Of course she's mine," Bert said.

"And this is supposed to be a free country, right?" I said.

"Well, yeah," Bert said. "But there are laws."

"Sure there are," I said. "But we're not going to break any."
Bert wasn't quite convinced. "Okay, on the outside chance we do get stopped, I'll swap places with you real fast," I said. "They can ticket me. Okay?"

"And if I pile 'er up?" Bert asked.

"Nonsense," I said. "Let's go."

Bert slid across the seat. I got in, closed the door, and winked at him. Bert glanced up at the Saint Christopher medal, pushed the clutch in, and shifted into gear.

We drove slow motion through town, the windows rolled

all the way down, the air blowing through Bert's white hair, filling his shirtsleeves, a starburst of sunlight riding along out in front of us on the chrome hood ornament.

I leaned over and turned on the radio. Classical music flowed out and filled the car. I turned the volume up so loud everything going by outside turned into a motion picture, the two of us part of the motion picture, driving across a giant screen. The streets were clean and black and wide as runways, and the plum trees going past on both sides were all of a sudden in full bloom—bursts of pink cotton candy growing up out of the sidewalks. Spring had erupted. *Hallelujah!*

At the intersection by the bridge, Bert signaled to turn right, back toward the Hogan House. "Not yet," I yelled over the music. "Let's go around one more time. The day's so perfect. You don't get many like this. Come on, Bert, one more time around! Just for the hell of it."

Bert smiled, clicked off the turn signal, and accelerated straight through, buildings going by, music loud all around, blue sky everywhere. Then Bert came up off the seat and floated in the air, hanging on to the wheel to keep from blowing out the window. Then I was coming up off the seat, too, music and that sweet warm air filling the car, filling our heads, the two of us floating alongside each other the way astronauts do in outer space.

We drove down past *The Appeal* office and the library to the A&W Drive-In where we turned around and came back through town. I spotted Mrs. Beasley getting out of her shiny yellow Cadillac near the now defunct American Federal Savings & Loan. I leaned over and honked the horn and waved at Beasley. Bert waved too. Both of us waving through the windshield, a couple of goddamned teenagers. Mrs. Beasley squinted into the sun, raised a hand to shade her eyes, her earrings and bracelets glittering all around her face, but she didn't recognize us.

We drove on down Second Street to the Thriftway and

rolled through the big parking lot, the tires of the Hudson up off the pavement now, the chrome hubcaps spinning around below us. Over by the automatic doors, a little boy in black rubber boots was riding the mechanical pony, the little boy's face glowing the same way Bert's face was glowing. The music got louder still as we pulled back out onto Second Street, all the people in the Thriftway parking lot waving white handkerchiefs, watching us drive away.

As we came back through town again, everything slowed even more. People on the sidewalks and in shop doors stopped and turned to watch us go by. Little kids pointed and tried to run along with us. Bert waved and smiled. It was a goddamned parade! And we were in it. Grand Marshals! White gloves, the whole shebang! Lights flashed and the music played louder still. The hood of the Hudson was a huge black mirror, curved shapes of plum trees and people and neon signs sliding down the hood, out across the fender, and dropping off out of sight into the street. More lights! Fireworks! Everything spinning.

Hallelujah! I reached over and held down the horn just for the sheer hell of it. Bert pushed in the clutch and revved the engine so high it backfired a couple times. Then a short blast of siren hit us from behind. Everything scattered off the hood. The paint wasn't as shiny or black. Colors faded. Our white gloves were gone. The music stopped. An ad for bags of Steer-Plus bark dust on sale at the PayLess Garden Center blared out of the radio. The air in the car smelled of mildew and must. There wasn't a plum blossom blooming anywhere.

I must have come back to earth a second or two before Bert, because I was climbing onto Bert's lap, yelling for him to move his ass out of my way. "It's a goddamned cop!" I yelled. "Let me take the wheel!"

Somehow the two of us—one on top the other, four hands on the wheel, four feet thrashing at the pedals down on the floorboard—managed to pull Bert's only child to a stop at the curb as Bert slid out from under me and into the passenger's seat.

"But I didn't *do* anything," Bert whined. "Nothing! I swear it. I swear to God."

"I know. I know. Relax, will you?" I said. "It'll be okay. Maybe he just wants to talk. Let's just play it cool, okay?"

The cop's blue uniform came up to the driver's side and blocked the light coming in through the window. "Good afternoon, gentlemen," the cop said. "And what might we be up to today?"

Bert freaked. "I swear, I didn't do anything wrong," Bert yelled. "Did I, George? Tell him! Tell him!"

I elbowed Bert, who was damned near on my lap now trying to talk to the cop out the window.

"Well, we were just out for a drive, sir," I said. "With this kind of weather, how can you pass it up?"

"Looks like you haven't been out for a drive in about fifteen years," the cop said, tapping his pen against his palm, his black book under his arm, "judging by those expired registration tags."

Shit. The tags of all things. I wanted to tell the cop he ought to have something better to do with his time than driving around watching for expired tags. But I held my tongue.

"May I see the vehicle registration and operator's license please?" the cop asked.

Bert started rifling through the glove box, pulling shit out onto his lap and all over the seat. I thumbed through my wallet for my driver's license, thinking it could be worse. Expired tags were no big deal. A small fine. A hand slap. We should take the ticket and be happy the cop hadn't seen Bert behind the wheel and was hauling us in for driving with no license.

"You know, Officer, you're right," I said. "Gertie here has been in storage for so long we forgot all about checking the tags before we took her out today. The nice weather must have done something to our common sense." I held out my license. "Guess we deserve this one, huh, Bert?"

"I need to see *his* license, sir," the cop said. "*He* was operating the vehicle at the time I pulled in behind you way back by Square Deal Lumber and turned on my lights."

We were sunk—Saint Chris and all. I couldn't think of anything to say or do, so I just sat on the wide front seat blinking at Bert. Bert was staring out through the windshield, that little-boy look long gone from his face.

Then Bert's face bloomed, his eyes went wide, and he was out of the car and hurrying around the hood so fast I was sure he was going to yell at the cop, or start throwing punches. But Bert did neither. He leaned against the fender of the Hudson, folded his bony arms across his chest, and started talking to the cop as if the cop were some longtime hunting buddy.

"I'll bet you're a hunter," Bert said.

"I go every year," the officer said. "But right now I need to see your operator's license."

"I'll bet you get one every year, too," Bert went on. "A buck."

"I've only been skunked once," the cop said. "Your license please, sir."

"Not bad," Bert said. "Big ones, too, I'll bet."

"Four or five points," the cop said. "One year I pulled down an eight."

"No kidding?" Bert said. "I'll bet you have that one mounted and hanging on the living room wall, don't you?"

The officer glanced down at me. I shrugged.

"Listen," the cop said to Bert. "I need to see your operator's license. And I mean *now*."

"I'll tell you what," Bert said. "I'll make you a deal . . . ."

I shoved my face into my hands. I couldn't believe Bert was going to try to bribe an officer of the law.

"You see, I'm a taxidermist," Bert said. "Licensed. Certified. Had my own shop."

"I'm running out of patience, sir," the cop said.

"Okay, okay," Bert said, holding up a hand. "The next buck you bag. Oak plaque. Engraved brass plate. The whole deluxe package. I'll mount it completely free of charge. Now, how's that sound?"

I couldn't stay sitting in the car any longer, so I opened the door and got out, deciding honesty was the best card to play. "Listen, here's the scoop," I said to the cop. "Bert here's not supposed to be driving because they claim his eyes are a little weak, although he can see just fine. Anyway, we're bringing his Hudson home from storage. I had no idea the tags were expired. I doubt Bert knew. I just thought Bert might like to drive his own car across town. That's all. I encouraged him. He didn't *want* to drive. I'm the one at fault here. I pushed him into it." The cop was listening. Bert was scratching at his ear. "Is there any way you could ticket me and let Bert here off the hook?" I said. "He's innocent."

The cop didn't say anything for a minute. "With expired tags, I usually just give a warning the first time," the cop said. "But I should cite you both for attempting to elude, although it wasn't much of an attempt. How far you going?"

"Just a few more blocks," I said.

"All right," the cop said. "But get this vehicle registered, okay? It's a beauty." He paused, then looked at Bert.

Bert grinned. "Oh, my offer still stands. We live in the old Hogan House. All I need's the head."

"The Hogan House?" the cop said. "I've heard about you folks."

"All good, I'm sure," I said, hurrying to get back into the car and the hell out of there before the cop changed his mind. "Thank you, Officer," I said. "We'd best get this rig off the streets until we get it registered legal." I slammed the door. "Hope you enjoy the rest of this fine day."

Bert shook the officer's hand, giving a few tips on how to store a deer head, then came back around and got in.

We pulled away from the flashing lights in silence. Gertie's hood was shining again. The starburst was back. Trees and houses and blue sky were sliding across the black paint and down off the fenders. Bert reached up, straightened the Saint Christopher medal on the headliner, then winked at me.

CLARA PAULSON

FIFTY-ONE YEARS. Snap. I finally got it. That's how long they've been married. Fred and Emma. Married. Fifty-one years is a long time. Longer still if it's Emma you're married to. I'd say that's worth double time. A hundred and two years! I can't imagine. That mouse Fred deserves a medal for still being alive. Fred and Emma's marriage seems to be mostly mutual tolerance, though, like so many marriages. But Fred and Emma are still together, which is more than I can say for myself. I failed at marriage three times. Three strikes. I'm out. And now it's too late. Late. Only half a body, no voice, and way too many wrinkles to bring men around now. I'm out.

Somehow Fred talked Emma into moving up to Oregon after he retired. I can tell Emma hates change. For thirty-odd years Fred and Emma lived in the same house on a dead-end street called Pimpleton Place in the suburbs of San Diego. Fred said they never once rearranged the furniture or changed the bathroom wallpaper—yellow and blue angelfish swimming through foil kelp. I know this because Fred told me so one night when he was well lubricated. I could tell Fred was feeling good by the scent on his breath. I know that smell. I know that wallpaper, too. That wallpaper's in some backstage dressing room somewhere, the kelp shining bright from all the lightbulbs around the mirror.

Who knows what Emma did all day on that dead-end street. Fred says she never worked. They had two kids, but the kids moved to the Northeast and they hardly ever see them. I'll bet Emma just watched soap operas on the television, wiped off the Formica, and sat around a lot. That's no doubt why Emma agreed to the move up here to Oregon. Afraid when Fred retired he'd catch her sitting around on her butt all day. The thought of moving that much weight around would cause anyone to want to just sit. Sit.

Fred says he never liked working for the Department of Defense all those years, but I'll bet it paid pretty well, and got him out of the house. Out of the kelp. I haven't figured out yet if it was the job or the wife that made Fred fall in love with gin. It could have been either. Or both. But Fred's quiet about the gin. I don't think anybody else in the house notices, but I do. The first time I met Fred, just before we left the Gardens, I knew right away he was a drinker, his Rudolph-red nose was a dead giveaway, blinking right smack in the middle of his face. But Fred's a harmless drinker, if there is such a thing. I know how Grace hates the stuff, so I hope Fred keeps his gin under wraps. If Grace finds out, she might kick him out. Out. And then we'd be left to deal with big Emma on our own.

The night Fred was lubricated up, he told me the reason he moved was because he was ready for a big change in life. Something wild. And wild for Fred was a move up here to Oregon where he didn't know a single soul. Fred says he'd never been north of San Luis Obispo. Emma's originally from New Jersey. For her, Oregon was the wildest of the West, the ragged edge, complete with cowboys, log cabins, and grizzly bear. Emma must have thought moving north was borderline insanity. Fred says as soon as he retired, they sold their house, loaded everything they owned—including that beautiful Steinway baby grand Emma never played but wouldn't leave behind—into a moving van, and headed for Oregon.

When they crossed the border north of Weed, California, and found paved roads, regular houses, and no sign of bear, Emma calmed down. According to Fred, they drove through every single town in Oregon that sounded interesting: Happy Hollow, Harmony, and Hope; Paradise Park, Plush, and Persist; Silverton, Sweet Home, and a place called Sublimity. They even drove through some towns that sounded awful: Drain, Needy, Pulp, Zig-Zag, and Starvout. Fred claims they found a little hamlet outside of Portland called Boring. Which sounds to me like a worse place to live than Silver Gardens even. But names can be misleading.

When they rolled into Lookingglass, Fred says he knew right away he'd found the town he was after. He pulled the moving van to the curb and they checked into the Nordic Hotel—the only hotel in this whole town. "Nine rooms and an outdoor Pepsi machine that glowed red, white, and blue all night long," Fred said.

But the next morning Emma started complaining about pains in her chest. Fred says a doctor told them her blood pressure was way too high, and her heart needed to calm down. The doctor recommended Emma stay in a rest home for a month or so until her condition improved. But Emma flat out refused to go in alone, so Fred agreed to move in with her.

Silver Gardens wasn't anything like Fred and Emma expected a retirement home to be. The Gardens wasn't like places they knew about down in Southern California called Leisure World and Retirement Heaven. God knows the Gardens has nothing to do with retirement, leisure, or heaven. But Fred says Emma hates change so bad that once she was settled in their room on the C wing and her blood pressure was better, she didn't want to move back out.

But we're all out now. Aren't we? That's what counts. I have no idea how Fred talked Emma into coming along that first crazy night of the vegetable seminar, or how he convinced her to move in here for good. Sometimes I wish he hadn't. Emma's a hard one to share a house with. And this is a big house. Big. Emma can be a real bitch if she sets her mind to it. I don't know how Fred's shared a bedroom and bathroom with Emma for fifty-one years. That man deserves a medal.

When it gets too bad, Fred sneaks off and finds one of the bottles he has stashed in the nooks and crannies around this house and lets the gin blaze a trail of heat down his throat, refueling his resistance. I've heard the bottle clinking against Fred's teeth. Sometimes he carries a chrome flask that flashes. I hear and see everything. The raspy sigh Fred lets out after the swig, the glaze on his lips, the red tinge around his eyes. All the pills Emma takes for her blood pressure and heart and ankles.

But living here in the big red house has started to change Fred. I can tell. Just like living here's changing all of us. Slow and subtle. The other day Emma said she caught Fred singing in the shower, and then later heard him walking around humming. Emma claims Fred's never done that before. She's afraid the singing and humming will drive her batty because Fred can't carry a tune in a tin bucket, she says.

I suspect Fred's humming because this house is so nice and big. Because it has so much room, so many doors he can close, so many little nooks and crannies.

George Castor

I came into the living room and found Bert and that damned antelope head of his most the way up a rickety stepladder over by the fireplace. Bert had a whole mouthful of nails pinched in his face and some wire in one hand. He was either trying to string himself up, or fixing to hang that antelope head of his right there on the living room wall for all of us to enjoy. Bert's face was redder than hell, him grunting and breathing hard trying to keep from falling off that ladder, and all the while trying not to drop that damned head.

"Careful!" I yelled when I couldn't bear to watch anymore. "You'll fall and kill yourself."

Bert jumped, grabbed the mantel with one hand, and for a second it looked like all three of them were going down— Bert, his antelope, and that stepladder. But they didn't. Bert held on, and the ladder stopped swaying. A couple of nails bounced on the hearth below the ladder, and Bert looked around at me, those owl eyes huge behind his glasses slid down his nose.

"What are you doing up there?" I asked. "Trying to hang yourself?"

Bert started to talk, squeezing words out around and between the nails bristling from his lips, a couple more nails falling out and pinging down the steps of the ladder. "Trying to liven this place up a bit," Bert said.

Then Grace's voice came through the air from somewhere behind us. "Livening things up with dead body parts?" she said. "Most people prefer paintings or flowers to killing animals for no reason other than the fun of it."

Bert's mouth went wide open now, the rest of the nails a shower of silver pins headed for the floor, Bert's words coming out clear and loud above the nails singing and bouncing as they hit. "They were dead when I got them!" Bert yelled. "This is preservation. Plain and decent!"

"Preservation?" Grace said. "What are you preserving?"

"This here pronghorn," Bert said. "What do you think?"

"I think it's dead," Grace said, her eyes rocks. "When something's dead, there's no sense trying to preserve it. Everything's got to go back. Even that antelope head of yours, whether you killed it or not. Everything goes back, comes around. It's one big circle. And we're all part of it." Grace stopped talking for a second. She just stood there looking at Bert and me, both of us looking back at her, the air gone sticky all around. "All of us are going back into the earth sooner or later," she said. "Back down. No matter how hard we try to avoid that." Her words were coming across the room spaced out, each word a stone thrown hard into a muddy riverbank. "We all go around the big circle. The same way the sun goes," she said. "It's not a straight line. From A to the End." And then it was just Bert and I and that antelope head in the room full of too hot air.

"Gawd, what's up her poop shoot?" Bert said. "She's got no idea how much work went into this old guy." He stroked the antelope's forehead.

"I don't know, Bert," I said. "But you might want to take her serious. Grace has a thing for animals."

Bert came down the ladder and put the antelope head on Emma's piano stool. "You know, you might be right," Bert said. "The first time I saw Grace she had a cage full of canaries and a skunk on a leash."

"You knew her before you moved in here?" I asked.

"Not really. She came to the Gardens now and then and told stories," Bert said.

"What do you mean?" I said.

"She just showed up in the dayroom and started talking. I don't know how I heard about it, but I went. Something different to do. You know, a change from the everyday ho-hum of that hellhole."

"Did she come very often?" I said.

"Only two or three times that I recall," Bert said. "But I'll never forget her birds and that skunk. You see, we never saw animals in the Gardens—no pets allowed." Bert stopped for a minute and pulled on his ear. "Except for Mrs. Lockhart and her songbird over on the C wing. Same kind of bird Grace had with her when she told her stories. Canary, I think. Yellow at least."

"What kind of stories?" I asked.

"Well, let me think," Bert said. "There was one about a baby in a hospital, and some girl who ran away from home. And then something about a man who spent his whole life running away from somebody in a black coat, or was it pigs? I don't remember for sure. But I'll never forget those dang birds and that skunk of hers. I hadn't seen animals for so long, I couldn't take my eyes off 'em."

I didn't finish hearing what Bert was saying about Grace's birds, because I saw something outside and went over to look out the window. There was Grace, out in the garden, barefoot, wearing a dark raincoat walking along with a stick poking holes in the ground, dropping yellow seeds into the holes. On the top of the stick, just above where she was holding it, was a silver pig—a goddamned pig the size of a rat. Then the whole stick turned silver and started flashing so bright in the sunlight as she moved I had to look away.

CLARA PAULSON

I SEE George getting out of his pickup truck, then reaching back in and taking out a cake box. A pale pink cake box with little round holes in it. Holes. I wonder whose birthday it is. What kind of cake he's got in the box. I like cherry chip, the way the little pieces of maraschino cherry kind of bleed pink into the fluffy white cake. George is holding that cake careful, closing the door of his pickup truck with his butt and coming this way, making sure not to tip the box and mess up the frosting.

When he comes through the door and goes past me sitting here, I hear singing coming from inside the box. Perhaps it is cherry chip, and the cherries themselves are singing. Or it's one of those singing cakes I've heard about, with batteries buried down inside. Or perhaps it's just my head, and it's nobody's birthday at all. No cake. Just an empty box with nothing in it but a bunch of holes, the wind whistling through those holes making my head think somebody's in there singing.

GEORGE CASTOR

ONE MORNING after Clara and the others had been living here for a while, Grace showed up in the kitchen where I was making coffee. Without so much as a good-morning-how'd-you-sleep, she started in talking to me.

"I've been thinking," Grace said. "We still have a lot of room in this palace of yours. Especially up in the attic. Those four empty rooms are just sitting up there going to waste. Seems to me the attic would be the perfect place for a sanctuary."

I'd learned to live with Grace's candles, but I was drawing the line at building altars in the attic. I took a deep breath getting ready to tell her no when she went on. "A bird sanctuary," she said. "An aviary! What do you say?"

I exhaled. "You must have had a bad dream," I said, and went back to my coffee.

"We could have a whole attic full of birds," Grace went on, spreading her arms over her head, her little hands floating back down to her sides. "Think about it. We could leave the windows open up there and the birds would fly in and out as they please. A third-floor bird sanctuary! That's just what this place needs."

I could see it now: all the floors and windowsills covered with bird shit and rotting eggs, pigeons roosting in the closets, barn swallows building mud nests in the corners, woodpeckers knocking holes in the plaster, the whole attic infested with mites and fleas.

"Sorry, Grace," I said. But Grace kept going.

"Maybe some pigeons would move in," she said. "And some scissor-tail swallows! Hummingbirds and bats, too. Bats are good. Maybe even a pair of owls! Barn owls. Wouldn't that be wonderful? Birds of prey gliding in and out up there."

"No owls," I said. "And bats aren't birds."

"Doves then," Grace said. "Imagine that. Hundreds of white doves flying out the open attic windows every morning!" Grace was almost coming up off the floor she was so excited about her aviary-in-the-attic idea.

"No birds," I said, firm. "Sorry, Grace."

She deflated so fast I could almost hear the air going out of her. So I said, "Let me think on it. Okay?" Then she was gone.

♉

The next day, I picked up a box of yellow chicks at Wilco Farmers and snuck them up to the attic. Then I found Grace and told her I had a surprise for her, but she'd have to climb all the way up into the attic to find out what it was.

"Here you go!" I said, handing her the box as she came to the top of the attic stairs. "A little something for your aviary." The chicks inside the box were making so much noise I could hardly hear myself talking. "Except they only get to stay up here in the attic for a week or so, until we get a coop built out back. And then their job is laying eggs. Everybody earns their keep."

Grace peeked inside the box, then looked at me, that grin of hers spreading fast across her face, all the excitement I'd watched drain out of her yesterday now flooding back in.

"A whole flock!" she said.

I shrugged. "A dozen was the best buy. Besides, I figure we might lose a couple before they start in laying."

Grace reached into the box and brought out a chirping yellow fluff. The chick poked its head out between Grace's thumb and forefinger, chirping so shrill and loud you'd have thought Grace was squeezing the poor thing half to death. But then Grace touched the chick's tiny head with her lips, and that chick went still. And right away all the other birds in the box stopped chirping, too. Not a sound in that attic. Just Grace staring at that little head poking out of her hand.

I saw how Grace must have looked as a little girl. Five or six years old. A girl getting a pet bird, or a pony, for her birthday, nothing else in the whole world mattering.

Then the light went strange and Grace looked up at me, quick—that little-girl look gone away.

"They're so young, George," Grace said. Her words and dark eyes pinned me. Held me and wouldn't let go. "A pig-colored box full of sunrise," she said. "A bunch of little souls just starting out. Tiny spirits singing to be alive again." And then all at once the chicks went crazy mad, filling the attic room with such a high-pitched screeching I thought for sure the windows were all going to blow. So I shut my eyes and covered my ears.

When I looked again, Grace and her box of sunshine chickens were gone, and I had the chills—my undershirt clammy and cold against my skin. And in my boxer shorts a wet spot I knew without looking was the color of rust.

CLARA PAULSON

I DON'T know what happened upstairs, but Grace came down a few minutes ago carrying that singing cake box, her face glowing the way it would if the box were a birthday cake covered with dozens of candles burning. Except there weren't any candles. Nobody's birthday. No cherry chip cake. Just a pink box full of holes and Grace's face aglow.

And now, here comes George down, but his face is anything but glowing—his face is drained the color of cold cream and looking scared to death. I wave at George, but he doesn't even look my way, just keeps going, right out the front door and down the steps.

George's face stayed washed out for a day or two. I thought he was getting sick. But he seems better now. He and Bert and Fred are outside banging and sawing—building a chicken coop. A chicken coop for what I thought was a store-bought cake. Silly me. Baby chickens instead of birthday candles. Life is strange and wonderful at times.

The toilet flushes and Emma comes up the hall, headed

back into her room to watch more television. I wave her over to where I'm sitting on the flagstones in the entryway. She comes. I scribble a quick question on my pad. Hold the letters up. PLAY ME SOMETHING? I point to her piano, the baby grand over in the living room.

Emma rolls her eyes. "Good Lord no! I haven't played in years and years," she says. "I had a few lessons as a girl. But then my mother took a liking to the local minister and we moved away—without our piano or my father." I look up at Emma looking into the living room at the Steinway. Her hand's hanging at her side a foot or so away from my face. Her nails are chewed down, dimples where the knuckles should be, a diamond wedding ring biting so deep into the skin it looks painful. "When I finally saw my father again years later, he was on his deathbed," Emma goes on. "He asked me why I'd never answered any of the letters he'd sent. I told him Mother had never showed me any letters from him. He said he'd sent one a week, always asking if we had room for the piano yet. A week or so after he died, that piano showed up at my house in a huge wooden crate." Emma stops and takes a deep breath. "When Mother died, I got all the letters. Suppose I should get rid of the piano, like Fred's been after me to do for years. Lord knows I'll never play it. And nobody here plays. Just something else to dust."

Emma shrugs and walks back down the hall to her room. The television gets louder when she opens the door. Then quieter again. The bed squeaks. I take my glasses off, use the hem of my nightgown to wipe my eyes.

GEORGE CASTOR

I TALKED Fred and Bert into helping me build the coop for Grace's chickens out in the far corner of the backyard. We used scrap lumber and old pieces of corrugated tin roofing I'd brought down from the farm months ago. I knew it didn't take much to keep chickens in, chickens being dumber than hammers. And living here in the middle of town, I was sure we didn't have to worry too much about weasels or other animals getting into the coop at night and killing the chickens. During the day, we could turn the birds out so they could scratch and peck in the yard.

I used a couple of tree branches for roosts, and bolted an old toilet to the middle of the floor for a feeder. Grace said the toilet seemed to fit, since the coop looked more like a privy than a home for her "baby girls." But you don't need anything fancy for chickens.

When we were done, I strung an extension cord out to the coop and hung a lightbulb down low to keep the chicks warm. Grace got up so often during the night the first few weeks to go out and check on her new girls you would have thought she'd given birth to the damned things herself. But at least we didn't have an attic full of bats and barn swallows.

185

All was well, until nine of the dozen started looking a lot more like roosters than pullets. Three hens would keep us in more than enough fresh eggs, and Grace didn't seem to mind that her "girls" were three-fourths boys.

But then the nine boys became men, figured out how to strut their stuff and crow, and a cop showed up at our front door. The cop said some of the neighbors were complaining about the early-morning noise coming from the shack in our backyard, and that there was a city ordinance against keeping farm animals inside the city limits. I told the cop our chickens were pets as opposed to farm animals, but the cop didn't buy it.

So the next morning at breakfast, I told everybody it was probably a good time to turn the crowing into frying. Grace stood up and gave me one of her looks that seemed to bore all the way through.

"The hens will lay better if we get rid of the roosters," I told her. "And hens don't crow, so the neighbors won't bitch."

"Then let's take the roosters out of town and turn them loose in the wild," Grace said.

"That won't work," I said. "Chickens have been bred so helpless over the years they'd never survive in the wild. I'm afraid our only choice is a plucking party, first thing this morning."

Grace stared at me a little longer, then dropped her napkin on her plate and left the room without saying another word. A few minutes later the chickens started making a racket out in the coop. I thought for sure Grace was letting the chickens out so we'd never catch them. But when I hurried out to the coop, Grace was nowhere around. All twelve chickens were there, and burning around the rim of that toilet were nine votive candles in clear glass holders. For a second I was a kid again, kneeling at Mass in that windy shack of a church in Ceresco, Nebraska, wondering who'd lit all the candles for all the souls. Then I was just standing in the doorway of a chicken coop I'd built for a woman who seemed to be getting stranger by the day. Just those nine candles burning around the toilet, and when I leaned closer, what looked to be a little pile of cornmeal sprinkled on the rim next to each candle.

⟲

I was the only one with any experience killing chickens, so I supervised the plucking party. Emma was so repulsed by the whole idea I had to twist her arm hard just to get her to stay in the kitchen and boil up the water for us. Clara didn't seem to mind, so I nominated her master plucker and outfitted her and her wheelchair with a blue tarp that covered everything except her one arm and her head. Fred said he'd never killed anything bigger than a housefly in his life and therefore didn't think he could bring himself to do it now. Bert claimed that all the animals he'd ever worked with were already dead when they got to him. Grace was nowhere to be found. So that left me on the end of the axe. I did talk Fred and Bert into taking turns holding the chickens down on the block for me, reassuring them that a lifetime of chopping firewood had honed my axe aim pretty close to bull's-eye on. If they didn't want to watch the axe fall, I said, they could just close their eyes.

The problem was, that's exactly what Fred did on the very first rooster. Shut his eyes and tensed up so bad, he pulled the bird back a little between the two bent nails I'd driven into the chopping block. That made my hit an inch or so high, which left the voice box in the headless neck of the poor creature. And when Fred heard the gurgled crowing coming from the bloody neck stub, he dropped the rooster, and turned away, covering his face with his blood-splattered hands. The headless rooster flapped to the ground, flopping and crowing in a blur of white feathers and spurting blood, then took off half running, half rolling down the driveway to where it collided broadside with Mr. Blankenship's white golf cart going by on the sidewalk, leaving a huge red starburst shining on the fiberglass fender. Mr. Blankenship slammed his golf cart to a stop, jumped out, and started inspecting the cart for damage. Of course, that's when the heap of feathers near his feet burst into a final, crowing seizure that sprayed his white double-knit pants and funny looking shoes and more of his golf cart the same color as the starburst on the fender. Then Mr. Blankenship saw all of us standing in the driveway staring at him.

"Castor!" Mr. Blankenship yelled, pointing a finger arrow-straight up the driveway at me. "I'll have your hide!" And in the silence that followed his words, the sunlight caught what must have been a diamond ring on his little finger, and the ring flashed.

I don't know if it was the flash of his own ring, the four of us standing there with our mouths hanging open, or the dead chicken lying at his feet, but something made that big man squeeze back into his tiny golf cart without another word, pull a U-turn, and head back down the sidewalk to his house—most likely to change his white pants, wash the blood off his cart, and come up with an alternate route to the golf course where he went every Sunday.

"That wasn't the best of timing," I said. "Fred, you have to hang on tight till it quits moving. Takes a while for the muscles to stop twitching. And normally there's no noise."

Fred blushed.

"Ah, a little blood never hurt anybody," Bert said, walking out to get the dead chicken. "Cold water will take it right out, slick as a whistle."

"It's your turn to hold," I told Bert. "Fred, check to see if Emma's got the water ready yet."

We killed the remaining roosters, helped Clara pluck, and singed the birds over a portable gas stove I had set up outside. When Emma came to the door and started whining about the foul odor that was coming into the house and making her nauseous, I was tempted to say something about her perfume blowing back in her face, but instead I just held up a naked chicken by its feet and shook it at her. Emma slammed the back door so hard one of the panes cracked and fell out on the porch.

When we were done, the four of us were quite the sight, dried blood and feathers sticking to our clothes and boots and Clara's blue tarp. The driveway was a sea of white feathers blowing out into the street and piling up along the gutters, mixing with the fluff off the cottonwood trees along the river that was coming down thick that spring.

CLARA PAULSON

IT'S A big change here from living at the Gardens. Sometimes I forget how big. In my head, too, things are different. Some of the fog has cleared up, the loose wires seem a little tighter. Time's passed. Time. Faster here than in the Gardens. Lots faster. Probably because there's always something going on. George getting nuttier all the time. But living with George beats the heck out of living with the Rhino.

Funny how time can go so slow for so many years, and then so fast. Like good music, I guess. Largo and then Allegro. Sometimes Passionato! I'm glad distances don't get longer and shorter, like time. A good mile or so separates me, here, from the Gardens up the creek. I'd hate to look out the window one day and see the Gardens standing right next door to this house, fence, floodlights, and the smell of fish sticks. That would be awful. But the Gardens won't move. And neither will I.

It's a strange lineup here, though. We don't have much in common. Nothing, really. Except our age. It's as if somebody grabbed a handful of old poker chips off a blackjack table in some casino, threw the chips in a red shoe box, and put the lid on. Of course, this is no shoe box. Grace calls it a palace.

I suppose this is as close as I'll ever get to being a princess. George is the king. Nutty king.

We all pitch in with the housework and cooking and cleaning here at the shoe box palace. I help where I can, which isn't much. Grace doesn't seem to mind helping me get along. Bert and George and Fred have all said to let them know if they can do anything for me. I don't think Emma knows quite what to do with me.

I never thought I'd be into the communal living thing, especially at my age—it reminds me of hippies or something, none of us married, except Fred and Emma, but all of us living together, sharing food, sharing toilets. That's basically what this is, I guess, communal living, gray-haired hippies. All of us under one roof, together. Poker chips in a big red house. I'm even figuring out how to put up with Emma's constant complaints about living in general.

Emma's the only one I haven't noticed much change in since we all moved in here. When Emma starts bitching, I flip though my pad to a page I keep handy just for her and hold it up: "RATHER B N THE GARDENS? THE RHINO AWAITS U!" That usually shuts Emma up quick, and she waddles off to watch more television. That woman sure watches a lot of it. Television. I for one am glad the television set's in her and Fred's bedroom. Emma likes the sound so blasted loud you can hear it from all the way out at the chicken privy, as Grace calls it. Only three chickens now. Three girls. Three eggs a day. George claims television's poison, and we'd all be better off had it never been invented. I agree. I agree with George on quite a few things, considering we're totally different and he's nuts. George put a little dot of black paint on the screen of Emma's television set where the green bar shows up when she presses the volume button on her remote control. George told Emma she couldn't turn the sound up past that black mark. That was a good move by George. He's no dummy. Guess that's why he's king of this palace. King of the red shoe box.

A few days ago, some friends of Fred and Emma's showed

up in their mobile home on their way up to Canada. I had never thought about Fred and Emma having any friends. George connected the mobile home to the house with what he called life support lines, an orange extension cord and a bright green hose. "Might as well put wheels under a god-damned house and drive it around," George grumbled. The mobile home is almost as big as this house. Except Fred and Emma's friends don't call it a mobile home. They call it a coach. George calls it an RV. I'd call it a bus. Converted Greyhound. The coach takes up half the block, makes the Cadillac they have hitched behind it look like a toy car. George had to bring the tractor around and move a trailer full of irrigation pipe and a couple pieces of farm machinery he had parked in the street to make room for the mobile home, for the coach. Legs came down out of nowhere near the wheels, went up and down automatically to level the coach. Now the coach is sitting out there with two wheels off the ground, making the bed inside nice and level, I guess. They raised a remote control satellite dish from the roof and covered the tires with funny vinyl skirts. I saw it all because I've been watching from right here in the living room.

Emma saw that satellite dish come up and I knew what Emma was thinking: hundreds of channels! I hoped maybe Emma'd watch television out there in the coach and give the set in her and Fred's room—and all of us living with her—a breather. But she hasn't yet. And their friends are leaving tomorrow, taking the coach and the satellite dish and the toy Cadillac with them.

A letter came the other day from the city that said any vehicle parked in the street has to be moved every three days. I don't understand that rule. Why would anyone want you to drive every couple of days if you didn't have to? We live so close to town you don't need to drive, you can walk most anywhere. It's probably so the street sweeper doesn't miss a spot. This is a pretty tidy neighborhood. But the letter wasn't referring to the coach. The letter had the words "including farm implements" in parentheses next to the word vehicle.

George has quite a few farm implements parked along the curb out in the street. Some neighbor probably called in. Mrs. Beasley, perhaps. Or that guy with his golf cart and white pants. Chicken man, I call him.

George says he's not moving his farm implements out of the street, though, because he pays taxes for the streets. So he has every right to use the street. "I'm growing a garden, goddamnit," George boomed as he read the letter. "So I need my machinery. Next spring I'll let the side lawn grow up and bale it for hay, prove to God and the city both why I need it close by."

Oh, there goes Mrs. Beasley walking by with that huge dog of hers, acting like she's not looking. But she is. Mrs. Beasley's got eyes in the side of her head, the old flounder. So she won't miss anything. One day last week I noticed her standing in her yard down the street looking our way through a pair of binoculars. I played it cool. Real cool. I wheeled myself out so she had me in full view. I acted like I was looking up at the trees. Then I turned and made one of those faces kids make, my good thumb poked in my ear, my fingers wiggling alongside my head, my half-dead tongue pushed as far out as I could get it. I know Mrs. Beasley got a close-up shot of me making that kid face, because she lowered those binoculars quick and hurried back into her pale yellow house. I haven't seen Mrs. Beasley spying on us since then. But I know she keeps tabs on this place, just like she's doing right now, going by with her dog acting as if she's not looking. Mrs. Beasley makes sure the gossip goes around the neighborhood, a spoonful of lard on a hot skillet.

GEORGE CASTOR

IT HAPPENED in threes, the way I'd come to learn bad things tended to sometimes do. All three things took place on the same day, about six or seven months after Clara and the others had moved in. Taken each by itself, none of the three were a big deal. But together, one behind the other packed in tight, they added up, bugged me, made me wonder that maybe the way things were going was almost too good to be true—that the bubble might pop and I'd be blown all the way back to square one: the hayfield and peeling paint, an empty house and an empty promise.

First was *another* damned letter from City Hall, stating that I was now in "extended violation" of their ordinance about on-street parking. But I wasn't going to go out and hitch and unhitch and move things around every few days just for the hell of it. I threw that City Hall letter in the fireplace the same way I'd done with the other City Hall letters I'd been getting.

It couldn't have been more than an hour later when Will Richards the realtor showed up. That's when I sensed something starting to shift, the way you feel the first hint of fall in the late-summer air, notice the lower angle of the sun.

"How's this place working out for you, George?" Will Richards hollered, hurrying up the front walk trying to catch up to me going up my red front porch steps.

"Couldn't be better," I said over my shoulder without slowing down. Ever since I'd bought the Hogan House, Richards had come around now and then to see if I was ready to list the farm. Now here he was again, his nice shoes crunching on my brick walk behind me. At the top of the steps I stopped and turned around.

"Glad to hear that, George. That's great, just great," Richards said, pulling up short at the bottom of the steps, his belly moving in and out between the edges of his sport coat. A square black pin with a gold R was cocked crooked on his lapel. "I've got a quick question for you, George, if you've got a minute."

I didn't say anything. Richards took a long drag from his cigarette and spoke, blowing out smoke and words at the same time, a little smoke coming out through his nostrils, too.

"You know, you've made some nice changes around this place," Richards said. "The paint job really transformed the old girl, didn't it? Yessiree."

"Brightened things up a bit," I said.

"I'll say." Richards cleared his throat and dropped the half-smoked cigarette to the walk, then stepped on the cigarette with a shiny black wing-tip and put his hands in his pockets. "You know, George, I got wind of something about you turning this place into some sort of retirement home. Is that right?"

"Haven't heard that one yet," I said.

"They say you've got a few more people living here with you," Richards said. "You know, older folks."

"It's a big house," I said.

"Well, the zoning here wouldn't allow for that anyway, you know. It would have to be high-density residential. Which, of course, this isn't."

I didn't say anything. Richards cleared his throat and went on.

"But I got to thinking you might be interested in an apartment complex that just went on the market across town. Sixteen units under one roof, if you can believe that. And of course, it's zoned high-density. I thought it might be a perfect fit for you. That is, if you're looking to start some sort of nursing home, of course."

"That sounds real good," I said. "Only problem is, I hate nursing homes more than most cats hate ear mites. So I'd have to be loony to be wanting to start one up, now wouldn't I?"

"Well, good," Richards said. "I just wanted to check in. You know, thought if I could get you a jump on a good deal. I wouldn't want you going to lots of extra work here for nothing." Richards dug at change in his pockets.

"Oh, extra work's never for nothing," I said. "But I appreciate your interest. It's nice to know people are watching out for me. Makes me proud to live in a town like this." I pulled out a yellow handkerchief and blew my nose. "Say, where'd you hear that rumor, anyway?" I asked.

"Oh, I'm not sure," Richards said, smoothing his hand back over his hair. "In my line of work, I see so many people, you know. It's hard to say."

"Guess it wouldn't be a small town without rumors, would it?" I said. "But you know something? I've learned over the years that if you pay much attention to rumors, they can pretty well wreck a decent day. I wouldn't pay this one any mind if I were you." I turned and went inside, leaving Richards playing with the pin on his lapel.

Minutes later, I heard a knock at the door and thought it was Will Richards being pushy. But when I opened the door, I found another man standing on the other side of the screen, a man much younger than Will Richards and wearing a dark suit and tie, shirt pressed stiff and white just the way Jason used to wear his shirts.

"Hi there," the young man said. I could tell by those two words alone he was selling something. "You must be Mr. Castor," the man said. "I'm David Jack, with Mutual of Idaho Commercial Division out of Salem. I just wondered if you had a little time this afternoon."

"I've got plenty of time," I said, looking at the man through the screen. "How much of it you get depends on what you're selling."

"Well, Mr. Castor, I was just wondering if I could talk to you very briefly about our commercial real estate protection package, which is especially designed for a business like yours—you know, one that has the potential for lots of liability claims and lawsuits and that sort of thing."

"You must have the wrong place," I said. "This isn't a business. And I'm not expecting any lawsuits."

"Well, most people aren't, sir. And that's just the point. Of course, I realize you have our basic homeowner's coverage already, but when you enter into a living situation like this one that involves rent and meals and accessibility and those sorts of issues, then the homeowner's coverage simply isn't enough to protect your assets. Now, we developed the plan I'm referring to especially with nursing homes in mind, which allows you as the owner—"

"This is no goddamned nursing home!" I yelled. But the young man didn't even blink. He just kept going.

"I'm sorry, sir, perhaps retirement residence would be a more appropriate term. But anyway, if I could come in for just a minute, I can show you the details of our plan, which I'm sure you'll find not only cost-effective, but also very—"

I threw the screen door open and stepped out. The man and his suit took a couple of steps back.

"I don't think you understood me," I said. "This is not a nursing home! And it's sure as hell not a business! So we don't need your fancy insurance plan. Is that clear?" The man stood there blinking at me, but I could tell he was getting ready to launch into another pitch. "Now get the hell off my property!" I said before he had a chance to get another string of words out. The young man cleared his throat, swallowed, and then without another word, picked up his briefcase and went down the steps. But halfway down the walk, he stopped and hurried back toward the porch, groping for something in the breast pocket of that white shirt.

"Oh, here," he said. "Let me give you my card. Just in case you do happen to change your mind. If I'm not in the office, they can page me and I'll return your call as soon—"

"All the way off!" I yelled, pointing at the street.

The man dropped the card, turned, and ran to his car. I stood on the porch for a long time after he'd driven away, the blood slowly working its way back down out of my face. The white rectangle of business card was lying facedown in the middle of the brick walk. A few feet away was Will Richards's cigarette butt, smashed but still smouldering, the thin gold band just below the filter shining in the heat bearing down hard.

It had taken a year and a half to get here. But here I was. Everything going along pretty well. Five people living in my big red house with me and Shag William. But in the space of a few hours, the whole thing seemed a little shaky. Realtors and insurance salesmen telling me I was running a nursing home. The city on my ass about parking rights in the street my money helped pave. The neighbors still as standoffish as the day I moved in. And the summer heat that year hotter than hell, hotter than any summer I could remember living up in the hills with the blackberries. I wished it would cloud up and pour.

Then I was driving home that night in the pouring rain. I saw that moth struggling on the black water. Stars and pond water all around. And then, for the first time in months, I saw Ralph: clear and bright as a photograph. But Ralph wasn't in his bed at the Gardens, his huge feet under the bedspread, his face gone all to skull. Ralph was standing in our boat working a fly rod back and forth overhead, the yellow-orange filament floating in the air above the green water. Ralph's blank stare was gone, too, his eyes alive—alive the way ripples of sunlight were flashing like lures on the water. Doug fir growing up all around the shore. Everything green and bright and warm. And there he stood, the old Ralph. Grinning that grin. Working his rod in silence. Little circles making their way out from the boat, those circles catching the sun, and turning gold, and getting wider and wider, moving out away from the two of us rocking there at the center.

Then I remembered the circle Grace had talked about, how everything was headed back around, headed back to the soil, no matter what we tried to do. And all of a sudden the golden circles going out from the boat were gone. Ralph was gone. No fish rising. No sun. The water around the boat was choked with drowned pigs bloated up and votive candles bobbing in the current. I was sitting in that boat all alone, rain coming down hard, the current getting stronger, pulling me faster and faster across the shimmering silver surface of a lake gone to river.

CLARA PAULSON

I CAN see it building up. Coming this way. I've been watching. Way off on the horizon, a great big upside-down oboe spinning so fast you can't see the silver keys. But it's still all sunny around here, and not even any wind yet. Yet. If you don't look way off, you'd never see it in the air. But I see it. Because I've been watching. In George's face, mostly. Eating at him. And this blister-hot heat not letting up doesn't help. It's even hotter than it was in Nevada. So hot you can't sleep nights. But it's not just the heat. It's that look in George's face.

I first saw the look when he came down out of the attic the day he gave Grace the chickens in the cherry chip cake box. And then I saw it again, but different, when he was reading another letter from the city. I heard him blast that insurance salesman off the front porch, and when he came in after that, I saw it again. I'm not sure what it is yet. But I see the oboe. Way off on the horizon, spinning fast. Reed down, almost touching. Coming this way.

Perhaps it's Emma. I think Emma thought this place would be posh, that she'd be taken care of, served supper right at six, fresh linens on her bed every Sunday night, fresh flowers on the nightstand, bathrooms scrubbed down twice a week.

But not here. Not in George's Big Red House. The only people who will take care of us here are us, George says. And George believes that, deep. I can tell. Deep. George doesn't want help from anybody. He expects all of us to pull our share, earn our keep. So it bugs him that Emma bitches all the time, wants to get a maid or a cook. But I don't think it's just Emma's bitching. There's something else pulling the oboe this way, something else putting that look on George's face.

GEORGE CASTOR

THE HEAT'S what did it. Heat that hunkered down and latched on and wouldn't let go. A hundred degrees in the shade for the better part of two solid weeks. So hot at night you stuck to the sheets and sweated like a sow. Too hot to eat. We hardly ever got days that hot in Oregon, and when we did, it was usually only two or three days in a row. Not twelve or thirteen days piled up one right behind the other, hot day and night, dawn and dusk. The heat sapped and drained, took a toll on everybody's spirits in the house. The stranglehold heat got to me, too, because once I got that waterfall inside my head, I couldn't get it out. I knew right then we had to go. All of us together, going to find water. Getting the hell away from all that heat sucking the moisture out of everything.

The heat was so bad the Forest Service shut down the woods on account of fire danger. So the log trucks that normally rumbled through town coated with dust stopped coming through, which made everything quieter, and hotter still. The heat bore down so hard everything went sluggish, got muffled—the way things get quiet when it snows. Except I would have traded for snow any day. It got so hot Grace's tall candles on the kitchen table went soft and drooped over. The garden, watered at night, was wilted by three in the afternoon. Except Grace's corn patch. Her corn seemed to love the heat. It was so hot even the cicadas shut up.

I could feel the mossy stones under my bare feet, the mist against my face. I could see the ferns moving in the breeze, everything dripping and wet. We had to go. We had to get away from our own morale that was sagging bad. A trip up to the headwaters of the Abiqua would be the perfect antidote for everybody's wilted spirits. Although I hadn't been up the creek in years, I could see the water: shallow pools shaded green and dark by overhanging arms of alder and maple. Cool water flowing, whispering, calling to me.

After hitching up Clara's chariot—an old single-horse trailer I'd converted so it was easy to pull Clara and her wheelchair around behind Max—I rummaged around in the hot garage and came up with four or five camp stools, a couple of old fishing rods, some blankets, a mask and snorkel, and a metal ice chest full of old tennis balls. The ice chest is what made me think to pack a picnic lunch. Wouldn't be an outing without a picnic. So I dumped the tennis balls out in the driveway, put the camp stools and fishing gear and blankets in the truck bed, and hurried into the kitchen with the ice chest. I pulled anything that looked like it might make good picnic fixings out of the refrigerator and dropped it into the open ice chest. Sliced turkey, cheese, a head of lettuce, a jar of pickles, a jar of stuffed green olives, mayonnaise, mustard, horseradish, half a watermelon, half a Walla Walla onion, some cold quiche, a bag of apples, a box of plums, a glass bowl of green Jell-O and marshmallows, a leftover cherry pie, a carton of whipping cream, and the glass gallon jar full of sloshing amber sun tea that Grace always kept on hand.

The cool air flowed out of the refrigerator and into the ice chest, filled up the ice chest and then overflowed out down onto the floor where the cold pooled on the linoleum around my ankles and rose slow up inside my pant legs. The cool air on my calves felt so good I didn't want to close the refrigerator door. I wanted to climb into the refrigerator and shut the door, sit inside until I was cool all the way through. But the waterfall was calling. I carried the ice chest out and put it in the truck bed with the rest of the stuff, then slid in behind the hot steering wheel, fired the engine, and started honking the horn.

"Road trip!" I yelled out the window between honks. "Let's go, everybody! Bring your swim trunks!"

When nobody showed up, I shut off Max and got out. Silence. Just the hush of the heat. Where were they? I climbed into the truck bed and yelled again, cupping my hands around my mouth. "Let's go, everybody! Time to cool off." Still nothing but the sun bearing down and the shimmer of heat waves rising off the concrete all around. No sounds of anybody moving inside the house, coming to the back door. I pounded on the hot metal of the cab with my open hands. "Let's go, people! Road trip! Hup-hup. Come on. Day's a-wasting."

I kept pounding on the roof of Max. The thunking sound my palms made hitting the metal was kind of nice, floating out into the heat waves. I stopped yelling for the others, but kept banging the cab with my open hands. The rhythm pulled me in. Time blurred and the sun burned. I just kept pounding, picking up the pace a little, letting my eyes close. After a while, I was floating to the beat in the bed of the truck, sweat running off my face, my hands splashing sweaty palm prints on the hot metal. I smelled woodsmoke and juniper in the air. All around me, out in every direction, a flat desert stretched empty and dry in the light that had faded suddenly to evening. I looked for the wolf in Ralph's eyes, but couldn't see the wolf. A breeze came up, cooled my skin, blew through my hair. The sun was melting orange below the rocky horizon to the west. A Coopers hawk with a kangaroo rat limp in its talons flew overhead, the rat's long tail moving in the air, a string waving good-bye. I watched the hawk shrink to a dot and disappear into the sun going down.

But I didn't stop pounding. If anything, I pounded harder,

the sound swallowing me now, turning my arms to liquid, my arms and hands gone numb, beating on a drum out in front of me. The drum was an old cedar cattle tank from up at the farm, a hide stretched across the top of the tank. But I wasn't up at the farm, or in town at the Hogan House. I was out in a desert somewhere, but up high, looking down, and all across the plain, campfires burned orange, pairs of sandals in the sand near the fires. I heard cries in the distance. The cries made me pound harder still as night swept in and smeared the horizon dark, brought the stars out above—millions of pinholes. The fires burned brighter. I arched my back, no pain at all. No pain in my knees either. I slammed my hands down harder and faster. The cries rose, carrying me up into the cool night air, me going after the Cooper's hawk, going toward the sun gone down, headed for the pale spot on the horizon beyond the hills.

Then silence and heat rushed in, wrapped me. The pounding stopped. Drum gone. I heard my own breathing, smelled sweat and hot metal. Metal burned against my cheek and ear. Coals burned deep inside my shoulders.

"Good Lord, George. Who do you think you are? Tarzan?" Emma's words brought my head up off the cab roof. The daylight was blinding, the heat dense and choking. Emma, Fred, Clara, and Bert were all standing on the concrete in front of the truck, staring up at me.

I couldn't talk for a minute. My tongue coated with dust. I looked around, squinting into sunlight. My head swirled. Nobody said anything. The metal pounding rang in my ears. My fingers throbbed. Everything shimmered. Dozens of greenish-yellow dots pulsed all over the ground.

"You were on your way to plumb crazy," Bert said. "You didn't even hear us yelling at you."

"Crazy's right," Emma said. "I was sound asleep, trying to survive this heat wave. Your racket woke me up. You out here beating the dickens out of your truck like a man possessed."

"Yeah, George, what's wrong?" Fred's voice was a high

squeaking. All these words coming at me from faces through the heat. I still couldn't say anything.

Clara stared, working her mouth as if she wanted to add something about me being loony, too. Her eyes were spooked again, the same look her eyes had that first night glaring at me over the teacup. Then Clara held up her notepad with the word "GO!" written on it twice in big black letters. She shook her pad at me through the air. I wasn't sure if Clara wanted to get going, or wanted me to get the hell out of her sight, out of the house and out of her life. Just the same word twice. GO! GO!

But right then, everything came together again, and words filled my mouth. "Clara's right," I said. "Let's go! Time's a-wasting."

"Where on earth are we going?" Emma asked, her hands on her hips, just daring me to make her go anyplace she didn't want to go. "I can't take this heat," she said.

"Get in, then," I said. "Because we're going away from the heat. We're going swimming. Go get your trunks and let's get the hell out of here."

"Hey, where's Grace?" Fred asked. Everybody looked at each other, looked around.

Then Clara started slapping her pad on her leg, pointing at the windshield with her pad and those two little words, stomping her one foot on her footrest so hard the bell on her wheelchair jingled. I leaned over the cab and looked in through the driver's side window to see what the hell Clara was getting so worked up about. There was Grace, a shadow sitting back against the seat where Dora'd always sat, staring straight ahead, that skunk a black and white ball on her lap.

I hung there letting the blood pulse against the backs of my eyes, watching Grace staring straight out through the dusty windshield, past the dried bugs and bird shit to where the others were standing, Clara's mouth still going open and shut, but no words coming out.

Then Grace pushed open the passenger door with a squeak and got out. She walked up to the front of the truck where the others were standing. "You heard the man," Grace said. "Get your suits!" She pulled her blouse partway off one shoulder and there in all that sun and heat burning was the bright purple shimmer of a swimsuit strap.

CLARA PAULSON

THE COMMOTION in the driveway's what made the only words I have tangle and knot and seize up inside the finger bones and knuckles of my good hand. So when I noticed Grace sitting in the cab, all I could scratch down were two letters that didn't mean anything and slap the letters against my leg, my mouth moving but nothing coming out. Out. I couldn't get ahold of my crystal knob to get away, either. Away from Grace's face behind that filthy windshield, staring straight at me, tennis balls lying all over the cement. I'm not sure, but I think Grace was sitting in the pickup truck the whole time George was beating on it like a fool. If so, that's too strange, too odd.

But that's over, and right now they're all up ahead in the pickup truck and I'm back here in my chariot that George built out of an old horse trailer especially for me and my chair. George calls it my chariot. The little window in front is the size of a television screen, so when I ride in here, I'm watching a television program up ahead. On my television right now, Bert and Fred are sitting on lawn chairs in the bed of the pickup truck. The wind's blowing their hair every-where. Everywhere. George's big forearm is out the driver's

side window, and Grace, she's squeezed in the middle between George and big Emma. Every now and then Emma lets
a saltwater toffee wrapper go out the window. The wrapper
flies around behind the cab where Bert and Fred are sitting
before the wind catches the wrapper and whips it away. Shag
William and that skunk are up there in the cab, too. We're
kind of a little family. Going on a field trip. George is the
father, I guess. I'm not sure who the mother is. Emma'd like
to be, but nobody'd stand for that. Emma's too bossy. And
Grace too odd. Which leaves me. But I'll never be a mother
again. I already had my chance at that. I'm the worst mother
in the world.

It feels good to be on the road. Downtown's deserted. We
turn north on Water Street and I realize we're going to pass
right by the Gardens on the way to this swimming hole of
George's. On the way to find water, as George says. I turn a
little to be sure I get a good view out my side window when
we go past. But George slows down as we get close, and at
first I think he is going to turn in, the fool-idiot. Bert and
Fred are slouching down in their lawn chairs, probably afraid
they'll be spotted by the Rhino and forced to go back to the
Gardens.

I get ready to watch the Gardens go by. George slows down
even more and I feel myself slide a little lower in my chair.
But I notice they're building a whole new wing onto the Gardens, so I sit back up to see better. The new wing pushes out
into the parking lot, a skeleton of new boards with holes for
windows spaced along the side. It looks like there's going to
be dozens of new rooms. Dozens of too high windows.

I imagine all the people who will pretty soon be living in
those new rooms. And all of us here with nutty George, piled
into his pickup truck on our way up into the hills to find
water. It doesn't seem fair. Fair. But life isn't fair.

As I'm thinking about windows and water and life not
being fair, George brakes hard and turns in to the parking
lot. Just like I was afraid of. George *is* a fool-idiot. Fred and
Bert slide down off their lawn chairs and disappear low in

the bed of the pickup truck. Now George starts honking that blasted horn. Bert's trying to cover himself with an old blanket. I can't believe George is doing this. He cuts through the gravel parking lot, getting so close to the new wing that I could reach out and touch the brand-new boards, all those little ribs going by. But I don't. Because I see an ambulance backed up to the front doors. The Rhino's there, and a couple of aides, watching somebody being loaded out. Not disappeared. When you die, they don't use the front doors in broad daylight. So whoever it is must still be alive. I can't tell who because hoses and straps are running all over where the face should be. Several people who look familiar are standing around in their robes with nothing better to do than gawk.

I look up at my television set and can't believe what I see. Now I know George is nuts, just what Bert said back in the driveway—plumb crazy. George is holding a pistol out the window! Pointing the pistol straight up into the sky that's smoky from all this heat. The sun catches the barrel and lets off a glint, a little blue butterfly. At first I think George is going to shoot the Rhino, take the Rhino out once and for all, but George just holds the pistol straight up, and as we go on by, he fires off three or four shots in a row. I smell burnt hair on the wind coming in hot through my television and want to be unhitched. This is going too far. I'm scared bad. Everybody by the front doors falls to the ground and holds their heads under their hands. Even the ambulance drivers in their white shirts and patches on their shoulders are lying flat, flinching, not wanting to die. Everybody except the Rhino, that is. The Rhino stands there, made of concrete, just staring at us as we drive on by.

All of a sudden, George stops honking the horn. I look at my television and see why. Piles of boards, a plastic outhouse, a forklift, orange traffic cones everywhere. The other entrance out of the parking lot has disappeared, blocked off by construction stuff. George brakes hard and tries to turn sharp, but the new wing's in the way, making the parking lot smaller, and several cars are parked here and there, so George can't cut it sharp enough to make a big U and go back out the way we came in. We stop dead still, dust rising, no sound but the engine mumbling low. I twist around and look out the open back of my chariot. The Rhino's standing there smiling. *Smiling!* We just sit here in the heat, the mumbling. I wonder what George is doing up in the cab, but I don't look. I can't pull my eyes away from the Rhino watching us.

Then the gears grind loud and awful and George revs the engine a few times before we start moving. Back. We're backing up! I never could back a trailer, so I brace myself for the worst: my body and bent chair tangled in the middle of jackknifed chariot wreckage, waiting to be cut out by the paramedics on those television shows. The Jaws of Life. Life flights. But I forget George was a farmer. George backs me and my chariot and all of us around and between parked cars and piles of boards as easy as going forward. I can see the faces near the lobby getting bigger and bigger as we pick up speed backing their way. Everybody's on their feet now scrambling to get away from us, afraid we're coming right in through those big glass Star Trek doors. Everybody except the Rhino. The Rhino's still standing there with her hands on her hips, just challenging George to squish her flat as a prairie dog. Flat. All over those big burgundy welcome mats.

Then I realize George is going to do just that. George has gone berserk! We're all going to die! I see the Rhino's face, a balloon getting bigger and bigger as we race closer, going faster and faster, the engine whining loud now, my chariot bouncing over potholes so hard I'm coming up off the seat. Thank God George cinched my chair down with that contraption he calls a come-along before we left the house, but I don't think it'll do much good now.

I close my eyes and get ready to hear that awful sound, the dead thump against floorboards when you hit a cat and then the sick feeling that follows. But the sound never comes. The next thing I know, George slams on the brakes. I'm thrown against the back of my chair. Hard. Gravel hitting everywhere, up under the fenders of my chariot. And then nothing. We're stopped. I look around again. I'm inches from that face. For a split second, everything's completely still. Just the Rhino and I. Staring at each other. Staring. Neither of us breathing. The heat swirling in around us mixed with parking lot dust and the gritty taste of gravel on the good half of my tongue.

Then from out of that silent dust swirling I hear a bird singing, shrill and pretty as bone china. China! I remember all the birds I've known. The blackbirds in my treetops. Mrs. Lockhart's yellow songbird she kept in her room on the C wing in a wicker cage. The birds Grace brought in with her skunk when she was the skunk woman. The baby chickens in that cake box.

The dust clears, and I see a wicker birdcage tipped on its side next to the ambulance, a yellow bird fluttering inside. I know that cage, that bird, and now I know who's being loaded out, who's underneath all those hoses.

George grinds gears again, everything jerks, more gravel flying, and we're racing away from the glass doors and burgundy mats. The Rhino's face is shrinking back down, somebody letting the air out of the balloon.

Then I see something. A small darting. A streak of yellow against blue. Mrs. Lockhart's bird! Flying straight up out of the dust and heat, away from that wicker cage tipped over. Mrs. Lockhart's bird singing as it goes higher, a shooting star in broad daylight, a soul headed for heaven.

George fires off two more shots. The new wing blurs past and we're out on Water Street again, headed away at full speed. Fast. Too fast. Hot air's pouring in through my television set again. Bert and Fred are so low in the pickup truck bed I can't even see them. Perhaps Bert and Fred fell out and got run over. But I didn't feel any thumps. In the rear window of the cab, Emma's profile is black and angry, her mouth going open and closed, her thick finger stabbing at the air near George's face. I can't see Grace at all.

I imagine a row of cop cars gaining on us, their flashing lights wavy through the hot air, sirens getting louder and louder. Just like in the motion picture shows. But for some reason the cops don't show up. George takes back roads and turnoffs, and a half hour later we come to a squeaky stop in deep shade. Everything's suddenly quiet. The road we're on has petered out. On my television I can see a narrow path that disappears through trees and brush up beyond the front of the pickup truck. I think George must have made a wrong turn and now we're all lost. I don't hear anything for a long time and think perhaps this is just a dream, or one of my wires. But the air smells too good. Good. Green and lush and cool.

Then George's words come clattering through the silence and I know this is all real. "Last one wet washes dishes for a week!" George yells.

I hear bones and shoes clunking in the pickup truck bed. Fred and Bert coming up for air. One of the pickup truck doors squeaks open. But nobody's saying anything. They're probably all wondering the same thing I am—about George. But then George comes back, pulls down my ramp, unhooks my chair from his come-along, and stands there waiting for me. I roll out onto the ground, my bell jingling. The shade feels good. George is just George, no gun, no balloons, no birdcage spilled over. No shooting stars.

Minutes later we're going down the path single file, George pushing me along over the bumps and roots. Still nobody's said anything. Not a word. I don't know what's going on or where we're headed. I want to shout to find out. Emma's mad, hornet-mad, but she's waddling up the path, too, ahead of us, using a stick she found for a cane. Fred's in front of Emma, so it looks like Emma's driving Fred to market the way you'd drive a little pig. Grace is lagging behind us back at the end of the line. Every time the path makes a bend, I look to see what Grace is up to, but she's just walking along, a little sliver of smile riding just below those two back eyes. The only sound other than my bell is George whistling an off-key rendition of "When the Saints Go Marching In" just above my head. George whistling all of us over roots and moss and rocks trying to find water.

And sure enough, pretty soon we find water. A waterfall and a swimming hole. Lime-green ferns are growing out of rock walls. The ferns are feather boas moving on the breeze and mist billowing up from the waterfall. The rock walls are wet and black and shiny. The water in the pool's pretty and clear, smooth as a piano, flowing off downstream in a little creek. The waterfall at the far end of the pool is a white veil. I look at George and he reads me.

"Pretty nice, huh?" George's voice is quieter than I've ever heard it.

I nod and see that the others are all spellbound, too. The mist is cool and moist, soft kisses against my face and neck. The mist is magic, floating around us, holding us all right here in this moment, everything unreal and fogged at the edges. After the heat and dust and shooting, this place has to be heaven.

We all just stand here staring out at the pool as if we've never seen such a beautiful place before. I know I haven't. I want to say that this is as close to heaven as I'll ever get. And the next thing I think I hear *is* my own voice saying close—close—but I know the word's only in my head, and will never squeeze out around my half-dead tongue no matter how hard I try.

But perhaps Grace heard me, because she wheels me through the deep gravel to the edge of the water and stops. I now have a front-row seat, and sit here letting this whole scene come in through my eyes and skin, never ever wanting it to fade. Never. It's as if the little side trip through the parking lot back at the Gardens never happened and we all took a shortcut straight up to the pearly gates.

Then my chair moves forward some more. Grace is pushing me out farther! Deeper. The water flows cool around my ankles, my calves. I can't move. Grace pushes me farther out into the current until the water is flowing across my lap, blue sky and green trees floating on the water. My gown fills with creek water and floats up, the pink flowers on the cotton blooming through blue sky and branches, blooming on the shiny smooth surface of the piano.

I kick my good foot straight out through the water. I want to lunge out and swim through the piano toward that waterfall. But just my slipper bobs to the surface and floats away downstream, a little pink boat.

Then George comes splashing past me and dives into the water, setting all the flowers on my lap dancing. All I see is George's bare heinie diving through blue sky and flowers.

I turn around to see where the others are, but what I see is Grace gliding by, stripped naked except for the purple bandanna around her head. Grace splashes a handful of water at me as she goes past, the gold around her teeth a pinch of sunlight below those black eyes. Emma's standing on the bank holding her face in her dimpled hands. Fred's next to Emma, shifting his weight back and forth, not sure what to do.

Bert's tearing his clothes off as fast as he can, and I can tell by the look in his eyes that Bert's never been skinny-dipping before either. Bert spits his dentures into his hand, then tosses them onto his pile of clothes where they land with a click and stare at me. I wonder if any of us has been skinny-dipping before. Besides George. George has probably never owned a blasted bathing suit in all his life.

Bert lets out a yell and wades in up to his waist. I wave to Emma to come help me, but Emma glares and stomps off, pulling Fred along with her. At first I think Emma's going back to the pickup truck, but I know Emma would never trust herself or Fred to find the truck again. They disappear up the bank. I imagine Fred and Emma sneaking off to get it on in the bushes, and I start laughing. I can't imagine that.

Grace is standing on a rock under the falls now, white water splattering hard off her head and shoulders, water shooting out all around her through sunlight. Cool water. I want to go in! I start slapping the vinyl arm of my chair. Bert's the only one who hears, so I wave him over. What the heck? Bert looks down at himself, shrugs, then comes wading toward me, wincing at the rocks underfoot. I pull at my gown with my good hand to let Bert know I want it off. Off. Bert just blinks, twice, his eyes big. I beg Bert with my eyes, but Bert just stands there. I want to scream at him. Bert looks around. George is swimming across the pool at the far end. Long slow strokes. Grace is still standing under the falls, the water splattering off her, a halo in the sun. Bert looks back down at me, his body skinny and white as the falls. Then a decision crosses his face, and Bert's tugging and pulling my gown off over my head. I manage the bra one-handed, whip the bra over my head onto the bank where it catches on some brush. I slap the arm of my chair again, quick. Chop-chop. And Bert pushes me out toward the center of the pool, rubber tires of my chair jarring on the bottom. When the water's up to my neck, I lift my good arm up out of the piano, breaking through the blue sky and branches to signal that it's far enough. Bert stops me, wiggles me a little to make sure my chair won't roll out any farther, then Bert dog-paddles past me, out toward Grace and George, toward the waterfall and mist blowing, out toward the music and feather boas and sunlight. Out toward the halo.

When we pull up back at the big red house and I see the cop car parked at the curb through my television, I know the side trip through the parking lot at the Gardens really did happen after all. And the paradise of George's swimming hole was only a magical moment in life that's now gone. I'm sure they have some law against shooting off a gun in town, so I prepare for the worst: I imagine the cops leading George off in handcuffs, his head hung low.

And sure enough, a few minutes later that's exactly what's happening, except they don't use any handcuffs, and George's head is anything but hanging low. George winks at me as they lead him to the cop car. He gets into the same cage I rode in on my way back to the Gardens after that night downtown so long ago. I get a sick feeling and wonder if this is the end. We'll all have to go back to the Gardens for good, back to the Rhino and her new wing. But the wink George throws us as he goes by says not to worry, everything will be okay. And for some reason I know George is right, although I don't know how on earth it can ever be all right now.

Bert must be thinking the same thing about having to go back to the Gardens, because Bert starts whining that if they take George, they'll have to take him too. But the cops ignore Bert, skinny without a shirt. We all stand here on the baking hot driveway watching as they drive George away. I can see George waving through the tinted window. But then my head goes light as a feeling rolls in me. The exact same feeling I had when I drove away from Amy at the hospital. Except I'm not the one driving away. And George is more like a brother, or a father, or an uncle. Not the only child I'll ever have.

My gown's already dry and stiff, that piano water all evaporated back to air and heat. I look down at my one bare foot where the slipper floated away. The veins forking across the top of my foot are ugly and tangled, my toenails the color of old ivory, elephant tusk, and too long, just like my fingernails.

Then I see the keyboard of the old Chickering upright I used to play at the Starlighter Club outside Reno. My fingernails are painted bright red, clicking across the ivory and ebony, my toenails red, too, peeking out from where they're squished together inside my open-toed patent-leather shoes, my feet working the brass pedals in the footlights. But then the curtain falls, and it's all gone. Just heat pushing me down, trapping me here on this blazing slab of driveway littered with tennis balls. I long for the waterfall again, the halo. I want to be a flower blooming deep in the current, an under-water blossom drifting along—mist and blue sky and trees going by overhead, on the other side of the shiny-smooth piano surface.

S w i n e   i n   T h i s t l e   B l o o m s

Along a narrow country road outside town, the old woman strolls in the heat snipping tiny pieces from a newspaper with a pair of scissors. The scraps of paper, each containing a single letter, flutter to the ground behind her. As the woman walks along, she hums, looks up from time to time, stops, breathes in, and smiles.

She continues walking and cutting, passing mailboxes and ditches full of thistles blooming purple. As she goes by a dense thicket of scrub oak, a loud rustle comes from the bushes and dry leaves. The woman stops, lowers the scissors and newspaper, and listens. The rustling continues, louder now, accompanied by a grunting sound. The woman steps off the blacktop into the gravel and squats down. She wears a sleeveless, pale blue dress. Her arms are eggshell-brown. The greens and purples of the thistles are brilliant in the late light. The woman does not move.

Soon, the low oak leaves at the side of the road begin to shake, the grunting grows louder. Then the nose and ears of a large pink pig poke out of the brush. Acorn juice drips foamy from the pig's chomping mouth. The woman slowly stands up. The pig sees her and starts to bolt, but stops and looks back through the thistles.

"Get along home, you silly old pig," the woman says. "Your mudhole's on fire and your children alone." The woman starts laughing, then reaches into her bag and holds a handful of cracked corn out to the pig. The pig sniffs the air and comes closer. The woman lowers her hand and lets the corn sift into a pile on the ground. "Unless they plan to turn you into bacon," the woman says in a whisper. "If that's the case, then come live with us!" She adds another handful of corn to the pile on the ground, then tugs at a blue bead attached to her bag until the bead pops off. She drops the bead on the pile of cracked corn. Then the woman stands, and starts walking back toward town, once again snipping with the scissors. But now no scraps of paper fall to the ground.

At the crest of a steep hill, the woman throws both arms into the air above her head and is engulfed in a fluttering shower of tiny paper scraps that freckle the blacktop white. She twirls around once and several more white flakes take flight from her braids and blue dress and drift off into dry grass and thistles going to seed along the ditch.

GEORGE CASTOR

WALKING HOME through the dark, the heat was still bad, coming strong up out of sidewalks and off of buildings, heat from the sun soaked in all day now seeping back out, warming the night, the cool headwaters of the Abiqua a whole nother world away. The smell of air-conditioned police station and stale coffee was still in my mouth, my mouth dry. Goddamned cops.

But at least they'd let me off. No bail. No fines. Just a hand-slap. Took away my .22 and told me I might think about seeing a psychiatrist, a shrink. Those cops trying to tell me in a roundabout way that they thought maybe I was loony. Maybe I was. None of their business. I hadn't hurt anybody. Just having a little fun, going to find water, cool down, get away from all this heat.

The night air on my skin felt good. I passed the Nickel-odeon with its jukebox throbbing on the other side of the cinder-block wall, music seeping muffled out of that wall along with the day's heat. A neon Olympia Beer sign burned in the window, plastic water flowing out from under a horse-shoe made to look like real water running. I thought about going inside and having a cold one, or a shot of the good

Doctor, a toast to Ralph. But it was nice to be walking in the warm night. So I walked on by.

I wanted to get on back to the house, see if the trip had put back a little of what the heat had been sucking out of all of us the past couple of weeks. I knew the water had done me good. My skin felt clean. My back wasn't too bad. A fresh feeling all through me. And my mind seemed clearer, too. The cops could keep my .22. I'd had one of the best days I could remember having in a long time. The only thing that could have made the day any better would have been Dora showing up and walking along with me, her arm through mine, me telling her all about it, Dora laughing. Or if not Dora, then Ralph, so I could tell him, Ralph grinning and slapping me on the shoulder with that big hand of his the way he always used to do. Talking about the wonder of it all.

One morning after summer had come and gone and the rain had set in pretty solid, I came downstairs and went into the kitchen to get the coffee going the same as I did every morning. Except this time I wasn't two steps through the swinging door when the hairs on the back of my neck went to cobwebs. I stopped and stood still in the half-light. The refrigerator kicked off, leaving a deep silence all around. The wind threw a blast of rain against the panes in the French doors, and then nothing but quiet again. That's when I heard it, or didn't hear it—what I was used to hearing every morning. Sounds I'd been hearing for almost twenty years: tail thumping against the wooden box, jingle of tags, clicking of paws on cold linoleum.

A low whistle came out through my teeth—the whistle I'd always used only for Shag William, two decades of that whistle. But Shag William didn't move, no tail starting to thump, no jingle. I could see him curled in his wooden box by the refrigerator where he always slept. But not hearing those sounds, I knew.

Being a farmer, I'd seen lots of animals die over the years, more often than not for reasons I couldn't figure out. Like the twin Black Angus calves I bought at the yards over in Mount Angel, hauled home, and then two days later was dragging side by side behind the tractor down into the timber, each black body leaving a muddy streak across the pasture. Or the Shetland pony Dora and I bought for Jason when Jason turned sixteen. But Jason wanted a car and only rode the pony a couple of times. I dragged Jason's pony down into the timber, too, years after Jason left home. There were the lambs and ewes I lost every lambing season. Half-eaten litters of rabbits the mothers sometimes killed. Dead cats and birds and rats. But it had been a long time since I'd lost a dog. And I'd never had a dog quite like Shag William.

He was just a pup when I brought him home inside my coat a month or two after Jason went away to law school. Dora saw that pint-sized pup peeking out and broke down crying, but Shag William kept licking at Dora's face until she was laughing, one of the few times I'd seen her laugh since Jason went away.

Shag William had lived with me for twenty years—longer, it seemed, than my own son had.

I lifted the dog out of his box and turned to carry him outside, but Bert came in through the swinging door and flipped on the overhead light.

"What's wrong with him?" Bert asked, his face all puffy with sleep, glasses cocked crooked, whipped-cream hair a mess.

"He's dead," I said. "Shut off the light."

Bert blinked but didn't say anything. He switched off the light. The room went back to early dawn. Bert came across to me and held his glasses straight with both hands as he looked at Shag William lying in my arms.

"Wonder what of," Bert said.

"Who knows?" I said. "Died in his sleep."

"How old was he?" Bert asked.

"Almost twenty-one," I said.

"That's old for a dog," Bert said. "That's about a hundred and forty in human years."

The refrigerator kicked back on. More rain blew against the house. Bert shoved his glasses up against the bridge of his nose and cleared his throat. "I'm sorry, George," Bert said. "I'd be more than happy to—you know. . . . I mean, if you'd like. That way you'd always have him around. Of course, I've never done up a dog before."

"Thanks, Bert," I said. "But I think I'll pass."

Bert swallowed and looked down.

"I mean it's a nice offer," I said. "But it just doesn't seem right. Not with Shag William. I'll take him up to the farm and bury him by the pond. He always liked the pond."

Bert stood looking at the floor, nothing but bones under his pajamas. "You can come along and help if you want," I said. "But I'm going right now."

Bert looked up at me. "You don't mind?" he said.

I shook my head.

"I'll go get dressed," Bert said. "Won't take but a minute."

I wrapped Shag William in a burlap gunnysack and put him on the seat between me and Bert. We drove through the rain without talking for those thirteen miles I hadn't driven in who knows how long, just the sound of the wipers slapping the rubber stripping at the bottom of the windshield, and the engine taking us around curves and over hills.

I slowed down at my driveway and turned in, cut the engine, and let Max coast to a stop in the carport. The blackberries were everywhere, thistles and tansy gone to seed, the white fluff beat flat by the rain. I got out and handed Bert a set of rain gear and two shovels, then lifted Shag William out of the truck. The dog was heavy.

I headed down the path toward the pond, Bert following along behind me in the rain, dragging the shovels, the shovel blades clanking together. At the clearing where the pond was, I stopped. Bert must have stopped, too, because the shovels stopped clanking. The surface of the pond shimmered silver with the rain and first light. I stood there looking out at the water, my dead dog getting wet in my arms.

I walked out onto the dock and should have just thrown

Shag William in and called it good. Just a dog. A mutt. Burial at sea good enough. But I put Shag William down on the wet wood and then noticed a white stub of a candle shoved into a crack in one of the posts. *Grace and her goddamned candles had found my pond!*

But I was wrong. It was my candle, from almost two years ago. Two years already gone.

I stood up, my hundred-and-forty-year-old dog a lump under the burlap sack on the dock near my boots.

Bert was still standing over on the bank, his yellow rain gear glowing against the green, his head so far back in the yellow hood I couldn't see his face. The rain had stopped. The surface of the pond had gone from silver to a smooth pale green, except for where the wind was brushing flashes of light across the water. And that's all I thought it was at first—what I saw floating out in the pond—just wind and light. But something about it didn't look right. So I got down on my knees and leaned out over the end of the dock. I blinked, looked again. *The koi!* The goddamned koi were still here! Alive! All three of them! Smears of copper and cream floating blurry just below the surface about halfway out. Except the fish were huge now, a foot or more long. Not the two or three inches they were when I'd let them loose that sunny afternoon all those years ago. Here they were, patches of copper, and pearl white, and black shining up through the green water bright as fresh paint.

I waved for Bert to come down, watched him drop the shovels and make his way down the bank, a yellow tin man trying not to slip. When Bert was standing on the dock next to me, I pointed a finger and whispered, "Out there."

Bert looked, but didn't see the fish.

"Lower, in the water about twenty feet out," I said.

"What?" Bert asked.

"Koi," I said.

"What's a koi?" Bert asked.

"Fish," I said. "Goldfish."

"Goldfish?" Bert said. "They're huge!"

"Beautiful, aren't they?" I said.

The fish were floating toward the dock now, one out in front, the other two a length or so back.

"They're coming closer!" I said.

I got down onto my knees. The fish were so close I could see their gills and dorsal fins moving in the water.

"Look at them, Bert!" I said. "They're still alive! Hallelujah!" But my voice must have scared them, because the koi turned and swam fast out into the pond, sinking out of sight near the middle.

I'd forgotten all about Shag William until I looked over. The burlap sack had blown partway off, so the dog's gray muzzle was showing, tiny drops of water hanging on his whiskers, the skin of his mouth pulled back a little to where I could see the white of one of his teeth showing, the tooth broken off.

🌀

When we had a hole about three feet deep dug, I stabbed my shovel into the grass. "Good enough, Bert," I said.

"Thought it had to be six feet," Bert said, breathing hard.

"For people, maybe," I said. "But this is deep enough for a dog."

I picked up Shag William. Muddy water had filled the shovel marks at the bottom of the hole.

"You sure you don't want to keep him around?" Bert asked.

I knelt and laid Shag William in the hole, tucked the burlap sack in around him, then stood up again. "I'm sure," I said.

I threw in a shovelful of wet dirt. But as the dirt hit the burlap, it turned into chunks of turquoise, bouncing and clicking, rolling down off Shag William and piling up bright blue in the muddy water puddled all around. Then Bert threw in another shovelful of dirt, and the blue was gone. Just a muddy hole filling up with water from below and hunks of mud shoveled down from up above, no color anywhere, everything gone to black and silver, the rain starting in hard again.

CLARA PAULSON

I CAN tell right away something's wrong. Wrong. George and Bert both look cold and wet and faraway as they stomp in out of the rain. Their glasses fog. Fog. George pulls his off. Bert doesn't. Bert's eyes almost disappear behind the white fog. We've all eaten breakfast but are still sitting at the table. None of us knew where they'd gone. Emma said that George's pickup truck driving off this morning at the crack of dawn woke her up. But nobody knew if Bert was along. Or where George was headed.

It's an odd thing that goes on here. Nobody would ever admit it, but we all kind of watch out for each other. Only nobody says anything, unless someone's late, or doesn't show up. And then it's only mentioned in passing: "Hmmm. Wonder where Bert is?" Although everyone else is wondering the exact same thing. It's what they say happens in good families. Solid families. Everybody takes care of each other. Brothers watch out for sisters. Sisters for brothers. We're a family of sorts. An odd family. A poker-chip family living in this big red shoe box together.

But this thing is different still. An unspoken fear or something, that whoever's late might never show up. Perhaps they fell, or slipped in the tub. Or something worse.

I'm not used to this. All my life I've done my own thing. Nobody kept track of me, except me. If I was late for a show, it was my fault, my own tough luck. The stage manager either chewed my butt or fired me on the spot. It's hard getting used to other people keeping track of me, making sure I'm counted—not the way they did in the Gardens, but what seems to be genuine concern. Perhaps we're becoming a good family. Good.

"Where have you two been?" Emma says loud, the brat of the family. "We thought something happened."

I didn't, I think to myself. They're grown men. They can take care of themselves.

"Something did!" Bert shoots back from behind his fogged lenses. "Shag William."

Then I know. Because Shag William's not jingling and sniffing around my wheels and feet for whatever I dropped.

"What about the mutt?" Emma asks.

"He's dead!" Bert yells. "We buried him up at George's farm. He's dead."

"Good riddance," Emma says. "He stunk." Her words are little ice picks flying end over end through the air. Times like this I get sick of Emma. I wish she'd died instead of Shag William. Then I regret wishing that.

Bert and George just stand there, staring at us, that tired look I haven't seen in a while back on George's face, little pink footprints on the bridge of George's nose where his glasses usually ride.

Then Grace stands and speaks. "The animal was old," she says. "His time to go on had come." Then Grace turns and goes upstairs, her words sagging in the air above the table. Her words stopping everything. Except for the little willies going down my spine, and Emma, just sitting there chewing, not enough sense to say she's sorry.

George goes into the kitchen, the door swinging back and forth behind him going slower and slower until the door stops. Bert turns and climbs the stairs up to his room. Then I hear a jingle, feel Shag William nosing at my dead ankle under the table and want to shout out to all of them that Shag William's back. But the jingle's not Shag William. At first I think it's the little bell on my chair, but I'm not ringing my bell, not moving, so it can't be. It's coming from somewhere else, upstairs perhaps, or some tiny toy church far away. I swallow a bulkiness swelling in my throat, try not to look at Fred and Emma sitting side by side across the table, a little family of two, part of our poker-chip family as flawed as all the other families out there.

GEORGE CASTOR

I DIDN'T know what made me flip on the bathroom light after I flushed in the middle of that February night. I got up to piss almost every night, but I never turned the light on. Just flushed and felt my way back to bed. But this time I flipped the switch, the bathroom exploded full of light, and I looked down at the toilet—saw pink foam disappearing through that throat of white porcelain. I leaned and looked closer, but the pink was gone. Or never there.

I slammed the seat down so hard something cracked. I wanted to punch a hole in the mirror above the sink. Or throw the scales out the window, lean out and watch the scales hit the driveway two stories down, a burst of springs and sparks and numbers flying everywhere through the night. But instead, I stepped up onto the damned scales and stayed standing there waiting for the black numbers to stop whirring past the little red line. I'd noticed my pants getting looser the past month or two, me having to cinch my belt in, first one hole, then another. But I hadn't paid it any mind, never thought to weigh myself. I figured losing a few pounds was healthy.

The numbers stopped moving, the red line just to the left of one sixty-five. The scales had to be broken. I bounced up and down. Stepped off, then back on. But the red line read the same. Just shy of one sixty-five. I got off the scales and turned to the sink, the numbers whirring to a stop behind me. I looked in the mirror, then shut off the light and went back to my room. The scales were most likely just out of adjustment. Moisture in the air. Rust on the springs.

CLARA PAULSON

I'VE NEVER seen her, because I'm not one of those around here who gets up before the sun. Sun. But George talks about her. They have some game they sometimes play in the morning with the newspaper. Desiree is her name. George says she's got a good arm. I hate sports.

I know it's the papergirl as soon as I pull the front door open and see her standing there in front of me, her face right at eye level, red hair hanging out from under a black baseball cap, the hyphenated words *Appeal-Tribune* stitched into the front of the cap in white. But one of my loose wires touches, shorts out, sparks in my head, and sends everything spinning. It's her! Mine! I try to stop her name, but it rushes in out of nowhere. Shoots into my half-tongue, and wants to fly out at her, at those blue eyes and all that red hair.

Amy!

"Hi. Is George here?" she asks.

I manage to shake my head, but inside I'm blowing apart. Apart. Pieces. Pipes. Piano wire. Everything letting loose.

"Well, I just need to collect for the paper," she says. "Maybe you can help me."

I can't. So many thoughts are crashing through my head

caving in that I'm almost sick. I can't move or smile or feel for my pencil. I can't reach up and ring my little bell, either. No way to call Johnny Q to come get me, roll me away. I just sit here looking at this little girl's beautiful face flooding over with confusion.

"It's only eight dollars," she says.

But it keeps coming. That horrible day rushes back into the space I've managed to keep blank and white for so many years. Every detail comes back in full color, my own motion picture. The smells of that hospital. The finger smudges on the glass of the nursery. The parking lot hard and black beneath my leather shoes as I walk to my car. The sharp soreness when I sit. The chill of the steering wheel beneath my fingers. My breasts almost ready to burst as I drive away.

"I can come back later," the small voice says. "Do you know when George will be home?"

I shake my head again. Amy's still here. This is all real. Right now. A radiance comes through those blue eyes that dives straight inside my lungs. Then I'm sobbing, unable to stop, or breathe, my tongue rolling around inside my head. A grimy little hand is stroking my arm. Back and forth. Back and forth.

"It will be okay," Amy tells me. "I heard about Shag William. Don't cry. I can come back later."

But I keep being pushed back into that hallway outside the nursery. Watching the nurse hold her up. Again and again. Her scrunched-up little face and red hair peeking out of that pink blanket. That nurse didn't know, or she wouldn't have ever let me see her. I told them I didn't want to see her.

So I know she can't come back later. Amy can never come back now. Because she doesn't know where I am. I don't know where she is. And I can't even talk into a telephone to try and find her. So even though she says she can come back, I know she can't. Never! I'm shaking, and the tears are falling onto my lap, smearing all the black letters on my pad. The dead side of my face tugs all horrible the way it does, drool coming out with the tears.

Then I feel a little arm around my shoulders and am sure it's Amy. But that can't be. That was too many years ago. Sixty? Amy would be sixty! Not ten or eleven like this little girl. Amy is a woman now. Almost old, like me. If she's still alive. This isn't Amy. I gave Amy away, walked away from Amy's little face looking at me through that glass, kept walking away out of that hospital and across the parking lot and drove away from Amy forever.

Then it all spins away, water going down a drain, swirled window smudges and nurses' uniforms and bits of broken wire going down with the dirty water, me chasing it all away with a long black stick, splashing, shoving the tip of that pink blanket down through the dark holes of the drain.

Then the girl is gone and I'm sitting here in front of the open door. Perhaps it *was* just a wire! All in my head. I hope! Thank God.

But a breeze comes in from outside, and I feel wetness cooling on my face and wrists. The black letters on my pad are all smeared. I try to write her name, those three letters, but my pen just tears a hole in the soggy paper.

PART FOUR

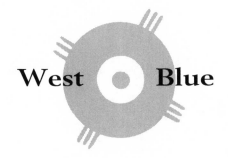

West **Blue**

Do not go gentle into that good night,
Old age should burn and rave at close of day;
Rage, rage against the dying of the light.

—Dylan Thomas

CLARA PAULSON

AT SUPPER George is solemn, something bugging him. I see it. That tired look on his face again. Oboe spinning on the horizon. Getting closer. Coming this way. Way.

"Everything okay, George?" Bert asks, between bites, a dab of mashed potatoes oozed out the corner of his mouth.

Everybody except Emma stops eating, waits for George to answer. Waits. All of us with silverware stopped in the air. George finishes chewing, swallows, then answers with a question that doesn't make any sense.

"Do mealtimes around here remind anybody else of a cafeteria?" he says. None of us say anything. Just George's question hanging there, odd and out of place.

After a while, Fred clears his throat. "Why, what do you mean, George? This is nothing like a cafeteria."

"I'll say," Bert says. "You ought to try the cafeteria at the Gardens. That was like eating with the dead. If you could call what they served there food."

I can smell fish sticks and vanilla pudding. I wonder if it's Friday at the Gardens. Wonder if Henrietta's working her black beads.

Then George starts talking about his college days, the dor-

237

mitory and the cafeteria where he used to eat. I don't know why he's talking about this. But he keeps going, that look on his face staying right there, his words coming out edged with a tone I've never heard in his voice before. I don't care about George's college days, or what he had to eat back then, but he keeps telling us about it. Going on and on. Then George says a word I don't know. Foodfight. He's saying a foodfight broke out in the college cafeteria one night. I want to ask him what's a foodfight. But Emma jumps in.

"What started it?" Emma asks. Her question stops George. The skin above Emma's lip is wet. Emma always sweats when she eats. George stares at Emma, that look inside his eyes now, too.

"Somebody fired the first shot," George says, picking up his spoon and scooping up a spoonful of mashed potatoes. "Kind of like this." He pulls back the top of his spoon with his finger and launches a ball of mashed potatoes across the table at Emma. The glob of potatoes slaps against Emma's forehead and sticks just above her left eye. Emma's mouth falls open.

"Good shot!" Bert shouts, and starts clapping his hands.

Part of the potato glob drops off Emma's forehead, but Emma doesn't move, her mouth still wide. George fires another spoonful that goes right into Emma's open mouth. She closes her mouth for a second, and I think she's going to gag, but she coughs up the potatoes and tries to blow them back across the table at George. But the glob falls out of her mouth and lands with a blurp in her glass of milk. Bert claps some more, and somebody starts laughing.

Emma's face is a dark red, and in her eyes embers have started to glow. She grabs a handful of salad drenched with blue cheese dressing and hurls it out across the table full force at George. The soggy wad of salad breaks up and scatters midflight, landing mostly on Bert and me. A piece of carrot pings off the rim of Bert's wineglass, and falls in. Bert stands up, grabs his wineglass, and throws the red wine and bobbing bit of carrot back at Emma. The liquid stretches pink and shiny through the air below the chandelier. I see the piece of carrot in all that pink headed Emma's way. But Fred reaches his open hand out in front of the wine coming through the air. The wine hits his hand and sprays the white tablecloth and Grace, sprays all of us. Pink everywhere.

I look for the piece of carrot, but can't find it. Food's flying all over now. So I jump in, too. I pull over a bowl of buttered peas and start tossing handful after handful straight up into the chandelier. Warm peas hailing down and bouncing off everything, landing in people's hair, catching behind their glasses, little green whole notes. Peas and pink and more potatoes flying. A few slices of bread go by. Grace mashes the cube of butter into Fred's face, then starts laughing harder than I've ever heard Grace laugh. She's laughing and rubbing the butter into Fred's hair with both hands, slicking Fred's hair down onto his head. Fred's laughing, too. He leans over and pours salad dressing all over Grace's lap, and Grace laughs even harder.

And then it's over. Over. The dining room table's a disaster area, and everyone except Emma is laughing so hard we can't breathe. That hysterical kind of laughter you can't stop, me laughing, too, my face tugging and drool leaking out the corner of my mouth, but I don't care.

"This is disgusting!" Emma says, spitting the words out of her mouth as if the words were strands of hair caught on her tongue. She's wiping at her blouse with a napkin. "You're all behaving like a bunch of fools," Emma says.

"You should know," George yells. "You're the biggest damned fool in this whole house!" His voice is icy and jagged, no sign of laughter left, that look all over his face, inside his eyes, under his skin. Everybody goes silent. A pea drops out of the chandelier and wedges against the wick of one of the two white candles burning in the center of the table. The flame sizzles and goes out, the smell of burnt toast in the air. Burnt fish sticks. I roll back from the table a little. My bell jingles, the only sound in the room. A wet tea bag caught up by its string on one of the upper rods of my steering mechanism dangles back and forth, dripping a little on my neck. Fred shrinks down in his chair. Bert blinks, a piece of lettuce stuck to his eyelid. Then Grace's voice comes loud through the burnt pea smell.

"George!" Grace says. "What's eating at you?"

Her words seem to stop George, smashing into him so hard I hear the wind being knocked out. And on his face that look is spreading, flooding all through his skin, that look stronger than I've ever seen it before. A look that scares me, because I can tell for the first time ever that George is scared of something.

Then George stands up so fast his chair falls over backwards and cracks against the floor.

"Nothing," he says. "Not a goddamned thing!" He turns to go and trips on his chair and almost falls. But grabs hold of the dining room doorway and stays up. He throws his napkin into the air behind him and stomps down the back hallway. The napkin floats down and lands—a little white tent on one of the gray flagstones in the entryway. The back door slams loud and the little tent collapses flat on the stone.

GEORGE CASTOR

I WALKED the ten blocks to the city park almost at a run, wiping salad dressing and wine and sweat off my face. My back was burning bad, but I didn't give a shit. I wanted to put distance between me and the house, between me and Grace and her witchy ways. I had to get the hell away from that goddamned toilet bowl. Grace was probably putting the pink in my piss. Burning it in with all her candles and circle talk. How else would she know? Asking like that in front of everyone. The way she said those words, *eating at you*. All I saw was Uncle Bill in that bed in Omaha, the cancer eating him up from the inside out. Goddamned Grace. She was playing with me, a hooked fish, wearing me out. Black magic, or voodoo, or some such shit. Well, I didn't need any of it.

I got to the park and slowed down. It was dark out. The air smelled of rotting oak leaves and late winter, but felt good going into my lungs. I wanted to run into Ralph right now, sit on a bench and talk with him. Tell Ralph about Grace driving me loony, and Emma, too. Tell Ralph the city was still on my ass about my equipment in the street, sending letter after letter, a half-dozen letters so far. Every single one of those letters going into the fire. Including the one that came yesterday with the big words TERMINAL WARNING printed out across the top of the page. I'd tell Ralph I was still a farmer. Tell him about Shag William dying last fall. Tell him I was seeing rust in my piss and having nightmares. Ask Ralph what to do.

Stars sparkled through the bare oak branches overhead. The red and green lights of a plane went across the sky.

A little blood was probably perfectly normal. A dab of blood now and then in your piss was just part of living. Like your teeth bleeding a bit once in a while. You just wash the spit down the drain and go to bed. No big deal. Blood gone the next day. And losing a few pounds was the same thing. Just part of it. No big deal. Hell, I might not piss any more blood for a year or longer, or maybe never. In fact, I still wasn't a hundred percent sure I'd even seen right. Maybe there wasn't any blood at all. Just my mind working overtime, or my eyes getting worse, colors going wrong.

I walked over and pissed in the moon-shadow of a picnic shelter. At night everything was black or white or a shade of gray. Bert, and Fred, and even Kenny down at Chuck's Paint Floor 'N More, probably passed a little blood now and then. Maybe even Grace and Emma did. Hell, women passed blood once a month for years! My little dab of rusty pink was nothing. Or maybe it was some genetic thing that linked men to women that even the scientists had yet to discover.

I sat down on a bench and was thinking about all the extra room we still had in the house when a car pulled into the park. A white Ford Falcon, shiny in the night, chrome wheels flashing, rear end jacked up, engine rumbling low. The car stopped and the engine and headlights shut off. Then the running lights blinked back on and glowed orange in the dark. I heard music and laughter. High school kids out carousing. I remembered school back in Omaha. Seemed only yesterday I myself was out carousing. Now, here I was past eighty, sitting on a park bench thinking about my school days. Dora dead. Jason all grown up and gone. Already dead, too. But only yesterday Jason being born. And before that Dora and I making love on the beach. It all went too fast, too quick. And no way to slow the son-of-a-bitch down. I remembered reading about some village in the Andes where people lived to be a hundred. Nineteen more years. A long time.

Laughter came through the dark from the parked car.

But I didn't live in that village. I lived in a country where making it to a hundred was such a rare thing you got your picture in the paper. I once saw a whole book full of pictures and interviews with a hundred people who were at least a hundred years old. Whoever wrote that book must have criss-crossed the country a dozen times to come up with a hundred people who'd lived that long. Hell, my chances of making it to a hundred were as good as me going to the goddamned moon.

Maybe ninety, though. Nine or ten more years. But what if I only had two years left? Or less than one year? What if all I had left of living was one single month? Thirty days?

What the hell was I doing, sitting around trying to guess when I was going to die? I stood and walked a little closer to where the white Falcon was parked. The windows were down. I stopped in the shadow of a huge oak tree and listened. Two couples. Drinking. Laughter. Music on low. I bent down and picked up a few acorns and held the cold kernels in my hand. The acorns were alive. These seeds the size of my own nuts. I threw one of the acorns. It bounced on the roof of the car and rattled down the front windshield. The music clicked off. I threw another one. It hit the hood with a ping. Then two more, fast. Ping. Ping. The driver's door opened and a boy in a T-shirt got out, looking around. I threw the last acorn and hit the boy in the back. He jumped.

"*Psssst*," I hissed in the dark. The boy spun around. I stepped out from behind the tree. "Over here," I said.

"What do you want?" the boy said, trying to make his voice bigger than it was. One of the girls inside the car giggled.

"I've got a question for you," I said, walking over to the car. The boy stepped back toward the open door. "Are you living it up?" I asked.

"Get out of here, old dude," the boy said. "I don't have any spare change."

"No, wait," I said, holding up my hand. "I don't want your money. You're young, right?"

"I'm old enough," the boy said.

"No," I said. "I'm the one who's old. I'm eighty-one."

"So?" the boy said.

"So you'll be old tomorrow," I said, taking another step closer.

"You're crazy, dude," the boy said.

"Think so? Well, you might be right about that. I've had the same thought myself more than once." I paused. "Say, have you ever heard of the Hogan House?"

"Of course," the boy said. "That haunted house just down the street."

"I live there now," I said. "Drop by sometime. And bring your pals."

The boy looked at me through the dark.

"No thanks," the boy said. "You're a looper." The boy turned and got into the Falcon. I had no idea what a looper was.

"Maybe," I said going toward the car. "But I was your age one day, too. Young and strong and thinking I had the world by the ass." The boy slammed the door and started the engine. I hurried up to the window. "But remember what I told you. You'll be eighty tomorrow!" The car drove off squealing the tires. "And then you get to die, too! You hear me? Die!"

☽

Less than a week later, Emma started bitching about being overworked, how the house was so big it was hard for us to keep up with all the cleaning and cooking. I let Emma's words go in one ear and out the other—until she started talking serious about hiring somebody to come in and help out a few days a week in the kitchen. That would be breaking the one rule I had for the place: we do it all ourselves.

"We all cook once a week," I told her. "That's the deal. And we split up the other chores. No loafers."

"But cooking for six is so much work," Emma whined. "And I cook for Fred on his day, too, so I'm cooking more than anybody else."

"That's your problem," I said. "Fred can cook."

"Are you kidding?" she said. "Fred doesn't know how to hard-boil an egg."

"He can learn," I said. "You drop it in and boil the hell out of it. It's not that tough."

"Yeah, but what about cleaning? It takes forever. Just dusting this place wears me out. And running the vacuum makes my bursitis shoulder hurt for days."

"Then move the hell out," I yelled. "Nobody's forcing you to stay. If you don't like it, go back to the Gardens. We're not hiring any cooks or maids or anybody else to take care of us. We take care of ourselves. Period."

"Then I'm calling a house meeting. Tonight. At dinner," she said, then turned and stomped off to her room.

But when Fred didn't show up that night for dinner, Emma's house meeting never got started on account of everybody trying to figure out where Fred might have gone off to.

"This happens now and then," Emma said. "It's nothing to worry about. Once a year or so the crazy man has to go off and get it out of his system. Okay? Now, can we talk about getting somebody in here to help with all the cleaning and cooking around this place?"

"Where does he go?" Grace asked.

"Who knows?" Emma said. "He never tells me where he's been. He just doesn't come around for a while. You know, like an old tom."

I raised my eyebrows and looked over at Bert. "An old tom cat, huh?" I said.

"Not that," Emma snapped. "He just disappears now and then for a few days."

"Disappears?" Grace leaned forward. "For a few days?"

"Sometimes," Emma said. "Other times he's back the next

morning. I've quit worrying about him. Fred's a big boy. He can take care of himself."

I thought of Fred in his white socks, bow tie, and breast pocket full of mechanical pencils, and wasn't so sure. "I'll go see if I can find him," I said, standing up.

"Hey, wait one minute," Emma bellowed. "I want to talk about house chores first."

"What about them?" I asked.

"Well . . ." Emma paused for a second, drew a breath. "I think it's high time we find somebody to come in a few times a week, you know, to help us with the cooking and the cleaning. We wouldn't have to pay them much. Maybe Fred and I would even pay for it."

"Damnit, Emma," I said. "I already told you. We do it all ourselves! Now what's wrong with you?"

"Me? I think you're wrong and we should have a vote," Emma said. "Right now. Majority rules. All those in favor of—"

"No hired help, goddamnit!" I yelled, slamming my fist down onto the table. "And if you're going to bitch and moan about pitching in and pulling your share around here, then move the hell out! Take your lazy fat ass with you and let the rest of us live in peace!"

CLARA PAULSON

I DON'T know what's happening. An explosion. Bones and body. Dishes jumping up off the table. He's blowing up. George. Exploding. At one of us. Big Emma. Right here in his big red house. A side of George I've never seen. A mean side. Him stomping out of the room. That look on his face. I want to shout at him to get back here and sit down and talk this through like a grown man, but I can't even get my good hand started trying to find my pencil. My hand just lies in the flowers on my lap.

The back door slams shut and George is gone. Gone. Bert's sitting across the table not even blinking, just staring straight ahead out through those glasses of his, pulling at his chin the way he does. Emma's bawling, tears running down her round cheeks, on down her two or three chins, tears dropping off and landing on her arms, little splashes on her too tight skin. I've never seen Emma cry before, that huge woman shaking, more tears coming. Watching Emma crying makes me pity her. All she was asking was for a little help with the dishes. Nothing to blow up about.

Grace's black eyes are dry and distant, staring off into space without a single blink, looking hard at something faraway.

Then Grace gets up and without saying a word blows out the two candles on the table, a little half-moon shell of burnt pea from the foodfight last week still floating in the wax next to the wick of one candle. The smoke curls up into the chandelier, that burned-out piece of pea smouldering, too, the pea smoke going up into the glass diamonds shining and clinking in the air and silence.

The clock starts bonging. I close my eyes, count each bong. It takes an hour to get out nine, nine bongs ringing in my ears and running around inside the metal tubes of my chair.

When I look up, everybody's gone. Gone. I'm the only one at the table. The television's going in Emma and Fred's room. But Fred's not in that room. That's right. Fred's been gone all day. That's how this whole mess started. Everybody worried but nobody saying much. Nobody wanting to say what we were all thinking.

Well, I'll say it. Perhaps Fred's dead. How's that? D. E. A. D. I write the four letters on my pad, a period after each letter. Two Ds, one at each end. There. I said it. But nobody's here to read it. So I tear the page out of my pad, wad the page up, and throw the ball of paper across the room. That word—four letters and four dots wadded up and wrinkled— bounces off the wall and rolls across the floor. Shag William doesn't go sniffing after the wadded-up word. Shag William's dead. Just like Fred is now. D. E. A. D.

GEORGE CASTOR

I HAD a pretty good idea where I'd find Fred: the nearest bar, the Nickelodeon, just across the bridge downtown.

The front windows of the Nickelodeon were so thick with condensed body heat and breath, the water was beading up and running down the glass. I went into the restaurant side and saw mostly the color brown. Brown vinyl booths, brown Formica tabletops made to look like real wood, and brown plastic baskets lined with waxed paper full of chicken strips and french fries, hamburgers and onion rings. Dinnertime at the Nickelodeon. Everybody's breathing and all the hot food making the windows run.

I went straight back and made a left through a doorway into the lounge side. A lit-up jukebox was churning out a country western tune. Lights up in the ceiling above the bar were throwing blue cones of light down through smoke and music and the sounds of glass clinking to where a bartender was mixing drinks, a cigarette hanging bright white from his lips as he squinted through his own cigarette smoke twisting up into those cones of blue light. The color in the lounge side was black. Black booths and chairs. Black tables. The bar all black, too, with diamond-tucked vinyl pocked full of cigarette burns along the edge. All that black made it hard to see much, but I looked around, scanned the faces. And sure enough, there he was. Fred. Sitting at a table in the far corner, talking to a red-headed woman. An old tom, just what Emma said. I crossed the room and slid into an empty chair at the table next to the one where Fred and the redhead were sitting. I tried to make out the words they were saying over the music thumping loud.

"Wait a minute. I heard about that place," the woman said, snapping her finger. "Yeah. Somebody said it was a nuthouse or a nursing home or something. Run by some crazy old rich guy?"

"That's George!" Fred said, his face alive in all that black. "George is the one who started it." I could tell by the way Fred was talking that he'd been here awhile.

"Is he really wacko?" the redheaded woman asked.

"George?" Fred took a slurp of his drink, wiping his chin with the back of his hand. "No. He's just a little strong-headed. Has a mind of his own. Doesn't like people telling him what to do. But he's a good egg."

I leaned over close to the redhead. I could smell her perfume. "Don't believe him, ma'am," I said. "This fellow George he's telling you about, well, he's beyond wacko, he's loony as a bat in broad daylight! Hundred percent loony all the way to the marrow. And dangerous, too!"

The woman pulled back away from my words, her eyes going big.

"And Fred here," I said. "He's one of them loonies, too. Don't let him tell you otherwise. He's been living there for months now. They're all loony! Ought to be locked up. Every one of them."

The song on the jukebox ended and the clatter of dishes and voices went loud.

"And you know something else?" I said, getting up and putting my face only inches from hers. "They kidnap people. And stuff 'em. The place is full of bodies mounted to pieces of plywood and hung on the walls. They especially go after redheads!"

The woman stood up and backed away fast toward the door, knocking over a chair and ripping her raincoat on a table as she turned and ran. I slid into her chair that was still warm and slapped Fred on the back.

"Got cha!" I said. "Figured I might find you in here."

"She was a very lovely lady," Fred said, his lips rubbery and wet. "Why'd you go and frighten her away? She—" Then Fred stopped, his mouth hanging half-open, as if he wanted to go on but couldn't remember what he wanted to say.

"Your wife's worried sick," I said.

"Emma?" Fred asked.

"No, Dorothy," I said. "In *The Wizard of Oz*."

"Who?" he said.

"Hell yes, Emma," I said. "She says you never miss dinner. That this is so unlike you. She's probably got the cops out looking for you by now."

Fred pawed at his shirtsleeve trying to find his watch. "Oh, am I late?" he said.

"Too late," I said. "We ate everything—including your share and Emma's. Emma said she was too worried about you to eat."

"She did?" Fred said. He drained his glass and put the glass on the black table. The ice cubes fell. Fred licked his lips, then sat up straight and leaned toward me. "You know something, George?" he said. "I love Emma. I've loved her from the very first day we met—when I was twenty-one and she was nineteen. Oh, she's a little bossy and could stand to lose a few pounds. But you know something else? Everybody has their little flaws and scars. For whatever the reasons. Whether your mother kept you from seeing your father, or your older brother always outdid you at everything, or ... " Fred stopped, sat back. "Well, I just love her, George. All of her."

The jukebox started in again as a waitress showed up and asked me what I was drinking.

"The good Doctor," I said. "Jack. Straight up." She turned to go. "Make that a double, will you? I've got a little catching up to do here."

☺

By the time Fred and I came out of the black side of the Nickelodeon, it was tomorrow. Two A.M. and nobody but the two of us on the streets. Walking was a challenge. The good Doctor in my blood and on my breath. Gin and tonic in Fred. But we helped each other, holding on, feet headed for home, arms and legs trying to keep up. Stay up. Keep us from falling over. Bodies bumping. Both of us burping and laughing headed for the Hogan House.

When we were crossing the bridge, I stopped, reined Fred in with my arm around his neck.

"Hold on a minute," I said. "Listen. *Shhh.*"

It was too dark to see the water down below. But I could hear it moving.

"You hear that, Fred?" I said.

"What?" Fred asked.

"That whistling sound down there," I said.

"Not really," Fred said, resting his forehead on his arms on the bridge railing.

"That's water pushing through vine maple and salmon berry on the banks. You can tell it's high tonight, headed for the Willamette, and then the Columbia, hightailing it back out to the Pacific. With all the rain lately, I'll bet it's halfway up the bank and the color of milk chocolate."

"Chocolate?" Fred said. "Emma loves chocolate."

"You ever wonder how fish can see when the water's so muddy?" I said. "Or how they breathe with all that silt making soup of the river? Or how they breathe air out of water in the first place?"

"One time I came home early," Fred said. "And caught her with a whole sampler box, those little wrappers all over the front room floor."

"But you know what's even more amazing, Fred?" I said. "Something I don't think they'll ever figure out? The way a salmon can spend years in the open ocean and then somehow find its way all the way back up the same little creek it was hatched in. The same goddamned pool. Now how the hell do they do that? How do they know when it's time to go home? To start swimming hundreds of miles against the current, beating themselves to pulp on the rocks? And only to die when it's all over. Goddamnit, Fred, if that ain't a miracle, I don't know what is. You know what I mean?"

"Emma does indeed love chocolate, George," Fred said. "That's for sure."

"Hey, Fred" I said. "You ever think about dying?"

"Huh?" Fred said.

"You ever wonder what it would be like?" I said. "You know, to wind up like the salmon?"

Fred didn't say anything for a long time. Something splashed in the water below. The shadow of an owl hushed by.

"Oh, I haven't ever been fishing, George," Fred said. "And Emma dislikes the smell of fish, so we never ate much of it."

"I'm talking about dying," I said. "Not fishing."

"Oh," Fred said. "Well, Emma'd probably like to die eating chocolate."

"I mean *you* dying," I said. "Not your wife."

"Oh," Fred said. "Guess I've never given it much thought."

"You ever pass blood?" I asked.

"Blood?" Fred said.

"Yeah," I said. "You know, in your piss."

"I did once," Fred said. "When I was a kid and got run over at home plate."

"You played baseball?" I said.

"Well, I wasn't very good at it," he said. "But I played. Outfield."

"Well, I'll be dammed," I said. I couldn't imagine Fred playing any sport. Chess, maybe, if chess could be called a sport. But not baseball. "Hey, Fred?" I said. "I just got a hell of a good idea. We ought to get a game going."

"What?" Fred said.

"A baseball game!" I said. "I used to play. And Desiree the paperboy, she plays. She's got a hell of an arm, I'll tell you. And I'll bet maybe Bert played, too. We could field a whole team! What do you say?"

"Oh, I don't know," Fred said. "I wasn't very good."

"Who cares how good any of us were. I'm sure we're all lousy now. But we'll just get out and have some fun. Knock some balls around. Move the bones a bit. You know, exercise! Stay in shape and all that shit. How about it?"

"I can't remember the last time I exercised," Fred said.

"Well, hell, it's never too late to start," I said. "I'll bet you weren't half bad at the game. Little wiry guy like you."

Fred didn't say anything.

"We'll get everybody to play," I said. "Bert and Grace, and everybody. We'll even get Emma suited up. Clara can keep score or something. Come on, Fred, what do you say? Let's get a game going."

"Right now?" Fred asked.

"Hey, there's an idea! Why the hell not?" I said. "It'll be getting light soon enough. We can at least get started on the field. And maybe this little project will get the City off my ass about my machinery being parked idle in the goddamned street. We'll have to use the disk and the tiller to work up the infield. And we can move some of the irrigation pipe around and lay it out to keep the outfield green this summer. We'll have ourselves a regular baseball season in our own backyard! What do you say?"

"Well . . ." Fred said.

"Oh, come on," I said. "A little baseball won't kill you."

"I guess I can give it a try," Fred said.

"That a boy!" I yelled, slapping Fred on the back so hard I almost knocked him to his knees. But Fred caught his balance, staggered, and came up grinning, straightening his glasses and fiddling with that bow tie of his.

"Come on! High-five!" I said. "Like the pros."

Fred tugged the bottom of his jacket straight, then, frowning with full concentration, tried to give me a high-five. But our hands missed by at least a mile and we both started laughing so hard we had to reach out and hold on to each other to keep from going down. But we went down anyway. Except not all the way. Our legs just gave way slow and we wound up on our knees, side by side on the wet sidewalk in front of that bridge railing, laughing so hard tears came. And for a second Ralph was right there with us, and Ralph was laughing, too, and everything was okay in the world. Everything a wonder.

CLARA PAULSON

I wake to darkness and an awful racket outside. The sound of a motor, rocks hitting metal, the voices of men. Men. I lie here in my bed, my ears wide in the dark wondering where I am. Then I recognize George's voice. Outside. On the side lawn. Words in the night. Tractor sounds. Is this a dream? The words *infield* and *baseline* and *goddamned rocks* come to me. Then Fred's voice, too: *I don't know, George . . . guess that looks pretty straight. Straight enough.* Then there's a knock on the wall. Or is it my door? It is. My bedroom door squeaks open and hallway light makes Grace a black paper doll standing in the doorway. She asks if I'm okay. I nod. Grace goes to my window and pulls back the curtain. A flashlight beam sweeps outside. More rocks against metal. Laughter. More words. *Spring training, goddamnit. Salmon. Chocolate.*

"They're tearing up the side lawn," Grace says. "Crazy men."

I nod in the darkness.

"Go back to sleep, Clara," Grace says. "They're full of devil water."

But I can't sleep. I lie here after Grace has gone out and closed my door. I listen until there is only silence outside. I keep listening until the curtains begin to brighten, faint notes of a piano rise.

Perhaps it was all just a dream, and I'm nothing but a silly old woman, half-dead, lying here having to go pee.

GEORGE CASTOR

AFTER FRED and I did what in the light of day turned out to be a pretty shoddy job of tilling up the infield after our night at the Nickelodeon, I got a book out of the library and spent a good week measuring and staking and laying everything out right. The side lawn was plenty big enough to fit a ball diamond onto, especially if we put home plate all the way back against the chicken coop, making the outfield as deep as possible. The street would be the fence. If anybody popped one into the street, we'd call it a home run fair and square.

Using the front-end scoop, I made a pitcher's mound. From Hal's Sports Shack downtown I bought puffy white bases and a real rubber home plate that I anchored to the infield at what I paced off to be about the right distances. I built a backstop by attaching some old cyclone fencing and leftover tin roofing to the south wall of the chicken coop. This gave the backstop some height and width. I even chalked lines on the diamond, just the way they showed in the book, including a batter's box, and first and third base coach boxes.

When the diamond was looking pretty good, I made a scoreboard out of a half sheet of plywood that I painted red to match the house and lag-bolted to one of the fir trees near

the chicken coop/backstop. The yellow T-shirts I'd special ordered at Hal's Sports Shack came in. Each shirt had "Hogan's
Spring Chickens" printed on the front and back in big red
letters. The shirts looked good, and I was sure it wouldn't
take much convincing to get the others fired up about playing
ball with Fred and me. Although Fred's enthusiasm seemed
to have cooled a bit since that night after the Nickelodeon.

○

"Baseball Bashes!" I announced one morning at breakfast.
"Fred and I have decided that playing a little ball once a week
will not only be fun, but will be the perfect way to get our
blood churning good, our joints limbered up. You know, a
little exercise to work the kinks out and keep us fit. I even
got T-shirts made up for everybody."

I held up one of the yellow shirts.

"I hate baseball!" Emma said. "It's boring and dull and
stupid, if you ask me."

"Nobody did," I said.

"I still hate it," Emma said. "You do too, don't you, Fred?"
She elbowed him.

"You know, George," Fred said, clearing his throat. "After
sleeping on this lately, I have come to the conclusion that
perhaps it might be best for me to just watch the first few
games from the sidelines. You know, see how it goes."

"What?" I said. "I thought we were in this together."

Fred just shrugged. Emma had worked him over good.

"How about you, Bert?" I said. "You must have played
when you were a kid."

"Played a little. Sure did," Bert said. "But the way they tell
me my eyes are shot now, I doubt I'd be able to catch *or* hit
a white marble of a ball moving at the speed of light."

"You drove that car of yours just fine. Remember?" I said.

"Gertie wasn't moving anywhere near the speed of light,"
he said. "She's big and black and slow and beautiful."

"Clara!" I said. "How about you? I mean I understand you can't play exactly, but you can keep score for us. Be part of the game." I thought I saw Clara nod her head a little, so I shouted, "Clara's in, everybody! Come on, who's next? Clara and I can't play by ourselves."

But nobody said a word. "Look," I said. "I'll tell you what. Give me one game. Just play one game and we'll go from there. I have a hunch you'll all get so hooked that these Baseball Bashes will become the highlight of your week. You'll probably want to play more than just once a week. Come on, what do you say? One game."

After a long silence, Grace spoke. "I've never much liked sports, myself," she said. "But I'll play, under one condition. And that is that everybody plays. All of us. Together."

When Emma still flat out refused, I bribed her by promising she could play catcher for both teams.

"The catcher's the one who gets to sit down, right?" Emma asked.

"That's right," I said. "We'll even put a lawn chair right behind home plate for you."

That tipped the scales for the big gal. Emma agreed to give it a whirl. I leaned close to Fred and promised him another night out at the Nickelodeon if he'd sign on. He glanced at Emma, then nodded.

"I'll probably bust my neck," Bert said. "But what the heck."

"All right!" I said. "We've got ourselves a baseball team just in time for spring training. If the weather holds, this Sunday's the day!"

☙

On Sunday the weather was on my side, warm and sunny, damned near balmy. I broke out the T-shirts and hurried through the house banging on bedroom doors. "Hup. Hup. Game day! Let's play ball!" I said, tossing everybody a T-shirt and a mitt, and telling them to be dressed down and out on the field by three o'clock. "No slugs."

I went right out and got Emma a lawn chair set up behind home plate. I even stood an apple box on end next to the lawn chair and put a box of chocolates on the apple box. We needed a catcher.

I was on the pitcher's mound ready and waiting when sure enough at just before three o'clock, five other yellow-shirted souls came trickling out onto the field, Emma bringing up the rear. But that made only six of us total. Not even enough for one full team, let alone two. But we'd make it work. The others were out here ready to play, so the last thing I wanted to lose was my momentum.

I led everybody jogging three laps around the bases to warm up, making sure they tagged each base and stepped on home plate. I then paired people off to play catch, had them stand a few feet apart, and told them to step back little by little as they got the hang of it. Pretty soon everybody was three or four paces away from their partners, balls going back and forth. Not bad.

After catch, I sent everybody out into the outfield and I hit grounders and fly balls for them to retrieve. Fred and Grace were pretty good, Bert was mediocre, Emma was downright lousy, and Clara, of course, couldn't participate, but she seemed to be enjoying watching. I didn't want to push things too hard on the first day, so I called it quits early and fired up the barbecue.

I spent the next week trying to round up another team, putting bright pink posters up at the junior high, the high school, the Nickelodeon, and on the telephone poles around the neighborhood. I even put up posters at the City Hall, who, ever since I'd given the mayor an earful over the phone, had stopped sending me letters about my farm machinery being in the street. The posters showed the time and place of the Baseball Bashes, and offered free hot dogs and drinks to anybody who wanted to come out and play. I was tempted to drive down to the Gardens and tape a couple on those sliding glass doors, but decided not to push my luck.

I had a whole load of posters left over when I was done, so I covered the columns of the front porch with them. When the wind blew, all those posters ruffled and fluttered, making it look and sound like the whole red house was about to lift off and fly away on the pink-feathered wings of some giant bird.

CLARA PAULSON

GEORGE IS up to it again. I swear he thinks he's still a kid or something. This time it's baseball, of all things. Baseball. Ever since that night he and Fred were out on the tractor drunk as skunks George has spent every waking minute making that field of his look almost as good as the ones you see on television, green and crisp, with bright white lines. Except George calls his baseball field a diamond. Diamond. George mows the grass on his diamond two or three times a week, keeps the dirt raked smooth and soft. He dotes on that diamond, worse than Bert on that old car of his. Men and their toys.

George even put up a bright red scoreboard. My job's using the scoreboard to keep track of who's ahead. Innings and outs and runs, and other baseball words I'm not sure I understand. I hang yellow wooden numbers on the red nails sticking out of the scoreboard. George made me a long-handled stick with a hook on the end. I lift the yellow numbers up using my stick and hang them where George tells me. It's kind of fun.

That first Sunday we all went out onto George's new diamond, I was sure this baseball idea wouldn't last more than a week. George claimed it was a form of exercise and good for us. But as far as I could tell, it was mostly standing around, everybody tossing balls, and dropping balls, and swinging at balls with the bat, but hitting mostly air. Air. The only thing getting any exercise was George's jaw, him blabbering on about how great we were all doing, how these Baseball Bashes were going to be the highlights of our weeks, saying how if we practiced hard enough, we just might make it to the major leagues and live forever.

And some of us do seem to be getting better. Grace especially. She can really send that little ball flying. Baseball's a nutty game, if you ask me, hitting a dinky ball with a wooden stick and then running around in a circle. Grace says that's what she likes best about the game, the circle. Grace talked George into letting her keep a candle burning in a quart Mason jar at the center of her circle, George's diamond. Grace's candle jar sits out in the dirt just beyond the pitcher's hump. When it's windy, her candle smokes, turns the wide-mouth glass of that jar black. They're both nuts, Grace and George. Candles and circles and diamonds.

I also "keep stats" as George calls it. He made up some stat sheets for me to fill in with numbers. When we're done playing Sunday evening, he takes the numbers and does some calculations and averages and announces the results Monday night at supper. He's even posted a baseball chart in the dining room that shows how everybody's doing. He graphs it all out with colored markers. And the little lines are starting to go up. Which means we're getting better, just like George said we would. Perhaps we will all live forever.

Emma just barely tolerates the game, though, sitting in her lawn chair behind home plate, barking out strikes and balls, and trying to catch the pitches—if the ball happens to land in her lap. If the ball doesn't, the batter has to go fetch the ball and throw it back out to George on the pitcher's hump. Emma doesn't budge from that lawn chair. George calls Emma our Catcher-Ump, whatever that means. Catcher-Ump, Pitcher's Hump, George and his umpteen baseball words. But I haven't seen that look on his face lately.

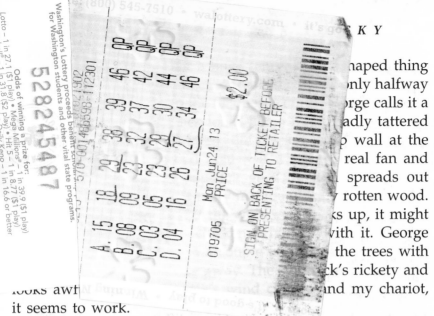

...aped thing
only halfway
...rge calls it a
...adly tattered
...p wall at the
real fan and
spreads out
rotten wood.
...s up, it might
...ith it. George
the trees with
...k's rickety and
...and my chariot,
...ooks awf... it seems to work.

My other job's running the barbecue, which I have a feeling is the only reason Emma plays. Food. George says if you don't play, you don't get to eat any hamburgers or hot dogs after the game. So Emma plays. I usually light the briquettes when George tells me to hang a yellow five on the nail in the innings box. Box. I have a hunch it's the smell of the barbecue that ends the game, although George swears we need to go a full nine innings every time.

Even though I don't officially play, I have to wear my yellow Spring Chicken T-shirt. George calls the T-shirts mandatory gear. Says we're all part of the same team. Everybody wears their T-shirt, including Emma. Kind of funny, really, all of us out here in our yellow Spring Chicken T-shirts playing baseball like a bunch of schoolkids. And the yellow looks good against the green grass and white lines, our big red house in the background and blue sky up above.

A few other kids from around town have started coming out to play with us lately, including that papergirl. At least she stuffs all that red hair of hers up under her baseball cap. But I still can't help seeing Amy when I look at her. So I try not to look. Look. Instead, I keep my eye on the ball, just like George tells everybody to do. I watch the ball dropping and rolling and being caught, and sometimes flying up into all that amazing blue sky, that ball a little white globe getting smaller and smaller way up above George's baseball diamond. Sometimes I wish I were that ball, sailing so high and far I'd never have to come back down to my half body, no music, and Amy gone forever.

☉

It's summer now, and the baseball thing of George's is getting out of hand. Hand. It's like that's the only reason we all ever moved in here—to play ball with nutty George on Sundays. Every Sunday morning George comes downstairs for breakfast wearing his Spring Chicken T-shirt, popping the inside of his mitt with his fist, whooping that it's game day and all of us should eat a big breakfast and be ready for action. All morning long he hurries around getting the bats and balls in order, the white lines on his diamond back to bright and straight, the dirt inside the lines raked smooth, the bases dusted off so white they hurt your eyes out there in the sun.

George puts briquettes in the barbecue for me and makes sure we have plenty of hot dogs and hamburgers and potato chips on hand. And then, at three o'clock sharp, rain or shine, George stands out on the pitcher's hump and blows a chrome whistle loud and long three times. S.O.S. Then, using a bullhorn he made from what was once an orange traffic cone, George tells the world the great Baseball Bash is about to begin. He pushes as much fanfare and enthusiasm into the air as he can through that silly plastic cone. These baseball games seem to have become George's sole reason for living. Nothing but baseball on his brain and in his blood.

George put benches on both sidelines for the players to sit on, and plumbed in an old porcelain drinking fountain next to the stopback. He even found an old popcorn maker—a big one, the kind they use in motion picture theaters and department stores—so now popping corn is on my list of baseball duties, along with hanging yellow numbers, and flipping burgers. George says it wouldn't be baseball without popcorn. But popcorn gets under my plates.

A couple weeks ago, George bought some old bleachers, hauled it home in pieces, and put it back together on the third-base side of his diamond. If anybody going by on the sidewalk slows to watch us, George calls a time-out and hurries over to fast-talk the onlooker onto his diamond, introducing them around, and promising he'll get them a T-shirt of their very own in time for the next game if they'd be so kind as to come back. Back. Nobody ever sits in the bleachers.

In addition to the whistle George wears on a string around his neck night and day, he's started carrying a little whisk broom around in his hip pocket all the time. He uses that little broom to swish off the bases three or four times a day. Every day. Not just Sundays. Sometimes I hear his broom swishing out there in the middle of the night, too.

When summer's over and it's pouring and cold out, I don't know what George will do with himself. But at least for now he's got a passion. Everybody needs a passion. God knows I'd love to be able to play and sing again. Spend every waking minute at Emma's shiny black Steinway in the living room. We could have Sunday afternoon concerts! With tea and cookies, and a fire in the fireplace. Then a nice supper after that, with brandy afterward, and cigarettes.

If I could sing again, I'd even volunteer to do the "Star Spangled Banner" from the pitcher's hump at the beginning of each of George's Baseball Bashes.

But George has gone overboard. The other day he found an honest-to-god flagpole somewhere, and put it up next to the drinking fountain. Now he runs a faded Old Glory up that flagpole before every game.

Right now I can hear George out there on his diamond blowing on that whistle of his, and it's not even two-thirty yet. He's standing on his pitcher's hump next to a big cardboard box the size of a dishwasher. I wonder what he's up to this time, blowing that whistle and waving like a fool-idiot for us to all come out. We should make him come get us. Go on strike.

But I go on out along with the others, Emma grumbling about how it's not even close to three o'clock, pulling her chicken shirt on, stretching her letters tight.

When we're all standing around the pitcher's hump, George says he's got a surprise for us inside the big cardboard box. Box. I can't imagine what it is. Perhaps he's got a whole team in there; a bunch of grade-school sluggers. He slits the box open with his pocketknife while he's going on about how we've made it to the big leagues and how we deserve this on account of how good we're all getting. That's all a line of bull, because nobody's really very good as far as I can tell. The kids who've been coming to play with us aren't even coming much anymore.

Then George lifts a bundle wrapped in clear plastic from the box, tears the plastic open, and holds up a baseball uniform—an honest-to-God real McCoy just like they wear on television, red pinstripes, funny yellow stirrup socks, the whole sonata. George tosses the uniform to Bert, then pulls out two more. Just above the numbers, each person's name is stitched onto the backs of the uniforms in wavy yellow lettering. And there's matching red baseball caps with yellow bills, and yellow belts, too. George tosses my uniform to me and I smell the brand-newness, see the tight stitching, my own name staring up at me from my lap, sunshine pouring down on all of us. That's when I know for sure something's not quite right with this baseball thing. With George.

But George is still digging headfirst in the cardboard box talking about how he wants to put up lights so we can play some night games, which gives the sport a whole different feel. Then he lifts the last uniform out of the box, pulls the plastic wrap away, and holds the uniform up for all of us to read the name. Name. Above the number 00 is the name "Beasley, B." The spy from down the street! He's talked her into playing with us! And right then, as if he'd cued her to enter stage left, I see Mrs. Beasley out the corner of my eye coming around the front of her school bus Cadillac, marching onto the baseball diamond with that huge dog of hers, waving her bracelets and yelling.

"One game! That's all I promised him," Mrs. Beasley is saying. "To get him off my back, I said I'd come play *one* game. But that's all. One game!"

Bert starts clapping, as if Mrs. Beasley's some star player we've all been waiting for, and then Fred and George and even big Emma join in clapping. I look over at Grace. But Grace isn't clapping. Something's wrong with Grace. I can feel it, see it in her eyes gone funny. Her new uniform's lying in the dirt at her feet, and she's trying to unbutton her blouse. But her fingers are getting all tangled and twisted in her yellow T-shirt that's covering her blouse, covering the buttons. Buttons. Her fingers keep digging, and there's a faraway look on her face that scares me. Grace is lost, gone somewhere else, a hollow shade of gray I've never seen before in her eyes.

But George blows his whistle right then and yells for us to go get dressed down and play ball. Bert starts wheeling me through the soft dirt, past Grace's candle already burning in the quart jar, across George's white lines. I look around and find Grace. But she's back to normal. She's picked up her new uniform and is starting toward the house with the rest of us, that hollow grayness in her eyes gone away, the sparkle back in the black.

GEORGE CASTOR

THE BARBECUE was smoking good, Clara almost disappearing in her apron and slippers turning burgers behind smoke, the smell of barbecue drifting out onto the diamond where we were all finishing up, everybody wearing their new uniforms and caps, the flag hanging limp on the pole, the day perfect.

Grace stepped up to the plate and took two practice swings. I wound up and pitched one slow. The ball arced high, bounced once, and landed in Emma's lap. "Ball one," Emma yelled, and threw the ball back to me.

I pitched another one that felt good. But Grace didn't swing. "Strike one!" Emma said.

I let go of the next pitch and knew right away the ball was gone. Grace swung hard, the wooden bat cracking loud as it hit the ball, popping the ball up toward the sun. The ball kept climbing, too, higher and higher. Way the hell up there. High above Hogan's star. Until, at last, the ball slowed to a stop, a tiny white speck hanging in the cloudless blue sky, nothing else up there but a single crow flying way off.

Then the ball gave in to gravity and started coming back down to earth, headed for Fred standing in the outfield. Fred started moving, looking up, concentrating, his engineer mind no doubt trying to calculate the speed of the ball falling, the arc it was making across the sky, and how far he had to move to be where the ball was going to wind up. The ball was so high up it took a long while to drop, giving Fred plenty of time to find the right place, raise his mitt, and wait. At the last minute, Fred took a small step to the side, moved his mitt a little higher, and the ball landed inside with a pop that echoed off the house. We all cheered. Emma bellowed to Grace who was already coming around second headed for third, "You're outta there!"

And then, as everybody was still cheering and clapping, I saw it. A heap of laundry lying on the grass in the outfield where Fred should have been. From the pitcher's mound, I knew. All sounds stopped and fell away. I heard only my own breathing. Dropped my mitt to the ground with a puff of dust. Tried to run. My feet not going fast enough across the infield. The soft dirt gone to mud or quicksand, pulling me back, holding me. Then I kicked glass and fire. Hot wax sprayed stinging up onto my face and hands. And everything broke to full speed again.

I ran to where Fred was lying in the outfield. But when I got to Fred, I barely slowed down. His face looking up out of that green grass told me what I already knew. No need to check for a pulse, or breath, or try CPR. None of that. No use. No reason to stop. So I kept going. Stepped right over Fred lying there dead on his back, and headed for Max. To get in and drive the hell away from the red house forever once and for all.

But that's when I saw white splattered all over my boots. White wax on black leather. Angel blood. I stopped. Fred lying not more that two paces behind me.

My body turned around, knelt down, and gathered Fred up. Then I was half running, half stumbling, half floating toward the front porch, a strength I had no idea where it came from holding on to Fred, carrying him. Fred's little-boy arms and legs flopping rag-doll-loose all around me. My body taking Fred's little-boy body up the front steps, past that barn-owl door knocker staring me down, and in onto the slate stones of the entryway. My knees and back were burning bad, but I only stopped for a second. Instead of putting Fred in on his bed, or on the couch in the living room, I kept going up. Up that cherry staircase. Past my own bedroom door, past Grace's and Bert's, past the bathroom with the red hairline and spinning numbers. On up the attic staircase. Up into the same empty attic room where I'd given Grace her box of sunrise. I wanted to keep going up farther, too. On up through the lath and plaster ceiling. Up through the rafters and shake roof, way up past the brick chimney where Hogan's wooden Christmas star was still rotting in the sun. I wanted to go up into the goddamned sun itself, taking Fred with me.

But the house stopped. No way to get any farther up. So I just stood there breathing, my lungs and throat full of flames, the pain in my back now shooting clear down both legs. My arms burning so bad I had to put Fred down on the dusty floor. I kicked the stairwell door shut and locked it, then went back over to Fred and knelt down beside him. I sat there on my knees, me alive and breathing, looking down at Fred, dead, headed on down the river.

Fred's uniform was spotless, as usual. His face clean-shaved, a red bow tie pushing up out of the neck of his uniform. His glasses cocked a little crooked on his face, but still held on his head by the black elastic strap. Clipped to the breast pocket of his uniform were the handful of pens and pencils and the folded piece of graph paper Fred was never without. In fact, the only thing I could see different about Fred lying there dead in front of me right then was a smudge of grass stain on his forehead where he must have hit when he fell, that and a few blades of grass poking out of the left hinge of his glasses. Fred was even still wearing his mitt. When I saw the white ball of Grace's pop fly cradled down inside Fred's mitt, I couldn't help but smile a little. Then I had to take my glasses off and wipe my eyes.

Footsteps sounded in the stairwell, and Emma hit the

attic door pounding on the wood and rattling the knob, screaming her husband's name over and over. Except calling him Freddy, instead of Fred. Crying, "My Freddy! My Freddy!"

CLARA PAULSON

IT'S GETTING dark out by the time George and Emma come down the big curved staircase. Down. George has his arm around Emma. Grace is coming behind, higher up the stairs. Three white baseball uniforms coming down. Angels in pinstripes with faces washed out descending to where Bert and I are down here at the bottom of the stairs looking up. I don't have to write down or hold up any words. Just looking at those three faces coming down the stairs, I know. Fred's dead.

Seeing George with his arm around Emma this way seems strange. Bert doesn't say anything. Nobody does. All five of us moving toward each other in silence, five angels coming together on the flagstones just inside the oval window in the front door.

Then the spell breaks, and Emma is wailing again, trying to fight her way past George and back up those stairs, calling out to Fred, begging her Freddy to come down, too. Grace helps George get Emma turned around and we all go into the living room and sit down. And that's all we do, just sit here, nothing to say, the only sound, Emma sniffling into George's red handkerchief and the ticking of the clock.

After a long time, Bert stands up. "Should I call somebody?" Bert asks. "The funeral home?" Bert's words are no more than a whisper, but too loud.

"No!" George says. "Just sit down." Bert sinks back into his chair. "No strangers are coming in here and taking Fred away," George says. "Not yet, at least. Not tonight."

Emma starts crying again. But quiet now, the way people sometimes cry without making any sound at all.

It gets darker outside. Grace goes over to the fireplace, strikes a match, and starts lighting candles one by one on the mantel. Then she gets a tray and puts all the candles except for one on the tray. The tray covered with candles burning looks just like a birthday cake. Grace carries the cake upstairs, taking all the light with her, except for the one candle burning in front of the mirror. And then George is gone, too, a blur hurrying down the back hallway and out the back door. The screen door slaps shut, then it's just Bert and Emma and I sitting here, each of us in our new mandatory gear, that solitary candle burning on the mantel. Grace's single flame shining a little on Emma's wet cheeks and eyelashes. Shining on all of us.

GEORGE CASTOR

I DIDN'T know what to do that night, everybody just sitting in the living room, stone-cold silence all around, all of us knowing Fred was still lying upstairs on the floor, dead. But I couldn't just sit there. So I decided to go up to him, take Fred some flowers up the way Grace took him a whole load of candles up.

Outside, I found a white five-gallon bucket in the shop, and cut as many flowers from around the house as would fit into the plastic mouth of that bucket. Marigolds, roses, dahlias, nicotiana, everything that was blooming. I even threw in some dandelions. Then I filled the bucket partway full of water and carried the flowers upstairs. Put the bucket on the floor at Fred's feet.

Grace was in the room with Fred, the window sill crowded full with her candles. Down on the floor, a circle of candles went all the way around Fred lying there in his baseball uniform, his mitt still on, that white pop fly of Grace's still peeking out of his mitt, a tiny crescent moon glowing dim.

I don't know why I nodded to Grace's words coming through the candlelit air heavy with roses and nicotiana. But I did.

"We ought to wash him," Grace said. "Get him dressed and ready to go." My head was still nodding when I noticed Grace already had soapy water steaming in a pan, and bowls of clear water sitting on the floor over by the window, candle-light shining off the bubbles and water. Next to the bowls were several towels.

"I'll go get some clothes," Grace whispered. And then it was just me and Fred in that room full of flames and flowers.

This was my chance to get out of there, to run one last time for good, the way I'd run off from my uncle Bill's funeral. But I just sat there looking down at Fred, at the little moon he was holding in his mitt.

So that's where I started while I was waiting for Grace to get back with the clothes. Fred's mitt. I eased the mitt off, being careful not to let that moon roll out. I put the mitt on the floor, pressed the leather closed. Fred's hand was moist but still a little warm. Putting Fred's hand back down on the floor palm-up is when I saw the nailheads—hundreds of nailheads scattered all across the attic floor burning the color of fresh-filed steel, burning my eyes so bad I stood up and almost fell trying to get over to the door fast. But Grace was coming in through the door as I was trying to go out, so I stopped, stepped back, stood there. Grace looked into my eyes. Then she lifted one of those tiny hands of hers and put her hand on my chest, the weight of a moth an inch from my heart. Grace stood there in the doorway, stopping me from running with just that one tiny hand steady against my ribs.

And then she spoke. "Emma helped me pick out the clothes," Grace said. So I stayed, a powdery handprint on the bib of my overalls.

We took off one of Fred's shoes and then the other, and then his socks. We unbuttoned his baseball shirt, Fred's bow tie underneath tied around the neck of the regular shirt he was wearing under his baseball jersey. I took Fred's pens and pencils out of his pocket, each pen making a little click when I pulled it loose from the pocket. I laid the pens and pencils on Fred's piece of graph paper over by his mitt. I unbuckled

Fred's baseball belt, and found another belt underneath, a belt and another pair of pants. Fred had been wearing his regular clothes under his baseball uniform all season long, through the heat of summer and everything. I had no idea. I pulled off the baseball pants, and then the other pair of pants, being careful to not let any of the stuff in Fred's pockets fall out on the floor. I folded the pants and put them by the mitt where Grace had folded his shirts and undershirt.

Fred looked smaller than I'd ever seen him, lying there in his underwear. His underwear soiled. I pulled off his underwear, put his underwear in a bowl of water. Then we cleaned Fred up down there, washing his skin with the warm soapy water, then rinsing him with the clear water, and then drying him off with fresh towels. We kept washing Fred all the way down to his feet. There was nothing to say. It was right. We did the same thing to Fred's upper body, his arms and his hands and his chest. I took off Fred's glasses so we could wash his face. I fogged the lenses with my breath, wiped each lens clean on my shirttail, then put Fred's glasses back on, sliding the earpieces gentle through his hair above his ears, easing the black strap over his head.

Then we dressed Fred, from his socks and shiny black shoes all the way up to a nice white shirt and a yellow bow tie I tied the best I could get. We combed Fred's hair. Smoothed his clothes out. Put the pencils and graph paper back in his breast pocket. Fred looked pretty good lying there.

I put Fred's mitt back on.

Grace tucked a tiny ear of dried corn into Fred's breast pocket, then gathered up the towels and bowls of water. "Leave one of the candles burning, would you?" she said. I nodded. Then Grace said good night, and left me alone with Fred, with the smells of soap and roses and moon on mitt leather.

☙

I sat there next to Fred most of the night. By the time it

was getting light outside, I knew what I had to do. I went out to the shop and rummaged around until I'd found a set of black iron gate hinges, some pine one-by-twelves, several cedar two-by-twos, a quart can of varnish, some wood glue, and a box of black sheet metal screws.

Back in the house, Grace and Clara and Bert were up sitting at the dining room table. So I told them what I wanted to do with Fred. Emma hadn't come out of her room yet, but I could hear the muffled drone of her television going already. She was up. Nobody said a word for a long time when I told them. Not even Bert. Then I heard Grace's words coming through the air across the table, the chandelier overhead jingling a little.

"That's fine," she was saying. "How it should be. Headed on around, all of us helping him get along."

Bert looked at me.

"I don't know, George," Bert said. "I'm sure there are regulations about stuff like that."

"You know something, Bert," I said. "I don't give a damn. All I know is that Fred belongs here, on this land, not in some marble orchard clear across town."

"How it should be," Grace repeated. "Going on around."

After a minute, Clara tapped her pad where she'd written the letters O and K. Bert swallowed, looked at Grace and Clara, back at me, then Bert nodded.

☙

By two o'clock, I had the outer pieces cut, sanded, varnished, and standing outside to dry. I'd glued and pipe-clamped the two-by-two frame together on the table saw. Sitting up on the saw like that, the frame reminded me of the model airplanes I built as a kid back in Omaha. Except this one was almost big enough to fly.

I was light-headed from the smell of varnish and fresh-cut pine and cedar. I knew I should open the door, or a window. Get some fresh air. But I didn't. Because Grace did.

She pushed the door open with a squeak and stepped into the shop. I smelled mowed grass, and summer. Standing there in the doorway, sunlight bright behind her, Grace could have been a girl, her knobby elbows, pigtails hanging down.

"Let's use this to line it," Grace said, shaking open a folded white cloth and holding it up, everything except her fingers disappearing behind all the white. "My mother's wedding tablecloth," Grace said. "I never used it." Her words came through the cloth at me, that tablecloth that was older than either of us. So white. Creases sharp and straight. Packed away in some cedar-lined hope chest for two lifetimes.

"Clara says she has an afghan we can use for a pillow," Grace said, lowering the cloth back down. "And Bert wants to read something."

I couldn't find any words in my mouth, so I just stood there watching Grace refolding her mother's tablecloth, being careful to use the same creases. "We haven't told Emma yet," Grace said, laying the cloth on the workbench. "But I will." And then she left. The shop door shut again. The smell of varnish burned in my nose and eyes.

I turned around and slammed my fist down hard on the workbench. Dust swirled up through sunlight coming in through the window above the bench. I hit the bench again and again until the side of my fist hurt and tingled and the sunlight coming in was a slanted shaft of solid dust floating.

"Goddamnit, Fred!" I grabbed a tape measure and threw it as hard as I could at the window. One of the small panes of glass in the window exploded and the tape was gone, dust and air and the smell of varnish being sucked out through the jagged hole in the glass, a river of dust gushing out that hole, sunlight and sawdust trying to pull me out, too. I wanted to punch my fists through each of the other panes of glass in that window, two panes at a time, shoving my arms out all the way up to my armpits, then pulling my arms back in, the glass tearing my shirt and slicing my arms to ribbons.

But I saw a spider hanging upside down on a web in the lower left corner of the window's peeling frame. The web shined in the sunlight. I leaned close and saw that the web had been patched here and there, places where the even, circular pattern was out of kilter. The spider didn't move. Such patience, waiting days for dinner to fly in and get tangled up. Or was this spider dead, too? Just like Fred. I blew into the web. The glass behind the web fogged, and the spider scurried down into the corner of the window, then stopped. The glass cleared. I wet a small wood chip with my tongue and flicked the chip into the web. The strands rainbowed as the chip caught and hung in the air. The spider hurried out toward the chip, then stopped an inch away. I blew on the web to get the chip going again, but the spider didn't move.

"You're no dummy, are you?" The sound of my voice sent the spider crawling down into a crack in the window frame and out of sight.

I went outside to check the varnish. The sunlight coming up off the concrete driveway was so bright I had to squint. But it was good to be outside. The pieces of pine leaning up against the shop wall were spotted with black gnats, but I didn't bother to pick the gnats off. I'd sand the bastards off and put on another light coat. The varnish would dry in time.

I went back into the shop to take off the pipe clamps. I didn't have the first clamp off when the shop door blew open and Emma came in yelling at me. "I won't stand for it!" she said. "It's a sick thing you're doing! Sick! Sick! Sick!"

"Wait a minute, Emma," I said. "Calm down. People used to do this all the time."

"Well, nowadays we have funeral homes!" Emma said.

"And I can't stand them," I said. "You know why? When my wife Dora died, they wanted a picture. So I gave them a goddamned picture. You know what they did then? They painted Dora up like a whore and kept her in a cooler for the better part of a week. I couldn't sleep, knowing she was lying down there by herself, ice-cold."

"Well, that's better than having him right upstairs in the same house!" Emma cried.

"You slept in the same bed with the man most your life, didn't you?" I said.

"Yeah, but he wasn't dead!" Emma said, her last word slamming into me. "I mean, it's like you're keeping him a secret up there!" she yelled. "It's sick!"

"A secret? What the hell are you talking about?" I said. "Fred's one of us, Emma—family! He doesn't belong to anybody else."

She dabbed at her eyes with a Kleenex.

"We have the right to bury him any way we want," I said.

"I don't want to bury him! I want him back!" She started sobbing. "I want him back! I don't want my Freddy to be dead."

That word came again, harder. I reached out and grabbed Emma by the arms and shook her.

"Goddamnit, Emma! Don't you know that's not the way it works? When somebody dies, they're gone! You hear me? Gone. Forever! You don't get them back! It's done. Over. Fred's gone! He's never coming back. Not today, not tomorrow, not ever! Like Ralph, and Dora, and my uncle Bill . . . all of them gone! *Forever.* Gone down the river and never coming back!"

I stopped and sucked in varnish fumes and dust.

"They're all gone! Just like Fred. So there's no use sniffling about it. Let's get him buried and get on with life!" I was slamming the workbench again, my throat raw. Emma had stopped breathing, and was backing away from me toward the door, her eyes gone huge, no sound at all coming out of her open mouth. When she was through the shop door, she turned and ran to the house, one hand on each side of her head. Then Emma's wailing let loose again, coming through the air in loud gushes as she went up Clara's ramp, threw the screen door back against the house, and disappeared inside.

In the time it took for that screen door to fall shut, I tasted rain and cottonwood in my mouth, heard the hushed whisper of river water flowing swollen in the middle of the night. I closed my eyes and saw the surface of a river running silver beneath a full moon, Fred or somebody floating away face-down. Then the screen door slapped hard into place and there was nothing but the smell of varnish and body odor and my aunt Bertha's perfume burning the raw spot at the far back of my throat.

CLARA PAULSON

I HEAR her loud out on my ramp. Loud. She's coming this way. Hurrying, which Emma never does, so I roll around to see what's going on, but she's already on me. This huge woman draped in a dotted smock drops to her knees in front of me, reaches her doughy arms out, and squeezes. She squeezes my steering wheel, my armrests, my tubes, my dead skin. My pencil and pad go flipping off into space. Emma shoves her face into my lap and bawls like a little girl, making my chair tremble, my bell jingle a little.

My lap's wet and warm when Emma at last lifts her head. Staring up at me I see a woman I do not know, her eyes pink and puffed and begging me to say something, anything. But I can't because she just knocked my voice to the floor. Floor. So I reach out my good hand and hold Emma's round cheek in my palm. Her cheek is wet and warm, big as a grapefruit. I sit here, holding half her face, not knowing what to do next. Emma keeps kneeling there looking at me with stuck-together lashes and bloodshot eyes that seem more lost and scared than any eyes I've ever seen before in my whole life. For the first time, I think perhaps Emma did love Fred on some level the rest of us couldn't see. But it's hard to know for sure.

Grief makes people do strange things. Like George right now out there building a casket for Fred so we can bury him ourselves.

When I look down, Emma's gone out of my lap. Lap. Just a damp place on my robe. I hear the organ music soap operas use between scenes swelling up loud, but can't tell if the music's coming from Emma's room or from inside my own head. My pad's on the floor halfway across the room flipped open to the page with those two letters I think now perhaps I should have never written. That black O and black K. Saying OK to George's insane idea about burying Emma's dead husband in our own backyard.

GEORGE CASTOR

I HAD never dug a grave before, not for a human being, but I didn't figure there was much to it. A hole about the size of the door, straight down, six feet or so. I talked Bert into helping me dig Fred's grave out in the side lawn, way back behind the chicken coop among the fir trees. It was dark, and I was tired, but I wanted to get it done before morning. I lit two lanterns, put one on the ground, and hung the other from a nail in the scoreboard. It wasn't five minutes before moths were bouncing against the glass chimneys. Hundreds of moths, pulled out of the night by hot mantles glowing white. Those tiny moth bodies threw shadows the size of bats all over the ground and across Bert's face and arms, moth shadows all over both of us.

We cut and peeled back the sod, stacking the pieces of sod at the base of one of the big firs. We started shoveling dirt out, throwing the dirt to both sides of the hole. The soil was good, this part of town being so close to the creek.

I moved the one lantern closer so we could see down inside the hole as we went deeper. We worked with our backs to each other, which gave us plenty of room for our shovel handles to clear each other. We kept digging down, stopping often to catch our breath, my throat still sore, my back stiff. But I wanted to get Fred buried and get on with things.

We carved the walls straight as we went down. The smooth marks our shovels left in the dirt walls caught the light from the lantern, dozens of half moons shining all around. We went deeper, our piles of dirt growing higher on each side of the hole, the smell of dirt and sweat heavy inside my nose. By the time the moon rose through the trees, Bert and I were standing chest-deep in that doorway headed for China, both of us breathing hard, my back throbbing bad.

"Look at that moon, will you, Bert?" I said. "Gorgeous as hell up there, isn't it?"

Bert pulled a sleeve across his forehead, but didn't say anything.

"Hard to believe there's been people up there walking around on it," I said. "Walking on the goddamned moon. What will humanity think of next?"

Bert went back to shoveling. I wondered why he was so quiet tonight. Probably just tired, like I was.

A while later, the lantern hanging from the scoreboard ran out of fuel. We both stopped digging and watched the mantle's glow fade, the moths in the air fading away, too, going from bright white to gray to gone altogether. I reached out and turned the other lantern off. Everything went black for a second, then shadows and edges came back. No moths at all anymore.

"Ought to be enough moonlight to see by," I said, looking up at the moon hanging just above the trees. The sky around the moon was a pale purple-blue, the stars washed out a little, but shining decent for in town. The moon was just a little over half-full, but I could see the face up there. That old man, half a face staring down at us, one eye watching the two of us digging a goddamned grave.

"Think heaven's like this, George?" Bert's voice came loud and sudden out of the quiet.

"Heaven?" I turned. "Who the hell knows?"

"Fred must by now," Bert said, his teeth and hair glowing in the moonlight. "Don't you think?"

I didn't answer Bert, because I saw that picture in Aunt Bertha's black Bible again. Except that Bible was floating faceup on a river, moonlight and water making the picture ripple a little, the flames and chunky angels all dancing and shimmering, the current pulling the Bible along.

✺

An hour or two later, I stopped and threw my shovel out, heard the shovel bounce on the grass. "Deep enough," I said. Bert threw his shovel out, too. Then I realized we'd dug ourselves in, got lost in the digging and forgot all about getting out. My head was a ways below the top of the grave. I tried pulling myself up the side, but my arms were too shot from digging half the night, my back pretty much gone. Bert tried giving me a stirrup lift, but as I shoved down, Bert yelped like a dog, and my foot slipped through his hands. Bert fell back, holding his neck.

"What happened?" I said.

"It ain't serious," Bert said. "Happens every now and then. Dang neck goes out." His voice was coming up out of the black where the moonlight didn't reach. "But it hurts like nails going in at first. I just got to lie here still for a while till the pain eases up. I'll be okay."

I tried to climb out on my own a few more times, but it was no use.

I could just make out Grace's bedroom window at the far side of the yard. From this distance, I knew yelling wouldn't wake her. Probably just wake the neighbors and bring the cops. So I scooped up a handful of damp dirt from the bottom of the hole and packed the dirt into a ball. I lobbed the dirt ball at the house. It was a lousy position to throw from, and Bert lying between my feet didn't make it any easier. I threw a couple more dirt balls, but they fell short of the house. I tried a different position and this time hit the flower box below Grace's window. The dirt ball left a dark mark on the yellow paint that I could just barely see in the moonlight. I scooped up more dirt and threw again. But I hit one of the windowpanes and heard glass explode inside. *Shit.*

Grace pulled back the curtain and opened the window. She leaned out, the skunk held in her arms, the moon making the white stripes bright as paper.

"Out here!" I yelled as loud as I could, throwing another dirt ball that fell apart before it even got close to the house. And then the hens in the chicken coop started squawking and making such a racket I was sure a fox was inside. But then the chickens went quiet, and Grace's window was empty, just the curtain moving a little.

CLARA PAULSON

IN THE morning I come out and see it over by the piano in the living room, sitting on a low cart made out of what looks like bicycle wheels and an old door. I stop. Fred's casket. The wood's beautiful, shiny blonde with dark knots the color of a bassoon. And running along all the edges are black screw-heads that look almost like stitching from here.

I roll over to have a closer look, and see three agates glued in a cluster to the lid. Then I recognize the rocks. They're the ones Fred found when all of us went swimming up at the waterfalls last summer. I remember Fred showing the agates to me, proud as a boy, explaining how the running water had worn the edges smooth, polished the stones. The agates on the lid look wet, the way they must have looked with water flowing over them when Fred found them. Just below the agates, somebody's decoupaged seven words, each word spelled out using single letters cut from newspapers or maga-zines and glued on side by side:

FAREWELL FRED, DEAR FRIEND.
GOING ON AROUND.

The three Fs are black. The big D's bright green. The two
Ls and the comma's a sort of mustard yellow. The periods
are square and black, too big, and glued on a little crooked.
The letters making up the bottom three words are all the same
color—turquoise. I know who did the decoupage. Reading
those seven words I want to cry. Say good-bye to Fred. I feel
crying starting to swell in the back of my throat. But I swallow, blink hard, try to swallow the swelling back down. Then
I see a pile of yellow powder on the lid a little ways below
the words.

I reach out my good hand and touch the wood first. Smooth
as piano keys. I touch the agates and feel cool water. The
seven words are smooth beneath the finish. I take a pinch of
the yellow powder. Cornmeal. I rub my fingertips together
and the powder falls back onto the wood, leaving my fingertips silky and covered with a pale dust. I lick my fingertips
clean.

My hand moves to the edge, feels stitching, the screws. My
fingers find the crack, and push in, lift the lid a little. The
lid's light. Through the crack I can see Grace's white tablecloth
dimpled with silver staples along the edge. Then I see a black
dress shoe shining like the ace of spades and jump back. The
lid bangs shut. He's already in there! I want to roll away!
Quick. I struggle with my steering wheel, try to find the crystal
knob. But then I see Grace sitting on the chair over by the
piano. She's been there the whole time! Watching me reading
her seven words, touching Fred's agates, messing up her
cornmeal.

Before I can get away, Grace is saying something.

"Emma picked out his favorite clothes," Grace says. Her
words are slow coming across the room, each word calm. I
don't know what to say or do, so I just look at Grace, tiny
on that big chair. "He's all ready to go," she says. "Following
the sun on around. Where we're all going. Nothing to be
afraid of. Just a big hoop going around and around."

I want to get out of the room, away from the black shoes
and black screwheads, and Grace's black eyes talking about

circles going around. But my arm won't move right. Can't find my crystal knob. So I look away and just sit here. Emma's television isn't mumbling away on the other side of the wall the way it should be. The whole house is hushed this morning. Outside it looks like it's going to be a nice day. Day. Sunday, I think. George's wind chimes moving a little, but not enough to make any music.

"Nice day for a departure, isn't it?" Grace says, smiling now, as if she's somehow happy Fred's dead.

My good hand finds my knob and starts to crank, but before I move very far, there's a knock at the front door. I look. It's her! The oval pane of glass is a picture frame holding a little girl in a white dress, flowers in her hands. She's looking right at me, red hair shining. My hand lets go of the crystal knob and comes up in front of me, waves for Amy to come in, come home to me at last. My darling girl. She does. But a gray pony lunges inside behind her, almost knocking Amy over, sniffing the air, rearing and jingling. Wait. It's not a pony. It's a dog. The size of a pony. Then Mrs. Beasley is coming through the door and the pony fits. Except Mrs. Beasley's not dripping in colors the way she usually is. She's dressed in black from hat to shoes. A huge white mum pinned to her hat bobs as she sneezes. Amy blesses Mrs. Beasley and closes the door.

☙

They roll Fred out the back door, down my ramp, across the driveway, and out onto the side lawn, George and Bert pushing from behind, Grace on one side, one of her hands on the casket lid near the agates and turquoise words and the pile of cornmeal going flat and sifting down over the edge, her other hand holding a flame in a red glass, the kind Fish-eaters use to send up prayers to souls.

Emma's walking right behind George and Bert, big as ever in a long pink dress, carrying a bouquet of red roses, the roses quivering in her hands. Emma looks more like she's going to a wedding than her own husband's funeral. Mrs. Beasley's walking along next to Emma, the white mum bouncing and bobbing up on her black hat, her face lost somewhere inside the dark shadow of her hat brim. A black handkerchief going in and out of that shadow, dabbing as if it's her husband in this shiny blonde box instead of Emma's. The papergirl's walking alongside me in her *Appeal-Tribune* baseball cap and white dress, the two of us bringing up the rear.

Bert and George roll Fred over to the grave they dug last night and all of us gather beside the casket. I can tell nobody knows what to do next. Next. The casket's shiny bright in the sunlight, except for a dull spot the size of a supper plate where the cornmeal dust is all spread out. In the middle of the dull spot a small handprint is shining bright, too.

Then, with no count or downbeat, I hear music coming out of nowhere. Singing. No organ. Just an a cappella soprano voice wavering weak at first, but then getting louder and louder until that voice is strong and full and singing out the words of "Swing Low Sweet Chariot," some of the sweetest singing I've ever heard. I think perhaps the good Lord has sent an angel down to help us out with what to do next, but that voice is not an angel singing. It's Emma! A voice I never knew she had coming out from behind her bouquet of quaking roses, Emma's eyes closed, her mouth a perfect choir-boy oval, tears rolling down her round cheeks and dropping into those roses. Emma! Begging that chariot to swing low and carry her home. Bless her sweet heart.

When Emma finishes singing, nobody says a word, the others probably thinking the same thing I am. How I never in my life would have thought Emma could sing like that. A gift of pure gold hidden away deep down inside that obese body.

Emma's words are still in my head when George clears his throat and starts to talk.

"Fred . . ." George says. "We'll miss you, buddy. But . . ." George tries to say something more, but he can't, because his chin and bottom lip start quivering and he has to look away, wipe at his eyes. Grace takes a step over closer to George and finishes his sentence with a handful of such short and simple words I know they are some of the truest words I've ever heard. . . .

"But we're all right behind you," is what Grace says.

⑤

George on the verge of tears at Fred's funeral was the last I saw of George's grief. It's taken the rest of us some time to come back up after losing Fred, but not George. George jumped right back in following the funeral. And for the five or six sunny Sundays that were left of summer, George was out on that diamond trying to get his baseball thing going again, plunging back in as if nothing had happened, as if Fred never died. Doing his Sunday morning whooping routine through the house, whacking his mitt, shouting for all of us to get a move on. And everybody but Emma went along and played. But it wasn't the same.

George started handing out fancy awards for most improved player, best batting average, most RBIs. He handed the awards out at Saturday night banquets. Got us all baseball shoes with steel teeth on the soles. Had Fred's old uniform framed and hung on the wall in the living room, Fred's number and name behind glass. George even hooked up an outdoor speaker system and played classical music starting a couple hours before the games were supposed to begin. Then pretty soon George was playing music through the speaker system most of the week, standing out on his diamond in his baseball uniform all by himself, listening to the music.

George told me from now on we were barbecuing steaks instead of hot dogs. He brought home expensive wine, smoked salmon, and gallons of ice cream. He brought home balloons, too. The shiny kind that look like aluminum foil. He tied those balloons to everything—the barbecue, the bleachers, the stopback. He even tied a balloon to the back of his baseball belt. That balloon floated above George's head everywhere he went, flashing and shining. George tried everything he could to breathe life back into his baseball games. But it didn't work.

It's almost November, and the fall rains have washed everything out, put a stop to George's baseball. The rains have turned his diamond to mud and puddles and leaves blowing and floating. Washed away all George's straight white lines. Left his bases standing in water, his pitcher's hump an island.

But George hasn't given up. Right now, in fact, he's standing out there on that muddy pitcher's hump in the wind and pouring rain all by himself, blowing his silver whistle for the game to begin. Then he stops blowing and a baseball drops out of his mitt and rolls down off the pitcher's hump into a puddle. The ball bobs and floats. George doesn't move. Thunder shudders loud. I can't bear to watch anymore, so I spin my wheel and come in by Emma's beautiful black piano. I sit here and listen to the rain outside, feel electricity in the air, gathering in the hairs on my arms and neck. And then my good arm reaches out slow toward the glowing row of keys, and with one finger I play middle C. I hold the key down for a long time, listening to the note fading away, not enough courage to play another. Then thunder cracks loud outside and I pull my hand back.

George Castor

STANDING OUT on the ball diamond getting soaked to the marrow was when I got the idea. The wind had just blown Clara's scoreboard out of the fir tree, shearing my PA speaker off the tree, yellow numbers spilling everywhere, the music all of a sudden stopped. Maybe it was the sudden silence that put the idea in my head, helped me figure out a way to keep the baseball games going all winter long no matter what the weather. The same way they did it in the big leagues: a roof. A huge domed roof over the whole goddamned diamond. That way Grace and the others wouldn't have any lame excuses about lousy weather keeping them from coming out and playing ball.

So I stood there on the mound thinking how to rig up a roof, my jersey splattered to the knees with mud, my mitt soaking wet, the water standing all around the mound being beat to a froth by rain coming in buckets. Thunder cracked and rolled loud, the storm socking in, wind whipping the trees, the sky damned near black. But I just stood there. Maybe a charge of lightning would strike me down and I wouldn't have to think about my new roofing project, or about Ralph, or how I'd pushed Fred into playing ball in the first place.

The wind got worse and the backstop shuddered and groaned. One of the yellow ropes snapped, a thread floating free out in the wind and rain. Then another of the yellow ropes broke loose. I could hear the wind working on that backstop, whistling through the rusty Cyclone fencing, through the old nail holes and tears in the corrugated tin, the rain hammering so loud against the tin the sound was louder than the thunder booming all around.

The wind blew harder still, that backstop creaking and pulling against the other two ropes, the wind trying to push me off that pitcher's mound. But I stayed put. Then a lightning bolt flashed white-hot bright. The earth shifted. Those last two yellow ropes snapped at the same time. And that whole goddamned backstop started coming my way, tearing loose from the chicken coop and falling forward. I couldn't get my legs engaged fast enough to run because I was cold clear through. So I shut my eyes. The next thing I heard was a slap that blew both eardrums out, filled my mouth and nose and eyes full of water and mud and uprooted chickweed. And then I was down on my knees, water washing over me. Silver water! Me headed on down that river once and for all. Grace's Rhode Island White chickens gone loony squawking and flapping out through a hole ripped in the south wall of that coop, those goddamned chickens turning into pudgy white angels coming down to help take me up. *Hallelujah!*

White Hens in a Rainstorm

It is night. An old woman wearing a white blouse, a dark skirt, and a scarf tied around her head hunches forward and hurries through rain and wind. She is barefoot. Under one arm, she carries a dark blanket. The woman splashes through standing water until she comes to where the ground is littered with twisted sheets of tin and splintered wood. A yellow rope floats on a muddy puddle. She pauses, then hurries around the wreckage toward a small wooden shack near a handful of large fir trees. Outside the shack she stops, looks around, and calls out into the rain ringing loud on the tin. She waits a moment more, then ducks and disappears through a dark hole in the side of the shack where some boards have been ripped away.

After a short time, a yellow-orange light begins to glow from inside the shack. The light builds. A shadow moves. Scraps of muffled voice drift out through the glowing hole into the rain—someone calling a dog or cat.

A few seconds later, three white chickens streak one by one across the yard, flap up, and disappear into the hole. Shadows flutter and dance inside. The voice comes again, but higher-pitched now, as if spoken to small children. Then the blanket drops down from inside, closing the yellow-orange mouth in the wall. The blanket moves a little, billows, then stops moving and hangs motionless. A light-colored ring woven into the center of the dark blanket and now illuminated from behind by the light inside the shack glows out into the dark. Below the luminous ring, a yellow zero floating on a puddle rocks in the wind.

CLARA PAULSON

EMMA'S HOLED up in her room. Ever since Fred died, Emma stays in there for hours on end. End. Back to watching her soap operas. I hear the television, the organ music. Emma hardly ever comes out. It's as if she doesn't live here anymore. Oh, she comes out to eat—God knows Emma wouldn't miss that—but she doesn't say much, and then she goes right back into her room, to her television, and closes the door. Right after we buried Fred, she used to walk out across the side yard to Fred's grave, that widowed woman huge and teetering on those little feet, walking through the grass and mud and old baseballs. I'm not sure what Emma did out there, pray perhaps, or cuss Fred for dying on her. Emma just stood out there under those big old trees for a while, then turned and came wobbling back toward the house. But Emma doesn't go out to Fred's grave anymore. Ever since that storm blew George's stopback down and gave George that awful cold, I haven't seen Emma going out at all.

I feel sorry for Emma in a way, but you can't help somebody like Emma. They don't want your help. Perhaps they like to suffer. When you try, Emma just waves her big arms at you and bellows to leave her alone. I asked Emma once,

"U WANT 2 TALK?" but she just waved her arms and was gone. So who knows? Perhaps this is Emma's bitter pill for being such a bitter person her whole life. Grace claims Emma'll come around, with time. But I'm not so sure. When Emma was crying on my lap that one day, I thought maybe she was going to change. And then the way she sang at the funeral. But dying only seems to change the living for a week or two. And then life goes on. On. Everybody back to normal, thinking you're never going to die.

I never thought I'd be thankful for this drenching Oregon rain, but I am now. Because it's finally put a stop to George's baseball rampage once and for all. This morning, another gray Sunday, George didn't even bother to come downstairs until almost noon. He looks awful, still in his robe, hunched over a bowl of oatmeal in there at the table, his spoon clinking, his lips slurping loud on his coffee. I've never seen George like this before, bony and washed out. Out. Perhaps we should have kept playing baseball with him. Perhaps us refusing to play in the rain is what's wrong with George. But I don't think so. I think it's something else. Like Grace said, something's eating at him from the inside.

GEORGE CASTOR

I WOKE to a humming sound coming up through the floor from downstairs. Three A.M. Thanksgiving just a few days off. I lay in bed and listened to the humming. Outside it was raining, but this sound wasn't the rain. This was more like the dishwasher running downstairs in the kitchen. But I'd started the dishwasher myself last night after dinner. It had run its cycle and shut off before I went to bed. Maybe the dishwasher had shorted out or something, kicked back on in the middle of the night.

I'd finally licked that cold, but still didn't feel a hundred percent. My stomach was bothering me. And ever since getting soaked that day the backstop blew down, my back was worse than ever, as if moisture had somehow worked its way inside my backbone and now had no way out. The vertebrae rusting and flaking and grinding away.

It had been raining solid for a long time now. I didn't know what to do with myself. The house was cold and damp, seemed too big and quiet. People shuffling around without saying much, Emma no more than a ghost. Maybe the whole thing was starting to unravel. I knew I had to do something before the others lost interest and moved out on me, but I wasn't sure exactly what.

I'd never get back to sleep without knowing what the hell was making that humming sound, louder now that the rain had stopped, so I got up to go find out. I checked the bathroom down the hall to see if somebody'd left the fan on, but the bathroom was quiet and dark. Halfway down the staircase, I stopped. Moonlight coming in through the window above the front door was skim milk on the steps. The moon was half-full, the same way the moon was the night Bert and I were digging Fred's grave. Except dark chunks of clouds were blowing across the moon now, a break in the storm. Winter socking in.

Downstairs, I pushed the kitchen door open and looked in. Nothing but the blue numbers on the stove glowing, moonlight shining silver on the dogwood branches through the French doors. I checked the downstairs bathroom. That fan was off, too.

The humming got louder as I came to the basement door at the end of the hall. The sound was coming from behind the door, somewhere down in the basement. I opened the door, the light from the bare bulb in the stairwell blinded me for a second, the sound louder now from down below. Then I recognized it. The washing machine. Somebody'd turned on the washing machine and the damned thing was stuck. I went down the stairs, the air smelling of damp concrete and dirt. More light was coming from under the laundry room door. I stopped and listened. Sure enough, the washer was running on the other side of the door. I pulled the door open, took two steps in, then my blood went to ice.

Standing in front of the washing machine was a skin-covered skeleton. Buck naked. Back to me. Long gray hair hanging wild from its head. Hogan's ghost! I wanted to slam the door shut and run. But then the ghost turned its head and looked right at me. I stopped breathing altogether. No clothes. No braids. Nothing but those black eyes telling me who it was.

"Hello, George," Grace said—except it wasn't Grace's voice. "How are you doing today?" She smiled. I tried not to look at her breasts hanging down to the middle of her stomach, two bladders with the air gone out. But I couldn't help myself. And lower down, a patch of gray hair so thin it barely covered her. And then the legs coming out, bony stilts, her tiny hands hanging beside the stilts, nothing moving but her mouth.

"What's wrong?" she asked, coming across the room toward me.

I took a step back. "Nothing," I said. "Just heard the washer and came down."

"Of course," she said. "I'm doing my wash."

"At three in the morning?" I said.

Grace went still. I could see her thinking. "What?" she said.

"It's three in the morning," I said.

"But—it is?" Grace said. "I have to do my wash. I don't have anything to wear."

I took a bedsheet from a basket, went closer, and held the sheet out to her. "Here," I said.

"What's this for?" she asked.

"Wrap yourself up," I said.

"Why?" she said.

"You don't have any clothes on, Grace," I said.

"I'm doing my wash," she said. "I don't have anything to wear."

In her eyes something had changed in a horrible way. "Grace," I said. "Are you all right?"

"Of course, George. I'm fine," she said. "I'm doing my wash. I don't have anything to wear."

"Here," I said again. "Wrap yourself in this."

"That's not dirty," she said.

"It's cold down here," I said, moving over to put the sheet around her shoulders as the washer shut off and spun to a stop. But as I touched her, she jumped, and my name came out of her.

"George!" she said, her voice different now, the old Grace back. "What brings you down here?"

I didn't know what to say, so I repeated what I'd already said. "I heard the washer."

"Oh, you need to use it?" she said. "Well, I'm just about

through. I'll be up in a minute. It must be about time for dinner. Who's cooking tonight?"

"It's three in the morning, Grace," I said.

"What?" she said, slowly looking down at herself.

And then she was gone, just the sheet lying in a pile at my feet, the floor overhead creaking a little, and the harsh light of the laundry room's bare bulb shining up at me from dozens of tiny round mirrors spilled on a dark cloth on the concrete floor.

CLARA PAULSON

I HEARD people up last night. Voices below me in the basement. Rumbling coming through the floor. Footsteps light as a cat's. Perhaps it was my head, because this morning everything seems normal. All of us eating breakfast. George a little quiet. And he keeps glancing over at Grace. Perhaps they were the ones up last night. Wonder what those two were up to. Sneaking around the house, a couple of teenagers. Grace and George, I can't imagine. Funny how sex means so much when you're young and foolish. How it's no big deal later on. It's kind of sad what sex does to the world, what one night of it did to my whole life.

GEORGE CASTOR

TWO WHITE tugboats with pink crosses painted on them float at the curb in front of the house. The tugs are ambulances, lights and sirens on top. The streets are full of water. Purple water. All the streets are canals. I stand on the front porch watching the tugs. I can't move because the soles of my boots are nailed and glued to the porch boards. Two bodies are being loaded down into the dark hulls of the tugs, each body draped in a huge waffle, whipped cream and a great big maraschino cherry on top of each waffle. Then the tugs chug off one behind the other through the purple water. But the tugs don't head up the hill toward the hospital. The tugs go downtown instead, toward Bingham & Bristol, no lights flashing, no sirens, just the sound of diesel engines churning water.

I look down. My arms and legs are broomsticks inside my clothes, all my flesh gone away. And my boots aren't just nailed to the floor. My boots are nailed to bathroom scales that are bolted to the floor. The scales show ninety-eight pounds, and there's a tiny picture of me as a boy standing next to my uncle Bill in the little window below the numbers. I turn to run, to get away from the scales and picture. The screeching of nails and wood splintering are loud all around

307

as I pry my feet loose and stumble into the house through the front door screaming names, almost tripping on the splintered wood and silver nails, springs and numbers flying everywhere.

The slate entryway is licorice. The smell of licorice in the air.

I run into the living room. Dozens of little moving men dressed in yellow coveralls and black waistcoats with the words *B & B Funeral Directors* stitched in silver onto the backs are packing up the house. My house. Filling yellow boxes with everything we own. Grace's candles going in. Bert's dead cat. Emma's TV. Clara's wheelchair in pieces going into one of those yellow boxes, too. The moving men all look the same: four feet tall, stocky with blue hair, red eyes, pig noses, and thick, pointy ears. The moving men all jerk as they work, all of them whistling in unison, some catchy tune I recognize, but can't place.

In minutes, everything in the house is packed up, carried outside, and loaded into two huge, pink semi trailers idling in the driveway. Then the back doors on the trucks roll shut and the trucks drive off through the purple water. The little yellow men swim along behind, their hands and boots splashing in sync, their voices all singing the same catchy song, the silver words on their waistcoats turning dark purple in the water. Then there's nothing but bubbles floating on the purple water where the men were. Bubbles and black coats and silver letters.

I run back into the house, a few pieces of porch boards still hanging on to my boot soles. A realtor with red lips the size of hot dogs is pointing out all the "charming" features of the house to a young couple. The man keeps saying, "Terrific! Fantastic! We like it. We like it." I yell at the couple and the realtor that this is my house, and for them to get the hell out. But they can't hear me, no matter how loud I yell. I try to grab the blabbering realtor and shake her, but she is air, or my hands can't quite reach. The realtor keeps talking and smiling and batting her eyelids that are covered with ants. A little smudge of lipstick on her front tooth keeps flashing, a stoplight blinking between those huge lips.

Then the realtor stops talking, and the couple laughs, a toothy, nervous laughter that comes out purple in the air. The same color as the water outside. The couple says they will take it, then they kiss each other. Newlyweds, still in their wedding outfits. They kiss again and say they plan to have children. The house will be perfect. Their dream house. The realtor smiles. I yell "NO!" into the couple's faces, but they don't hear me. They just smile. The realtor smiles, too, then pulls out a huge contract from inside her dress, along with a silver ballpoint pen the size of a fence post. The man takes the pen with both arms and touches it to the contract.

⟲

I woke up, breathing fast, the neck of my nightshirt wet. The light was so bright I knew it was late. I'd slept in again, damnit. I lay there awhile before getting up, letting the dream fade, thankful it was just a dream.

Downstairs, nobody was around. Just Dora's grandfather clock ticking, its Communion-plate pendulum swinging back and forth behind the glass. Everything still there, the oak table, the piano, the couch and reading lamp, the leather wing-back chair, Grace's candles along the mantel, none of them burning.

"*Bert! Emma!*" I yelled. "*Clara!*" The names echoed through the house and disappeared. "*Fred—*" The name was out of my mouth and in the air before I could stop it. Fred wasn't here. What was I thinking? A siren was wavering somewhere across town. I went into the dining room and yelled again. No answer. Into the kitchen. Where were they? Maybe the others had all died, too. Baseball killed them. Just like Fred. My goddamned baseball games.

Fred now gone. On down the river. The first one of us to go. Only four others left. And me. Me next? If Emma died of grief staring at that damned television, there'd only be three. It was coming apart at the welds. I hadn't kept on top of my promise. The house was dying on me, Ralph. I had to find new people. Younger people. Fast. Before I wound up in the Gardens after some neighbor kid selling Scout cookies found me huddled in a corner. The same way I found you.

No, this house had to go on living. Living and breathing. Red and yellow. Someday Desiree the paperboy would live here, when she was sixty or seventy, and her kids, too, and their kids. So this house had to keep going. I'd make sure of that. And other Hogan Houses like this would spring up all over the country—farmhouses and apartment buildings, old barns and converted warehouses, all of them painted bright red! All full of old people just like us, living together. Living it up. We'd put every goddamned nursing home in the country out of business for lack of people willing to go in and die all alone! As sure as the salmon came back upstream and the geese flew south, this house would survive.

I hurried back upstairs, pulling myself up the banister, feeling weak in my legs. I wiped my forehead and throat with my handkerchief as I went down the hall shoving doors open and yelling names into bedrooms. Nobody. Where the hell were they? The bathroom! Somebody must be in the bathroom. But my knocking on the door only pushed the door open with a squeak. Nothing but porcelain fixtures, those goddamned scales, and the smell of soap and mildew.

I turned and hurried back down the hall, stopping on the top step. Through the window above the front door, just below where the moon had been that night, I could see the top of a sweet gum tree across the street, the last handful of leaves a bright red. I'd never noticed the tree before. While I was watching, the highest leaf broke off and cartwheeled away in the breeze.

I went through the bedrooms and bathroom on the main floor. Nobody. Had the others all died, and I'd forgotten? Were they buried out by the chicken coop, too?

I went out the back door, down the ramp, and out onto the

side lawn. The grass on the ball diamond was ragged and uneven, the backstop still lying where it had fallen, weeds growing up through it. I walked across that backstop, caught my boot on a piece of tin and went down, the sound of wire stretching and tin creaking, breath coming out of me. I lay on the rusty mess breathing fast. *Slow down, George. You have to slow down.* A Christmas beetle came climbing up out of one of the nail holes in the tin, its back shimmering green and blue in the sunlight. Where was it going? Trying to get away from me, my breath? It was too late in the year for Christmas beetles. The beetle fell through another nail hole and was gone.

I got up and hurried on across the backstop and around behind the chicken coop. But what I saw where Fred's grave should have been was the scoreboard. Maybe Fred wasn't dead either! Maybe I'd been dreaming for months! I started to turn and run, but a corner of the wooden marker Emma'd wanted me to put on Fred's grave caught my eye poking out from under the scoreboard. I lifted the scoreboard by the edge, a few yellow numbers seesawing back and forth on their bent nails. Ninth inning. Score: nothing. I flipped the scoreboard all the way over on its back and looked down at the flattened marker. Only one. Okay. Only Fred. So the others were still here. Somewhere. Worms and sow bugs moved on top of the grave. I wiped my face again, then remembered Ralph was buried in the cemetery at the edge of town. Maybe the others were buried there too. I stumbled back across the backstop to the house, yanked the door of Max open, and started to get in. Then I saw my own eyes staring at me out of the side-view mirror. Eyes gone wild. Loony eyes!

Running around like a goddamned scared rabbit. Get 'hold of yourself. I stood there a long time, one foot on the running board, my hand on the steering wheel, my own words working their way in, everything slowing down.

I shut the truck door and went back inside the house. Going past the dining room table, I noticed a note scrawled on a page torn out of Clara's pad: "WE WENT 4 A WALK. U WR

ZZZING. C U SOON." She'd signed it, C, G, & B. Those three letters rushed up at me. Three! Only three of them left! Not four! And then, as I looked at the G, I remembered the humming, my trip down to the basement, Grace's naked body. Grace gone loony!

I stumbled through the hall and out the back door, half running, half falling down the sidewalk. I went up to the little yellow house and pounded on the door. I didn't hear anybody moving inside, so I pounded again, harder and longer. Both hands, my palms stinging. Still nothing. I stepped into the flower bed next to the door and cupped my hands against the window glass trying to see inside.

"She's not in there!" a voice came from behind me. I turned. Standing on the sidewalk leaning on a rake, wearing a purple dress, red knee socks, and a pair of beat-up white sandals, was Mrs. Beasley.

"There you are," I said, hurrying over to her so fast I caught my boot in the short white wire fence running around her flower bed and ripped the flimsy thing halfway out of the ground.

"What's wrong?" Mrs. Beasley asked. "You want the uniform back?"

I stopped. That's right. She'd played baseball with us. But other than that, I didn't know her from Eve. What the hell was I doing, standing here tangled in white wire panting like a dog?

"Well, what is it?" she said. "I don't have all day."

Words came flying out of my mouth before I could stop them. "You want to move in with us?" I said. "Move into the big red house and live together?"

Mrs. Beasley stared at me for a minute, blinked, then spoke slowly. "First you asked me to dinner. That was a couple years ago, remember? I turned you down. Then you asked me to play your silly ball game. So I did. But if you think I'll just up and move in with you, you're crazy!"

"Not just with me," I said. "With *us*."

We both stood there on the sidewalk in the winter sunshine

without saying anything. The breeze moving Mrs. Beasley's purple dress a little, the breeze up in my hair, too.

"What brought this on?" she said. "They all dying off on ya?"

The sun went thin. My throat went shut.

"You know, it looks to me like you've been dieting," she said. "Or the food's lousy down there. Look at yourself. You're wasting away." She made that clicking sound with her tongue.

Just when I thought for sure I was going to pass out for lack of air, my throat opened with a gush, my feet came free, white wire and leaves and spent flowers falling away, concrete hitting my heels, me headed for the house—my big red house going empty on me, dying off—Christmas star, front porch, and all of it.

"Besides, I don't think you could stand me!" Mrs. Beasley's yelled words came chasing after me, but I didn't look back.

I rushed into the house, pulled down a beat-up suitcase, and started packing, running into one bedroom after the next, jerking open drawers and closet doors, pulling out a sweater here, a blouse or shirt there, a handful of socks, shoving it all into that same suitcase, toothbrushes, turtlenecks, underwear, extra pants, bras. I didn't know whose was whose, what fit, or what they liked. It didn't matter. I just wanted to have enough, because I wasn't sure how long we'd be gone, or if we were ever coming back. That is, if any of them were even still alive and wanted to go with me when they got back here.

I went outside, hitched up Clara's chariot, climbed into the cab, and waited, the engine running, me and Max ready to go. Maybe me and Max should go alone. Forget the others. Just go. Get the hell out of here and never come back. But I just sat there staring out over the steering wheel at the empty street, the world dead still.

Then something moving down the block made me look. People walking and rolling. Arms and legs going. Clothes moving. People living. People I knew! Coming my way! *Hallelujah!* I shoved the stick shift so fast into first the gears ground and Max and I shot out into the street. I gave it gas until the engine was screaming and we were bearing down on them hard. Then I hit the brakes and shuddered to a stop at the curb next to them.

"I packed for all of us!" I said, climbing out. "Come on. Let's go! Get in!"

"Where are we going, George?" Bert asked.

"To the coast, goddamnit," I said. "It's such a gorgeous day, we have no choice! Get in."

"What about Emma?" Grace asked. "Planning to leave her behind?"

I hadn't noticed Emma wasn't with them. But it made sense. She was the number four. No E on Clara's note. "Well, she's not in the house," I said. "Her room's empty. So it looks like she's going to miss out." And then I saw Grace staring at something off in the distance. Bert and Clara saw it too, so my eyes turned the same way. Back toward the house. There she was, Emma. Standing on the front porch, polka dots billowing out all around her, one thick arm up in the air waving a tiny white handkerchief in the sunlight.

"Where the hell was she?" I said, reaching in to hold down the horn and waving Emma over. Emma started waddling down the steps, headed this way. I dropped the ramp on the chariot, and got Clara loaded in. Bert agreed to sit back with Clara, since he would have froze to death sitting in the open truck bed, and there wasn't room for all of us up front. When everybody was in, including Emma, I climbed into the driver's seat and we roared off headed for the Pacific, that big red house getting smaller and smaller in my side-view mirror, the front door standing wide open.

CLARA PAULSON

I SMELL a saltiness in the air. We must be getting close. I have no idea why we all agreed to get in, but you know George, he can be convincing. And why not? At our age why not do whatever comes up? Up.

Now we're stopping. Through my television I can see the ocean and a long gray beach. Bert gets to his feet and starts banging on the inside of the chariot, telling me we're here, as if I can't see that for myself. Then George comes back and pulls down my ramp. He looks bad, exhausted, and a little angry.

"Let's go," George barks, and we're all walking down a path toward the sand and that glorious roaring musical sound of surf. There's no ocean in Nevada, so I never knew the ocean had so much power. The one and only trip I ever made to see the ocean before right now was with some fellow I woke up lying next to in a fleabag hotel halfway between Vegas and L.A. He claimed I had told him the night before back in Vegas that I wanted to see the ocean. So that was where he was taking me, in my car. We left the hotel and kept driving west, but by the time we at last pulled over and looked down on all those crashing waves, the sun was already down, and I was drunk again. He had to carry me down and scoop out a place in the sand for me to sit. In the middle of the night, I woke up, still sitting in that sand chair, and heard for the first time the music of the ocean, the magical roar of surf through the dark. The next time I heard the music, it was morning and the sun was coming up warm on my back. I opened my eyes to discover I'd been left with no car and not a penny in my empty pocketbook. Just a vodka bottle full of sand sitting on the beach next to me.

We're walking down toward it now. The roar. The ocean music. The path ends and my chair stops so fast I almost fall face-first out onto the sand. But the deep sand doesn't stop George. He tips me back and pushes hard from behind, Bert pulling in front and Grace helping on one side until we get through to some sand that's wet and hard, and I roll along smooth again, every now and then hitting a shell that sends a little crunch up through my pipes and into my ears.

Out in front of me the waves are dancing! The air's full of mist and salt air and seagulls, and where the sky meets the water, everything's churning and splashing a frothy white. But we don't stop. Stop. We keep going, straight on toward the beautiful crashing waves. When I look around, though, I notice it's not we anymore. It's just George and I. The others stopped farther back. George is pushing me as fast as he can right toward the waves. My wheels are throwing up little trails of water and sand spraying on us. I lick my lips. Salt. The sun's so low, the light on the waves hurts my eyes. I think George is going to run me right in all the way up to my neck. Back behind us on the beach, the others are waving their arms and yelling. But the surf's too loud to hear what they're saying. Then George and I stop.

All I hear is "Holy shit!" those two words whispered a few inches above my head. I look up. George is staring out at the waves, his mouth dropped open so far I can see the roof of his mouth, the fillings in his top teeth. George still has his own teeth! I look where George is looking, and I see it too.

Just beyond the waves. This huge dark mass rolling up out of the water. I think perhaps it's a rock. But it's moving. Perhaps it's a piano being tossed by the waves. The biggest Steinway grand I've ever seen. Then I hear a gasp and a white shot of mist shoots straight up out of that piano and hangs in the sunlight for a few seconds.

"A whale!" George whispers.

I tip my head back again. George is still staring, a little kid on Christmas morning. And then everything tangles. Wires short and something blows. I see that hospital, the glass and fingerprints, the pink blanket. I've never seen a kid's face on Christmas morning! I'll never know what that's really like! Not ever! Because I gave my only child away and drove off without looking back. I try my crystal knob, but my wheels are sunk down in the wet sand. I start slapping the arm of my chair. I want George to keep going. Push me in! Go! Push me all the way out past the waves and seagulls and roaring water. Out past where the piano-whale was. *Way* out where it's deep, and dark, dark blue.

Push me out, George! Push me! I slap my chair until my hand stings. Go! Now! But George doesn't. He's not behind and above me anymore. I'm watching his back moving away from me. He's going in himself! He's leaving me here in the sand the way that other fellow did. I'll have to go on living with my sin staining my ex-Fisheater soul without George. The water turns the bottoms of George's overalls a dark blue. But he keeps going. The water's up to his knees. His chest. The waves are washing into him, almost knocking him down. His chalky hair is lost in the surf churning white, but he keeps going out. I sit here surrounded by roaring, by ocean music, watching George going away from me for good.

And then, farther out I see another whale break the surface, another little puff of steam and breath. Then two more whales, close together. A tail comes out, dark and glistening against all that water. George is almost gone now, the water up to his neck, only the tops of his overall straps and the collar of his red flannel shirt showing. I know it's over. And I'm scared

317

because I now know why he wanted to come to the beach so bad today, why he didn't care if we left Emma behind. So he could walk out into the sea, float away, get pulled off by the currents, and never come back. Never. I don't want to lose George on this beautiful day. But he's gone now. Just waves moving in sunlight and the crying of seagulls.

A little wave comes all the way in to where I'm sitting, a few inches of water going through the spokes of my wheels and under my chair, grains of sand moving in the water making me dizzy. Perhaps if I wait here long enough, the tide will come in and wash me out. Out to where George went.

But then somebody grabs my chair and wheels me up the beach. It's Bert. Pushing me up toward Emma and Grace. He parks me facing the sea again, and we're all standing here in a row watching the whales that are now way off.

I hear someone crying, and think at first it's me, but I'm not crying. It's Emma. Emma's whole body is shaking and she's pushing at the bags under her eyes with that little white hanky she was waving from the front porch. Bert moves over next to Emma and puts his arm around her. He's nothing next to her. All bones and skin. I watch the big polka dots on Emma's dress fluttering in the wind, Bert's bony hand going back and forth across the dots, Emma's shoulders shaking.

And as I'm sitting here listening to the seagulls and Emma crying and all the waves roaring, I see something in the surf. An animal. Crawling out of the waves. A baby whale perhaps that got too close to shore. Or a dead seal. But then it stands up. Dark blue. Red flannel. My heart takes off! I crank my steering wheel so hard I pull free and go shooting out across the wet sand. My own name comes yelled from behind, but I keep cranking. Again and again. The wind's heaven in my face. I keep going, the crystal knob a rock in my hand, sending me faster and faster out across the flat sand, through the roaring and gulls, the sun on fire sliding down behind the churning watery edge of the world.

GEORGE CASTOR

SEEING GRACE pushing Bert up the back ramp and down the hall in that wheelchair—the same hospital-type of wheelchair they'd given Ralph a ride to the Gardens in—Bert's heart still going, Bert still alive but forever changed, I knew what I had no choice but to do. Fred dead and now both Clara and Bert in wheelchairs. The time had come.

So I dug my Husky out of the shop, filed the chain, filled the tank, and fired that old saw up, blue smoke and the smell of gas everywhere. I hadn't run a chain saw in a lot of years, but it all came back. I became part of that saw, both of us tearing a four-foot-by-four-foot hole through the middle of Hogan's big house, starting down in the basement and working our way up through all four floors clear to the attic. Sawdust flew out of the screaming saw as the chain tore through floor joists and subflooring, lath and plaster, nails and knots. That old Husky made the work easy. All I had to do was hang on. Took me twice hitting wires, fireworks falling toward the basement through that dark shaft, before I shut off the juice at the box. But I kept going, by lantern light, only stopping when I ran the tank dry, or the chain got so dull I had no choice but to stop and file the teeth. When there wasn't any metal left to file, I put on a new chain. I went through three chains cutting that hole in the house. One chain for each of the days I was cutting.

I hit a water pipe on the second floor, ice cold water damned near knocking me on my ass. But I just went out to the street, shut off the main at the meter, and kept cutting.

A little past noon on the third day, I finished cutting through the floor of the attic, shut off the saw, and looked down. Three stories below, through that ragged four-foot hole, I could see the concrete floor of the basement covered with sawdust and plaster dust. I spit and watched my spit floating down through the shaft, wavering a little as it fell.

Halleholylujah! Now all I had to do was find an elevator to fit.

I read the want ads in *The Oregonian, The Appeal-Tribune, The Nickel Shopper,* and *The Beaver Advertiser.* I went to junk-yards and junk shops up and down the valley. I even called Otis Elevator's World Headquarters in Farmington, Connecti-cut, but I'll be damned if I could find a secondhand elevator anywhere. So I had to rig one up myself.

I bought an old pulley system that had been used on a shipping dock in Portland. Built a wood platform a shade smaller than the shaft I'd cut, but big enough to hold a wheel-chair and one other person. Put in four three-inch pipes that ran from the roof all the way down to the concrete floor in the basement. Greased the pipes heavy, then mounted U-bolts to each corner of the platform, those pipes running through the U-bolts. Then rigged a bunch of ropes up. For counter-weights, I filled gunnysacks with walnuts and tied the sacks to some of the ropes. To keep people from falling off, I built a cedar fence around the platform, a fence post in each corner, and a gate on one side. The gate on the platform matched up to gates on every floor where more cedar fences kept people from falling into the shaft. I thought about Sheetrocking the shaft and framing in doors on each floor, the way a real eleva-tor has, but it seemed a lot of extra work for not much gain in function. Also, by leaving the whole thing open, whoever was going up or down would get an unobstructed view of the house going by. Which might be kind of nice.

You ran the elevator by hand, standing on the platform and spinning a big ship's wheel I'd had up at the farm for years. Dora was always after me to make that ship's wheel into a coffee table, but I never got around to it. With the walnuts and the pulley system working together helping you spin the wheel, you could ride that platform all the way from the basement up to the attic without hardly breathing hard. A lever locked the elevator in place and even with the floor for getting on and off.

If you wanted to go from the attic to the basement, you simply let go and the ship's wheel would slowly unspin itself, blurring a little, the platform floating down nice and easy, the braking mechanism and the walnuts keeping things from going too fast.

Calling the elevator to you if it was on another floor was a tricky problem, but I took care of that by wiring up a row of four small lightbulbs near the gate on each floor. If the elevator was up in the attic, the fourth lamp in the row would be lit. The attic was the fourth floor, the basement being the first. I painted numbers above each of the lightbulbs. The numbers told you how many times you had to spin the car steering wheel mounted to the wall on each floor in order to call the elevator to you.

It wasn't as complicated as it sounded, but I decided to write up operating instructions and post a copy on all four floors next to the car steering wheels, and one next to the ship's wheel on the platform.

My homemade elevator wasn't pretty, but it sure as hell worked. Better, as it turned out, than I figured it would. Hell, high water, or every last one of us in wheelchairs wasn't going to put an end to this big red palace.

CLARA PAULSON

I SAW Bert's heart stop. Stop. Through the oval window in the front door. Bert had just come up the front steps. He saw me through the glass and smiled. Raised a hand to wave. But then Bert's face changed. The smile cracked apart and fell off. The hand he was waving at me with dropped along with the rest of him. Then Bert was on his back rocking back and forth, both Bert's hands twisting his shirt into a knot at his chest, his face turning purple.

Emma saw it too, because she went past me going faster than I've ever seen Emma move. She pulled the door open and Bert's words came in. In. "God this hurts!" Bert was yelling.

After what seemed like forever, an ambulance arrived and two men in white pants and blue jackets ran up onto the porch. One of the men jerked Bert's shirt open, sending buttons bouncing across the porch boards. One of Bert's buttons made it all the way in to me, bounced off my good ankle and lay there, a little happy face without a mouth, staring up at me from the flagstones.

Bert's bare chest was pale with a patch of gray hair between his nipples, ribs flaring sharp under the skin. I knew Bert was dying. Emma stood to the side biting at a thumbnail. One of the men in white pants pushed his fingers into the side of Bert's throat. Bert's mouth still open, but no words coming out anymore. The other man pulled a green plastic mask over Bert's nose and mouth. Smeared goop on Bert's chest. Sparks in my head. Sparks all over Bert's chest. Bert flopping once, and then nothing. The red and white lights on top of the ambulance down in the street turning slow and pale.

The men lifted Bert onto a folding bed, pulled a blanket up to his chin, then carried him away, Bert's eyes wide open above that green plastic mask. I knew people sometimes died with their eyes still open. So I thought for sure Bert was dead. Dead.

But Bert didn't die. He came home a week or so later sitting in a wheelchair, just like mine, but newer, and without a crystal knob or steering wheel, or little bell.

The morning after Bert came home in that chair I woke up to the lions on my bedposts roaring mad, the window glass rattling, no water or lights, the house full of blue smoke and fine white dust and Emma bellowing like a bull elephant that she was moving out. George gone cut-time crazy.

But Emma hasn't moved out. The dust is all cleaned up. Steinway back to black. Glass balls and air bubbles shiny again. And now Bert and I have an elevator. Our elevator's not like any elevator you've ever seen before. In fact, it's downright ugly. No other way to say it. But Grace has been busy putting potted plants around here and there, hanging scarves and weavings and feathers on the railings George built around the holes he sawed through the floors. I try to think of the elevator as one of those fancy glass elevators in the big hotels down in Vegas. Except there's no glass in George's elevator.

George about killed himself putting it in. Overdid it, I think, the fool-idiot. Just yesterday, I heard him on the phone making an appointment to go see a doctor. I don't think George has seen a doctor in all the time I've been living here. Perhaps he's never been to a doctor. George calling a doctor and talking low so none of us will hear means something's not right.

But thanks to George being nuts, I now know what this house looks like upstairs. I know how Grace's room smells and that she lets her yellow birds fly around loose in her room during the day. I know where Bert keeps his dead cat and his car keys. I know that George's room is a mess and what he and his wife looked like on their wedding day, a pretty silver frame sitting on his dresser, his wife in pearls. I also know there's a claw-footed bathtub in the upstairs bathroom that's so big you could go swimming in it.

Sometimes I take the elevator all the way up to the attic and roll myself over to one of those windows that are curved on top. I sit and look out onto the treetops and the houses all around. I see whales and music notes. This spring I'm going to plant marigolds in the window boxes up there. I love marigolds, lots of little suns, all bright orange and shining. I'll go up and water my marigolds, break off the dead and shriveled suns and throw them out into the sky so more suns will bloom. Bloom. Then I'll sit back and watch the other sun shining bright on the green treetops. I'll watch for blackbirds flying across the blue-sky sheet music of summer. Perhaps I'll try to sing again, up there in the attic where nobody will hear the nothing coming out of me.

GEORGE CASTOR

A SINGLE word was all I heard fall from the doctor's mouth, that word landing between my legs on the crinkly white paper of the examination table where I sat. There were other words in the air around my head, lots of doctor words, but I didn't hear any of the other words. That one word lying there bleeding into the white paper was more than enough.

And then I was sliding down off the table, taking with me as much of that crinkly paper as my two hands could rip away, wadding the paper into a ball the size of a basketball against my chest, that single word rolled deep inside, me walking out leaving the doctor standing there saying more words like radiation and remission.

There was nothing wrong with me.

I should have never called in the first place. Never agreed to having tests run. Never pissed into that plastic cup or let them take blood. I should have never come back for the god-damned test results.

It was already dark by the time I was walking across the bridge, still carrying that wadded-up word with me. So I stopped. Listened. The creek was moving pretty good below me, water flowing fast.

I pulled out a book of matches, lit one, touched the flame to that ball of paper, then blew until the fire was going good and hot—roaring right there in my hands, my own breath making the flames burn hot, heat against my face. Then I dropped that fireball over the railing and watched it fall, sparks and glowing pieces of paper coming loose and floating down, too. The flaming wad of paper landed on the water, hissed a little, but kept burning as the current took it downstream fast. Watching that word burning up between air and water, floating away on the current, I swore I'd never breathe that word to a single soul. Nobody was going to tell me I had something I didn't have. I was stopping that word right there. Not ready for the river yet.

So I had no idea how Grace found out. But the minute I saw three red votive candles burning on the toilet tank when I made my midnight run to the bathroom a night or two later, I knew Grace knew. I lifted the toilet seat lid, looked down, and saw words floating on water, a whole bunch of words written on a piece of purple paper in Grace's handwriting, a circle going all the way around those words. I slammed the toilet seat down hard and was about to flush those words away. But I couldn't. Because enough of the black letters had worked their way into my brain, spelled out names I knew, Ralph's name, Jason's name, Dora's name. Aunt Bertha and Uncle Bill. Bud and Fred and even Shag William. I thought for sure I'd seen all those names spelled out somewhere inside that circle going around the words. So I lifted the lid, dropped to my knees. But the only name I saw was my own goddamned name spelled out in capital letters curving across the top of the circle. Inside the circle were other letters, other words, but none of the names I thought I'd seen. I knelt there in the candlelight, my hands holding the cold porcelain of the toilet bowl, my eyes reading words that took hold and wouldn't let go, the words almost reading themselves out loud to me:

There was once an old woman who raised pigs. She lived in a small house on the edge of town and took her pigs for a walk every day, making a big loop around the town. She used a silver cane to direct her pigs, tapping them gently on one side or the other to turn the pigs, placing the cane across their noses to stop the pigs before crossing streets. The townspeople did not like the old woman walking her pigs about on the sidewalks. But the old woman did not care. She loved her pigs. And loved being outside.

One day the old woman fell ill. She was too weak to get out of bed or take her pigs out for walks. But the pigs loved the old woman. The pigs waited.

A few days later, the old woman died in her sleep. The pigs let themselves out of the sty and walked the same loop through town by themselves, stopping here and there to root for food. In the evening, the pigs returned to their sty.

This went on for many years. The townspeople no longer noticed the pigs wandering through town, always taking the same circular route, always returning to the sty at the old woman's house at nightfall. After seven years, only one old pig was left. One Sunday, this old pig went out for its daily walk. Except this time, the pig took the old woman's silver cane in its mouth as it walked. The sun shone on the silver cane. The townspeople all stopped to watch the pig walk by, sunlight playing on the cane. The old pig went up to an old farmer who was sitting in the town square in the sun wearing a black coat. The pig dropped the silver cane at the farmer's feet, nosed the cane once, then turned and went back to the sty at the old woman's house. The pig died that night.

The old farmer took the silver cane home with him, where he found that two of his own pigs had just given birth to large litters, all the piglets the same color as the cane. The next morning, hanging from a limb of an oak tree in the barnyard, the cane had become a seamless hoop, a silver circle, catching the rising sun.

When I finished hearing those words about pigs and silver canes that didn't make a damned bit of sense, I reached out and pushed the handle on the toilet tank. But that purple piece of paper wouldn't go down. It just swirled around in the bowl. I flushed again, but it still didn't go down. Then my hand reached in, grabbed the dripping wet piece of paper, squeezed toilet water out. Goddamn her! I blew the candles out, then took the candles and the soggy wad of paper down the hall to Grace's room. Without even slowing down to knock, I charged in. Grace was sitting in her chair by the window with that skunk on her lap, the sill jam-packed full of candles blazing bright.

"What the hell's all this supposed to mean?" I said, holding everything out to her, wax from the candles spilling hot onto my hands and wrists, hot wax and toilet water dripping on the floor.

"Just trying to help," Grace said.

"Help? Candles and crap about circles and pigs? You're as helpful as the goddamned doctors who think they know it all!" I yelled. "I don't need any help!"

Grace's eyes swung and struck me. Two headlights bearing down. She leaned toward me, those eyes pushing me back until I bumped into her bed and sat down, the candleholders clinking together as they rolled out of my hands onto her quilt.

"I have something you need to hear," Grace said, the skunk disappearing down off her lap. "You could have healed your cancer, if you'd wanted to. That's just up here." She tapped a finger against her temple without blinking. "But nobody can heal old age. Because old age is not a disease. Old age is part of being born, part of living. And dying is part of living, too. Without dying, there would be no living, George. It doesn't matter what you die of. A car wreck, cancer, old age. Suicide. Don't you see? It's not a straight line that starts here and stops there. It's one big circle. A hoop. No beginning and no end. Going around and around. Coming up in the east and going down in the west. It's the path the sun takes. The circle birds fly every year. The cycle water follows when it's steamed into air by the sun. Your river's partway right, George. But it's more than that. Because even rivers flow in circles. Every river turns to sky." She stopped, stood up. "So there's no need for any of us to be afraid of dying."

I wanted to yell at Grace, tell her I wasn't dying. Tell her doctors didn't know jack-shit and that I was getting sick and

tired of all her bullshit about candles and hoops and goddamned pigs. I wanted to tell Grace to pack her bags and
move the hell out of my house—right then, in the middle of
the night. Except I couldn't get my tongue to make words in
my mouth, and her birds started in flapping, the little bell in
the cage jingling in the frozen air.

"It's up to you," I heard Grace say, then I either fell asleep
or passed out. Because when I came to, the birds were silent,
and Grace was nowhere in the room. Just the skunk sleeping
curled in her chair. The candles on the sill were all out. But
the three candles off the toilet tank were burning again, sitting
on the floor out in front of me, around that piece of purple
paper now dried out and curled up at the edges.

Outside I thought I could hear the faint honking of Canada
geese going over. Were the geese headed north already? Or
south? What day was it? What month? The skunk stirred and
stretched. I heard the jingle of a bridle. I blinked. A silver pig
flashed in bright sunlight. I shut my eyes. A black Bible. A
barn on fire. A bloodred bull. Flames burning on river water.

CLARA PAULSON

I SMELL coffee and somebody coughs. I hear a cup clink against teeth. A lump of butter catches my eye as it goes sliding down my stack of pancakes—bump, bump, bump—riding along in a little stream of syrup. But I don't watch the lump of butter slide all the way down onto my plate, because across the table I notice Grace's fingers—small as a girl's—smearing blueberry jam onto the front of her nice cotton blouse, just below her throat. She's trying to undo the buttons on her blouse! She gets the first button undone and moves down. Down. More smeared jam. Bingo, she gets the second button, too. A little V of her brown skin shows where her cleavage should be, but Grace is too skinny for a cleavage. I can see the lumps of her ribs under the loose skin. Perhaps she's going to strip right here at the breakfast table because her tiny fingers are still working—now all the way down by her stomach. The blouse has fallen open more, and I can see a little piece of bright yellow skin showing on her breast. I move my eyes up. Wham! There are her eyes! Those two obsidian quarter notes shining and stabbing into me. But no, not really. She's staring through me, at something somewhere behind me. As far away as the moon. And then I recognize the look in those eyes! Out on the pitcher's hump. It's the same look! Except that time there was a yellow T-shirt between her fingers and the buttons. And no blueberry jam. It's not Grace in there looking out at the moon. It's somebody else.

But Grace doesn't strip. Instead, she stands up, mouth full of pancake, a little jam oozing out between her lips at the corners of her mouth. Grace turns and goes upstairs, her arms leading the way, her little-girl fingers tearing at those last few buttons. Nobody else has noticed. They don't watch her go. Bert's got something under his top plate and is working his tongue trying to get it out, his eyes closed with concentration. George is stirring his coffee, frowning at the paper, his spoon the sound of a tiny triangle. Emma's talking to nobody listening about how she slept bad last night. I want to yell at all of them, tell them what I just saw, cuss them for not noticing.

But perhaps Grace's bra was hurting her, gouging in a little, and she's just gone upstairs to change her bra. Perhaps that's all. Then I remember Grace doesn't wear a bra. That was one of the first things I noticed about Grace, those breasts hanging all loose beneath her clothes. That, and the way her shoulder blades stick out of her back, the nubs of wings.

The lump of butter's all melted into a puddle. I push my fork down through the cakes. Syrup oozes out everywhere. Across the table, Grace's chair is empty. I try to tell myself it's okay. Grace just had a hot flash and went up to change. I had them. They hit you like a spotlight and you're all of a sudden sweating so hot you need a window to throw open, or a cold shower. Perhaps Grace found a window, way up in the attic. And she's up there leaning out into the cold air, cooling down.

A few minutes later, I see a shadow move at the top of the stairs. It's Grace, carrying a wicker laundry basket piled high with wash. Everything's okay, after all. Good. I go back to my pancakes. But Grace never does her wash in the mornings. George does, at the crack of dawn. But Grace does her wash before supper. Every Friday. I look back up at Grace. A spoonful of sand spills down my spine between my blouse and skin. Grace isn't wearing any clothes! Not a stitch! The bite of pancakes in my mouth swells way too big. I almost gag on the sick sweetness, but manage to swallow it all down. I don't stare at Grace's nakedness, though. Because I can't. My eyes are locked on a little yellow sunflower that's riding along on her left breast. As Grace gets closer, I can see some green in the sunflower, and the dark center, too. It's a tattoo! Ink in her skin! Grace has a tattoo on her tit! I always wanted one. A turquoise-blue butterfly on the inside of my thigh, where my skin's milky and soft. My little secret friend most people would never know was there. On Sunday mornings I'd let my blue butterfly flutter around the room in the sunlight as I drank coffee in bed and listened to the radio.

The others start turning around in their chairs now, trying to see what I must be gawking at. At. But Grace is almost to the bottom of the stairs by now, a little volcano of wash rising up out of that basket. And lying on the volcano, beside where the lava should be shooting up, is that skunk of hers, riding along below the sunflower. The skunk's yellow eyes glow right at me. George lunges, pulling an afghan off the chair in the entryway and holding the afghan out to Grace, but Grace puts up a hand. "Sorry. Got a full load right here," she says, and goes on down the hallway, her butt all saggy and small. I hear her footsteps, cat paws, going down the basement stairs. We're all frozen here, steam rising up from the cups of coffee and pancakes, the ticking of the clock loud, the beautiful tinking of that tiny triangle fading away.

Then Bert's top plate drops out of his mouth and lands in his pile of cut-up pancakes. "Good Gawd!" he blurts. "What's wrong with her?"

But nobody answers Bert or says a word. George comes back over to the table, dragging the afghan, his blue eyes all swirled and out of kilter. George sits down. "I don't know," George says, his voice so far away I can barely hear it. "Same thing happened a while back. It's like something snaps."

And I know exactly what he means. It's just like my wires. Although they seem to be getting better lately.

"Exhibitionist!" Emma hisses.

"Shut up!" George spits. "Shut the hell up!" Emma must see the same thing I see churning in George's eyes, because she shuts right up. Her big body shrinks down. "Give her some time, goddamnit!" George says. "She needs time. She'll be okay. We'll all be okay. She'll snap out of it. I know she will."

But I don't think George does know. Not really. Not this time. I can see it. For the first time since I met George, I can tell he's not sure. George is scared. So am I. Of what's going on right here. Right now. With Grace down in the basement not wearing any clothes. It's really happening and there's nothing to do. Not a thing. Except swallow my own syrupy saliva and look over at Grace's half-eaten pile of pancakes suffocating in blueberry jam.

A few minutes later, Grace is passing by again, headed for the stairs, still naked, carrying that basket full of volcano, her wash still dirty and dry. But no skunk. I can't see the sunflower, either. Grace says "Good morning!" as she goes by us, as if everything's back to normal. But it's not. Because Grace is still naked and she never does her wash in the morning.

Grace turns and climbs the stairs. But halfway up she stops, right in the middle of a step. She's skinny from here. The skunk streaks up the stairs past Grace, its claws catching on the carpet, little tearing sounds falling all around us down here at the table. Tiny jingles from that pig charm on the skunk's collar come drifting down on us, too, soft as snow. Grace slowly turns and looks back over her shoulder at all of us staring up at her, a bunch of fool-idiots around a blackjack table. Then Grace drops the basket and the volcano blows. A river of colors spews down the stairs, tumbling and blurring. The empty basket bounces against the front door with a burst of wrenched wicker. Something crosses Grace's face. Face. Right away I know she's back in there. She snapped out of it just like George said she would! The way she did out on the pitcher's hump. I want to stand up and let out a big cheer. Cheer Grace on for having the guts to get that tattoo. Cheer her on for walking naked through this big red house. But I don't. Because it's not that kind of thing. Instead, I watch a darkness gather on Grace's face. She turns and hurries up the stairs, running away from that long, colorful river flowing down onto the flagstones all the way to the front door. Peeking out at me through the crook of Grace's arm as she goes up is that little yellow sunflower, bulging a little, blooming bigger, because of how Grace is holding herself so tight.

GEORGE CASTOR

BURNING THAT word up and throwing it into the creek must have done something, because I hadn't noticed any blood for the better part of two weeks, and I was pretty sure I'd gained some weight back. I'd prove that doctor wrong yet. Grace was right, it was all up here.

But then the weather went to pot. Winter turned on us and came back mad as hell right when spring should have been breaking open balmy. A dose of freezing cold and snow and wind all the way down from the Arctic, the radio said.

The cold snap had been socked in and dumping snow for the better part of a week when Grace didn't come downstairs for breakfast one morning. I'd been keeping my distance from Grace ever since our run-in about the note in the toilet. Maybe Grace was upstairs writing me another note.

But like Clara said, Grace wasn't one to miss breakfast. So I went up and checked Grace's room. But her room was empty, her bed made, just that skunk sleeping on the chair and Grace's birds in their cage, still covered up. I checked the rest of the house. But she was nowhere. Grace wouldn't have gone outside in this weather. It was so cold and blowing so hard a person wouldn't last long out there. But I checked the chicken coop just to be sure. No Grace. Just the chickens huddled together.

Hell, knowing Grace, she probably ran out of candles and made a trip to the Circle-K to restock. Or she needed birdseed, or skunk food, or who the hell knew what with that woman.

Most of the morning we all just waited, the snowstorm raging white outside. I tinkered with the elevator, kept stoking the fire, trying to keep the cold from seeping into the bones of the Hogan House. Bert sat staring out the big front window, the light making his eyes and face the color of the sky outside, making the new chrome of his wheelchair dull. Clara sat over by the piano, tapping the eraser of her pencil against her pad or on her glass steering knob. Every now and then Clara shifted in her wheelchair, setting the bell of hers ringing a little, the only sound other than the fire popping now and then and the clock chiming out the quarter hours. Emma sat on the couch doing cross-stitch, the small black polka dots on her yellow dress hundreds of holes.

"Where the hell is she?" I said when the clock was done bonging out noon.

But nobody said a word, Emma and Bert and Clara all just sitting there looking at me as if I was the one who should have the answer. That's when I saw three people looking back at me. Only three. Two in wheelchairs, and one full of holes. No Grace with the gold around her teeth shining, her eyes shining. No Fred wearing his bow tie and pocketful of pencils. No Shag William and his tags. Only three. Four total counting me in this big old house. Three of them left, and me. I got up and ran out into the howling center of that storm.

I hadn't made it more than a block before I ran into a sheet. The sheet glowed a blinding white, rising up in front of me, silver-gray daylight all around. I turned back toward the house. But the sheet turned, too, surrounded me, wrapped me tight, made it hard to get air, the wind icy in my mouth and nose. I hadn't even grabbed a jacket on the way out of the house. Damned fool. I needed gloves in this weather, and a hat. This was a winter storm unlike any I'd ever seen in Oregon. The kind of storm I'd moved here to get away from.

The red house was barely visible through the blowing snow. Where the hell was she? I could at least make it to the Circle-K, see if she was there. But this was insane. What was I doing? Grace wasn't wandering the streets in this storm. Grace was fine, probably sitting in some closet with her candles going all around her to stay warm. I hadn't looked in the closets. I turned back to the house, the sheet snapping in the wind behind me. A pair of barn owls flying off into the moon.

That's when I heard it. A single word Grace had said the other night when I was sitting on her bed. I swallowed, the word rising from my memory until the S and the C were hissing loud in my head. I hadn't heard the word when she'd said it that night, this single word, slipped in among all her other words about circles and lines and growing old. But now it blared, burned my ears.

I hurried back to the house and went upstairs to Grace's room, my mouth chalky, my hands and face stinging with cold turning back to warm. But I didn't see anything unusual on Grace's dresser or nightstand. I shuffled through a pile of papers on her desk. Nothing. No sign. Grace's windowsill was cluttered with candleholders and stubs of candles cocked at all angles. Some candles in glass votive holders. Reds and greens and blues. None of the candles lit. On the dresser was a paper grocery bag full of new candles, long ones and short ones, all still wrapped in cellophane, wicks white. Grace hadn't gone after candles.

What the hell was I doing searching her room for clues? The way they did in the motion pictures. Grace was probably sitting downstairs with the others by now. I hadn't even checked when I came in. So I started out of Grace's room to go back downstairs. But something made me stop. I turned back. Slow. Something calling me. Pulling me. I crossed to Grace's bed and stood looking down at the quilt, my heart knocking hard up into the back of my throat.

337

I reached out and threw the quilt and blankets back. Fast. And then I saw it. A small piece of corn-colored paper fluttering and twirling to the floor in front of me, a dry maple leaf. Grace's birds moved in their cage. I pulled in air, shut my eyes, hoped some breath of wind would blow that scrap of paper away, out the window, out into the snow. I stood for a long time like that, both my eyes shut, birds pecking at their bell in the cage behind me. Then I opened my eyes. But the piece of paper was still lying there on the floor. Maybe it was blank? Just a scrap of paper? A receipt? Nothing?

Grace's skunk was nosing the piece of paper now, smelling it. I bent forward, reached for the paper, the floor coming up to meet me, my own breath blowing that paper, turning it over. Letters. Grace's handwriting. Words in a circle. The floor hit my knees. My fingers found the paper. The birds went still. The skunk gone. The storm outside all of a sudden hushed. The yellow scrap of paper coming up to me. Those letters working their way into my head, telling me something I didn't want to believe.

CLARA PAULSON

THE SNOW has stopped outside. No wind. There is calm and a little sunshine. A few smudges of blue getting bigger up high. Everything else white, powdered sugar, and such a sudden silence. I roll across the living room to get a better view out the front door, but I don't see just white anymore. A dark figure is wading through the snow toward our front porch. He's got one of those Smokey-the-Bear hats on, all wrapped in clear plastic, everything but his badge dark blue. A cop. A big one.

The knocker bangs loud and I hear George coming down the stairs. He's been up there so long I thought he'd gone back to bed, tired of waiting for Grace to come home. We're all worried about Grace, but George was wearing the carpet out walking back and forth all morning, until he took off outside, then came back a few minutes later and went hurrying upstairs. I don't know where Grace could be. But I'm sure she's okay. One thing about Grace, she seems to know what she's doing in life. She can take care of herself.

George comes past me and pulls the door open. I roll back a little, away from the cold air that blows in between my ankles. In the doorway George and the cop stand breathing, neither one saying a word, just their breaths rising foggy between them. I notice how skinny George is, his pants all baggy in the butt, his ears sticking out. The cop steps inside. George closes the door with a clump. The cold air stops flowing between my feet. I can't see their breath anymore, but I hear words coming out of the cop. Words so hushed I can't hear them all. Something about a field up by a grange hall. A big tree. Cold frozen. A farmer found it. And then I hear her name loud and clear. *Grace*. They found her! She's okay! I want to get up and hug George and Emma and Bert. Hug the big blue cop.

But George doesn't turn with a smile for me, or let out a whoop. He doesn't say anything. He just holds a crinkled yellow rosebud up, trembling a little in his fingers. The cop takes the rose, then George turns toward me, his face gone to concrete, no light in his eyes, no blue. And right then I know it's something awful. Something bad. This is one of those moments you'll remember for the rest of your life, where you were and what you were doing. President Kennedy. Dr. King. Everything I've come to know and love about George's face is gone, wiped away, nothing left. He just stares at me, his mouth hanging open a little, his head bony. The cop puts a hand on George's shoulder, a big hand. The papery yellow rosebud sagging in the cop's other hand down by his gun. George just stares through me, as if I'm glass, or not here at all.

I slap the arm of my chair, loud. Shake my chair. My little bell rings. George doesn't move, but I see his eyes slowly pulling me into focus. His eyes so empty and faraway I'm not sure I know this man. I'm not sure I'm here. I slap my chair again, twice. Push the question from my half-dead tongue onto my face, out through my eyes and skin. No sound. No words or voice or song coming out. But George gets it. Words start forming slow in his mouth, his lips moving apart, teeth, his tongue pushing those words out in my direction. Words I all of a sudden know

I don't want to hear. But it's too late. Late. The words are already coming through the air from George to me. I slap my good hand to the side of my head, cover my ear. But the words come inside anyway, off-key notes, broken strings, echoing and bouncing and hissing inside, over and over and over.

GEORGE CASTOR

COMING DOWNSTAIRS—the sound of knocker beating loud all through the house, beating loud inside my skull, the uniform standing on the other side of that oval pane of glass—all I could think was that the trooper was here about Jason. To tell me they'd made a mistake. Goofed. Jason wasn't dead after all. It wasn't Jason's fancy green car they'd found at the bottom of the Columbia. Somebody else's boy.

But it wasn't Jason the trooper was here about. The trooper was here about what I already knew but didn't know how. What I wanted to not know. About Grace. All I could do was hold up the note I had wadded up in my hand, give the trooper Grace's little crumpled-up circle with her last words in it. Turn away. Past Clara and the other two. Down the hallway and through the back door out into the snow to go see for myself. The only way I was ever going to believe what Grace had done.

I drove Max out into the snow-covered hills without thinking. I couldn't think. Just words tumbling, Grace's inky words on that yellow paper, the trooper's words about where they'd found her, and other words I had no idea where they were coming from. Voices in my head. Everything caving in and blowing apart at the same time. So I just drove, riding on nothing but the drumming of the chains against the packed snow below me, the words rattling around up in my head, and a bad pain burning low in my guts. Cold air came in through the rolled-down window. The sun out, but low. A white so bright all around I couldn't hardly tell where the road stopped and the ditches started. Everything washed wedding-dress white.

I had to find the tree. Because I couldn't believe Grace would have done this to me, to our big red house, to my promise, to the others. I couldn't believe what I'd read in her own handwriting, and then what the trooper'd told me in cop talk.

Driving along through all the white, I knew it was over. The Hogan House was history. Only three left back at the house. Three. Too few. It was over, Ralph. Sorry, buddy. The whole thing that Grace had started by showing up on my front porch that Saturday morning forever ago was crumbling before my eyes.

We weren't college kids. Or tribes in Africa. We were nothing but a handful of old folks, waiting to die. And in this country you died in hospitals or nursing homes. Not in big red houses like mine. So now we'd all wind up at the Gardens, the Ad-ministrator smiling as we all checked in at the front counter. Me getting ready to find out how Ralph had lived those last two years of his life. Me ramping up to die in a nursing home all by myself.

But right now I had to find the tree, the place where Grace had sat down and let the freezing storm take her away.

Evans Valley Grange wasn't very far from town, maybe a mile, or two. I slowed down as I came to the grange. But the fields all around the grange were full of trees. Fir and cedar, maple all bare, a row of poplars, a big sugar pine. That's all the trooper'd said: under a big tree out by the grange. It could have been any of the dozens of trees. But I'd find Grace's tree if I had to look under every last one.

Cresting the hill by the grange is when I saw it. The blue thread first. Going across the snow. Then the big oak. I hit the brakes so hard the engine died. Snow silence all around. A ragged, pale blue thread went winding up a hill to the east. Tracks. A trail. And where the trail ended at the top of the hill was a giant oak tree, one of the biggest oaks I'd ever seen, its bare branches reaching up above the horizon spreading into the sky.

Holy shit.

I let off on the brakes, went coasting squeaky down the hill a ways to a wide spot on the shoulder. I pulled over and sat there looking at the trail of pale blue footprints leading up the hill to that huge tree.

By the time I made it up to the tree, I was breathing hard, sweating pretty good, my back and knees aching from wading through the snow. I leaned against the tree to catch my breath. Then saw that the snow all around one side of the trunk was trampled, covered with footprints. I'd found it! The place Grace had come to die. Kill herself.

Or was it?

I dropped to my knees and started searching the snow for some sign, but all I saw were bootprints. Heels and toes and tread on soles. Every print white and clean. I slammed my arms down onto the snow, leaned forward and swept my arms back and forth, rubbing away the prints, Grace's name spilling out into the snow, over and over. I crawled forward on my knees, sweeping back and forth, as wide as I could reach, faster and faster, erasing the footprints of all the people who'd been here and taken Grace away, people who didn't even know Grace. The same way they'd taken Dora.

When I couldn't get enough air into my lungs to keep going, I stopped, sat back. Lying all around me in the snow were pieces of snow angel wings. Some broken. Some whole.

Then I saw something. Dark marks. In a row. A pattern. A semicircle of dark spots in the snow. Seven spots. I poked a gloved finger against one of the spots. The snow collapsed into blue darkness and the spot was a hole. The other spots were the same. Perfectly round holes about three inches across that disappeared down into the snow.

I dug at one hole with both hands, throwing snow into my crotch. But all I found was frozen grass and dirt and leaves a foot down. Nothing else. I pulled off one glove and shoved my bare hand into the snow, feeling as I went deeper, groping. I felt something. Something hard. A rock. I closed my fingers around the rock and pulled it out of the snow, but it wasn't a rock. I was holding a hunk of quartz, or a huge diamond. I thumped it against the heel of my gloved hand. The inside fell out. It was hollow. I looked inside. Stuck to the bottom was a silver clip and a tiny piece of blue stone, and poking out of the clip was a thin black tail.

A wick. It was a fluted crystal votive light. *Grace!*

I dug to the bottom of each of the other dark holes and found six more. Grace had carried these all the way out here last night during that snowstorm, then sat up here under this oak tree all night, seven candles burning, these seven glass votive lights sinking into the snow in front of her. It was true. Grace was gone for good. Never coming back. Gone on down the river after Ralph.

I stood and looked out over the valley. From the top of the hill, I could see all around, three hundred and sixty degrees of valley rolling out away from me. The air was clear, clearer than I remembered seeing it in a long time. The Coast Range to the west and the Cascades to the east were powdered white. I could see the Benedictine Abbey perched on its hill in Mount Angel, six miles away. Everything was white, sparkling, beautifully painted. I breathed in the taste of fresh snow. And other smells, too. Of sunshine and earth and things stirring, the way it always smelled every winter just before spring. Down in the valley, the sun reflected a pale gold off a frozen pond.

I heard a faint honking. At first I couldn't see the geese. But then there they were, floating overhead, a jagged V pattern, their cries drifting down to me. Hundreds of geese going over, headed north, the huge V wavering and shifting as it floated across the blue.

I sat in the snow watching the sun moving low across the southern horizon, snow melting in through my overalls and boots. Me sinking into the snow little by little. But I didn't care. I just sat there looking at the winter scene stretched out in front of me, the most beautiful view I'd seen in a long time, a painting—the colors still wet, everything quiet. I wanted to stay right there forever, part of the painting, sitting under this huge oak tree, its black arms spreading open into the sky above me. Sap stirring beneath me, starting to climb up from the dark, cold roots.

Grace's body was downtown at Bingham & Bristol, being prettied and prepared for the funeral. They'd probably found some hang-tail remnants of her family who would fly into Portland on a jet plane, rent a car and drive down, go through the motions of putting a relative they didn't really know in the ground, then fly off again to lives still going full tilt, their obligation fulfilled. I knew a funeral like that was the last thing Grace would want, but it was too late this time. The authorities had found Grace first. Not like Fred. But something told me it didn't really matter. It was different. Grace was different. She was long gone, out there ahead of the geese going north.

I looked over at the votive lights I'd dug up lying in the snow. I squeezed my pockets for matches, but I didn't have any. Besides, there was hardly any wax left. The candles had all burned out. Before, or after Grace died?

Razor-cold air stiffened the hairs in my nose. To the southwest, another front was blowing in, its smooth edge arcing across the sky, pushing toward me, a giant blade ground silver-gray pulling a dark blanket across the blue behind it.

An urge so strange came over me I shivered. I tried to push the thought out of my head, but it wouldn't leave, a stray cat in winter. Should I stay here? Let the front blow in, dump more snow, take me, too? I could feel my heart picking up below the layers of flannel and wool. I alone could decide. Right now, by myself. Nobody else. I thought about the others. The house. Fred was gone now. And Shag William, too. Bert wasn't doing too well. Why not follow her?

I sat under the ancient oak tree as the storm front covered the sun and the wind came up, steady and cold. The first flakes of snow started to fall, small icy pieces that bounced against my jacket. Each flake a tiny crystallized star. I wanted to curl up and sleep here, until the storm blew over. Burrow into the tiny stars and sleep the way sled dogs did. Just until morning, when the sun would come back and make everything glisten and sparkle. I pulled my hat lower and rested my head on my forearms. The storm gusted, blew sand against my face.

☾

When I lifted my head again, it was dark, but everything was light—the strange glow of snow at night—and the flakes were blowing almost parallel to the ground, the wind baying. But the cold seemed far away, almost warm now. My neck had gone stiff. My back, too. Had I dozed off? Deep in my body I felt a chill, but I was warm. I let my head settle back down onto my arms. That was better. I was too sleepy. Morning would be here soon enough. The sun would come back.

Something woke me. A shout, faint and high on the wind. I lifted my head and listened. Just the wind in the branches overhead. But the sound came again, a yell or a cry. It was a voice! Grace! I'd left her in the truck all this time! She must be freezing cold! I tried to stand, but the grease in my joints had gone stiff in the cold. I couldn't move. My hat blew off and tumbled away across the snow, disappeared into dark. I rolled onto my hands and knees and tried to stand. Got my feet under me. I crouched, balancing myself with my hands. The wind was so strong I wasn't sure I'd be able to stay up. If I could stand at all. But I straightened, bent into the wind, a deep pain thrusting up my spine, burning in my knees. I took a step forward, squinting into the wind, then my legs were gone, and I was in the snow. I couldn't feel my feet. My feet were frozen! I lay in the snow listening to my heart in my ears.

After a long time, I saw something. A glow. A flicker. Light. A house, maybe! With a woodstove and a pot of stew bubbling. I pulled myself back up onto my feet and then saw what was making the strange glow: the candles! The votive candles were burning at the base of the oak tree, throwing light up the great trunk, shadows dancing on the bark. Grace was still here! She wasn't dead after all. She'd lit her candles for me! So I could see my way out of the river. I stepped closer to the candles. But there were many more than the seven I'd dug up. Dozens of candles burned at the base of the tree. Maybe hundreds! Was Grace hiding? Teasing me? Playing with my brain? Reaching out, I found the trunk, solid and hard in all the wind and blowing sand. I leaned against the bark wall, panting. I stood for a long time, watching the flames burn, the candleholders melting down into the snow, sinking, disappearing, the light all changing, the white changing, too. Soon the snow on the ground all around the tree was glowing blue from down underneath, a warm blue-orange trembling. The wind gusted through the branches overhead, the branches now lit up from the underside, flickering yellow veins running all through the black sky.

Then I was tearing at my overalls with frozen fingers, my bladder swelled to bursting down inside me. I pulled myself out, let a torrent of warmth flow out of my body, flowing forever. Flowing so much that when I looked down and saw a patch of dark snow, I was sure it was the ground showing through. Pissed so much I'd melted a hole through the snow clear down to the soil. The earth.

But then I looked again, saw a shade of color in the candlelight, and dropped to my knees. The darkness wasn't the black earth showing through at all, but a rich rust-colored stain on the snow. I scooped up a handful of the dark snow and rubbed it between my hands, opened my hands and saw a glistening reddish pink on both palms!

Words in a language I didn't know gushed out long and ragged from the back of my throat. Both my fists slammed down into the rusty slush. Over and over, my fists pounded, beat, drove the rust deeper and deeper into the snow, down through the white toward the black earth where the roots of that great tree lived. I kept beating the snow until I could no longer breathe, until I was burning up and freezing at the same time.

When I lifted my head, the candles were all out. Gone. The night was ink again. No rust or pink. No yellow flames. No holes in the snow. I pushed my face into my hands, my hands so cold my cheeks caught fire. More words came out of me, a slur of sound not human, my breath melting the ice crystals pinched between my hands and face. Then light! My hands dropped away. The candles were burning again! The snow glowing from down below! I tried to warm my hands above the candle holes, but the flames sizzled out one by one as I crawled, cupping my dripping fingers over each glowing hole.

Then there was just darkness all around. I fell forward, snow pushing in around my face, filling the hollows of my eyes and temples, holding my head in its frozen blanket, my ears so cold they would break off if I moved. I breathed snow. Opened my mouth and chewed snow. The icy crystals bits of glass between my teeth, against my tongue and gums, cutting, numbing, making my teeth ache into the bone of my skull.

Lying facedown in that frozen bed, I knew I was at last floating on river water. But not out in the current yet. Still over by the bank, in the cattails and willow. I could pull myself out, drag myself up onto dry ground. Or else I could let go of the bank, float away. The blood was real. That doctor had been right. Cancer was eating me away. So why not just lie here and let the snow float me away? Beat the cancer to it?

You could have healed your cancer. That's just up here. But nobody can heal old age. Grace's words were whispers in my ears. *Because old age is not a disease.* Not a disease? But cancer was a disease, and cancer was what was killing me! Not old age! Grace was loony. *It's part of living.* What the hell was she doing? Was she out there right now, talking to me through my ears full of snow? *One big circle. The path the sun takes.*

Something moved close by. A rustle on the snow. Grace *was* here! She'd come back! I lifted my head, wiped snow out of my eyes.

But what I saw stopped the breath going in and coming out of me. Stopped my heart. A few inches away from my own face was the face of a wild animal. A wolf! Amber eyes glowing in the dark. Nose quivering, sniffing me on the wind, nostrils wet and flaring. A pink tongue flashed. White teeth. I looked into the burning yellow eyes, smelled the wolf's warm breath, smelled desert and dust, blood and flesh. Smelled the Gardens.

Then wetness brushed my forehead. Cold and hot. The smell of steel. And I knew I couldn't lie there, go the way Grace had gone. Go ahead of the geese. I wasn't finished with what I'd started. To go now would be to fail all the way around. Fail Ralph. Fail the others. Fail Grace. If I quit now, the Gardens would win. Bert and Emma and Clara would all wind up back at the Gardens where they'd come from. And if the Gardens won, nursing homes would keep on springing up all across the country, packed to the rafters full of people who had nothing more wrong with them than being old. People locked away with nobody interested in learning what they'd learned in life. *Wisdom. Wonder.* If Grace was right, if dying was part of living, part of some circle, and not just a one-way river, then why the hell not live it right up around to the beginning? The way Fred had. Go out playing baseball or swimming after whales? Or go out when and where you chose to if you felt yourself slipping. It didn't matter. If the young didn't have time for the wisdom we'd learned by living through the wonder, why not live in big old red houses like the Hogan House and keep our secrets to ourselves, take our secrets with us when we went? Or pass our secrets only to the very young, to kids like Desiree, before they were told that getting old wasn't good. Before they started believing they'd never get old.

And then the wolf was gone and I was on my feet again, stumbling down the hill toward Max as fast as an old man can run, down that thin thread of blue, slipping and shouting, beating my cold hands against my legs and stomach, Grace's votive lights clinking together in the pockets of my jacket, dawn breaking the color of salmon above the Cascades, the river flowing inside my head starting to rise up into the sky, arching through air, the color of the water changing from dull silver and gray into a piercing sky-blue turquoise that shimmered gold in the hot, hot sun.

Waterlight in Late Winter

The water in the creek runs clear, thin collars of ice ringing the round rocks rising here and there above the flowing surface, each black rock topped with a smooth white mound of snow. Along both banks, deep snow rounds down to where the water moves. Snow dusts naked branches of vine maple, covers blacktop and bridge railings, hushes the frozen morning air.

Without a sound, a black cloth floats out from under the bridge on the water. Tiny round mirrors on the cloth wink, throwing up flashes of light as the cloth drifts on downstream, moving around rocks, twisting, slowly spreading open, a dark blossom ringed in light blooming on the water. The glittering mirrors float into a wide band of sunlight that sparkles across the surface of the creek. It becomes impossible to distinguish the mirrors from the sun on the water.

CLARA PAULSON

IT'S ALMOST eight in the morning when I hear his boots clomping on the back ramp. I sigh and feel some of the worry flow away with my breath. Bert and Emma hear the clomping, too, and I can see worry flowing out of their faces, as well, all of us sitting here in the front room half the night, worried sick about George. None of us ate breakfast this morning. Not even Emma. It was a night from Hell, wondering where George was. Why Grace killed herself. What we were going to do now. We all thought George was dead, too, just like Grace. But I recognize the clomping of George's big old boots. Boots. Sweet music in my ears. Nutty George is back from the dead!

I brace myself to see the zombie that disappeared yesterday afternoon, nothing left of his face but skin gone to concrete, leaving the rest of us here with that cop apologizing and backing his way out the front door.

But when George comes into the entryway and stands looking at the three of us sitting here in the living room, his face is nothing at all like concrete. His face is full color and glowing like I've never seen George's face before. Something big's happened, I can tell that right away. But I have no idea what.

George is just different, standing there looking at us, the chandelier burning in the dining room behind him, his jacket covered with melting snow, sequins flashing a little as he breathes. Even his eyebrows sparkle, wild hair and whiskers full of snow, too, looking like he just rolled in a pile of sequins, his whole body sparkling and twinkling.

Nobody moves. We all stay right where we are, George staring into the room at us, Bert and Emma and me staring back at George shining, a snowman in sunlight. Nobody says a word. All of us breathing.

All of a sudden, the light changes. Blue sky breaks outside. The sun hits the chandelier. The storm's over! The sunlight and snow make everything in here seem brighter than ever before. I know I'll never forget this moment. Not ever.

What finally breaks the spell is the sound of George's hand brushing sequins off his coat sleeves, spraying ice and snow and water all over the flagstones, throwing sparks everywhere as he starts making some announcement about being awake, or saying good-bye, or something I don't quite understand.

I blink, look again, and George has been transformed. He's an oriental angel with white whiskers almost down to his knees! He stands there looking at us with a grin so big his eyes have disappeared. And George the angel is smoking! I've never seen George smoke. But there it is, the half-gone cigarette between his fingers, the blue-white smoke, a serpent curling up around his arm. I smell it now, too. Tobacco. I'm back onstage! Smoke drifting across the piano. The spotlight a solid beam of blue smoke above the crowd.

But this isn't George smoking. It's somebody else standing where George was only a second ago, before I blinked. Somebody I've never seen before. I wonder who. Where George went. I blink again and George is back, but he's standing next to the oriental angel, slapping the angel's back, the angel grinning even bigger, looking up at George, the angel's long white whiskers hanging there between the two of them like the horsehairs of some broken string bass bow.

"Hey, everybody!" George yells at us. "This is Clayton Liu! He's come home at last. Hallelujah!"

But George's words don't make any sense. All of this is too confusing. Smoke and mirrors and ice water. I want it to be warm again. Sunny and hot. So I can plant marigolds upstairs in the window boxes.

Then George yells two words so loud I almost jump out of my chair: "The Gardens!" My little bell rings wild. George is sending us back! Calling the whole thing quits! Boarding up this big red shoe box. He's going to drive off into the sunset with this oriental angel named Clayton Loo. Leave the three of us behind for the Rhino.

"Everybody at the Gardens!" George is saying. "I'll even invite the goddamned Ad-ministrator herself down here!"

It's true. The Rhino herself. George is inviting the Rhino to come get us in person! It's all over. A dream too good has come crashing to a stop. Stop. Back to the Rhino and fish sticks on Fridays. Back to my too high window with the tree-tops. Back to handfuls of blackbirds hurled past.

Emma's saying something about morbid. The word "wake" flies around a couple of times. Wake? We're all awake. What are they talking about? Perhaps I'm asleep and they're telling me to wake up. But I'm not asleep.

Then I hear the word Irish and get it. The piece clicks in. Good God. George must be planning to bury Grace out in the backyard with Fred. And this time he's going to have a wake first. An Irish wake. I don't know if I can take that. I try to imagine Grace laid out on the butcher block in the kitchen and all of us standing around drinking and crying and trying to sing, the way I've heard they do it over in Ireland.

But I'm too tired to imagine. I just want to fly out through the window and up into all that brand-new blue, through the ice-cold air and on up toward the sun, where it's warm. Warm. One big marigold blazing in the sky.

"You're not dead till you're dead!" Bert yells, and starts whooping, the fool-idiot. But Grace is dead. The blue cop said so.

Then I hear one word shoot out of George's mouth and streak across the room into my ears. Off key. Out of tune. *Cancer*. I hear George saying he's got it—that word—and won't live much longer. *Cancer!* George has cancer! Now I see it, all through him, his clothes and skin hanging on him. The pieces snap together so loud and fast my ears hurt.

"I'm dying, goddamnit," George says. But he's smiling, waving his arm through the air in front of him as if he were talking to a huge crowd. "Like all the rest of you," he says.

Nobody breathes. I want to ring my bell and have Johnny Q take me away. Back to B31. To anywhere but right here with George telling us he's going to die on us, too.

"Only difference," George blasts on, "is that I know what's going to take me out. And that it won't be too long. So I want to have a wake! Except not after I'm gone. Hell no! That wouldn't be much fun for any of us. I want to have my wake while I'm still alive and breathing. Make a toast to going on around."

GEORGE CASTOR

I PICKED the date of April Twelve. Not only was it my eighty-third birthday, but it gave me a good month and a half to make all the arrangements. Ever since the night out under Grace's tree, my energy had been dropping off pretty steady. The blood was back for good now, but it didn't bother me. I tried to think of it as little splashes of me going on ahead, making their way back toward the sea, like the salmon and the rainwater. I'd catch up soon enough. Emma begged me to go to the hospital for treatment, but I flat-out refused. The last thing I wanted was to spend my last days in a god-damned hospital. Die in a hospital.

We buried Grace in the cemetery on the edge of town, the same one where Ralph was buried. Some relative of Grace's flew in from Spokane and took care of the details. We all went to the funeral, went through the motions. But I wasn't letting anybody mourn Grace too long. Grace knew exactly what she was doing.

I gave in and started taking naps. Sometimes twice a day, which I hated. But I got so tired so fast I had no choice. Spent all my time working on plans for the party. Clara talked me into calling it a party instead of a wake. I liked that idea. I was having a party. A going-away party. A going-around party. I made up invitations and the whole bit. Passed the invitations out to the others in the house. Gave a handful to Desiree. Walked one down to Mrs. Beasley. Stapled the leftover invitations to the porch pillars. Even put a few up around town, down at City Hall and at the Nickelodeon.

Clayton Liu showing up saying he was going to move in and stay here for good made me know for sure the Hogan House would keep going. Four left, instead of three. Clayton said California was okay, but he'd gone farther south, down into Baja where he lived in a small town called Espíritu Santo something. Clayton said one night he woke up dreaming about pigs and his short visit here with Grace and me. He got out of bed that night and looked in the mirror and for the first time in his life he said he saw an old man looking back at him. He left before it was light out the next morning and hitched all the way up Highway One and came back. Right here to the red house with the huge front porch. Said he never did forget our front porch. Showed up wearing thin white cotton in the middle of the worst snowstorm ever to hit Oregon. Loony guy still chain-smoking Camel straights and saying how he could surely use a good strong pot of hot coffee. I could almost hear Grace whispering in my ear that Clayton Liu's soul was at last ready for the big red palace now.

CLARA PAULSON

IT'S TAKEN me a while to give in and go out there with him in the cold every morning. The snow's gone and the trees are starting to leaf out, but it's still cold that early.

I've been going out, though, every morning for the past couple of weeks to do exercises with this Clayton Loo. He claims it's officially called Tie Sheet, but I don't see where it has anything to do with sheets or tying. Clayton Loo just calls it "exercises." I wouldn't even call it that. Clayton Loo hardly moves. I move even less sitting in my chair.

A few days ago, I looked over and saw Emma coming our way through the fog, big as a cow, a black scarf tied around her pink face. I was sure Emma was going to bark at Clayton Loo and me for something, for being too loud, or too early, or too slow. But Emma didn't. She just came up and asked if she could try it, a little girl wanting to play.

I couldn't believe it. Emma was never up early. I thought perhaps she was sleepwalking and just happened to wander outside our way. But Clayton Loo helped Emma get started, helped her find her balance on those little feet. And Emma's been coming out now every morning regular since. I've noticed something sneaking onto Emma's face, too. A softness. A slight glow.

So it's the three of us out on the side lawn at the crack of dawn every morning. I move the good half of my body real slow, trying to hook up with my sheet, or life force as Clayton Loo calls it. I haven't found my sheet yet. Clayton Loo says that takes time. But I have been feeling a little tingling sensation in my dead hand lately, just the tips of the fingers. A buzzing, the sound a fly makes under waxed paper. And I've noticed the same buzzing sensation in my tongue, too. In the dead half.

Who knows? Perhaps if I keep doing Clayton Loo's exercises every morning, I'll hook up with my sheet, get my whole dead hand back. Perhaps my arm and my tongue, too. George would be out here with us, too—I know that. But it's hard for him to get up early anymore. He cusses having to take naps and sleep in. But he gets weak so fast he has no choice.

George's party is still a couple of weeks off. But he's all fired up about it. He says he's serving Irish whiskey and Henry's Ale, and we'll all dance till the sun comes up. Knowing George, he'll probably make sure we do, too.

GEORGE CASTOR

ALL THE invitations I had left over went into a shoe box. The shoe box went onto the seat in Max, where Shag William used to always ride, and before that, Dora. Then I fired up Max and drove up Water Street to the Gardens trying not to think about the pain shooting up through my bowels.

The new wing was finished, painted and everything. I was surprised at how well it blended right in with the older parts of the building. The whole parking lot was paved now, too. I pulled up and parked right next to those big glass doors, shut off Max and got out, taking the shoe box with me.

The lobby was carpeted now, a dusty blue, which made everything seem quieter, less echoey, a little smaller. There was a new clock hanging on the wall above the counter. Looked like walnut and brass. The new clock said it was just past noon. I smelled hot food and heard dishes rattling in the cafeteria. The receptionist sitting behind the counter looked up and asked if she could help me. The receptionist wasn't much more than a girl.

"Just dropping by to see some old friends," I said. The receptionist smiled. I moved down the hall to the swinging doors of the cafeteria. I pushed one of the doors open. Rows and tables of white-haired old folks eating lunch off plastic trays. Some not eating, just staring off into space. Some being fed by younger people dressed all in white.

I went in, walked to the nearest row of tables, and started working my way down, handing each person an invitation out of my shoe box, telling them my party was going to be a good time, that they should try to make it if they could. Some of them smiled and said thank you. Some of them didn't even look at my invitation, didn't notice me giving it to them. One man wearing a military hat and medals on his robe started shouting, "Propaganda! Propaganda! Stop this man! Stop him! Guards!" But an aide came over and calmed the man down. I gave the soldier's invitation to the aide. Another old woman wearing a rosary around her neck and another around each wrist reached out and took my invitation, crossed herself, then held me in her eyes and asked God to bless me, making a little cross in the air with her hand. Bless her heart.

I passed through the lobby on my way back out to Max, but in the middle of the dusty blue wall-to-wall carpet I stopped. I was so tired I knew I should sit for a spell. I could feel the tired, aching in my knees and pulsing up behind my forehead. The pain in my bowels was bad today. I shook the shoe box. A rattle. One left. The new clock said twelve-twenty, the gold second hand bouncing its way around, going down past the two and the three and the four. That's when I saw something gleaming the same color as that second hand, and turned. A big brass plate on an oak door, a single word etched onto the plate, capital letters going all the way across: ADMINISTRATOR.

Was she still here? The door was ajar, so I walked over and pushed it open a foot or so. There she was, red dress and all, sitting behind a big oak desk reading some papers. She didn't look up. Everything about the Ad-ministrator was the same, except for some new silver streaks running through her hair. I pushed the door all the way open, the hinges not squeaking a bit. The door hit the stopper and the Ad-ministrator looked up. I could tell she recognized me right away, but before she could say a word, I started talking, putting all the energy I had left into the words.

"I'm throwing a little bash for myself next week—a going-away party," I said. "A real ripper. If you can make it by, please do. It would be good to have you there. I kind of feel like I know you, although I'm sure you can't stand me. Here's an invitation." I held the shoe box up.

She looked at me over her glasses, puffed out her chest and started to say something. But before she could, I kept going.

"Should be a hell of a good time," I said. "I just now invited everybody here. I'm sure they'll all come. And Ralph will no doubt show up, too. You remember Ralph. Hope you can make it, too."

I took the lid off the box and slid the open box with the invitation inside onto the desktop. Then I winked at the Administrator, and walked out of her office leaving her no time to say a single word back.

Going out through the sliding glass doors, the silver words I'd cracked all to hell years ago rolling apart to let me through, I was all of a sudden so tired I thought I might go down, right there in front of the Gardens, wind up in one of those lousy beds after all. But I made it to Max, climbed up into the driver's seat, and drove back toward the house.

Going across the bridge, I slowed down. The water in the creek was moving pretty good. But I couldn't hear the water over Max running. The sun was high and strong, and the vine maple all leafed out, the leaves that bright, bright green of early springtime. Two goldfinches, one chasing the other in circles, flitted in the air, then dove down and disappeared below the bridge railing. I honked the horn twice and kept going. *Hallelujah!*

CLARA PAULSON

THE CLOCK in the entryway finishes chiming out eight long bongs as Mrs. Beasley appears in the oval window, rapping on the glass and squinting, trying to see inside. She's wearing the same black outfit she wore to Fred's funeral, except instead of a mum on her hat she's got a huge burgundy peony pinned up there. A couple of petals have fallen off and are lying on the black brim. Brim. Her patent leather purse in the porchlight is the color of midnight rain. Her nails and lips match the peony on her hat—the same color as the welcome mats back at the Gardens. Mrs. Beasley doesn't wait for one of us to get the door. She just comes in blabbering a blue streak. It's hard to tell if she's just talking to herself or wanting all of us here to hear.

"Lordy, Lordy, I hate to admit it," she's saying, closing the door behind her. "But I think I just might miss the poor old boy, may his soul rest in peace." She closes her eyes and kisses a red thumbnail.

"Well, I'll be damned!" George yells from where he's sitting in the dining room dressed in his baseball uniform, one of Fred's red bow ties tied around his neck. "I don't believe I'm hearing right."

Mrs. Beasley turns and sees George sitting there, red and yellow from head to toe, a big grin on his face. All color slides out of Mrs. Beasley's face, just her burgundy lips hanging open a little. The peony on her hat stops moving. Another petal drops off and lands on the black brim without a sound.

"Welcome to my wake!" George yells, holding a bottle of beer high in the air.

Mrs. Beasley points one of her red nails at George, stutters, puffs. "You ... !? You ... !?" she says. "You're supposed to be dead!"

"Now, now, let's not rush things," George says. "But here's to it. Welcome to my wake!"

It's the same old George coming out of George. Except not on the outside. On the outside, George is so skinny his baseball uniform's just hanging on him, his eyes are bigger than ever, and his too big baseball cap on sideways and pulled down to his ears makes him look like a kid. That's what George is right now. A little boy at a birthday party. And Mrs. Beasley's all mixed up, thinking this was George's funeral instead of his living wake.

People keep showing up in the oval window, coming in through the front door. Two high school kids I think I remember from the baseball games come in with a couple of other friends, all of them dressed in black leather and silver metal.

"We're the band," they say to me because I'm the one sitting closest to the door. "Where should we set up?"

The band? I think. What band? But I like the idea, so I point to an open area over by the Steinway. They seem satisfied, start bringing in instruments and amplifiers and microphones. This is getting good. I should have known with George behind it.

Desiree shows up, looking more like a young woman than the spindly little papergirl I've seen before. She's even wearing a dress. A green dress. Red hair done up nice and pulled back. She's going to make a pretty woman someday.

I don't even recognize some of the people who come in.

George did the inviting. Who knows who all will show up here tonight.

A small man with an even smaller woman on his arm introduces himself to me as Chuck Brandenburg and his wife Annabelle. Then he leans close and whispers, "From the C wing down at the Gardens," as if that's the special password tonight. Hearing the name of that place stops me. But Annabelle says, "We've heard tales about this place, so Chuck and I decided to come check it out for ourselves." I smell the Gardens in the air around Chuck and Annabelle, fish sticks and air freshener, ammonia sloshing in mop buckets. But I'm glad they're here. I smile, give them a thumb-up. They're in.

Another woman comes through the front door a few minutes later. Her lips are fuchsia, and she's wearing earrings so bright and big they don't stop bouncing. She says she's from the Gardens, too. Now I start to wonder. Speaking with an accent, she tells me her name's Linda Maria Elizabeth Estebán. But she says I should call her Leenda. *Leenda*. I nod, electricity coming out her eyes and face, flowing into the pipes of my chair, filling up the room. I write my name on my pad, hold it up, try to smile. Linda Maria takes my dead hand in her hands. Squeezes, gentle. The flies in my fingertips go nuts. She smiles. Says nice to meet you, Clara, and looks inside me, where Grace used to look. Except Linda Maria's eyes are brown, not black, and there are flecks of gold in the brown. Linda Maria's young—sixty-eight or -nine, I guess. But it's hard to say. Her hair's electric, too, shining coppery, but light, the color of brand-new piano wire. "I walked down from the Gardens," Linda Maria says, still holding my hand. And I believe her. I don't smell the Gardens on Linda Maria. I smell apple blossoms and lilacs and cut grass and makeup.

"It's such a lovely evening for a walk," Linda Maria says. "And to be walking away from the Gardens for a change makes it all the more lovely, don't you think?" I want to reach up and kiss her, touch her electric hair, touch her sparkly earrings. But instead, she lifts my dead hand higher off my lap and kisses my hand. The flies go wild. I wave Linda Maria Elizabeth Estebán in.

Then I see George looking at Linda Maria from across the room. Then George looks at me, winks, and grins—a little-boy-baseball grin.

The band starts up. The music's different, but good. A little loud, but I don't care. It's live. I haven't heard live music for so many years I wouldn't care what it sounded like. I want to get up and dance. Dance. Cut the rug a little. Feel a hand in the small of my back. I want to play the piano and sing along.

The dining room table's piled high with salads: pasta salads, green salads, three-bean salads, and a huge fruit salad in a cut-glass bowl. Trays are heaped with carrot sticks and broccoli and cauliflower, marinated mushrooms and asparagus, cold cuts, and all kinds of cheeses. More food than I've ever seen in one place. Bowls mounded full of Swedish meatballs and chicken wings and green olives. Breads and rolls and crackers overflowing out of baskets onto the tablecloth. The china hutch is cluttered with bottles of everything, from Kahlúa and Grand Marnier, to Henry's Ale, pink champagne, soda pop, and the Irish whiskey George promised.

For the first time in years, I'm drinking a White Russian tonight.

George is throwing himself a humdinger, every last stop pulled all the way out! Fortissimo!

♫

A couple hours later, George beats on the green glass neck of his Henry's Ale beer bottle with a fork handle. People stop talking and the house calms down. In the sudden hush, George lifts his beer bottle high and takes a breath, getting ready to say something, tell us something important, make a toast. But whatever he's planning to say gets stuck inside. I see it. The words won't come. George just stands there, his fingers bony against the green and gold label on the bottle, the beating of George's heart in his throat making Fred's bow tie tremble a little. George's hand starting to tremble, too. Beer sloshing inside the green glass. Not a sound in the house.

He's trying to bring the words out. But he can't. George swallows and lowers the bottle, waves Clayton Loo close, whispers in Clayton Loo's ear. Clayton Loo looks around, a question mark on his face, then shrugs and hurries off down the hall and out the back door. George wipes one of his eyes quick with a finger.

Then the words start coming, slow at first, as if George has just climbed a flight of stairs and is catching his breath between words. "Now, some of you don't know the real reason for this party here tonight," he says. "If I had told you, you might not have shown up. But, you're here. And that's what counts." He breathes a couple of times. Takes a sip of beer. The foam slides down the inside of the bottle. "Now, as you can see, I'm not quite as robust as I once was. I've lost a pound or two. Slowed down a shade." He stops again, looks down at the bottle in his hand, but doesn't take a drink this time. "You see ... the truth is ... I'm headed north, pretty soon. Downriver. On around. Into sky. So I wanted to throw a little going-away party. A wake, really. Now I know the order's a little backwards. But this was the only way I could figure to not miss out on all the fun."

A gunshot goes off. The back screen door slapping shut. Then the slow rumble of a train coming through a tunnel, down the hallway. Everyone turns to see what's coming, see who's driving their car through the house. But it's a box car, with Clayton Loo pushing it, coming across the flagstones and right into the front room, people backing out of the way. The wood's polished smooth and shiny. A great big casket riding on the same cart we used for Fred's casket. Except there's no agates or words on the top. Just a glass doorknob, the same as the doorknob on my steering wheel.

Nobody says a word. All of us just staring at this shiny box. Then Emma lets loose.

"Oh, good Lord, George!" Emma bellows.

"Now, now," George says, holding up a hand. "It's just a box. Nothing fancy. But I figured a wake wouldn't be complete without one."

"This is sick!" Emma says. "Sick!"

"Now, Emma," George says. "I put a lot of work into this box." I can tell he did, too. The wood's so smooth I can see people's faces and Linda Maria's earrings reflecting off the finish.

Emma puffs up to launch another attack, but right then the sound of door knocker starts pounding loud and at the same time the grandfather clock begins bonging. Emma deflates. Everybody's looking around. A murmur in the room. Nobody saying anything, just the clock bonging. Everybody counting. Wondering who's late for George's going-away party.

I turn and see two women through the oval window, one younger and one older, the younger one with red hair shining bright in the porch light and moths fluttering. The older woman gray-haired. Clayton Loo moves over to the door, pulls the door open, bows a little and gestures for the women to come in. But the women just stand outside the wide-open door, scanning the faces staring back at them from all around George's casket sitting up on wheels. The clock stops bonging and then there's just silence.

"Come on in," George booms, slapping the casket, his voice suddenly loud and rejuvenated. "Join the party!"

The older woman steps inside, into the brighter light and what must be the smell of warm bodies and beer. The younger one comes in, too, and I notice she's pregnant. Then the older woman clears her throat and speaks, her voice almost a whisper. "I'm looking for a Clara Paulson," the woman says. "She's my mother." And the lights go out.

EPILOGUE

i hope i die
warmed
by the life that i tried
to live.

—Nikki Giovanni

CLARA PAULSON

IT'S LATE summer already, and I can smell fall not far off. I like fall. George always liked fall. We buried George a couple of months ago. Out there next to Fred behind Grace's chicken coop. Doorknob, boots, overalls, and everything. Emma sang real pretty again. I wrote up a few departing words and Bert read my words. Desiree came. Mrs. Beasley was here, too. Mrs. Beasley cried. Clayton Loo led the service. He was good at it. Early morning service this time, right after exercises. I'm not sure you ever get over somebody you love dying. It's like a little part of you comes loose and falls away. Leaves a hole. The hole never heals over all the way. Always a little tender. Always there.

That's what I've been doing since George died. Healing over. It's been hard, though, because of the way it all worked out. I mean, I didn't kill George, although in a way I guess you could say I did. Or helped kill him at least. But it wasn't the mortal sin type of killing. George said it was just helping him on around. Grace's words.

But before I did that, a few weeks after his wake, George called me into the living room where we'd set up a bed for him over by the Steinway. When I was near his bed, George asked me if I would do him a favor. I nodded, wrote ANY-THING on my pad, held the pad up so he could read it. Then George reached out and touched the arm of my chair, looked straight into my eyes, and asked me if I would play for him. "The piano," he said. "Anything." So I rolled over to Emma's piano, blinking back tears, and stopped in front of the keyboard. My own reflection stared at me through the gold letters. I took a deep breath. Then another. Squeezed my good hand into a tight fist. Opened it. Squeezed again. I reached out, my whole hand trembling, until my fingertips found the smooth keys and stopped shaking. And then I was playing. Pachelbel's Canon. With only one hand, and lots of wrong notes. But I played. Played. For the first time in years and years I played again. And I kept playing until my hand and arm got so tired I had to stop.

When I looked around, Bert and Emma were next to George, Emma's cheeks wet, Bert and George beaming, not a sound in the room. Then all three of them started clapping at the same time, and they kept on clapping, cheering, Bert whooping and hollering, me sitting there crying like a little girl.

☽

A few days later, George called me to his bed again, but this time he told me he didn't want to eat solid foods anymore. Said he wanted to have only juices. So I brought George all sorts of juices, anything Emma could put in the blender and churn into a liquid. Emma said George had to keep getting his vitamins one way or another. All the different flavors were her idea. Emma made George squash shakes and salad shakes and even T-bone-steak-well-done shakes. Emma couldn't bear to see George lying in bed in such bad shape, so I was the one who took the juices in to George, on a tray on my lap. Me, or Clayton Loo sometimes. Clayton Loo took care of George, kept George washed and shaved and changed. Clayton Loo gave George special teas to help ease the pain.

Emma kept making juices. Rainbow Juices, Emma called them.

But George must have caught on, because one day he told me he didn't want juice anymore either. Just water. Plain water, straight up, is what he said. So that's what I brought George, glasses of clear, cold water in the heat of summer. Emma tried sneaking liquid vitamins into the water, but George could taste it, and told Emma to quit.

And then one day George told me to stop the water, too. Cut it off, he said. So I did. I didn't tell Emma, though. She would have wanted us to rush George up to the hospital, hook him up to a drip bottle to keep him from dying of thirst. But I knew that's the last thing George would have wanted, so I poured the glasses of water down the toilet.

Three days after I stopped giving George water he started saying words that didn't make much sense: something about some fly fisherman named Ralph, something about catching up, and how Ralph better start running; something about salmon swimming, and geese going north, and water being steamed into clouds.

I was sitting by his bed with Clayton Loo when George struggled to get his last breaths of late June air. And then George left us, left his big red house to all of us and went on around.

⟳

George is gone. Gone. And I helped him go. But I know what I did wasn't a sin. Because George was pretty bad in the end, wearing diapers, hardly sleeping, cussing and calling out in the night because of the pain. Saying he wished it was winter and freezing cold out and he could walk again. George is gone now. His uniform hanging on the wall next to Fred's. Emma had George's uniform framed.

I know we'll make it here in George's big red house. Except it's not just the four of us anymore. Linda Maria Elizabeth and Chuck and Annabelle moved in a few weeks back. So

George and Grace's old rooms upstairs aren't empty anymore. And there's Clayton Loo, of course. Mr. Exercise. Mr. Tie Sheet. Clayton Loo lives up in one of the attic rooms. Says the air up there's better. Healthier.

The marigolds I planted in the window boxes up in the attic bloomed all summer and are still going strong. Window boxes brimming full of sunshine. Sometimes I take George's elevator up to the attic and pick bouquets for the supper table, or for when we have breakfast out on the terrace. Fill a vase full of those little suns blooming bright orange. Other times I just sit up there looking out one of the arched windows, out past my marigolds, just looking out into all that blue. Sometimes I hear piano music, see quarter notes and eighth notes and baseballs blowing across the sky. Sometimes I hear chickens, the clicking of blue stones, dog tags jingling in the wind. Sometimes I hear George's wind chimes all the way down on the porch. Now and then, I hear myself singing.

Just last week, Mrs. Beasley showed up with that horse-dog of hers and asked if we'd consider letting her take us up on George's invitation. Guess George asked her to move in here a long time ago, but she turned him down. George never mentioned that to us. Mrs. Beasley said her daughter took a job out of town and she didn't want to live alone. Said we could use her house down the block as an annex, or a guest house. Said we could even paint her house red and yellow to match this one, if we wanted. Mrs. Beasley said she knows how much George liked red.

I can't imagine living with Mrs. Beasley, but I've lived with Emma these last years. What's another poker chip dropped in the box? God knows Mrs. Beasley's got spunk. She'll be moving in next week, bracelets and all. Emma wants Mrs. Beasley to move into her and Fred's room with her. I can't imagine that. But who knows? The two of them might hit it off. In life, things surprise you all the time. Little things. Like Emma wanting to play the piano again, and asking me to teach her. And big things. Things so big they shock the living daylights right out of you. Like Amy showing up at the door in the middle of George's wake.

I'm still not all the way sure it happened, not a hundred percent. I won't believe it all the way until Amy gets here. Of course, her name's not Amy. It's Anne. But I'll always call her Amy in my head. That night was so crazy. Just a blur, really. Music and drinking and dancing. Somebody playing the piano. George showing off his casket. Clayton Loo smoking like a stack. That's why it's still hard to believe it was my Amy who showed up.

Even before she said a word, before things went black, I felt myself filling up fast with a knowing I still can't explain. In fact, as Amy stepped through the doorway inside this house, I knew two things at the same time: I knew that George wouldn't live much longer no matter what any of us did to help him, and I knew that this woman standing in the porch light and moths was the little girl I'd left behind the smudged glass of that hospital nursery and driven away from all those years ago. A lifetime ago, almost. Amy's going on sixty! My little baby girl! From across that big living room, I saw myself in her face, and in her daughter's face, too, and I knew.

After the wake, Amy and her daughter Rayanne stayed on for a day, then went back to Lincoln to pack things up, sell a house in a subdivision, quit their jobs, and move out here with me—with us. Who knows how they wound up in Nebraska, both unmarried, Amy working in the cafeteria of a meat packing plant, and Rayanne making beds at some Motel Six. Said it took years of phone calls and letters and dead-end leads to find me all the way out here in Oregon. In all this rain and green so far away from both Nebraska and Hawaii. Said they got into town so late that night the Gardens was locked up. But the night aide let them in. The aide told them he'd never heard of me, but that they should check back in the morning and talk to the Administrator. They said they were going back out through the sliding doors to find a hotel when a woman wearing three black rosaries came across the lobby, blessed herself, and told them to check a big red house downtown across the bridge. Henrietta, God bless her Fish-eater heart. Perhaps Henrietta's a saint, and there is a God after all.

The only hotel in Lookingglass was full, so Amy and Ray-anne were headed for Salem to find a place to stay that night. But this house was so lit up when they drove by they noticed the color, said there was a row of candles burning at the bottom of the front steps and way up high a star of tiny white Christmas lights. They could see people inside, so they decided to stop and knock before driving on into Salem. Amy says she's learned to follow her intuition, look into every coincidence. I suppose if you try hard enough to do something in life, you'll eventually succeed. Except live forever. Now that's something George would have said. I can almost hear him saying it right now. George's voice in my ear makes me smile.

Amy and Rayanne are going to live in the apartment out over the garage. Amy said she'll cook for us. Says she loves to cook. Of course, Emma heard that and puffed up bigger than she is, glowed all over to be getting out of cooking. Rayanne's been taking nursing courses at a community college back in Nebraska. Wants to be a nurse. I guess Rayanne can take care of what ails all of us. Emma's beside herself, can't wait till they get here. A cook *and* a nurse, just what she wanted. I don't think George would mind. They're family. Family taking care of their own. How it should be.

And before too long we'll have a brand-new member of the family here at the Hogan House. A baby. My great-grandchild. For the first time in my life I feel connected. Connected to the past and to the future. My daughter has a daughter—my *granddaughter*. And my granddaughter's going to have a baby in less than a month, and all of them with my own blood running in their veins.

Amy just called yesterday to say they're renting a U-Haul trailer, and should be here in a few days, depending on how long at a stretch Rayanne can sit. Rayanne must be getting pretty big by now. Good God, I'll be a great-grandmother.

And I haven't even been a mother yet. Perhaps you do get second chances in life.

Bert says he's never been a grandpa before, and wouldn't mind having a crack at it. I told Bert he won't have any choice in the matter. That child will be pushing the two of us all over the place before we know it, the way time goes so fast and kids grow up. In fact, this grandchild will have more grandpas and grandmas than any child in the country. Probably be good for the child, too, growing up with a bunch of old folks like us. Spring Chickens. Be good for us, as well. I'll teach my great-grandchild how to play the piano and plant marigolds. How to gather eggs and grow corn. And I'll make sure that child learns how to play baseball—even in the pouring Oregon rain.

At age sixteen, GREG KLEINER spent a year in the mountains of northern Thailand as an ASF exchange student. For a month of that year, he lived at a Buddhist monastery as a novice under the tutelage of an aged monk. He has worked as a dairy goat farmer, hotel concierge, freelance journalist, wildlife biologist, and technical writer. He now lives in western Oregon with his partner Lori and their two small children, Eli and Sophia. *Where River Turns to Sky* is his first novel.